MIDNIGHT BEACH

A Port Stirling Mystery

KAY JENNINGS

PARIS
Communications

Midnight Beach/ Kay Jennings. -- 1st ed.

ISBN (Hardcover edition): 978-1-7339626-3-6
ISBN (Paperback edition): 978-1-7339626-4-3
ISBN (e-book edition): 978-1-7339626-5-0

Publisher's Note: Midnight Beach is a work of fiction. While certain events and locales may draw on real life, they are used fictitiously to add authenticity to the story. The cast of characters is solely a product of the author's imagination, and bears no resemblance to real people, organizations, or gangs.

Cover image: Sandra Cunningham / Trevillion Images
Cover and interior design: Claire Brown

Printed and bound in the USA
First printing 2020
Published by *Paris Communications*
Portland, Oregon, USA

www.kayjenningsauthor.com

For Bonnie McIntee, who always said I could do this.
Of course, she said it in the context of "You're always making up stuff."
Thanks, mom. And, with my thanks to readers who write reviews
about books they like. Every writer appreciates you more than you know.

CHAPTER 1

the body

Friday, April 5

Clay Sherwin's decapitated head was found, in the reeds, about four feet from his body. The Chinook County marine biologist, who stumbled over the head while counting snowy egrets in the marshy estuary between Twisty River and the Pacific Ocean, took a split second to realize what he was seeing, and then promptly turned his back and threw up his entire breakfast.

♦♦♦

Matt Horning slowed his run on the hard-packed sand to an easy jog, and looked out to sea, using the sleeve of his black windbreaker to wipe the sweat off his face. The Pacific was sparkling blue with silvery whitecaps as far as he could see. This morning's soft wind barely touched his face under his "Hook 'Em Horns" cap.

Three months into his relo to Port Stirling, Matt found it difficult to remember what early April was like in his native Texas. But he knew it wasn't this crisp, this fresh, as this sunny Oregon morning. Running north, the rugged headland with its 300-foot cliffs was off to his right, and he squinted into the early morning sun just peeping up over them. Now awash in spring's greenery, the bluffs looked so much more alive than when he'd arrived at his new home in January's deadness.

He usually preferred to run south on the beach from his ocean-view cottage high up on the bluff so he wouldn't have to run by Emily's tunnel. But, every once-in-a-while, it seemed important to remind himself about the day

1

he'd arrived in Port Stirling to start his new job as police chief. This morning, Matt woke up thinking about that dead little girl left in the tunnel of a giant sea stack on Port Stirling's six-mile-long beach, and all his team had done to deliver justice to her.

He picked up his pace again and let the gentle air brush away his tears. Matt was proud to have come through for Port Stirling in one of the town's darkest moments, but there was no glee in the case's resolution.

But slowly, the town was beginning to heal. There would be a mayoral election soon, and Matt had been approached by a committee of the town's business leadership to run for the office. There weren't many natural-born leaders in a village the size of Port Stirling, and Matt's skills during their recent tragedy had stood out.

"Nope. I'm a cop," Matt politely told them, "not a politician."

A bona-fide hero in his new hometown, Matt had, instead, set to work rebuilding the police department after several years of inattention from his retired predecessor, Ol' George.

Matt's boss, City Manager Bill Abbott, had been determined to replace George Simonson with a younger, more aggressive police chief for Port Stirling, and had thanked his lucky stars every day since Matt's arrival. Smiling to himself, Matt recalled how many times in the past three months Abbott had enthusiastically slapped him on the back in City Hall's hallways and said, "What would we have done without you, Chief Horning?"

It looked like the new mayor would be one of the town's former teachers, Brad Souter, who had also been a big basketball star at Port Stirling High School in his younger days. Matt had met him just last week, and thought he was the ideal candidate...smart guy, funny, articulate, and a good leader. Although sacrilege in the Pacific Northwest, Brad admitted to being a Dallas Cowboys fan, and had remembered the year Matt Horning played cornerback for the Boys before blowing out his knee. For his part, Matt was impressed at how the 70-something man seemed so at ease with himself. *Wonder if I'll ever be that comfortable in my own skin?*

"Thanks for not running," Souter said, smiling and shaking Matt's hand at the end of their get-acquainted lunch. "There's no way in hell I could beat you right now. Everyone in Port Stirling loves you. Hell, I'd vote for you myself if you ran against me!"

Matt hoped Souter won; he had the empathy and comforting confidence that Port Stirling needed in a new mayor right now.

Back at his rental bungalow perched on the edge of the bluff, Matt cooled off outside on his patch of lawn in the morning sunshine. He stretched out his calves, quads, and hamstrings, holding onto the fence that separated him from a 300-foot fall to the rocks and beach below. He would never tire of this spectacular view, especially south where he could see the coastline for miles.

Inside, he ate a big bowl of yogurt and Oregon blackberries. He sprinkled some golden flax seed on top because he'd read a recent article in the NY Times that indicated flaxseed might help reduce inflammation of the joints. Matt could use any help with his right knee, which was painful more days than not since his old football injury.

The big stone fireplace at the center of the cottage was still warm to his touch from last night's fire, and the place was cozy. He stared out his huge picture window while eating his breakfast, searching the surf for his first friend in Port Stirling, Roger the seal. Matt still got a kick out of how often the seal appeared, and how he seemed to be looking right at Matt on the clifftop above him. He had named him once it became his habit to talk out loud to the animal about his theories in Emily's case. *Hope no one ever learns that little factoid about their new police chief.* No sign of Roger this morning. Off to the shower.

Towel-drying his hair, Matt stepped out onto the white terry bath rug just as his phone jingled on the vanity. He hesitated for a split-second, because at 7:20 a.m., it was a little early for a phone call, and it must be something bad. *Just like a cop; imagine the worst.*

He jumped for the phone, answered and heard silence then a cough on the other end. "Chief, this is Milton, the 911 dispatcher up at City Hall," finally said the caller.

"Hi, Milton, I remember you. What can I do for you on this beautiful Friday morning?"

"Well, uh, you're not going to believe this. I don't believe this." Milton pushed his black frames up; they kept sliding down his nose.

"What is it, son?"

"Just got a call from a county bird counter. Says he found a body. And a head," Milton choked out.

"Sorry, I'm not tracking that. Please say it again." Matt held the phone closer to his ear.

"This guy says he's out near Twisty River and he found a dead person...only, the head and body are separated."

"I see," said Matt slowly. "Where is he?"

"Do you know that wildlife refuge close to where the Twisty feeds into the ocean? That's where he is. He's scared shitless. I've got him holding on the other line. What should I do?"

"This is important, Milton, and you're doing great. Tell him to stay put, don't touch anything, and watch for my city police car. I'll be there in under 10."

"Ten minutes, sir?"

"Yes, 10 minutes. Please tell him to wave when he sees my car, OK? Oh, and tell him to not call anyone else."

"Got it." Milton hung up.

Matt threw down his towel, and grabbed the first pair of jeans and a sweater he could find. He snatched his badge, his briefcase, and his jacket off its hook near the front door. Just before he reached for the door knob, he jogged back to the bedroom and unlocked his Colt 1911 pistol with its box elder burl custom grip from the small safe deep in the closet. Then he ran for his police car parked in the gravel driveway in front of his house.

The unfinished bowl of yogurt sat forlornly on the kitchen table.

◆◆◆

"Jay, where are you man?" Matt said into his phone.

"City Hall," Detective Jay Finley answered his boss. "Why? Where are you?"

"On my way to that wildlife refuge out near the mouth of the Twisty River. We've got a body. Grab Rudy and whoever else is on duty this morning and meet me there ASAP. Also, call Bernice, and tell her we need some serious forensics – the whole nine yards. Step on it, OK?"

"Oh, crap!"

"Jay, one more thing."

"Yeah?"

"Bring your guns."

◆◆◆

Fifteen years in police work, and Matt Horning had never seen anything like what he was currently looking at. He was pretty sure it was the head and

4

body of Clay Sherwin. Pretty sure. It was hard to tell for certain because of the way the head had rolled a bit to the side.

Sherwin had been a tall man, at least 6'2", and, again, without seeing the whole length of him – together – Matt wasn't 100 percent sure of the ID. And, it had been a while since Matt had seen Sherwin.

What happened since then, Clay? Matt thought, as he stared at the open eyes of the dead man. What the hell happened?

The badly-shaken biologist stood by like a statue as Matt surveyed the scene.

"Why are you out here this morning?" Matt inquired of the man. "Seems like an odd place to be working."

"I..I..do an early spring count of the egrets in the area for the Oregon Fish and Wildlife department every year. Today was the day," he mumbled.

"Please speak up," Matt demanded, "I didn't hear the last part of what you said."

"I said 'today was the day'," the man shouted, drowning out the nearby surf. "For the egret count."

"Do you know a man named Clay Sherwin?"

"Is that who this guy is?" he asked, not looking at the body. Or head. Keeping his eyes locked on Matt's face.

"We won't know for sure until forensics does its work. Do you know him?"

"No, sir, I do not."

"Have you ever seen the victim previously?"

The biologist looked pained, stared briefly at Matt, and then risked a quick glance at the victim's head.

"No, I don't believe I've ever seen this man around town," he gulped out.

"Have you ever been here before?"

"I told you, I do this count every year."

"In this exact spot?"

"Pretty much, yes. ODFW likes it to be consistent from year to year."

"Are you usually alone?"

"Almost always. Sometimes a college kid or two will come with me as part of their curriculum, but mostly it's just me."

"Do you own a sword?"

The man looked incredulously at Matt and didn't say a word for an instant or two.

"I'm a marine biologist and a scientist, chief, and, if you must know, a bit of a wimp. No, I do not own a sword. Or any other weapons. I was counting egrets. Wrong place, wrong time, it appears."

"So it appears," Matt agreed. "Unlucky, huh?"

"If I'm to be caught up in a murder case featuring a decapitated victim, I think 'unlucky' is the understatement of the year. Can I go now?" the biologist said. "Not feeling so hot."

"I'm afraid not. Detective Jay Finley in my department is on his way here now, and I want him to take a formal statement from you with all your contact information. After that you can go home. Shouldn't take long."

Looking miserable, the biologist nodded. After a pause, he said "Do you have any idea what this is about? It doesn't feel right for our little town. For Port Stirling."

"Kind of feels medieval, doesn't it? Or like a page out of the jihadist manual. No ideas, but if it's the guy I think it is, I will know where to start," Matt told him.

"Where's that, chief?"

"Washington D.C."

CHAPTER 2

....

the promotion

"I want a raise," stated Dr. Bernice Ryder as she approached Matt and the biologist, clutching her black medical bag. The fifty-something, attractive woman was dressed casually in khaki pants and a black cotton sweater set, and, today, was wearing glasses with red frames that squared out her oval face. Chinook County's medical examiner frowned as she reached to shake hands with Matt. She nodded at the witness, but did not shake hands with him; that could wait until she'd dusted him for prints.

"You've been here three months, and this is your second murder," she continued. "That's precisely two more than I usually do in a year. At the rate you're going, I deserve a raise."

Matt smiled a greeting at Bernice, and warmly clasped her hand. Not everyone got Dr. Ryder's sense of humor, but she and Matt had hit it off the first day they met. They shared what some observers would call a gallows humor, but to the two of them it was a way to lighten the grim atmosphere of their shared work.

"Every night before I go to bed I say 'Nothing ever happens here', just like Bill Abbott told me during my interviews. Doesn't seem to be working for me," Matt said.

"Whatta we got?" Bernice looked around, saw the victim's head, raised her hand to cover her mouth and said, "Oh, Lord!"

Matt reached out a hand to steady his medical examiner, as she wobbled a bit. "I know," he whispered to her.

Bernice patted his hand and said in a firm voice, "I'm fine. Just a little shock to this old system."

Dr. Ryder turned and waved to three men who were parking their vehicle on the bank above the marsh.

"Is that your crew?" Matt asked. Another Port Stirling police car pulled up next to them, and Matt was very happy to see Jay and Rudy emerge.

"Yeah, I was told to pull out all the stops," Bernice said, "and these are the best technicians we've got. If they can't get you what you need from the crime scene, it doesn't exist."

She greeted her men and gave them instructions, and then turned to Jay.

"Officer Finley, how nice to see you again. I guess."

Jay smiled at Bernice; he liked her, too, and had welcomed her steady presence on Emily's case, his first experience with a homicide.

"Actually, it's Detective Finley now," Jay corrected. "I got promoted."

"So your time in the garbage dump looking for bloody shoes paid off," she deadpanned.

"Jay did more work on that case than just wade through garbage," Matt jumped in. "He deserved to be recognized."

"I wholly concur, chief," Bernice said. "Job well done. Congrats, Jay. Wear it well, OK?"

"Yes, ma'am."

"I thought we had outlawed the use of 'ma'am' since Tex got here," she nodded in Matt's direction.

"Only he can't say it," Jay said.

"Won't I ever be an Oregonian to all of you?" Matt asked.

"No," said Bernice.

"Don't think so," said Jay. The 28-year-old detective winked at the medical examiner. Buds.

◆◆◆

"If you're done making fun of my Texas upbringing, can we get to work please?" Matt said.

Serious nods all around.

Bernice pulled on latex gloves and joined her men who had encircled the body and the head with crime scene tape, extending it out about a dozen yards in each direction.

Jay, green face, whispered to Matt, "At least it's not a dead little girl this time, boss."

"Yes, there's that."

"But this…this…" Jay continued, waving his hand at the ground, "this is horrific. Barbaric. Not sure where to begin."

"I think it's Clay Sherwin," Matt said quietly to Jay. "I met him during Emily's investigation. He was the non-golfer staying at the golf resort."

"That guy we looked at for Emily's murder?" Jay asked. "Why was he still in town? I thought he was just a tourist." He looked puzzled.

"Yeah. Good questions," Matt agreed. "But let's not get ahead of ourselves. We have a lot of questions to answer about Clay Sherwin, but first, let's make sure it is in fact him – Bernice will tell us that. I'd like you to take a statement from our biologist who found the body, so the poor guy can go home. He's had better days." Matt indicated his witness, who was still standing stark still, arms at his sides, and following Twisty River with his eyes.

"Sure thing." Jay took out his notebook and pen.

"Rudy, my man, can you help Bernice and her guys? Whatever they need?" Matt was relieved to see both Jay and Rudy wearing their pistols. "Search the area, OK?"

"The body doesn't have a head attached to it, chief," Rudy declared.

"Probably what killed him, don't you think?" Matt said, trying to sound as normal as he could under the circumstances.

"I hope like hell he was drugged first or something," Rudy stammered.

"Bernice will tell us soon, gentlemen."

The medical examiner was squatting near the victim's head, her hands on her knees. She peered at the ragged neck area, and then stretched her own neck forward, moving in even closer for another look. She let out a loud burp, and Matt feared she might be sick, but she stood up and purposefully walked around the body, being careful to not disturb anything close to it.

"Lynn, hand me your pincers," Bernice said to one of her crew. She gripped them and pulled back the victim's jacket on one side, exposing a gunshot wound and a bloody shirt.

"Shot through the heart at point-blank range is my guess," she said, turning to Matt. To her colleagues, "Guys, let's start with the gunshot wound."

Waiving the pincers in Matt's direction, Dr. Ryder quietly asked him, "What the hell is going on with this one?"

"If it's who I think it is, I have the beginnings of a theory," Matt replied.

"You know the victim?" she asked.

"Maybe. It's complicated," was all Matt said now to his M.E. "And, I'm not absolutely positive it's him. He looks a little different than I remember."

"Perhaps because his head is in another zip code." Bernice paused, grimaced and then said, "If you don't want to say anything more just yet, I'm good with that."

Matt looked directly at her. "Thanks, Bernice. We'll need a positive ID first, and then I'll make a phone call. Can I get his wallet off him?"

"Not yet. We'll do our thing, and then take him to the morgue. You can come if you want."

"Yeah, I will. In the meantime, I'll help my guys search for shell casings. We're thinking 9mm, right?"

"Yep, and while you're at it, keep your eyes open for a 19th century saber."

"You're kidding me again, right?"

"No, Matt, no kidding this time."

"Why a 19th century saber?" Matt asked. "What part of your brain did that come from?"

"Not sure," Bernice answered, and her eye twitched. "I'm not an expert on swords, but the first thing I thought of when I looked at the victim's body near the neck was a naval cutlass sword from the mid-1860s."

"Okaayyy," Matt drawled, encouraging Bernice to keep talking.

"The cutlass was preferred by the U.S. Navy because it was good in close-quarters fighting," she added.

"Like on a ship?" Matt asked her.

"Yeah, precisely like on a ship. It was better than longer swords for hacking and chopping up an opponent when space was tight. I guess I thought of it here because our guy was the victim of a serious hack job. It wasn't a long, sharp, elegant sword that did this. It was shorter, like a cutlass. I'll know more when I get him on the table, but that's my first impression."

"You never cease to amaze me." Matt shaking his head.

"Oh, you have *no* idea of what goes on up here," Bernice said as she tapped the side of her head three times in quick succession. "Bottom line here, Matt, this is scary stuff," Bernice said, holding his eyes. "I'm tempted to go to the airport right now and get a flight to Maui."

"Can't let you do that, Bernice. Looks like our lives just changed again. We need to get a move on. And put a lid on what we've got here...do you trust your colleagues to keep quiet?"

"Yes, they won't breathe a word, and I couldn't agree more. I'll have to figure out how to get him into the morgue without calling attention."

"Zip him up in a body bag, and lock the morgue door while you're doing the autopsy," Matt said. "This decapitation business absolutely cannot get out, especially before I've made a couple of phone calls. I will personally stand guard outside your door until you've finished."

"That's a plan," Bernice said. "Even though I'm a brave M.E. and afraid of virtually nothing in this world, this case might test my skill set. I will feel better knowing you've got my back."

"Always," Matt smiled at this woman underselling herself. Dr. Bernice Ryder had been one of the first voices on the county crime team to mention the key that eventually broke open Emily's case. Matt recalled the dopey medical examiner the Plano PD had to work with, and he, once again, thanked his lucky stars that this small coastal community had someone of Bernice's professional demeanor and smarts in this key role.

Matt stepped away a few yards from the activity, and, alone for a moment, stared off in the distance at Twisty River flowing into the Pacific Ocean. The green of the river, as it approached, turned first grey and then muddy as it violently met the sea's waves head on. Then, a hundred yards or so out, it became one with the bluer-than-blue ocean. *Yeah, the tourist, Clay Sherwin*, Matt thought to himself. *That's what you all thought. And now, just as I've gained all your trust, I will have to explain why I lied to you. Why I wasn't forthcoming, and why I held back information from you. My team. Which means I don't just have another homicide to solve, I'll have to earn your confidence all over again. Shit.*

CHAPTER 3

the autopsy

The forensics team performed their grisly job, and the police officers completed their sweep of the area, coming up empty-handed. Matt escorted the biologist to his car once he'd been dusted for fingerprints.

"I need your promise you won't tell another living, breathing soul what you saw here today," Matt demanded, holding on tight to the man's arm to drive home his words. "Obviously, you're upset, and if you have family at home, you tell them you were a witness to a crime today, but you aren't at liberty to discuss it. I need a head start on this one before the harsh truth cranks up the rumor mill in this town. Do you understand me?"

"I don't want to talk about it," the biologist wheezed. "Please don't worry; I'll make up something to tell my wife. I'm not sure she could handle it if I told her the actual truth. Not sure I can handle it." He looked fearfully at Matt.

"This is a jarring, savage thing. You should be upset. I'm upset. But you can handle it. Promise me you'll keep quiet," Matt said, giving his arm a supportive squeeze. "I'll come talk to you when I've got some information. Once you know I'm following a lead or two, you will feel better. You'll see."

The biologist silently nodded, and Matt watched him drive off, waving when he saw the man look back in his rear-view mirror.

The transport of the body and the head to Buck Bay Hospital – the morgue was in the basement – was uneventful. Matt gave the same speech to his professional colleagues as he had given the biologist.

"If I wake up tomorrow morning to the news that Port Stirling has a killer on the loose who decapitates his victims, I will know it was one of you who leaked it. And I will not be a happy camper. I can be very nasty if this team acts in an unprofessional manner, and you don't want to see that side of me – do you understand?" He stared them all down, one by one.

Only Detective Jay Finley and Dr. Bernice Ryder knew their police chief well enough to know he was just blustering for emphasis. The gathered others weren't quite sure, and their nervous looks indicated they took Matt's words seriously.

Matt, Jay, and Rudy hung outside the morgue's locked door in the hallway while Bernice and her crew did their thing. Only a few hospital personnel wandered by, gave a quick look, but went about their business without questioning the uniformed cops.

Every trip Matt had ever made to the morgue reminded him that his job was to get justice for the victim; it was the lifeblood of why he'd chosen this profession. He had also chosen Port Stirling, hoping that in this small coastal village he could get away from the violence that had taken over his life in Texas. But that was not to be.

His first case in Port Stirling, although alarming and frightening for the town, could have happened anywhere under the same set of circumstances.

But what the hell was this? This was so unnecessarily brutal. Why was Clay Sherwin targeted in this manner? It wasn't a random murder, that much I'm sure of. It has 'message' written all over it. And if someone knew who Sherwin was and decided to dispose of him in this fashion, that meant that they were desperate about something. And a desperate killer willing and able to take out a man like Sherwin was a killer to be feared.

Jay went to get them coffee while they waited. Rudy and Matt talked about the recent "March Madness" college basketball tournament, which the University of Oregon Ducks had won for the first time since 1939. The whole state was still euphoric about the win, and everywhere he went Matt heard discussion about it.

"I always thought Oregon was a football school," Matt said to take Rudy's mind off what was happening behind that closed door.

"We are!" Rudy exclaimed. "But now I guess we're a hoops school, too! Isn't it great?"

"Yes, great," repeated Matt. Being born and raised in Texas, he was used to big sports wins, but he knew how much a truly big win like this one could do for a state's morale. The basketball coach had only been with the Ducks for two years, he'd read, so this was a stunning accomplishment. Matt hoped like hell he could give his town and his adopted state a few more days of joy to celebrate this win before word got out about Sherwin's murder and the butcher behind it.

Jay arrived back with the coffee just as Bernice unlocked the door.

"All done," she said to Matt. "Here's his wallet. The victim is a Californian, Clay Sherwin."

Matt gingerly took the wallet from Bernice.

"It can't hurt you now," she said.

"I know that," Matt grumped at her. "I'm just being cautious. It's very light. Did you photograph the contents?"

"Yes, we did. But what you see is what you get – only his California driver's license, and some cash - $78 – and one credit card. Nothing else in the wallet."

"Private guy," said Matt.

"He had a reason to be private, chief," said Bernice. "I did find something else." She turned and went to another table where Sherwin's clothes were spread out. She held up his outerwear jacket and motioned for Matt to come closer.

"When I removed Sherwin's jacket, it felt lumpy near the bottom hem," Bernice explained. "So I cut through the lining and found these." She held up a plastic holder with a photo of a woman and two children, a boy and a girl. In the other hand she held an ID of another sort.

"The wallet and these can go to his next of kin, which appears to be a very pretty woman named Arlette Sherwin. I'm guessing wife."

Ignoring Bernice's attempt at wit, Matt removed the photo from its plastic holder and flipped it over to inspect the back. It read "Arlette, Lily, Spencer, 2015". Bernice was right – Arlette Sherwin was a real looker. Long blond hair, wide-set blue eyes, eyebrows and cheekbones just the right distance from everything. The kids looked like the perfect melding of their parents – handsome children.

The plastic ID card in Bernice's other hand featured a recent photo of Clay Sherwin. Above the photo that stared out at Matt read the words "United States Government". He quickly reached out and grabbed the card out of Bernice's hand, and jammed it in his pocket. Matt didn't want anyone else to see Sherwin's ID just yet.

"You gonna tell us who this guy really is?" Bernice inquired of Matt.

"I'm not sure who the victim really is," Matt dodged.

"But you have suspicions about him?" Jay asked, pushing his boss.

"There might be more to Sherwin than met the eye back in January," Matt allowed.

"What aren't you telling us?" Jay insisted. "What's going on?" He looked hard at Matt, and held his ground.

"I'll explain what I know about Clay Sherwin when we get the county crime team together this afternoon. I didn't tell you the whole story about him during Emily's case, and I'm sorry for that now." Matt said, signs of muscle tension in his face and shoulders. His chest felt heavy and his heart was beating fast.

"Don't apologize, man," said Jay. "We'll wait for the whole story, but I'm sure you had your reasons for not telling us everything. It sure looks now like something was going on."

Jay's words were reassuring to Matt, but his young detective looked irritated.

CHAPTER 4

....

the women and the feds

Fern Byrne loved her new job with the Port Stirling Police Department. Her previous work at Chinook County as a victims' advocate had suited her, but she couldn't stomach her boss, the district attorney, David Dalrymple. He was a pompous, arrogant jerk in her view, with totally transparent political ambitions.

Dalrymple had responded poorly when she'd told him in February that she was taking a role with the Port Stirling PD.

"But that's a step down for you," Dalrymple argued. "Why would you want to leave an important county-wide job to go to work in that backwater town?" He was truly incredulous.

"Chief Horning saw the value of my contribution to the Emily Bushnell case, and he's created a new position," she told him. "I'll still be an advocate for crime victims, but I will also use some of my skills in a larger detective role. So, essentially, it's an enhanced job for me." Fern smiled at the D.A. "Also, I live in that backwater town, Port Stirling, so there's that, too." He had never bothered to ask Fern where in the county she lived.

Dalrymple ignored that remark. "What kind of transition are you planning?" he sneered. "Leaving us high and dry?"

"Of course not, sir. I'm giving two weeks' notice, and it's not like I'm moving to China. I'll be a phone call and twenty minutes away if I can help you. Rest assured that I won't leave you high and dry."

Fern thought back to yesterday when she'd accepted Chief Horning's offer and they had discussed the logistics of how the transition out of the county

17

and into the Port Stirling PD would work. Matt had told Fern, "There will be some overlap for a while, and you should feel free to use your judgment about when your previous role might take precedence. Just keep me in the loop." Fern was certain that the D.A. would not be nearly so generous in spirit if the situation was reversed.

Now, she sat with her hands folded primly in her lap, and looked sweetly at Dalrymple. "And, I'll be an active member of the county major crime team with you, so I'm sure we'll interact on occasion going forward."

"Do you know anyone who we should interview to replace you?" Giving up.

"No, I'm afraid I can't help you there. But I'm sure you'll find someone you like." Fern stood up and held out her hand. "Thank you, David, it's been a pleasure working with you."

That had been about six weeks ago, after Fern had passed Buck Bay Community College's 'Introduction to Criminal Justice' course. Matt, looking to rebuild his police department, had formally approached Fern with a job offer, but taking that course was a prerequisite to her hiring. She had found the intro course so fascinating, that she'd decided to pursue their Criminal Justice, Associate of Science degree. Fern held two degrees from Stanford, but Art History and Political Science didn't interest her as much now, after her exposure to Matt Horning and Emily's murder case.

"Where is everybody?" Fern said now to Sylvia Hofstetter, the small department's only other female employee, as she hung up her raspberry pink raincoat on the coatrack near the squad room door. It was sunny out now, but, hello!, it was April at the Oregon coast, and one didn't dare go out without a raincoat.

"We've got another dead one," Sylvia croaked, calmly looking up at Fern over her reading glasses. Sylvia, a devout non-smoker, had a voice that sounded like a two-pack-a-day-er. Plus, she was old. No one knew her exact age. But she was a darn good records clerk, and even after working with her for only a few weeks, Fern could not imagine how the PSPD could possibly survive without Sylvia Hofstetter for even one day.

"What?"

"A corpse. Found out in that marsh near where the Twisty River finishes its journey. Matt's out there, and called Jay and Rudy for backup – they just took off. Things are certainly more exciting since he got here!" Sylvia adjusted her purple and black silk scarf tied in the French manner around her neck.

"Good Lord," said Fern. "What should we do?"

"Stay put, Red, and close to our phones. That's my guess."

"You're probably right. And my name's not Red," Fern said, annoyed. "We should see if Matt wants us to assemble the county crime team, don't you think?"

"Good idea. I thought all redheads were called Red. Didn't mean to offend."

Fern laughed. "We are, but that doesn't mean we like it."

"Duly noted. Wonder if the chief minds my calling him 'Tex'?" Sylvia looked thoughtful.

Carefully, Fern said, "I doubt that he loves it. Kinda like 'Red'."

"We could call him 'Stud Muffin'," said Sylvia straight-faced.

"We most certainly could," agreed Fern, "but we won't," she said sternly.

"The chief and Jay had me call Dr. Ryder, and she was on her way with the forensics crew from Buck Bay, but I haven't notified anyone else yet," said Sylvia. "It must be bad because the chief wanted Bernice to bring 'her whole crew'."

"Yikes, that doesn't sound good," Fern agreed. "I think we need to take action, Sylvia – back me up unless you think I'm overstepping. I'm calling Ed Sonders with the state police right now," and she quickly moved to her desk.

"Go for it," Sylvia said. "Chief wouldn't want us to sit here like bumps on a log. And, we should leave him alone while he does his thing."

Fern's side of the room had nice windows that looked out to the river, the jetty, and the Pacific Ocean beyond, and she peered out now. The marsh area was further north, and she couldn't quite see that far, even with a squint. But the sun was glinting off something, and Fern figured it must be their cars at the crime scene.

How could this be happening again? Port Stirling was a quiet town except for the occasional drunken domestic abuse case or drug overdose. It occurred to Fern that Matt and the guys might be in some danger, but she grabbed her desk phone and firmly pushed that thought to the back of her mind.

"Ed, hi, it's Fern Byrne in Port Stirling," she said and paused. "I'm fine, and you? Listen, we have a situation going on over here, and it sounds like we're going to need the crime team here this afternoon. I haven't talked to Matt yet, he's at the scene of the crime, but it sounds bad."

Another pause from Fern while she listened to the ever-colorful Ed Sonders swear loudly and long. "I know, barely time to catch our breath. Where are you currently, Ed? Oh, good, so you could make it here easily, say, by 1:00 p.m.? I don't have all the details yet, but it appears that time is of the essence. Great, I'll call Sheriff Johnson, Patty Perkins, the Buck Bay chief, and the D.A. I'll let Matt know, and confirm with him that timing will work. Thanks, Ed, see you soon."

She worked her way through the crime team players, and then punched in Matt's cell number. He picked up after two rings.

"Is this a good time for you to talk?" she asked him.

"Yeah. We're finishing up at the morgue in Buck Bay, and I'll be heading to the office in about ten minutes. I was just about to call in. I assume Sylvia filled you in?"

"Yes, I had a meeting in Twisty River at the county courthouse first thing this morning, but Sylvia gave me the basics as soon as I got here. What's the story?"

"It's ugly, Fern. As ugly as I've seen. Don't want to discuss over the phone. I'll be there soon. Stick around, OK?"

"I'm not going anywhere, boss. Sylvia and I wanted to help you get an investigation rolling, so we've scheduled a 1:00 p.m. meeting for the county crime team. Does that work for you?"

"You read my mind. Thanks for doing that, Fern, and, yeah, that's good timing. I need to make a couple of phone calls first, and give Bernice time to write her autopsy report. Do me a favor and call the Bell County sheriff, too, can you? Think his name is Les Thomas or Thompson…something like that. I haven't met him yet, but I want him at this meeting today if he can get here."

"I believe it's Les Thompson, and I will call him. His office is in Silver River, and that's only about an hour from Port Stirling. If he can't come to the meeting, what do you want me to tell him?"

"I will need to fill him in soon, so tell him I'll be calling him in the next 24 hours if he can't make our meeting today."

"Will do. The other team members are all accounted for and will be here," Fern reported and paused. "Sounds big," she squeaked.

"It is."

"Are you doing all right? Be careful."

"Trust me…lookin' over my shoulder. Big time lookin' over my shoulder. This is different, Fern. This is sinister, creepy. Please don't tell anyone this, but I'm nervous."

Fern moved out of the squad room into a quiet corner at the end of the hall. "You know I would never tell anyone anything you tell me in confidence. But murder is murder, right? Isn't that what you always say? There's a victim and there's a killer with a motive."

"True. But this killer is particularly terrifying. And you will understand when I fill in the team. Please stay safe in the office, and I'll see you soon." He hung up.

The hair on Fern's arms stood up. He sounded…scared. *Matt can't be scared, he's my chief.*

◆◆◆

"Department of State, International Narcotics and Law Enforcement Affairs. How may I direct your call?"

"Joe Phelps, please. This is Police Chief Matt Horning in Port Stirling, Oregon, calling."

Matt sat alone in his police car in the jetty parking lot waiting for his call to be connected. A lone seagull landed on the asphalt near the car, picking at the remains of a french fry carelessly tossed on the ground. *What the hell was wrong with people? One of the most pristine places on the face of the earth, and some moron has to throw a fry out the window?*

The surf was angrier now than it had been this morning. The sea was increasing its reach on the riprap armoring the shoreline. Wood pilings on the Twisty River side were being pummeled by the grey, roiling waves, flinging spray high into the air. About every third wave was now breaking over the end of the jetty, all raw power. Where there was usually one big wave break just beyond the tip of the jetty, they were stacking up two or three deep today, some as high as 25 feet. Even inside his car, the roar was thunderous.

"Phelps here. How's it going, chief?"

"Not good, Joe," Matt answered. "I've got some real bad news."

"Aw, shit, it's Clay Sherwin, isn't it? We haven't heard from him in two days, and Rod is worried. He was going to call you today."

"I'm afraid so. Sherwin has been murdered, and it's brutal. His body was found this morning. I'm so sorry." *Why doesn't this part of my job ever get any easier?*

"Where was he?"

"In a wetlands marsh area, close to where Twisty River enters into the ocean. A marine biologist was out there doing a bird count and found him."

"Is that north or south of town?"

"North. Only about a mile or so."

"How do you know it was murder? How was he killed?" Phelps was clearly upset, but now it was all business for the head narc.

"Brace yourself."

"Tell me, Matt."

"First, he was shot at close-range through the heart. We're running ballistics tests now. My medical examiner thinks that's what killed him."

"And second?"

"Second, he was decapitated. His head was about four feet away from his body."

"Oh, for God's sake."

"Yeah."

The line went silent for a moment.

"He was on to something," Phelps finally said, his voice barely audible.

"Looks like it. We've done a post-mortem, and I'll get the M.E.'s report later this afternoon. We should have ballistics and some other test results sometime tomorrow. And, my department has called the county's major crime team in for a meeting at 1:00 p.m. my time. It's a small, tight group, and we're obviously keeping a lid on this as long as we can. I presume you'll want to come out."

"Headed to the airport as soon as we hang up, Matt. Rod will want to come with me, and I may bring another investigator, too, from the FBI."

"Why the FBI?" asked Matt. "I thought Clay was working for you."

"He was. But his investigation ramped up in the past couple of weeks, and he developed an additional theory that warranted me bringing in my counterpart at the FBI. I'll tell you more when I see you. Who's on this crime team of yours? Do they know how to keep their mouths shut?"

"They're good people, Joe, and they know what they're doing. Plus, they won't want this story getting out locally any more than you do. Guaranteed."

"No, I don't suppose they would. This has to be my case, chief. Do you understand?"

"No, Joe, it's *our* case," Matt replied forcefully. "I understand that Clay Sherwin was your guy, but we've got some maniac running around *my* town cutting heads off. You can't expect me to stand idly by, especially if you've been holding back information from me. I've started our investigation, and I can't keep Sherwin's real identity hidden from my team anymore. I should've brought a couple of key people into the loop back in January, and I'm regretting that now."

"This is bigger than Port Stirling, chief."

"I get that. And you're the man with all the resources. But we know this area, and we know our people. That can help you. But for now, what about next-of-kin? Clay once mentioned a wife and son to me, and we found a family photo in his personal belongings. Are they real, or part of his cover?"

"Unfortunately, Arlette, his wife, and the kids are very real," Phelps swore softly. "This is going to be a tough one."

"Send me his wife's contact info and I'll call her," Matt said. "You get yourself on a plane and get out here as soon as you can."

"I appreciate your help on this part."

"What else can I do for you on our end?" Matt asked. "I'll book hotel rooms, and arrange for a car at the airport. Anything else?"

"Good. Is there a place at your office we can set up and operate from?"

"Yeah, we call it our War Room, and it will work for you."

"It's war, all right."

CHAPTER 5

....

trust

At a few minutes after 1:00 p.m. on this now-raining Friday, Matt welcomed the Chinook County major crime team to their usual meeting place, a soulless, institutional, windowless room in the bowels of Port Stirling City Hall, the "War Room".

"You again?" Patty Perkins wisecracked to Matt as she took a seat around the table to his right. "We'd better be here for a murder, because if my vacation was interrupted for anything else, *I'm* going to kill someone."

"Apparently, it is me again," Matt replied, a grim set to his jaw. "I thought you might still be gone. Is the honeymoon officially over?" he inquired as he pulled out a chair for her and held it while she sat down.

"The trip is over; the honeymoon never," she grinned. Patty Perkins was the primary investigative cop in Twisty River, a small town that served as the Chinook County seat about twenty-five miles inland from Port Stirling. Patty was known throughout the county by her colleagues as one of the leading detectives in southwest Oregon. She was also a newlywed, and calling her in for a grisly murder was not exactly the wedding present that Matt had hoped to give her.

Bernice Ryder welcomed her old friend, Patty, with a bear hug. "Where did you two lovebirds go?" she whispered as the other team members were filing into the room.

"Switzerland, and it was arctic cold. We spent a lot of time indoors eating cheese fondue and drinking. Quite wonderful, actually."

"Well, welcome home. You got here just in time," said Bernice, casting a quick look at Matt before taking the chair next to Patty.

"That's what I hear," Patty said. "Is it bad?"

Silently, Bernice nodded, eyes wide open as she stared at Patty.

Big Ed Sonders came into the room. He clapped Matt on the back as he passed him to find a chair across the table from Patty and Bernice, and next to the sheriff.

Matt reached out to shake the hand of a man standing in the doorway, unsure of himself. "You must be Les Thompson. Come in, please." Matt closed the door behind the newcomer.

"I'm probably the only one who hasn't met Les before today, but just in case, Les is the sheriff of Bell County. I invited him to join us today. Take a seat anywhere, Les."

Matt sat at the head of the table, cleared his throat, looked around, and said "Looks like we're all here except for the district attorney. Did we call him, Fern?"

"Yes, sir. I talked to his admin and she promised she'd tell him about the meeting."

"Maybe Dalrymple's pissed because you got a better job," deadpanned Ed.

Fern blushed. "I'm sure that's not it."

"He's late," grumbled Chinook County Sheriff Earl Johnson, with his Mike Ditka haircut and broad belly straining his uniform buttons. "Let's go." Earl did not suffer fools gladly, his marked disdain for the district attorney rarely hidden.

Matt sat, shifted in his chair, and opened his dog-eared police notebook on the table in front of him. He paused for a moment as he glanced at his notes, and then looked up at his colleagues around the table.

"I appreciate y'all getting here on such short notice. We wouldn't have called you if we didn't have to, especially on your Friday afternoon. But we had to."

Just then the door opened and district attorney David Dalrymple strolled in. "Chief Horning," said the D.A., his navy suit, white shirt, grey tie looking as spiffy and overdressed as ever. "I thought we were meeting at 4:00 p.m. like we always do. Who changed the time?" he frowned.

"My department," said Matt. "We have a sense of urgency, and need to get this investigation rolling. Sorry if the short notice inconvenienced you, David."

"You're lucky I'm here," Dalrymple groused. "I had to scramble when my assistant told me about the new time when she realized I hadn't left my office."

Sheriff Earl rolled his eyes.

"Lucky us," agreed Matt. "We've started without you, so please take a seat quickly." To the assembled team, he continued, "At 7:10 a.m. this morning, a body was found in the marshy wetland area just north of Port Stirling. The victim has been identified – by me, and by identification on his person – as Clay Sherwin."

"Isn't that the guy we interviewed out at Port Stirling Links in Emily's case?" asked the sheriff. "I know you cleared him with a solid alibi, but I always felt there was something off about that guy."

"You weren't totally wrong, Earl. There's more to Clay Sherwin's story than I let on back in January."

"You hid facts from us?" Dalrymple demanded, pointing his finger at Matt. "May I remind you that I am the district attorney, and no one is allowed to keep the facts from me. What is Clay Sherwin's real story?"

"Chief withheld the details about Sherwin from all of us," Jay said, and there was undeniable frost in his voice. "You weren't singled out, Mr. Dalrymple."

Both Jay and Dalrymple looked pointedly at Matt.

"Hold on, please. Let me finish describing this morning." Matt scratched his nose, and continued looking at his notebook. "Dr. Ryder is going to fill in the details on the cause of death, but before she does, I need to warn you about a shocking detail. Sherwin had been decapitated, and his head was discovered about four feet away from his body."

A couple of hands flew to mouths, and Patty let out a loud, involuntary gasp. Bernice put her arm around her friend.

"Yeah, it was gross," chimed in Jay sitting at the far end of the table. "Blood everywhere, neck dangling…"

"Sweet Jesus," roared Ed Sonders, and his face turned beet red. "This really pisses me off. If you have to kill someone, kill them. But this!"

The district attorney's countenance went from a flushed, angry look to white as a ghost in a matter of seconds. He tugged at the neck of his shirt as if he was trying to loosen his tie to breathe. Fern, sitting beside him and seeing him turn pale and clearly agitated, touched his arm and said, "Are you all right, David?"

"I'm OK," he stammered. "But this is horrifying news." His voice was several octaves lower than usual. "How on earth will we tell the public about this? It's terrifying."

"I hope this isn't my fault," choked out the sheriff, looking down at the report in front of him. "I didn't blow it, did I Matt?" He looked pleadingly at him.

"Of course not, Earl," Matt assured him. "The only people that even knew you and I talked to Sherwin are in this room, and the desk clerk at Port Stirling Links. He was very nervous about his resort possibly being involved in a child's murder, and he didn't say a word to anyone. You did your job, sheriff, and these two cases are unrelated. Now, Jay, if you're done scaring everyone, can we let Bernice give her report?"

"Sorry, boss."

Sternly, Matt nodded at Jay.

"Clay Sherwin was killed by a close-range shot to the heart," Bernice cleared her throat and started. "The separation of his head from his body came after he was already dead."

"Thank God," whispered Fern, still patting the D.A.'s arm in a comforting fashion.

"Then that's a killer who wanted to send a signal to us," Patty said, frowning at Matt. "Who is this guy Sherwin? You need to level with us. Now."

"Well, the killer wanted to send a signal to someone, for sure. This is what I didn't tell you in January," Matt said. "Shortly after Earl and I interrogated Clay Sherwin separately regarding Emily's death, I got a visit in my office from two guys. From the United States Department of State."

"What the hell?" said Dalrymple, sitting up straight in his chair, and appearing to have recovered from the grisly detail. "Why wasn't I advised about this development? Honestly, chief, what the hell were you thinking not to bring me in on this?"

"He was probably thinking that this was a covert investigation, not a popularity contest," Patty said as sweetly as she could manage. "Let it go, David."

"Yeah," Matt continued, as if Dalrymple hadn't spoken. "Joe Phelps, Deputy Chief in charge of Narcotics Enforcement, and his lead investigator, Roderick McClellan. They flew all the way out from D.C. to tell me to back off Clay Sherwin. Not only was he not Emily's killer, he was here working as a special agent trying to uncover an international drug-smuggling ring that the feds think is operating in Chinook or Bell counties…probably both, which is why I've invited you, Les. They were afraid Earl and I were going to blow his cover and upend the mission."

Matt leaned back and let the team absorb this news.

Sheriff Johnson slapped his open palm on the table. "I knew there was something about that guy. But nobody deserves to die like this."

"I'm sorry I didn't include you guys, but the feds were adamant that no one else was to know about Clay Sherwin's true identity. They reluctantly told me what was going on, only because I might have really messed it up for them. I hope each and every one of you know that I would trust you with my own life, and I mean that, but I made a promise to them. I gave Joe Phelps a call this morning, and they are on their way out here. We're to proceed with our own investigation, but they'll be closely involved since the victim is a federal employee."

"You know, chief, we've handled drug smugglers on our own before," said the sheriff. "They were relatively small-time amateurs, but the county has worked with the Coast Guard on this kind of a deal previously. Maybe you could suggest to the feds that they stay put in D.C. and we give it a go."

Matt ran his hand through his hair. "I don't know, Earl. This feels like we should avail ourselves of their help. Murder. Decapitation. It's bigger than amateur smugglers, I think."

"Well, it's true we haven't dealt with this level of crime," Patty said. "But we do have some pretty darn good detectives. Like me, for instance."

Matt smiled. "Agreed. You all have skills that will be hugely utilized during this investigation, and we will certainly kick it off this very minute. But the reality is I won't be able to stop Phelps and McClellan from doing their thing. Just know that I am truly sorry for deceiving you in January, and that we'll take charge now and get going. We owe it to the victim, and to our community."

"Well, that's all fine and good, Chief," said Dalrymple, standing now and circling the big table. "A pretty speech. But it didn't work on me. We're supposed to be a team," he said, spreading out his arms to encompass everyone at the table. "How can you expect us to trust you when you've eroded whatever trust you built up by hiding Sherwin's identity from us? You're still new here, remember? We don't really know you all that well yet."

"David, I…" started Matt before Jay interrupted him.

"We are supposed to be a team," Jay said, looking down at the table and not at Matt. "It doesn't feel good to me that you didn't tell us about Sherwin and what he was doing here."

"Maybe if you had told us," piped in Sheriff Earl, "we might have been able to help the poor bastard."

"Exactly!" exclaimed Dalrymple, back at his chair and angrily pulling it away from the table before he sat back down, fuming.

"Guys, under normal circumstances, I never would have withheld the truth from any of you," Matt said, spinning his pen around his fingers. "But this was extremely sensitive, and the feds were adamant. I'm sorry. I understand it looks like I don't have faith in you, but I do. Every one of you. Maybe I made a mistake making that promise to Phelps."

"Maybe you did," Jay said softly. "If you don't believe in us, how can we believe in ourselves?" He looked up at his boss, and there was confusion written all over his face.

Agonizingly, Matt said, "I'm sorry, Jay. I don't know how many times I can say it. I'm sorry I lied to you." He looked around the table. "To all of you."

Ed Sonders coughed. Other than that, there was silence in the room.

"You did what you felt you had to do in January," Patty finally said, making her decision. "That's history, and we move forward from here." She shifted in her chair, and changed gears quickly, adding, "So, we're dealing with cutthroat international drug smugglers in our county. Nice."

CHAPTER 6

....

v r b o

"Do we know what Clay Sherwin was working on?" asked Ed Sonders. "Specifically? And, for the record, the feds should have notified the Oregon State Police the minute they had an inkling something was going on."

"I told them you'd be pissed," Matt said. "In their defense, they convinced me that they were fairly certain there was some sort of smuggling operation going on – they got an anonymous tip – but it was early days, and they had no idea who might be in on it."

"Still insulting," huffed Ed. "Do I look like a drug smuggler to you?"

The whole table laughed. Ed Sonders, all 6'4" of him in his imposing, starched khaki state uniform with his sharp blue tie, holster, and gun looked even less like a drug smuggler than Fern did.

"No, Ed, I wouldn't peg you for a drug pirate," Matt said. "But Clay Sherwin told me that when they first started investigating around here, they thought it might be a local operation, so everybody was a suspect. It was only a month or so ago that he told me they were now convinced it was international in scope."

"How did he know that?" Patty asked.

"I'm clueless, Patty," Matt admitted. "Even I was on a 'need-to-know' basis, and Sherwin was tight-lipped. But he came by last week and told me that his leads had dried up, and he was going to take off and go home to California for a couple of weeks. Spending spring break with his kids. That's the last time I saw him, and is really all I know. Phelps and McClellan should have more of an update from him, and we'll learn more about his latest activities once they get here. Phelps indicated on the phone that there was a recent new wrinkle."

"Was he still staying at the Links resort?" asked Sheriff Johnson.

"Oh, that is a piece I do know," Matt said hurriedly. "No, Earl, Sherwin had rented a VRBO cottage somewhere near the south end of Ocean Bend Road. Been there since early February."

"Can we search it?" asked Ed. "Do you know exactly where it is?"

"No, I was never there, but he did mention that it was on a private lane off to the right just before the road makes that hard left toward the highway."

"I know where that is," Jay said. "It's a dead end lane, and there's only one house on the property. It sits in a clearing once you pass through the trees that front Ocean Bend. Some buddies and I rented it for New Year's a couple years ago. So we could drink in private," he added, in case there was any question.

"David, please get us a search warrant ASAP," Matt instructed. "It will take too long to go through VRBO's no-doubt red tape. Ed, let's go tonight as soon as we're legal, and Patty, you come with us. Jay, round up Walt and Rudy, and Fern, you go with them."

"Don't you think we should wait for your best friends, the feds?" Dalrymple asked. "We could be stepping in something they don't want us to. Some of us aren't as cavalier with our careers. There could be ramifications if we step in where they don't want us to. I'll talk to Judge Hedges if you insist, but it's my opinion that we should wait until Phelps and his guy arrive."

The room got quiet. The D.A.'s remark about 'careers' was obviously a not-so-subtle dig at Matt's troubles in his previous role in Dallas. The circumstances that drove him out of Texas and into Port Stirling were not a secret in this room. He hadn't bowed down to politics then, and he wasn't about to now.

Matt looked around the table. "What do the rest of you think? Should we move forward or sit on our hands until Joe and Rod get here tomorrow?"

After a few moments as the team looked around the table at each other, Fern spoke first. "I agree with Matt – we need to get going and begin this investigation where we can. We have no assurance that the State Department will want to fill us in even after they arrive – they sure haven't so far. We could be operating in the dark on this for days."

"It seems to me you always agree with him, Fern," sniped the D.A.

"Perhaps that's because, so far, the chief's decisions have all been correct," sniped Fern right back. "All but one, that is," and she dared a look at Matt that said she agreed with her colleagues. "Everyone sitting around this table has a responsibility to protect our county. Surely you can agree with that, David."

"They cut off the head of a federal agent," piled on Patty. "That fact doesn't make me want to go home, cook a nice dinner, and get a good night's sleep. Get the damn warrant, David!"

David stared daggers at Patty, but didn't argue any further. Even bullies know when they're beaten. "OK, OK, I'll talk to the judge as soon as we're done here." He slumped back in his chair.

Matt and Fern shared a quick glance, and absolutely no one in the room missed it.

"Thank you, David," said Matt, nodding in the D.A.'s direction. "I believe our town is at grave risk, and we need to act and get this investigation underway right now. Someone's got a sword and he's not afraid to use it."

◆◆◆

Doug Fir Lane was pitch dark when Matt and the team turned off Ocean Bend Road onto the one-lane driveway.

"Would it kill the owner to put up a light out here?" Matt, jumpy, said to Ed beside him in the state cop's car.

"Maybe Texans are afraid of the dark, but Oregonians aren't," Ed said, his mouth turning up ever so slightly.

"We have this thing now called electricity. It's OK to utilize it."

"The Oregon coast is a dark place at night," Ed said, not humoring him.

"No shit, Sherlock. And, I know what you're doing."

"What am I doing?"

"You're trying to go all stoic on me. Take the edge off."

"Is it working?"

"Maybe."

The two cops shared a laugh.

"Are you afraid of anything, Ed?" Matt asked the big guy.

"My wife."

"Why is that?"

"She's smarter than me. And that's the only way people can beat me – they have to be smarter. Chances are some doped-up lunatic with a sword is not smarter than me. But you, you're smarter than me, and as long as you're heading up our team, the lunatic's going down."

"You still think I'm capable after I lied to all of you?"

"You made a mistake, Matt," Ed said gruffly. "I don't know what that feels like since I've never made one personally, but I understand that people make mistakes all the time."

Matt laughed in spite of how miserable he felt. "So, you trust me to move on from my lies, and not make any more stupid mistakes where our team is concerned?"

"I'm counting on it. Catching this lunatic, or, more likely, multiple lunatics is far more important than your personal angst at the moment. We'll get 'em."

"Hope you're right. I sorta like my head."

"No doubt, it's a pretty one. Fern seems to agree."

"What's that supposed to mean?" Matt turned to face him.

"We're here," was the state cop's only reply.

Ed pulled the car up in the driveway in front of the rental cottage. The Port Stirling police car driven by Jay pulled in immediately behind him, with Sheriff Earl and Patty Perkins behind it. A light shown from somewhere beyond the glass panels to the side of the front door.

Matt jumped out of Ed's car the instant it stopped, pulling his Colt pistol out of its holster, all in one smooth move.

"Be ready for anything, people," he whispered to his colleagues. All except Fern were armed and poised for action; she was only two months into her six-month academy training and had not yet been issued a firearm.

Matt had been surprised to learn that Oregon was indeed the 'wild west' when it came to weapons policy. In Texas, each chief of police was responsible for standardizing the policy, and making sure that each of his officers carried the same guns. But in Oregon, there was no mandate, and his officers could do their own thing.

Matt brought three weapons with him from Texas: the Colt 1911, which he wore now while in uniform, and a Smith & Wesson 5-shot snub-nosed 357 revolver, which he also wore now on his ankle. And, he had a scoped rifle, but had left that one locked in the trunk of his police car when he learned that Ed had a shotgun in his state car trunk. All three were old-school Texas choices, and represented his comfort level when facing potential danger.

Fern had asked Matt's advice about weapons when she started her training, and would eventually choose the same Colt 1911. All the other officers in his department used Glocks, which was fine with Matt. While he found the Glock to be a rugged weapon that wouldn't jam, it just wasn't for him because he wasn't as accurate with it.

At this moment, Matt was very happy he'd taken his team through a firearms refresher course just last month. Ol' George hadn't thought it necessary for the PSPD to be up-to-date with weapons training because they rarely had the occasion to draw a gun. To his relief, and to some surprise, Matt had been happy to learn his officers were mostly accurate, and showed good judgment when shooting. He'd also heard through the department grapevine that Fern might be the best shot of all of them by the time her training was finished.

"Ed and I will go in the front door first," Matt said, speaking quietly. "Earl and Patty, come with us. Jay, since you've been here before, please take the three officers with you and go around to the back. Is there another door on that side of the house? Do you remember?"

"Yeah, there's a large back deck that runs the length of the house and two sets of sliders – one into the living room, and one off the master bedroom."

"OK, you take Rudy and check the bedroom door to see if it's locked. Fern, you and Walt wait by the living room door, and I'll let you in once we're in the clear. It's quiet and there's no vehicle here, so I'm not expecting trouble, but do check around the back. Everyone have their flashlight? Let's go."

The house was owned by a couple in Sacramento, and they rented it through VRBO. They hadn't yet responded to Matt's request to open up the house, and they hadn't found a key on Clay Sherwin, so Ed had pulled his lock pick kit, including his sure-fire lock pick gun out of his glove compartment.

They headed up the four wide steps to the front door. Matt tried the front door and it was locked. He knocked and peered through one of the glass panels, while Ed did the same on the other side. It looked like the foyer light was the only one on. No answer. He knocked again. Still no answer.

"Step aside," Ed said to Matt. "I love this little toy." In less than ten seconds, the door's lock sprung open and they were inside. With their guns raised in front of their bodies, Matt and Ed cautiously and quickly moved through the empty house, going one direction, while the sheriff and Patty went the opposite way. They let in Walt and Fern, and the four moved to the back of the house, turning on lights as they went, and checking the three bed-rooms and two bathrooms.

Matt pulled back the draperies in the big bedroom on the back of the house, and let in Jay and Rudy. While the rest of the house seemed neat and tidy at first glance, the bed in this room was unmade on one side. In the en-suite bathroom, a forest-green towel was laying on the floor, and toiletries were scattered across the counter. A bar of soap laid on the bottom of the tub/shower combo.

On the wall near the slider, a suitcase rested on a hotel-style foldable lug-gage rack. It was open, and contained men's clothing, underwear, and a pair of black leather loafers. Matt rummaged through it, and found nothing out of the ordinary.

"No money or credit cards here either. But it belongs to Clay Sherwin all right. He was wearing this sweater the day I first interviewed him," he said, holding up a dark blue cashmere crew neck pullover. Moving to a nearby closet, Matt also recognized a long black overcoat hanging at one end.

And there were books on one nightstand, one of which Matt remembered from Sherwin's room at Port Stirling Links. Sherwin's reading taste seemed to veer to fiction.

Nothing in the house appeared to be disturbed. There was a small amount of coffee in the bottom of the glass coffee maker in the kitchen, but the older-model machine had been turned off. A bowl and a spoon were left in the sink, and the residue matched the cereal and banana peel found on the counter, and the milk in the fridge. There was also a wine glass in the sink, with remnants of red wine. Jay bagged the bowl, spoon, and glass.

In the garbage bin under the sink, they found an empty pizza carton from a restaurant nearby out on the highway.

"Too many carbs," said Fern.

"Maybe he had sausage on his pizza," Jay countered. "And maybe the delivery person came back last night, robbed him, and then dropped his body in the marsh."

"How many petty thieves do you know, Jay, who shoot their victims point-blank in the heart and then chop off their head?" Matt asked.

"Sometimes the answer is simple," Jay said, somewhat defensively.

"This is not one of those times," Matt barked. "But we will investigate the pizza anyway because it's evidence that Clay or someone was recently here.

Follow up with the restaurant, Jay, and see if you can nail down a day and time for this order, and any specifics about delivery or pick-up, OK?"

Jay nodded, but did not speak.

Ed spoke. "So, it looks like he took a shower, got dressed, drank some coffee, ate a bowl of cereal, and left the house of his own free will. You found no car keys on his body, and there wasn't a car at the crime scene. So, where's his car? Do you know what he was driving, Matt?"

"I walked him out of the office once to our parking lot, and I think it was a black SUV of some sort. I didn't actually see him get in it and drive off, but that's the vehicle he stood next to. I think it was a Toyota, like a 4Runner. Oregon plates, so likely a rental. I'm confident enough to put out an APB on it for our next step."

Lyft and Uber had not yet made their way to remote southwestern Oregon, and a car was a necessity. Finding Sherwin's car was crucial.

"I'll check the rental car companies first thing in the morning," Fern volunteered. "Was he using the name 'Clay Sherwin' exclusively as far as you know?"

"Yes, and he had all the ID to go with it, courtesy of the United States Department of State," Matt answered. "Pretty sure it's his real name, and Phelps referred to his wife as 'Arlette Sherwin'."

"Still, that's a good first question for your buddies when they arrive tomorrow," Ed said.

CHAPTER 7

....

flash

Saturday, April 6

Joe Phelps and Roderick McClellan arrived at the Buck Bay Airport in a chartered plane they'd arranged at Portland International Airport.

"Pretty place you got here," Phelps said to Matt, who picked them up, along with Ed Sonders, who had insisted on going. "Said that to Rod when we were here in January."

Matt introduced the feds to Ed, and waited for what he was certain would come out of big Ed's mouth. Sure enough.

"Ed Sonders, Oregon State Police," he said, shaking hands. "You know, that organization you should have notified about your operation."

"In some states, the state cops turn out to be the bad guys," Phelps responded. Not a shred of remorse.

"Not in Oregon. We catch the bad guys. And maybe we could have caught your bad guys before they chopped off your agent's head." All 6'4" not giving one inch.

Phelps had the humanity to look down at his shoes at Ed's remark. After a pause he said, "Maybe you could have. But we'll never know that, so it's best to move forward."

"That's what we're doing, Joe," Matt said briskly, "moving forward. We searched Clay Sherwin's rental house last night, and found nothing amiss. We've got an APB out on the vehicle we believe to be his rental car. It's missing."

"Did you call Arlette?" asked Rod, speaking for the first time.

39

"Yes, I did," Matt said. "I told her that we'd found her husband's body and that he had been positively identified."

"How did she take it?"

"I'm not really sure." Matt thought for a minute, remembering standing at his office window when he made the call to the victim's wife, with the low sun sloping across the sea beyond. She seemed upset at first, but then quickly – too quickly, he'd thought – turned all business.

"Are you sure it's him?" Arlette Sherwin had asked.

"Yes, ma'am. I'd met your husband previously on several occasions, and I identified the body. We also found his State Department ID and his driver's license on him when we did the post-mortem."

"You already did an autopsy? Shouldn't I have been notified first?"

"With all due respect, it wouldn't have mattered. When we have a suspicious or unusual death on our hands, we're required to do an autopsy. State law. I'm very sorry."

"Did you at least call his boss at the State Department?" she demanded.

"Yes, ma'am. Joe Phelps and Roderick McClellan are flying out here as we speak. They're very upset, and asked me to give you their sincere condolences. Mr. Phelps said he will be in touch with you once they get here."

Matt hadn't shared the gory details with Arlette Sherwin; Phelps had asked him to hold that back for now. Fine with him – let Phelps do some of the heavy lifting on his guy.

"What happens next, Chief Horning?" she asked. "Should I come up there now?"

"I would say 'no', not yet, Mrs. Sherwin. Your husband's body won't be released by the medical examiner for another day or two while they complete some final tests. There is really nothing you can do right now. Once we're finished, I or Mr. Phelps will alert you, and then we can decide together how you want to proceed. How's that?"

Matt didn't say that he couldn't guarantee her safety currently either. Until they knew why Clay Sherwin had been so brutally murdered, anyone connected to him might be at risk, too. He did tell Arlette to keep her wits about her as much as possible, and to not hesitate to call his cell phone if she wanted to talk for whatever reason.

It didn't occur to Matt until he turned out his nightstand light about midnight last night that Arlette Sherwin had not asked him how her husband had been killed.

Matt had relayed the conversation with Sherwin's wife to the two feds and to Ed, and the four continued their talk while Matt drove them to their hotel. Jay had arranged for a city car to be available to Phelps and McClellan during their stay, and it was parked out behind the hotel. Matt gave them the keys, and carried one of Phelps' bags into the lobby.

"I'm not in love with them," Ed said when he and Matt were back in Matt's police car.

"I didn't expect you would be," Matt smiled. "Hey, they have a job to do, Ed, and we're going to help them solve this puppy and right the world. Got any plans right now?"

"At your service, chief."

"Great. We're going back to Clay's rental house. I have a hunch."

♦♦♦

Matt and Ed lifted the crime scene tape they'd placed last night, and let themselves into Clay Sherwin's VRBO rental.

"What are we looking for?" Ed asked.

"Not exactly sure," Matt said. "But it dawned on me in the middle of the night that one of the books on Clay's nightstand was also on his nightstand back in January when I questioned him in his room at Port Stirling Links."

"So, he was a slow reader," suggested Ed.

"Maybe. But there was another book right next to his bed, and the book I remember was pushed back in the corner. If he hadn't finished it, why wouldn't it be handier? And if he was done with it, why wouldn't he stash it back in his suitcase?"

"So, we're going to look at a book."

"That's right, lieutenant. Follow me."

Matt picked up the book – *The Cartel*, a novel by author Don Winslow – and thumbed through it, looking for any highlighted sentences or sections that might give him a clue into Clay's thinking. Nothing.

But when he got to the end, the hardcover back felt bulky. Taped to the inside back cover was a USB flash drive.

"Bullseye!" Matt exclaimed.

"I'll be a son-of-a-bitch," said Ed, clapping Matt heartily on the back, and grinning from ear to ear.

CHAPTER 8

....

fern   byrne

Unearthing the car rental company that had rented to Clay Sherwin had been an easy job for Fern Byrne. She may not officially have the title of Detective Byrne yet, but, as a cadet, she was already head and shoulders above everyone else in the Port Stirling Police Department. Which Matt knew she would be, and was the reason he'd made an attractive offer to her after the Emily Bushnell case.

It was easy work because, if you didn't count the U-Haul neighborhood guy in Port Stirling – and Fern sincerely hoped it wouldn't come to that – there were only two rental car companies at the Buck Bay Airport.

Bingo! Door number one. Clay Sherwin had rented a black Toyota 4Runner on December 26 last year, and told the rental agency that he would need it for approximately two months. The clerk had been overjoyed because the full-size SUV was one of their higher-end models, and they never had rentals for more than one week. At Fern's urging, he remembered the customer, and described him as "tall, a big guy, with really broad shoulders and in shape, kinda quiet."

Fern asked the clerk to email a photo of the vehicle to her, which he promptly did. She had it on Matt's desk by 8:15 a.m.

Comments like the one her former boss, the asshole district attorney, made yesterday only made Fern more determined to succeed in her new role. Yes, she did often agree with Chief Horning, and, yes, she liked Matt. *So sue me.* Dalrymple's implication that her entire outlook was based on that was sexist and demeaning, which is the main reason she'd dumped his county job, and walked out with a smile on her face.

Everybody liked Matt. He had come into their lives at the very moment they needed him most. And while Fern knew better than nearly everyone that Matt had his flaws and was not perfect, he was a bona fide hero in Port Stirling. She wasn't taking the fact that he hid Clay Sherwin's real identity from the team as hard as the rest of them seemed to. It was, after all, the feds' case, and if they wanted to keep it secret, it made sense that Matt would respect their wishes. It would take more than a little white lie to shake her trust in him.

◆◆◆

Turns out there were a bunch of black Toyota 4Runners in Chinook County...at least eleven, so far. When the APB went out – only saying that the police were looking for this vehicle with no explanation as to why – several matching the description had been spotted around the county. Jay, Rudy, and Fern were out chasing down the owners and checking out each report. So far, none of them matched the license plate of Sherwin's rental, and all owners were accounted for.

Where the heck was his car?

Back at City Hall, the three PSPD officers, plus state cop Ed Sonders, crowded around Matt's desk. Out Matt's big picture window, it was still a fine day, but storm clouds were forming out to sea. He was beginning to recognize weather patterns, and the looming weighty clouds on the horizon, a sullen purple color, meant rain was coming.

"Thanks for pounding the pavement, you guys," Matt said to his department. "Here's an idea: Ed, does the state have a helicopter or two we could borrow? Do a flyover of Port Stirling and the surrounding area? See if we might get lucky and spot Sherwin's vehicle from the air?"

"Good idea, chief. I'm on it", said Sonders and left the room, pulling his phone out of its belt pouch. "Back in a flash."

"Where are the feds?" asked Fern.

"Dropped them at their hotel. They wanted to pick up their car, and see the crime scene. I gave them directions. They'll come here when they're done out there, probably about an hour, hour-and-a-half."

"Are they going to brief us on what Clay Sherwin was working on?" she asked.

"Yeah. They're coming to this afternoon's crime team meeting and will fill us all in. Now that their agent on the ground is dead, they know they need our local help on their mission," Matt said.

"The perpetrators must've known Sherwin was on to them," Jay added, fidgeting in his chair before crossing his long skinny legs. "Why was he working alone? Is that normal? Risky, if you ask me," shaking his head.

"Agreed, but on a stakeout like this one it's fairly normal," Matt said. "One agent can sneak around and be inconspicuous, whereas a team would be more likely to be spotted. I'll be anxious to hear exactly what Phelps and McClellan know about Sherwin's activities." He paused to guzzle some water from the plastic bottle on his desk. "You like to think the federal government knows what it's doing, but, depending on what Clay knew, it should have been clear that the opponent is likely very serious about whatever in the hell they are doing. I guess hindsight is 20-20."

"So, you think these guys, Phelps and McClellan, maybe didn't know that much about what Sherwin was actually doing?" Jay asked. "Shouldn't he have been keeping them up-to-date?"

"I don't know," Matt said thoughtfully. "Phelps acted like he didn't know much, but I'm not sure I bought it. We'll get our chance to quiz him face-to-face, and he will need to know that trust is a two-way street. If he's holding back on us, this isn't going to work."

"Are we going to assume Sherwin's death was related to whatever he was working on?" asked Fern.

"No, we are not," Matt answered firmly. "Tell me, what was the one thing you learned during the Bushnell investigation?"

Fern hesitated briefly and then offered, "That the obvious answer might not be the correct one? And that our first assumptions were dead wrong?"

Matt looked at her. A slow, admiring look. "Right response. Which is why we'll be looking into all aspects of Clay Sherwin's life – family, finances, past jobs."

"I'm always right," she said, and the corners of her mouth turned up slightly.

"I hate that about you," said Jay. "You're like that girl in the fourth grade always waving her hand when the teacher asks a question." He raised his arm and waved it to show how it's done, pulling a face for emphasis.

"I'm not *like* that girl," laughed Fern, "I *was* that girl."

They all laughed because they knew that was a true statement, and then Matt corralled them back to business, "OK, here's how we'll divvy this up. I'll work on the family angle. I didn't love Arlette Sherwin's reaction when I gave her the news, and I want to further explore her," he said. "And, I'll talk to his kids, too. I know he was pretty close to his son, but I don't know anything about the daughter."

"Just the two children?" asked Ed, coming back into Matt's office. "Helicopter is a go, but they can only spare us one, and not for very long. We've got a missing hiker in the Cascades, and my office has the other copters working up there."

"We'll take what we can get, and be grateful for one," said Matt. "Thanks, Ed. Let's finish this. Only the two kids that I know of." He broke off talking, and stroked his chin. "On second thought, Fern, you take the children – can you? You related better to the Bushnell kids than I did. Jay, you look into his business colleagues. See if he had any enemies at work. And, what did he do before this job? Has he always been a special agent?"

"Will your two fed guys help steer me in the right direction?" Jay asked.

"My feeling is that they will be cooperative," Matt said. "They'll be getting big-time heat in Washington – losing an agent is not going to be popular in the State Department. You should be able to connect by phone with his D.C. colleagues. Fern, you'll need Sherwin's personnel file. I have Arlette's cell phone. I've told her to not come up here just yet, mainly because Bernice hasn't released his body. If you need to go down there to meet with Sherwin's kids, do it. Get Sylvia to make it happen. I'll talk more to Arlette about how she wants to handle things once Bernice lets go."

Matt took a deep breath and sat back in his chair. "Ed, talk helicopter to me."

"We've got one leaving Salem now, and the pilot says he knows a place to land it in Port Stirling. He has the description of Sherwin's vehicle. Wants us to map out the area he's to cover when he gets here. I can do that, and meet him where he lands. He'll be here in about 90 minutes."

"Excellent. I will manage our relationship with the feds, so please, none of you worry about that. Phelps is a good guy. McClellan is a little prickly, but only because he knows what he's doing, and he's impatient."

Matt rubbed the bridge of his nose. "How can this be happening again?" he said to no one in particular.

"I just stopped having nightmares about the Bushnell case," Jay said, "so I needed something else to freak me out. It's my fault."

They all smiled, but the smiles were tense, not joyful.

◆◆◆

"I'll take these," Fern said, handing two bunches of spinach to the booth's vendor, and simultaneously pulling a wind-blown lock of red hair behind her ear. She had recently cut her formerly long, wavy hair into a sharp, angular bob, and she wasn't used to it yet.

Today would be a very quick swing through the market before she headed to the office, just to stock up on a few fresh things for the days ahead that Fern suspected would be intense and unforgiving. It occurred to her this morning that it might be useful to see if there was anything unusual going on in the center of town, which is where the market was held, on a surface parking lot. Would she see any people she didn't know? Hear any scuttlebutt from her favorite vendors?

Fern loved the Saturday Farmer's Market in Port Stirling. It used to only operate in the warmer months, from May – October, but last year the City Council kicked in with a small grant so the vendors could justify every-other-Saturday throughout the winter. She never missed one, and was so happy that swarms of town people seemed to show up every week, rain or shine, to support it.

The fish and seafood were the main draw – and those vendors sold out every week to the savvy shoppers who arrived early – but this time of year one could also snare some beautiful greens, early radishes and peas, and some over-wintering vegetables. Fern never took it for granted that she lived in a special part of the world, and had access to all this bounty.

Occasionally, she dreamed of buying a small farm somewhere over the hill to the east of where she now lived in Port Stirling, and growing her own vegetables. Maybe with a man she loved, and a couple of kids. But realistically, Fern doubted if she would ever be a mother. Time was not on her side, and neither was the local gene pool. Oh, the thought was always present, simmering under the surface, but it wasn't an obsession with Fern. In fact, when she *really* considered motherhood, she had trouble seeing herself giving up work, and raising children as her profession, as her mother had done.

Her mother had been extremely good at being a mom. Encouraging Fern and her brother every step of the way. Letting them get plenty of Port Stirling's wonderful fresh air, playing outside until sometimes it got too dark to even see what they were doing. And, along with her also terrific father, teaching them that there was no such thing as a free ride in life. That you were entitled to, and only got, what you earned by your character and your hard, smart work.

Fern learned from her parents how to do it right, but, deep down, she knew she wouldn't be as skilled at it as her mother had been. It wasn't that she was selfish, she wasn't, and she had a lot of love to give, but her mother gave up almost every aspect of her own personal life, reserving only her love of playing bridge and growing roses for herself.

At least, I haven't succumbed to getting a cat as a substitute baby.

Hurrying down one aisle to her favorite asparagus vendor, Fern almost literally ran into Jay. He was in uniform, and had an uncharacteristic scowl on his face.

"What are you doing here?" she asked him. "You don't strike me as the fresh vegetable type."

"Very funny," he smiled down at her. "Probably here for the same reason you are – checking out the scene. See anything funny?"

"No, and I'm paying extra attention this morning. So far, I know everyone I've seen – no strangers, no tourists, nothing out of the ordinary at all."

"Same here. Just another Saturday morning in Port Stirling. Not a single frickin clue." His scowl had returned.

"Listen, Jay," she hesitated. "Can I say something?"

"Not if it's about Matt."

"It is. I want to help you."

"Don't need it."

"I think you do. I can tell you are confused about him, and maybe even feel betrayed by his fib to us."

"Lie. He lied to us. Call it what it is," he said angrily.

"All right, Matt lied. Instead of taking us into his confidence – which, by the way, I agree he should have done, thanks for asking – he protected us from a difficult truth. For whatever reason, he made the decision that we didn't need to know Sherwin's real identity, at least, not at that point in time. And, if you'll recall, we had the homicide of a child to solve, and were up to our eyeballs on that case."

"He should have trusted us to handle the truth, especially you and me!" Jay whispered animatedly. He didn't want the market crowd to know he was upset. "We would have run through hot coals for him at that point. He was teaching me how to be a proper cop, for God's sake. Lying isn't in our procedural manual."

"Give us a hug, so everyone will know we're friends," Fern demanded.

It worked. Jay calmed down.

"I'll get over it," Jay said. "It's just a little raw right now."

"I get it. Don't shut me out, Jay. No matter what, you and I will always be on the same team. Right?"

"Right, Red."

"Don't call me that," she smiled at him.

On her way to her car, Fern briefly watched two young mothers with their kids in strollers talking at one end of the market's information booth, drinking their identical coffees, and probably comparing notes on junior. Nice for them, but Fern had to help catch a killer.

CHAPTER 9

....

real estate

Joe Phelps and Rod McClellan sat uncomfortably on either side of Chief Horning. The large rectangular table that sat 12 only had one empty seat for today's county crime team meeting.

"Because Clay Sherwin was working undercover for the United States government, it's likely to assume that's what got him killed," said Matt after introductions had been made. "However, Cadet Byrne pointed out that perhaps it's not totally smart to just assume that. We will look into all aspects of Sherwin's life, and my department along with the state police has started that process. But it's still highly probable that he met his end because of his undercover work, and Joe and Rod are here to fill us in on what they know in that regard. Gentlemen?"

Joe Phelps cleared his throat. "About six months ago, the Narcotics Division of the State Department got an anonymous tip that a group of individuals, most certainly foreigners, were bringing varied drugs into the U.S. by landing amphibious vehicles on small, remote beaches in southern Oregon and northern California."

"You mean like a water car?" asked Patty Perkins.

"More like a big water tank, military style," answered Joe.

"How'd the tip come in?" asked Matt. "Phone? Written? In person?"

"I received a written note in my office mail," said Rod. "It was mailed from Silver River, Oregon."

"Oh, shit!" said Les Thompson, Bell County Sheriff, and a proud resident of Silver River, population 2,342, and the county seat.

"Yeah," agreed Rod McClellan.

"Then why was Sherwin staying in Port Stirling and snooping around here if the tip came from south of here?" asked Matt.

"Because there's only one motel in Silver River," Les Thompson answered for the feds, "and it's a sad one."

"That was one reason," Phelps smiled. "Pretty sure Clay would be more comfortable at Port Stirling Links, plus a resort spread out like that would be more anonymous, and he could come and go without being seen all the time."

"And, the note said 'recent activity is north of here'," added McClellan.

"So we felt fairly certain that Port Stirling would be a good base for him – he could easily surveil south to the California border and north to the more populated areas of Oregon. Turns out there are about a zillion little coves and bays just between Port Stirling and Silver River, most of which have very little access. Clay was good at putting himself in the shoes of the criminals, and he told us this part of the Oregon coast would be so easy to take advantage of."

"Then he got lucky," Phelps said, leaning forward onto the table. "Or unlucky, I guess is more accurate, considering his death." He flicked both of his thumbs with his index fingers and paused. "One night about three weeks ago he'd hiked into a sheltered small bay about two miles south of Port Stirling. Had to make his way down a rutted single lane road, ditch his car, and then climb over a sand dune. When he got to the beach, he saw some big tire tracks in the sand right down to the water. He went back to the same spot five nights in a row, all to no avail. Then, on the sixth night, while he was watching from the top of the sand dune, a boat with no markings on it approached the shore. He'd watched it from out on the horizon with its light coming directly toward him."

Phelps stopped his narrative, and drank water from a glass in front of him.

"As the boat hit the beach, wheels appeared under it, and it drove up onto the beach about fifty yards. Four men jumped out of the boat, and all four held some sort of rifle or shotgun – Clay couldn't identify the weapons through his binoculars from the distance he was at. Two other men approached from the south, walking close to the shoreline. Clay didn't see them until they were about twenty feet from the boat guys, and wasn't sure exactly where they came from."

"All men?" interrupted Patty.

"Yes, four men off the boat, and two men on the beach. One of the men from the boat approached the two while his three companions all pointed their weapons at the two men. He appeared to check some sort of ID that the two men produced from their jackets. Then he waved at his compatriots behind him, they lowered their weapons, and went to the boat and pulled out four bales of something."

"Guess what was in the bales," said Ed drily.

"Yeah," said Phelps, "take your pick from a multiple choice – heroin, coke, fentanyl, or another controlled substance of your choosing. The deal went down. Cash changed hands, the two dudes, plus the four from the boat, all started walking inland carrying the big bales. Clay waited, and about 20 minutes later, the four guys got back in the boat and drove it into the sea, heading straight out as far as Clay could see them."

"Could he see any ships on the horizon?" asked Les Thompson.

"No, it was too dark, and he told us he didn't see any lights out to sea."

"Did he hear anything?" Matt asked. "Voices, accents?"

"Spanish."

"So, our Mexican friends are up to no good in my town," said Matt.

"Clay said it didn't sound like Mexican Spanish, more like Central American. There's a difference," Phelps said. "Like Guatemala, Costa Rica…somewhere like that."

"Are we dealing with a cartel, in your view?"

"Don't know. Clay went back every night for the next ten nights with an infrared LED night camera in an attempt to get some photos, but they never came back. At least, not to that same beach. The last time we heard from him, he was going to try another spot."

"When was that?" asked Matt.

"Four days ago. He was supposed to check in with us every 36 hours or so…nothing." Phelps looked down at his clasped hands resting on the conference table.

"Did he say where he was going to try next?" Ed asked.

"He said he was going north of town…Port Stirling. Nothing specific, though."

"We found his body north of town," said Matt, stating the obvious.

"And his head," added Bernice.

"Is there anything else you want to tell us?" Matt asked, after Phelps didn't say anything further.

53

"That's all we know, chief," McClellan answered. "Clay was secretive while he investigated until he felt he had solid evidence to present. We don't know what he was doing the past few days."

Matt looked directly at McClellan, and seemed to consider his response. He leaned back in his chair and tapped his fingers on the table. "He didn't share a list of real estate properties along the beach that he considered suspicious with you?"

Phelps and McClellan looked at each other, and then McClellan said, "No, he did not. Why?"

"And you haven't seen a photograph of two Latino men that Clay took?"

"What is this, chief?" Phelps said, looking puzzled.

"Or a photo of those same two men and four young girls being off-loaded from an amphibian tank?" Matt glared at the two feds.

There was some rustling in seats, and then dead silence in the room.

"If you have additional information on Clay's investigation, we'd like you to share it, chief," said Phelps stiffly.

"I was just about to say the same thing to you," Matt snapped back. "I found a flash drive in Clay's possession that contained a list of properties, dates, and photos. I'm having trouble believing that he hadn't shared this info with you boys. He was way further down the road in my town than you've let on. Care to comment?"

"We didn't know about this stuff," McClellan said. "We would tell you if we did. I was Clay's immediate supervisor, and I swear to you I haven't seen anything like what you just said. Where did you find it?"

"It was taped to the inside back cover of a book on his nightstand," Matt said. "The latest entry – two addresses south of town – was made last Wednesday. Ed, please share the lists and photos we printed off the flash."

Jay said, "We didn't find this last night, did we?"

"No," Matt replied, and shared his middle-of-the-night brainstorm about the book. "Ed and I went back to the house earlier today, and this is everything we found on the flash drive." He paused while Ed distributed the photos around the conference table.

"Obviously, the really troubling photos are of the men with the young girls," Matt continued. "It looks like they've been brought in by boat."

"Sweet Jesus!" exclaimed Patty. "Sometimes I hate men. Present company excepted, of course. To make sure I've got this straight: you found these photos on a hidden flash drive in Sherwin's rental house, and he was in our county to spy on a potential international drug ring. So now you believe we're also dealing with international human trafficking as well as drug smuggling?"

"We don't have enough evidence yet to make that definitive determination, but, yeah, it doesn't look good," Matt agreed. "Clearly, Clay Sherwin suspected something foul in his investigation. Beyond what he originally came for. At least, that's what these photos say to me. He uncovered something he wasn't expecting."

"Chief, we had no idea," Phelps said. "You need to believe me. We would have alerted both you and Homeland Security if Clay had shared this new evidence with us."

"Does State deal with trafficking?" Matt asked.

"Yes, and it often happens just like this – an investigation of one thing leads to this kind of discovery. We have a federal task force on human trafficking, and I will need to alert them."

"I thought the FBI handled issues like this," said the D.A. "Why wouldn't we call them?"

"They are involved in trafficking and forced labor, yes," said Phelps. "We approach it with a collaborative inter-agency effort. Homeland Security – which includes the Coast Guard, and we'll need them – Justice, and Labor all have a part, too. But we take more of a lead when it's a suspected international operation – anything to do with our borders. Clay knows – knew – the difference, and he would have brought it to Rod first."

"We work with the local Coast Guard HQ'd in Buck Bay on a regular basis," said Jay. "Mostly, it involves search and rescue in the ocean, but they've also helped us with identifying big marijuana crops by air, that kind of thing. I have a good contact there."

"Good to know, Jay," said Phelps. "When your boss agrees, please go ahead and talk to your local guy. If the perpetrators are doing what these photos of Clay's seem to indicate, the Coast Guard will be our partner in this investigation. I'll let my counterpart at Homeland Security know we're in touch locally."

"While the photos of these girls create even more of a sense of urgency to our investigation, I'd rather you not alert your task force just yet, Joe," Matt said. "I want some time to scrutinize Clay's notes, and see if we can come up with any hard evidence or clues. OK by you?"

"I'm afraid I can't do that, chief," Phelps said. "We have a 24-hour rule on notification, and I'm already pushing the boundary on that. But you don't need to worry about more federal employees descending on your town. I will be the point person on our investigation, it's more of a courtesy call than anything else. Only the DEA will want to send an agent once I alert the Justice Department of the drug smuggling. But I'll make sure it's only one agent, and I think you'll find that they will be helpful to us. DEA works our borders well."

"Do what you have to do then, and we'll do what we have to do. Let's break now, and we'll get our local team started on the ground," Matt said. "Joe, you and Rod can use the small conference room next door – it's all set up for you...dedicated, secure phone lines and computers. David and Bernice, thanks for coming, we'll see you tomorrow same time, alright? The rest of you please stay and we'll strategize about how we're going to find these girls and the bad guys."

CHAPTER 10

....

beer and chowder

Matt liked to cook, and finally had his cottage's kitchen set up with all his stuff. He had waited until he settled into his new job as Chief of Police to make sure there weren't any unpleasant surprises before having any household goods shipped from Dallas. So far, the only surprise had been the confounding lie told by his boss, City Manager Bill Abbott, that "nothing ever happens in Port Stirling".

Poor Bill, Matt smiled to himself, putting the rib eye steak he'd bought two days ago to cook tonight into the freezer. It had been a long day, capped off by a mostly contentious meeting of the county crime team and the two State Department guys, and he thought it was a good night to pop in to the Inn at Whale Rock, and let Vicki feed him.

His boss was horrified when Matt made the call to tell him about Clay Sherwin. Matt couldn't help himself; he had to get in a dig about nothing ever happening in Port Stirling.

"I didn't lie to you, Matt, I swear," Abbott had said. "A second murder is unbelievable! What the hell is going on?!?"

"The two homicides are completely different, Bill. The Bushnell case could have happened anywhere. Sherwin's murder is more because of our location, I'm afraid. I'm going to be blunt here – it scares the fuck out of me."

"It might be a trend. Is that what you're saying?"

"Yes, sir. We're just beginning to gather the facts of the case, but it looks like Port Stirling might be Grand Central Station for an international drug smuggling operation. And what we know to date might be the tip of the iceberg. The manner in which Sherwin was killed sent a message loud and clear that these guys don't want to be bothered, and that they have no patience for fooling around."

"Is the federal government going to help us?"

"Yes, it's essentially their operation, but they need us for obvious reasons – they don't know the local geography, people, issues, etc. We'll be boots on the ground for them. We've already helped – Jay knew the rental house where Clay Sherwin was staying, and we've already searched it. Fern was able to track down his rental vehicle, and we have an APB out on it now. Ed requisitioned a state helicopter, and we're using it to try to locate Sherwin's car – it's missing."

"I heard it overhead, and wondered what the heck it was doing," Abbott said.

"Yeah, no luck so far, but there's a lot of area to cover, and the pilot's working hard on our behalf. I'd really like to find that vehicle. It could tell us a lot."

"Like what?"

"Well, Dr. Ryder says that it doesn't appear Sherwin was killed where we found him," Matt said. "She says there wasn't enough blood at the scene, and that his body had been moved. I think there's a good chance that when we find the car, we find the murder scene. And maybe we can get some more physical evidence off his car."

"DNA?"

"Yes. Or the bullet that went through his heart. Or who knows what? Clay Sherwin and I weren't best friends by any stretch of the imagination, but I liked the guy. He was doing his job, and nobody deserves to die the way he did. Nobody. I want to follow where the evidence leads us and get these guys."

"Search down by the shoreline," Abbott suggested. "Dumb people drive their old cars into the surf believing that the tide will take them out. What usually happens is that they get stuck at low tide, and then it becomes our problem. Maybe your killer is a dumb guy and counted on the Pacific to do his dirty work for him."

"You got it, Bill – I'll have my team take a look. Clay Sherwin may have given us a starting point, and it's about two miles south of town, somewhere by a big sand dune."

"No! Do you mean that small cove that is sheltered by a big stand of trees and a couple of dunes?"

"I don't know, haven't been there yet. It's next on my "to do" list. Why?" Matt asked.

"Because there's an inlet just north of that cove, and my house is on the other side of the inlet."

"Can you see the cove from your place?"

"No, the land curves around a bit, and we're further back from the beach. That cove is hidden."

"So, you wouldn't have seen or heard anything in the last three or four days, huh?" Matt had to ask.

"Nothing out of the ordinary," Abbott answered.

"No lights coming in to shore from a boat out to sea?"

"Is that what happened?"

"That's what Clay Sherwin told his bosses the last time they heard from him."

Matt filled Abbott in on the story from the feds, and told him to keep his eyes and ears open when he was at home, especially at night. And, to keep all his doors and windows securely locked.

"I don't want to alarm you, Bill, but these dudes aren't fooling around. Watch your back, OK?"

Matt's next call was to a reporter he'd met at the local TV station in Buck Bay. He explained that they were investigating a case, and wanted to make an appeal to the public, asking for information from anyone who may have seen any suspicious behavior near the beaches over the last few weeks. Matt knew he was likely opening a can of worms, but a quick bite on TV could turn up a tip. Maybe 'the tip' would even materialize.

After bringing his boss up to speed, the media call, and with a clear strategy for how to proceed as soon as Sunday morning brought them daylight, Chief Horning decided to call it a night. The thought that there might be young girls in danger tonight was agonizing to Matt and his team, but they knew there was nothing they could do on a dark, foggy night with its fathomless grey haze. Better to get some rest tonight, and put their plan into action first thing tomorrow.

He quickly drove to the Inn at Whale Rock, just down Ocean Bend Road a few blocks from his house, so he could get some food before their 9:00 p.m. closing time. He needn't have worried; his first friend in Port Stirling, Whale

Rock's waitress, Vicki, would have made sure her pal, the chief, got dinner no matter what.

"You got your hair cut," Matt said to greet her, "it looks nice." Gone was Vicki's poufy Texas hair from last winter that had made him feel right at home. But she did look ten years younger with the more modern style.

"If this is the first time you've seen my new 'do', it's been too long since you've been in. Sit yourself down, and I'll bring you a beer. We've got a new one you'll love – Buoy Beer, NW Red Ale."

"Buoy, like those floating things they use on the water for navigation? Cute name."

"The same. The brewery is up the coast a bit, but it's darn good beer. Be right back, chief."

The beer in Oregon had been a revelation to the Texas boy. It was only one of many, many things he liked about his new home. Oregonians, while perhaps not as outwardly, immediately friendly as Texans, seemed somehow more authentic to him. Once you made it past their initial wariness, you always knew where you stood. And they were, deep down, tough as nails. Fern told him her theory on the native Oregonian toughness: The early Americans divided up into two categories, those who stayed on the east coast, and the real adventurers who headed west. Of those, some only made it to Missouri and the Midwest, but the brave die-hards were the ones who continued on to the Oregon Trail and kept going.

The longer Matt was here, the more he thought these Oregonians were the true pioneers – individuals all, clear-headed, and determined. And with a love for nature that was unmatched. They never took their state's natural beauty for granted, and the majority of the population seemed to be outside at any given moment.

"Try this," Vicki instructed, setting down a pint of beer in front of him. With hands on hips, she waited while he took a sip.

"Well? What do you think?"

"You're right, as usual – darn good beer. Tell me the name again. Buoy Beer, right?"

"You got it, chief. It's real popular with the locals right now."

"How is business? Tourists coming yet?" Matt asked.

"It's been good. March was terrific. Lots of Spring Break tourists in town, and they seemed to extend their vacations more than usual. It didn't hurt that the whale watching was better than usual this year, and, for once, the weather cooperated. The wind didn't blow as hard, and the golfers were all happy. I made good money and can't complain," she smiled. "April is starting out good, too."

"That's great to hear. You haven't, by any chance, had any Central or South American visitors have you?" Matt asked.

"What do you mean?"

"Customers speaking Spanish. Anything like that?" Matt said casually.

"Don't think so," Vicki replied. "At least not on my shifts. Why?"

"Just curious. Nothing out of the ordinary then?"

"Nope. Not really. You know me though, I do keep my eyes and ears open. Especially since little Emily's murder. That was a wakeup call for the whole town. You think murder can't happen here, and then boom! Killer on the loose." Vicki shuddered.

"People should remain vigilant," Matt said. "The Bushnell homicide was a one-off case, but it did make my job a little easier when people around here realized they aren't immune from the dangers of today's world."

Vicki looked askance at him. "There's not something you're not telling me is there?" she said. "And I realize that's a double negative." Smiling.

"No, ma'am," he lied and smiled back. "But I would like you to pay attention, and let me know if anything or anyone strikes you as funny, OK? You're in a unique position here. Everyone needs to eat, plus you have good radar."

"True and true. Will do. Now, what can I get you before the chef starts giving us both the stink eye?"

◆◆◆

Fern had bought some clam chowder from one of her favorite vendors at the Farmer's Market, and she heated it up now, adding a big pat of butter to the pot and one grind of fresh peppercorns. It was after 8:30 p.m. when she and the team had finally left the office, and she gratefully slipped into her favorite pink robe and slippers now. She poured a glass of chardonnay, and grabbed the newspaper off her coffee table as she waited for the chowder to warm.

Like most people in their thirties, Fern got the majority of her news online, but she felt it was an important part of her new job to keep track of all the local news. She subscribed to the Buck Bay News, and read it religiously. Her feet propped up on the sturdy oak coffee table, she scanned it now, and sipped her cool wine. She found herself absent-mindedly stroking her neck on occasion, as if to ensure her head was still attached to her body.

Nope. No one selling lethal sabers this week, she noted. Not that she really expected to see them advertising in the paper. There was one smallish ad written in Spanish in the Classifieds section, but with her rudimentary Spanish skills, Fern thought it was seeking an English tutor. She would check it just to be sure.

Sylvia had made copies of Clay Sherwin's personnel file that the feds had provided, and distributed them to Matt, Jay, and Fern. Matt had asked Sylvia to also get copies of it to Ed Sonders and Patty Perkins. All understood that it was for "their eyes only".

Fern looked over her copy of the file as she ate her clam chowder, part of a baguette, and some carrot sticks she'd quickly washed and chopped. Another glass of wine? *Yes, please.*

Clay Sherwin lived with his wife, Arlette, and their son, Spencer, in La Jolla, on a bluff overlooking the Pacific Ocean. A daughter, three years older than the boy, appeared to live on her own in a condo further inland from her family. Fern noted that the girl, Lily, was eighteen. There was no note in Sherwin's file about Lily, beyond her age, address, and cell phone number.

Fern opened her laptop and Googled Lily's address, and then compared it to the family's home. It was less than two miles away. Curious about why the girl lived on her own but still so close to her parents, Fern decided to start by calling Lily first thing tomorrow.

Mmmm, this clam chowder is totally delicious – wonder if Trudy at the market would give me the recipe?

◆◆◆

Matt felt something brush against his leg under the restaurant table. He reached down and felt fur.

"Mr. Darcy, come here!" said the Border Collie's owner, Lydia Campbell. "I'm so sorry, Chief Horning, but he remembers you as a friend." She smiled and stuck out her hand to shake with Matt, who had risen from his booth to greet the approaching older woman.

Matt brushed aside her hand, smiled, and gave her a big hug instead, saying "How are you, Lydia?" He reached down and scratched Mr. Darcy's ears, much to the dog's delight, who placed his head on Matt's thigh.

MIDNIGHT BEACH

Lydia Campbell had found the body in the previous case – or, more precisely, Mr. Darcy, her dog, had found the dead girl inside a tunnel on the Port Stirling beach. Once his department had recovered from the shock of the village's first murder in over 20 years, Matt had decided to honor Mr. Darcy by bestowing the title of "Port Stirling's First Dog" on the Border Collie. He now had a plaque with his name on it at City Hall, and the pooch, who had been so well-behaved during the televised ceremony, was now a beloved legend throughout Chinook County. The ceremony hadn't hurt the new Chief of Police's reputation either.

"I'm doing well, Chief, and you?" asked Lydia. "You don't eat here every night, do you?" She looked worried.

Matt laughed. "No, I just got out of the office too late tonight, and didn't feel like cooking. But I do like to check in with Vicki every once in a while. I don't imagine you're a regular here either. I seem to recall a good-smelling something in your oven the last time I dropped in on you and Mr. Darcy. I actually like to cook, and my mom taught me well."

"I enjoy it, too. It's a creative outlet, don't you think? I'm only here tonight because it's not healthy for seniors who live alone to not leave the house much. I force myself out the door to retain my social skills. Human interaction is very important as we age."

"You are not aging, young lady," Matt complimented. And, in truth, Lydia Campbell looked closer to 65 than the 78-year-old he knew her to be. That's what walking on the beach every day of her life, and the moist ocean climate likely contributed.

"Oh, you smooth Texan," said Lydia.

"Am I ever going to be considered an Oregonian?"

She took his hand in hers and said seriously, "It takes a while, Matt, don't give up. Oregonians are somewhat reserved and cautious when it comes to newcomers. Friendly, yes, but it took me a while when I moved up here from California before I was fully accepted. I should think you are way ahead of me, though, because Californians are viewed with great suspicion in this state." She smiled.

"Worse than Texans?" he smiled back.

"Considerably." Lydia paused and, looking down, pulled on her dog's leash. "Come along, Mr. Darcy, and let's let the chief have his dinner."

◆◆◆

Driving home up Ocean Bend Road in what was now a thick, drippy fog, Matt wondered: *Who was Clay Sherwin? Who was he really?*

Some people's lives presented immediately, but Matt felt there was more to Clay Sherwin than met the immediate eye. *What makes a tall, classically handsome, southern California family man want to work as a special agent for the government? What in his education and career path brought him to this point?*

The first time Matt had met Sherwin he thought the guy was secretive and a bit odd, but, under the circumstances − Sherwin was a suspect in a child's murder − he didn't think that much of it at the time. But now, on reflection, Sherwin's personality was strange even after they became friendly acquaintances. Matt realized there was also a sadness about Clay Sherwin, and he didn't recall ever seeing the man really laugh, or even smile much.

On the surface, it didn't appear that Sherwin had much of a personal life. In Port Stirling, he apparently worked, read books, and walked, first on the golf course, and then on the beach. He kept to himself, which was obviously within his job description. The only time Matt ever saw Sherwin was when he visited the chief's office to talk about his assignment. Even then, he didn't deliver many details. Matt had never seen him around town in the usual spots frequented by the locals.

One of the first things Matt had done after solving the Bushnell case had been to buy an Adirondack chair with a small matching table. The real kind made out of Teak so it would age gracefully in the sea air, like Lydia Campbell. He put the chair in his small yard, close to the edge of the bluff, and now took a small glass of his favorite Balvenie out there, wiped off the damp chair with the arm of his jacket, and plopped down. Matt had envisioned sitting out here in nicer weather and watching the sun drop over the horizon, but tonight he needed to clear his head.

The fog swirled around him, and while he couldn't see the ocean below or the sky above on this pitch-black night, he enjoyed the noise of the waves crashing onto the rocks below the bluff. The wind was blowing, not gale force tonight, but enough to ruffle his hair and nip at his cheeks. There wasn't much protection from the wind and water on Matt's part of the coastline, and the promontory to the north made the waves below him even fiercer. It was like a boxer in the ring who had his opponent on the ropes, and kept coming at him again and again. The warmth of the Scotch was welcome.

Matt regretted not being able to see up and down the beach tonight from his lofty perch. He now had a goal for the few hours every day he was actually at home – watching for bad guys out to sea. Were they out there tonight? Bringing in their cargo, whatever it might be? And what was Matt really dealing with? All he knew so far was what the feds and Clay's flash drive told him. What was really going on in Port Stirling?

It starts tomorrow at daybreak.

CHAPTER 11

....

coves

Sunday, April 7

Matt met Jay, Fern, Ed, and Patty at their previously agreed to location, a diner out on the highway, at 6:45 a.m. Phelps and McClellan were back at City Hall in their small conference room, and the two county sheriffs, Earl Johnson in Chinook, and Les Thompson in Bell, were to have a virtual meeting this morning to discuss dividing up their respective local searches.

Matt and his team wanted a break from City Hall, and the 24-hour diner was known to all of them. It was also a good jumping off point to begin their investigations of the properties south of town on Clay's list. The diner catered mainly to tourists on the highway, and had a series of small dining rooms attached to a lounge, whose main attraction was video poker, beloved by a certain percentage of the local population.

Matt's group found a round table in a small room near the back where they could talk freely without being overheard. At the chief's suggestion, they had all dressed in street clothes today so as not to attract undue attention.

The restaurant's décor consisted primarily of old, dusty glass floats strung with heavy-duty rope, with peeling wallpaper reflecting boats at sea. The overhead lights were from the 60's, and added no ambience whatsoever. The restaurant was going for a 'seafaring' theme, but it came up short and sad.

However, the sunny waitress brought a big pot of hot coffee when she came to greet them, and that was what mattered at this early hour. All five cops turned their cups up in anticipation of the strong brew.

"No luck finding Sherwin's car, chief," said Ed Sonders as soon as the waitress took their orders and left them alone. "The helicopter covered this place like a blanket, but he didn't turn up anything. Nothing remotely like Sherwin's Toyota except for the ones we've already identified. I'm afraid he had to fly the bird back to Salem. We're on our own."

"Shit. Where could that vehicle be?" Matt said to the universe, twisting his coffee cup in its saucer.

"The perps have either hidden it, driven it out of town, or destroyed it. If it's one of the first two choices, we'll have to get lucky," Ed responded.

"Yeah, and I hate luck. I'll assign two of my officers to keep doing a ground search, and I'll ask Les Thompson down in Bell County to do the same. Can you chip in some boots on the ground, or is the state strapped elsewhere?"

"My boss says this homicide is our number one priority, and it will be no trouble to relocate some troopers here to help us. I think he's afraid whatever operation we might be dealing with could become a cancer up and down Oregon's entire coastline. It's scared the bejesus out of all of us, Matt."

"I hear you," Matt said somberly. "The federal government is marshalling resources to investigate and they have the lead, I guess."

"You guess?"

"Well, it is our town, and I am the chief of police, and I did know the victim."

"This is not the time for a turf war, chief," Patty warned, wagging her finger at him.

"No, no, that's not what I'm saying," Matt said quickly. "I'll take my cues from Phelps. It's just that I can't sit here with my thumb up my ass and do nothing. We know our area better than they do, and we have to pull out all the stops to assist."

"Agreed. Are you in regular communication with Joe?" Ed asked.

"Yeah. He's the last person I talked to last night, and the first person this morning. We know we need each other."

"Good to hear. Last night, I rounded up six state troopers who work the southern part of the state, and they'll be in town this morning to help us."

"Thanks, Ed."

Ed took a big drink of his coffee and then said, "I didn't think anything could be creepier than our last killer, but this might edge into the top spot."

"Yeah," said Matt. "Let's talk about the addresses and property descriptions on Clay's list. I want to start there."

Jay said, "I got the name of the local realtor that Mary Lou always uses when anyone at City Hall needs local housing – Sandy Vox – and I talked to her last night."

"I know Sandy – she worked with Mary Lou on my house," said Matt.

"Right. I told Sandy what we needed to know, and I've arranged to meet with her at 9:00 a.m., once she has a chance to pull up recent transactions in her data base."

"She's going to look at sales and ownership between Port Stirling and Silver River? Properties that front the ocean?" Matt asked.

"Yes, I told her south of Port Stirling to beyond south of Silver River with some sort of beach access. That corresponds to Clay's scope, I think, looking at his list you found."

"This is good, Jay," Matt said, and he looked around the table. "The four of us will do some informal snooping around while Jay finds out what he can. Patty, let's take your car, you drive, and we'll try to look like tourists out for a Sunday morning drive. As soon as Jay's meeting finishes, we can reconnect and compare notes."

"How many properties were on Sherwin's list?" Fern asked.

"Three," Matt replied. "Two of them are adjacent, although the addresses have quite a gap, which tells me that they are big acreage. They start about two miles south of town. The third one is a lot further south, maybe even closer to Silver River."

"Nothing north of Port Stirling on the list?" Patty asked. "I'm curious about why that location was chosen to dispose of his body. But the more I thought about it during the night, I figure it's because the killer wanted to send us a message, but wanted it to be in the wrong direction to throw us off. What do you think, chief?"

"I think you're right. Misdirection. Makes sense," Matt said. "That's what I'd do – point you fine detectives in the opposite direction so it would take you longer to find me."

"Yup," concurred Ed. "All the action is south of town."

Everyone clammed up as the smiley waitress arrived with their orders.

"Ladies first!" she exclaimed, setting down scrambled eggs, toast, and fruit in front of Fern and Patty. Patty, her small handgun tucked in an ankle holster hidden under her black pants, winked at Fern.

With the table crowded with food for all, and the waitress beating her retreat, Jay dove into his big stack of pancakes, bacon, and fried eggs, saying "Let's eat. We may be missing our heads by dinnertime."

Outside the diner in the parking lot, once they all understood their part of today's investigation, Matt said, "I told Arlette I would call her again today, and I want to make that call first before we head south, since we're not sure what we may encounter. Patty, come with me to the car – I want you to listen in. Jay, good luck with the realtor. We'll be anxious to hear what you turn up. Call me as soon as you're done, and we'll figure out where to hook up. Ed and Fern, this shouldn't take too long, and then we'll take off."

Matt's second phone call to Arlette Sherwin didn't unearth much of interest. She told him that Clay had wanted to be a "secret agent" since high school, that they were as happily married as the next couple, and that he hadn't shared much with her about what he was working on, other than it was some sort of international smuggling operation. They had no financial problems; Clay's dangerous work was highly compensated, and Arlette had inherited their beach-front, cliff-top home in the La Jolla neighborhood, along with a lucrative string of luxurious senior living complexes in San Diego from her parents who had died together in a sightseeing plane crash on Kauai two years ago.

She and her children had been expecting Clay home for their son Spencer's spring break. Matt asked her if she was worried when her husband didn't show up as planned three days ago, and Arlette said that while it was unusual for him not to call if he'd been delayed, a change in plans was very normal in his line of work. She had been planning to call him if she hadn't heard anything by Saturday…and then Matt had called her with the news.

This time, Arlette did ask Matt how her husband had died, and figuring this calm, cool woman could handle anything thrown her way, he gave her all the gory details, requesting that she not share them with anyone just yet. She had gasped at the word "decapitate", but had maintained her composure. Arlette had implored Matt to not tell her children what he had told her, fearing it would be an image they could never get out of their heads. He agreed, and promised that the details were up to her to disclose, and he would do everything in his power to keep it as quiet as possible.

She asked Matt to notify her when the body was released, and she would send a private plane to bring his remains home. The kids were very upset, and Arlette wanted to stay with them in their home environment and not travel to Port Stirling. Perhaps one day she would come and see where her husband had died, but, right now, she was needed at home. As an honorably discharged veteran of the armed forces, Clay Sherwin would be buried in Miramar National Cemetery near their home in San Diego.

"Well, my first impression," said Patty as Matt hit 'end call', "is that Arlette seemed well in command of the logistics for being such a recent widow."

"Yeah, like she'd had more time to think it all through," Matt agreed.

The four 'tourists' set off in Patty's vehicle – a white Mazda CX-3 – for their destination – the first address on Clay's list, and the closest to town. Ed sat in front with Patty – more legroom for the big guy – and the other 'couple' sat in the back.

After one false start, they found the gravel drive they were looking for, and turned off the highway. The single-lane road wound through some dense trees, and then came out into the open in a pretty meadow, with bright orange poppies edging the road. After about a mile on the gravel road, Patty pulled up to a chain stretched between two posts, blocking any further access.

Matt got out of the back seat, making a point of stretching as he looked around in case anyone was watching their car. Ahead of them about 100 yards, the road made a sharp right turn and was quickly engulfed in another stand of big trees. He couldn't see any buildings, or any signs of life. Approaching the fence post, Matt saw that it would be easy to unhook the chain and drive over it, but he decided, for now until they got further intel from Jay's meeting, it would better serve their purposes to turn around and scope out the other properties on Clay's list.

"Let's keep going," Matt said, climbing back into the car. While Patty drove, Matt made notes in his police notebook.

CHAPTER 12

....

beach-front access

When Jay called Sandy Vox to explain the information they needed, she mentioned that the city had last used her to find a rental house for their new Chief of Police, Matt Horning, last January.

Was that only three months ago? thought Jay. *It feels like a lifetime has passed.*

Like everyone else in the police department and around City Hall, Jay often considered how they would have managed the Emily Bushnell homicide without Matt Horning. Under Matt's steady hand and grasp of investigative procedure, the PSPD had, within one short week, solved the case. Their new chief had shown himself to be smart, kind, and a real leader.

But to Jay, this felt different. And, as pissed off as Jay was that Matt had lied to him about Clay Sherwin's real identity, it wasn't just about that. Not that he would ever question his boss and friend, but somewhere deep inside he wondered if Matt had the chops for a crime of this nature. If they were truly dealing with an international crime syndicate, did he have the experience to guide them? Or were they all in uncharted waters, literally and figuratively? Bottom line: Did he trust Matt to protect his town from whatever this was?

Just do as you're told, Detective Finley, and don't worry about tomorrow until tomorrow comes.

Rays of sun came through the paned window and warmed Jay's back. The Crab Shack Café was sparkling clean, and Jay was comfortable at a bistro-style table topped with a blue-and-white checked tablecloth.

While he waited for his meeting with Sandy Vox, he went back over his notes from this morning's breakfast to make sure he was clear on his responsibilities. Sandy came in wearing a bright yellow raincoat over black leggings and a black sweater. Jay thought she looked rather like a bumblebee. He rose to greet her and they shook hands.

Settled in her chair, Sandy said to Jay, "I pulled all the sales for the past 18 months on the west side of Hwy 101 between Port Stirling and Silver River." She then turned to the waiter, who had sidled up to their table. "I'll have an espresso and one of your lemon tarts."

"You, Jay?" asked the waiter, who had known Jay since high school days.

"Coffee please, Tim."

"You got it."

"I need a sugar and caffeine hit to jumpstart my day," smiled Sandy.

"How's business?" asked Jay.

"It's very busy right now. I'm trying to find the right property for three Portland businessmen who love to play golf at Port Stirling Links, and have decided they need to buy a house here. Plus, I've got two couples of California retirees searching for their retirement homes, and I think one of them is going to buy one of my listings. So, life is good."

"What does your data base show for properties selling around here recently, especially south of Port Stirling?"

"Well, I'm not exactly sure what you're looking for, but there are two or three transactions that stand out."

"Why is that?"

"They're different for our market."

"Great. That's what I'm looking for – oddballs," Jay said. "Talk to me."

"The coolest one is the rock band Deep Love – do you know them?"

"Sure."

"They bought a ranch about halfway between Port Stirling and Silver River. A big, old, rambling ranch house on 150 acres. It's in the middle of nowhere, and it was an all-cash deal. 'Course, if anyone has the cash these days, I suppose it's rock stars, huh?"

"The truth. And NBA stars. Whose name is it in?"

"It's listed as 'Deep Love, LLC', with an address in Los Angeles. Looks like the band members all own a piece of it."

"I'll need the property address and the L.A. contact info ASAP," Jay said. "Were they represented by a local realtor?"

"Uh-huh, a realtor with Waterside Realty in Buck Bay. The deal was done about this time last year."

"I'll need that contact, too. Why do you suppose a famous rock band would want an isolated ranch in Chinook County?"

"To get away from it all? Maybe it's a recording studio. Don't know, but it's cool, isn't it?" Sandy said.

"It's cool if it's really them. We'll sure find out. What else?"

"A Seattle couple bought 50 acres surrounding that lake to the west of 101, closer to Silver River – do you know where I mean?"

"Yeah, Fauna Lake. Why did that sale jump out? I'd love to own 50 acres on Fauna Lake."

"I looked up the buyers, and they also own a small resort in an isolated part of Costa Rica. Also on a beach with a bay. I'm wondering what their plans are, that's all."

"You just said it: To get away from it all? As great as Seattle is, it's no place for quiet contemplation these days. I was there for some training last month, and almost got killed twice on the freeways. Are you thinking they may be planning to build some sort of resort? Good God, not another golf course, I hope!"

"Hey, don't you be bad-mouthing our golf course. I would've starved in real estate in this town without them. I have no idea what they want with the property. Just thought it was interesting that they already own a resort."

"Anything else of interest? Any foreign buyers?" Jay asked.

"Not that I could tell," Sandy answered. "The only other outside the area deal is a guy from Silicon Valley who bought 200 acres with a small house and several outbuildings, also south of here. His property is about six miles north of the rock band's property, also on the west side of Hwy 101. His name sounds Chinese – Zhang Chen. He's a tech entrepreneur, and has bought several properties on the west coast in the past two years. From northern Mexico all the way up to Vancouver, B.C. But he's from California."

"Hmm. Where do these people get all this money? Why don't I have any?"

"Cuz you're a cop?" Sandy surmised.

"Oh, yeah, that's right," Jay smiled.

◆◆◆

They hooked up with Jay at 10:30 a.m. at a wayside on the highway.

"Anything of use from our favorite realtor?" Matt asked.

"Yes, I think so," Jay said. The cops sat three to a side at a rough cedar picnic table hidden back by a galloping creek, well off the highway. Jay spread out the real estate listing sheets that had appeared to be the most relevant of the transactions that he and Sandy had talked about.

"Two of these relate to the locations that Clay listed," he began. "The third one has a couple of factors about it that make it possibly of interest to us."

"Why so?" asked Matt. "Start with that one. Where is the property?"

"It's further south than we think Clay's investigation took him…almost to Silver River. But the property changed hands within the year, and the new owners have a Costa Rica connection. Might not mean anything, but I felt it was too early to rule them out. They bought about 50 acres with both a lake and beach access."

"Is it that Fauna Lake area?" asked Ed.

"Yeah, that's it. The realtor thinks they might want it to build a small resort – that's what they did in Costa Rica. That's the connection."

"That property wasn't on the market long," Ed noted. "I noticed the sign one day, and then a week or two later it was gone."

"It was bought by a couple from Seattle, and according to Sandy, they'd been looking in this area for a while, and moved quickly when this parcel came on the market."

"We'll check it out," said Matt. "You have the address, right? What about the other two on Clay's list?"

"Yeah, and I know where the road to it is," Jay answered. "It looks like the two places Clay was eyeballing both sold recently, and both were all-cash deals, which is one reason Sandy pulled them out. Also, both of the new owners are from California, which isn't unusual for our area these days, but might be relevant since that's where our victim is from, too."

"We drove to the place that is closest to Port Stirling, but we ran into a chained-off road about a mile in from the highway," explained Matt.

"That one is now owned by a Silicon Valley rich guy. No one has lived there for months. New owner owns property all up and down the west coast. Sandy says it looks like he's an investor, but she didn't have time to fully research any of these transactions. I told her we will do that, but if she learns anything else, she'll let me know."

"And the third one?" Matt asked.

"The third property is between the two we've talked about, but closer to the Silicon Valley guy's…almost adjacent. Sandy told me it's the old Jarvis homestead, a big house and ranch on about 150 acres. Grandma Jarvis died last year, and the grandkids sold it."

"To whom?" asked Patty.

"Get this," Jay said, grinning. "The rock band Deep Love. Bought it late last year."

"Get out!" exclaimed Fern.

"I'm supposed to know who they are, right?" said Patty, straight-faced.

"Even I know that band," Ed laughed. "You are really out of it, woman."

"I don't follow pop culture," Patty smirked. "There's no point in it, and I have better things to do with my time."

"Have they been in town?" asked Fern. "I would have spotted them for sure! This is exciting."

"Sandy thought their agent and one of the band members were here to close the deal. November-ish, she thinks. Doesn't know if they've been back since, and it was obviously done on the quiet."

"Well, it's clear we've got a lot to follow-up on here. Nice work, Jay," said Matt. "Did you have to share much info with Sandy?"

"Nope. Played my cards close to my vest, and she didn't ask particulars. She only knows we're looking at beach access properties – not why we're looking."

"Well done, Detective Finley," said Patty, swinging one leg around the bench and getting up. "Let's go have a look."

On their way back into town, Matt said, "So, no signs of life at either the Deep Love ranch or the Fauna Lake property, the Wassermans. What do you guys think? Should we get a warrant and go past the chained-off road at the first one?"

"How big is that property, Jay?" asked Fern. "How close were we to the house, do you think?"

"It's 200 acres all together, Sandy said. Plus, if it's where I think it is, the highway goes inland about a mile around there, so you could have had another mile on the gravel road before you hit the beach," Jay said.

"And if we do saunter in with a warrant, and there's a bunch of armed villains, what do we do then?" Patty asked Matt.

"Good question," Matt said, looking directly at Patty. "But what if we suspect the young girls are being held there? It's a longshot, I know, but it is a possibility. I can't be the only one of you who feels a sense of urgency about the danger these girls might be in."

"Of course we feel it, too," snapped Fern. "But I think Patty's point" – she nodded in her direction – "is that we need more of a plan, and more information. We can't just barge in."

"We could take the chain down, drive up to the house, and if we do run into any bad guys, we just say "We're lost tourists looking for the beach, sorry for the trespass", or something like that," Matt said. "There is a house on this property, right, Jay?"

"Yeah, Sandy told me there's a small house, a barn, and some other outbuildings."

"Sorry, chief, but you don't look like a tourist, you look like a cop," said Ed. "I do not!"

They all laughed and said, mostly together, "Yeah, you do."

"OK, I'm ganged up on," said Matt. "Here's what we're gonna do. Ed, have some of your colleagues patrol the section of Hwy 101 between Port Stirling and Silver River tonight...at least two squad cars. Ask them to be obvious. If there's any – and I mean any – sighting of at-risk girls, they are to notify us immediately. In the meantime, we'll start investigating the owners, verifying who's who, check on alibis. Does that work for y'all, and are you clear on each of your roles?"

Nods around, and "Yes, chief".

"OK, not sure I'll sleep tonight, but I agree we need a plan," Matt said.

"Oh, and Ed?"

"Yes?"

"You look more like a cop than I do."

"The truth," agreed Fern, grinning at Ed. She loved Big Ed.

"I'll ride back to town with you, Jay. I want to find the cove that's around the promontory from Bill Abbott's house. He told me how to get to it. You game?"

"Sure. Let's go."

♦♦♦

They found it fairly easily. There was no road into it, but Abbott had told Matt about a narrow path through the trees and around the sand dunes. Once the two cops arrived on the spit of beach, they found zilch, however, and in fact, the secret cove was pristine. The waves crashed against the headland just to the north, allowing the waves to lap gently onto the cove's beach. It would be a safe, relatively easy beach on which to land a boat, and it was completely private, but there was no sign of any recent activity.

"If I ever get a girlfriend, remind me of this place," Matt said to Jay.

"I'm going to beat you to it," the young detective smiled.

"Oh? Are you holding out on me?"

"Maybe. One of my high school girlfriends who went off to college in Arizona and got married is back in town. Seems hubby was a creep, and the marriage was over quickly. It's no big deal, though."

"If you thought of her here in this romantic spot, it might be a big deal," Matt offered.

"Like I said, maybe," Jay said. "No hurry, right?" He looked uncertain.

"You're not getting any younger."

"Look who's talking. At least my prime is still ahead of me."

"Ouch."

"I'm not saying 40 is ancient, but…"

"You should stop while you're still ahead, Detective Finley," Matt laughed. "What's this girl's name so I can be careful to not horn in on your territory?"

"You're not her type," Jay deadpanned, "but her name is Stephanie. Stephanie Coben."

"That's a nice name. Try not to blow it."

The men could see a sliver of the next little bay south of them. They maybe could have scrambled over a big rock outcropping separating the two beaches, but Jay noted that the tide was coming in, and it was a risky maneuver. So, they trekked back out to their car, but repeated efforts to find a way into the cove off the road failed. Finally, Matt took off hacking his way through some undergrowth, and found his way to a small clearing. From there, it was a short hike through a dense copse of trees before it opened up to the secluded beach. Smaller than Abbott's cove, it had a steeper, more slanted beach that was protected by rugged rock formations that jutted out into the sea on two sides, and by the dense trees on the third side.

Smack dab in the middle of the small beach were gigantic tire tracks.

"What the heck?" said Jay, almost running into his boss when Matt had abruptly stopped in front of him.

"Get out your camera, please," said Matt quietly. "Let's get some photos."

The tracks were so big, there were shallow puddles of water interspersed in the ruts, which meant they had likely survived at least one high tide.

They led directly out of the ocean.

CHAPTER 13

....

U S C

Nothing happened Saturday night – thankfully, thought Matt. The Oregon State Police had been out in force on the highway, and reported it was quiet as a church on Monday.

The county crime team had decided to wait one day for their next meeting to allow the feds time to get acclimatized and work on a plan for how they wanted to proceed. But Matt and his team were hard at work, spending Sunday morning working on the real estate angle, and investigating Clay's background and family.

Jay had gone into City Hall, primarily because the squad room was more conducive to work than his apartment. Sylvia had come in, too, to catch up on some paperwork that Friday's excitement had pushed to the background. The two worked in companionable silence.

Jay started on investigating the Silicon Valley entrepreneur, Zhang Chen, because of a conversation he'd had with his best friend he'd met for a beer last night after work at Stirling Tavern.

His buddy understood that Jay couldn't talk about his work, and so they covered everything else, and it was a good outlet for Jay's stress. But last night, remembering that his friend lived south of town on his family's long-time farm, asked him about the areas with beach frontage that had changed hands recently. He knew about one in particular – Zhang Chen's – and it had been an interesting conversation.

Jay spent a couple of hours researching Chen online, and then called Matt, who was working from home.

"What's up, Jay?" Matt answered his phone.

"I've been gathering some information on Zhang Chen, who owns the chained-off property closest to town. He's the Silicon Valley entrepreneur – more money than brains, and he's a very smart guy."

"I remember. What did you find?" Matt asked.

"Along with his new digs that include the house, barn, and several out-buildings, Chen's 200 acres also contains a small river that feeds into a little bay. Apparently, that river contains one of the best fishing holes in the area."

"And that's relevant because?..."

"Because I was talking to a high school buddy last night who grew up south of town, and he knew the property in question. Told me that he and his dad used to pay the former owner $5 to access said fishing hole. There's an access road through the north end part of the property that's very popular with local fishermen. Zhang Chen closed it off so no one can fish there any-more."

"He probably just wants his privacy."

"Maybe. But, my buddy tried to fish there last week by slipping through the new gate – I know – and got chased off by big, mean dogs. Zhang Chen is working in San Jose – I checked – so who is feeding the dogs and taking care of his property? And why the extreme privacy measures?"

"Here's an idea," Matt said. "Let's hire a drone photographer and fly over Chen's property. In fact, do the same thing for the other two properties south of town that changed hands last year, too. Sandy Vox probably has a real estate drone photographer that helps her, talk to her. Our helicopters make too much noise and probably alert the bad guys."

"That's a great idea. We can take aerial photos of all three places, and see if there's equipment or anything else suspicious being brought in."

"Or, if we see any young girls," Matt added. "Can't stop worrying about them."

"Yeah, me too. It was a bad night."

"Same." Matt paused. "I don't have a lot of experience with drones, but don't you think they would be less obtrusive overhead?"

"I think so. I know they make some noise, but they're small and not as visible. It's sure worth a try. Plus, all three of these real estate transactions are south of town where we know Clay Sherwin was focused. And all three are on the west side of 101 close to the beach. If we're on the right track, one of these three properties might be the base."

"Likely," agreed Matt. "Although if our logic is flawed – like it's an out-sider and not someone local, or that we're looking for property with beach access – it could be almost anywhere south of town. But it makes sense to see if we can get some overhead photos of these three places. Two of them are on Clay's list, and, therefore, the most suspect. Can you get this done, Jay?"

"I am so on this! Stay tuned."

"I will. I'm investigating the rock band because, you know, rock 'n roll and drugs," Matt said. "Let's connect at my place later this afternoon – that work for you?"

"Yeah. See you later, boss."

♦♦♦

In between update calls with Patty, Fern, and Joe Phelps – Ed had gone home to check in with his wife, and was now in Buck Bay briefing his state police cops who had come to the county to help – Matt dug deeply into Deep Love's band members and history. He rounded up some current contacts for them, notably the band's agent and accountant. He also tracked down the real estate agent who'd handled the deal on this end.

Nothing he'd uncovered so far indicated that this purchase by the band was anything other than a "hideaway-from-the-world" place. But he was just beginning to scratch the surface of checking alibis for the time period around Clay's murder, and trying to learn more about why they bought the property.

Shortly after noon, and feeling restless, Matt decided to take a break from his computer, and scope out if anything was going on south of town on the highway. When he moved to his rental cottage and saw the 1950's attached garage, Matt knew his super-sized Denali SUV at home in Texas would not fit. So, he left it with his brother, and just last month had bought a smaller, but luxurious, black Lexus sport vehicle. He'd debated for several weeks what kind of car to buy, aware of how his choice might look to his new hometown. But in the end, he was true to himself: he had plenty of money, and he liked a nice car. Taking his new car out for spins to get to know his new locale was one of the few stress-relievers he had.

Today, he was drawn back down south to poke around some more. He had not been as far south as Silver River on previous jaunts, and drove straight there. The scenery on the coast highway was spectacular, but Matt didn't pay it much attention today. The town of Silver River, sprawling on both sides of the highway, was not much to look at on the surface, but he suspected it had hidden charms once you got away from the road.

Just before entering the town, the highway took him over a historic bridge that spanned the mighty Silver River just before its entrance to the Pacific Ocean. The sun came out for a minute, and it sparkled off the water. Matt pulled off into a wayside and watched the seagulls dive-bombing the river. The beach side of the road was special, and it was dotted with small motels, cabins, and restaurants. *Someone in this little burg mailed the anonymous tip about the smugglers to Rod. It looks so idyllic now, that seems impossible.*

Matt grabbed a burger at a drive-up, and then headed back to Port Stirling, meandering. He took several roads off the highway, and followed them to their ends, surprised at the amount of land that seemed to be owned by the Bureau of Land Management. He knew the BLM was responsible for managing many of Oregon's diverse landscapes, but their presence in Chinook and Bell counties was dominant.

The Wasserman property at Fauna Lake and the Deep Love ranch both showed no activity again today. Since there was no one around, he'd walked both properties a bit, finding the beach access. He drove as far as the chain fence on the Chen property, and there was nothing new there either. *All quiet on the western front.* He turned around and headed home. Jay called him, and they agreed to meet at Matt's cottage.

Matt quickly built a fire in his mammoth stone fireplace – Sunday had turned chilly, and he felt it in his bones from the ocean's spray while he was out walking on the windy beaches. He popped open a beer for Jay, and they sat at Matt's kitchen table facing the fireplace.

"Did you find a drone we can use?" Matt asked.

"Yeah, Sandy has a guy out of Buck Bay, and I talked to him, but his business is focused on real estate. He didn't seem too anxious to help us, and he told me to try the Coast Guard. Turns out, they have two drones, and I've arranged for them to assist us. Theirs are more elaborate and will work better for us anyway. They sound cool." Jay's face brightened and his eyes shone. "They will send one out before sunset."

"You've told them the area we're interested in?"

"Yes. They'll launch it from the Coast Guard boat in the Port Stirling marina and it will go south down the coastline. I'm going to watch them."

"I hope this works. Except for Clay's list and photos, we don't have any clues or helpful evidence yet. We need a starting point." Matt ran his hand through his hair. "Joe is running Clay's photos through State's database, but he didn't have anything to report as of noon. If we can't identify the people in those photos, and if these beach-front properties don't turn up anything, we've got nothing."

The two cops reviewed where their research had taken them earlier today, and made a list of questions that needed answers. They'd printed out the tire tracks photos from the cove, and Matt said, "Have Walt analyze these, and see if he can figure out what vehicle could make them." Jay nodded, and they took a few minutes to stare at the photos.

The buzz from Matt's phone brought them back to reality with a start.

"Where are you?" Fern asked into Matt's cell. "I'm at City Hall and no one is here."

"I'm at home. Jay's here and we're working on the case."

"I'll be right there. I have news." She hung up.

"OK," Matt said into the dead line, holding the phone away from his ear.

Matt lived about five minutes from City Hall – nothing was too far from anywhere else in Port Stirling – and, sure enough, in five minutes Fern's baby blue VW bug pulled up in Matt's circular driveway. As usual, it had a rose in its dashboard flower vase.

"You really should landscape that mound of dirt in the middle of your driveway," Fern said, entering after a quick knock.

"When have I had time to do any landscaping? People keep getting murdered."

"Point taken," she admitted.

"What have you got?" Matt asked her from the kitchen, as he poured Fern a glass of white wine.

The three of them had become comfortable in these more informal discussions. They didn't always meet here at Matt's; sometimes they got together in a café or restaurant, anywhere outside of police department headquarters. It wasn't that they tried to hide anything from their colleagues. But there was a level of trust among the three of them forged during the Bushnell case that wasn't present – yet – throughout the department.

And, while Matt felt a little guilt over his preference for working most closely with Jay and Fern, his honest assessment was that there wasn't a great deal of additional brainpower and talent on his force. He would remedy that situation over time, but it would take some careful maneuvering around City Hall. In the meantime, Matt had become adept at handing out assignments that took advantage of everyone's skills, making sure that no one was operating above their head or out of their comfort zone.

Matt looked at his two colleagues now and wondered, *have I broken that trust by my lies?*

"I've had lengthy phone calls with both of Clay Sherwin's children today," Fern started. "They are, understandably, very upset. The boy, Spencer, age 15, could hardly talk. Poor thing was trying to be brave, probably for his mom, who was also on the call."

"Yeah, I talked to mom, and she indicated that the kids weren't coping very well," said Matt. "I hate it when we have to do this so early in the investigation. It's so raw for the kids."

"Essentially, Spencer didn't have anything of value to add to what we already know. Doesn't really know much about his dad's line of work. He did say he called him 'James. James Bond' when they were alone or at home."

"Cute," Matt said. "Until it isn't."

"It broke my heart," said Fern, placing her hand over her heart and letting out a big sigh to compose herself. "Anyway, Spencer couldn't tell me much. He's a good student, good athlete, good son, good brother. Nice, smart young man. Doesn't deserve to lose his dad at such a young age, if you ask me. He's going to have it rough for a long time."

Matt reached across the table and put his hand on Fern's arm. "Next time I'll take the kids, I promise."

"There'd better damn well not be a next time!" Fern almost shouted, pounding her fist on Matt's hand. "I'm getting tired of dead and sad children. It's not the way life is supposed to work."

"Spencer will be fine in the long run," Matt said, withdrawing his hand. "Someday he'll be able to look back and he'll be proud of his father. If Arlette is smart – and she is – she'll let Spencer slowly grow into the man of the house. He will grow up stronger and tougher because of this. I've seen it happen, especially in the inner cities where lots of boys grow up without fathers."

"You're just trying to sugarcoat it for me," Fern said firmly, shaking her head and eyeing Matt. "I wish you wouldn't do that. I'm not some weak woman who needs protecting from life's bad stories. I'm simply expressing my empathy for the boy. Let's move on."

"OK, let's move on," Matt said, staring her down.

"By all means, let's move on," said Jay, smirking. "Did you talk to the girl?"

"Yes. Because she's 18, almost 19, I called her alone. No mom on this call. And this one might have unearthed something important," Fern said, leaning back in her chair, and tugging at the neck of her black turtleneck.

"What?" Matt asked.

"Well, first, Lily is a good kid, too. Like her brother. And smart. I was initially curious and maybe even suspicious about why Lily lives apart from her family, but less than two miles away. I looked up the Sherwin residence on Google Maps, and it's a big, palatial house. Looks very comfy. Why would you trade that for a small condo with no beach view, no beautiful grounds, etc?"

"Why did she?" Jay asked, stretching out his legs.

"Turns out it's a boring reason. Lily wants to spread her wings and fly on her own," Fern answered. "No fall out with parents, no trouble of her own. She's very mature, and just wants to be her own woman."

"Does she have a job? Going to school?" asked Matt.

"Both. She works part-time as a project assistant for a big advertising agency in San Diego, and goes to the University of California, San Diego. The campus is in the La Jolla neighborhood, close to home. She's studying business. And, she has dinner twice a week with her family, more often when dad is home."

"You're right, that is boring," said Matt. "What is this big news you said you had?" The fire crackled loudly, as if to punctuate Matt's question.

Fern placed two balled-up fists on the table, leaned forward and said, "Guess where Clay and Arlette Sherwin met?"

Jay and Matt looked at each other, and Matt shrugged. Jay said, "We give up...where did Clay and Arlette Sherwin meet?"

"They met while both were students at USC. Los Angeles," Fern said. Her eyes lit up. "Guess what class they met in?"

"Romance languages?" suggested Matt.

"Nope. Care to guess again?"

"Just tell us already!" Jay exclaimed. "What class did they meet in?"

"They met in fencing class," said Fern.

"As in swords fencing?" asked Matt.

"As in swords fencing."

"Did Lily tell you this?" asked Matt, astounded. "Does she know about the decapitation?"

"Yes, Lily told me and, no, she doesn't know. At least, she didn't hear it from me," said Fern.

"How did it come up?"

"I asked her about her parents' marriage. Were they happy? Did they fight much? That kind of thing. She said they seemed happy enough, and had been together since college. I asked where that was, and she told me USC. Then she said, "Meeting cute...they were sparring partners in their fencing class.""

"What did you say?"

"Just what you just said: 'As in swords fencing'? Lily said 'Yeah, cute, huh? Dad loves to tell that corny story'. I nearly dropped my phone," Fern said.

"I would have," Jay said, getting up to walk over to the window, staring out to sea. "Do you think the girl knows anything?" He turned around, hands in his pockets, and looked at Matt. "Does this change everything? Are we barking up the wrong tree?"

"In my view, Lily knows nothing. It's just a coincidence," Fern replied. To Matt: "And before you tell me for the umpteenth time that you don't believe in coincidences, I have to say that I think this is one."

"It's a freaky coincidence, if it is one," Matt said slowly, his Texas drawl coming out like it always does in times of stress. "Our victim has his head cut off with some sort of sword, and he and his wife were into sabers? And you think this is coincidental? You need to check this out, Fern. I want you to fly down there, meet the family, go to USC and find out if Lily's story is real. Check out the family home. Got it?"

"What am I looking for in the home?"

"Daggers. Swords. Whatever," Matt said irritably. "Was this just something they did in college, or was it a family hobby? And there are other questions we should be asking with this new tidbit. I won't call it evidence because it's not, but it certainly makes me want to probe more into the widow."

"What would her motive be for killing her husband?" asked Jay. "And, so violently."

"Could be lots of reasons," said Matt. "Like the classic one: Clay was having an affair and Arlette found out. Maybe he was planning to divorce her and she didn't care much for that idea. Maybe she grew tired of sharing her money with him. Maybe he has a huge life insurance policy. We won't know until we get digging. Let's look at her opportunity to commit the crime first – does she have an alibi? Then we'll thoroughly look into their financial situation, credit cards, etc. Phone records, the whole nine yards. Until we rule out Arlette, she's ruled in."

"Should I check with Joe Phelps first?" Fern asked. "Before I head down there?"

"Change in plans," Matt said brusquely. "The feds are quietly working on a plan, while we seem to be the only ones doing any investigating. I'm calling the shots now."

"I'll take that as a no," Fern smiled, set down her empty wine glass, and gathered up her coat and handbag.

"I'm confused about what I should be doing now," Jay lamented. "Who killed him? International drug smugglers or his friggin wife?"

"Let's walk Fern out to her car, and then you and I will come up with our own plan," Matt said, standing and patting Jay on the back. "Our town is at risk, and I've been a damn fool for taking other people's word that they're working on it. That shit stops here and now."

"It's OK, guys," said Fern, approaching Matt's door. She gave a little wave of her hand. "I'm fine. On my way home. Keep working and we'll talk later."

"Talk soon," Matt promised.

◆◆◆

Fern's low, cherry-red pumps crunched in Matt's gravel driveway. She threw her coat and bag into the passenger side of her VW, and walked around to the driver's side, inhaling the fresh, salty breeze before sliding gracefully into the driver's seat.

The anonymous person wearing a black hoodie sweatshirt in the Jeep pulled off to the ocean side of Ocean Bend Road overlooking Matt's cottage tugged the hoodie forward, already seeing what needed to be seen.

CHAPTER 14

....

cup o joe

In the deepening gloom of Sunday afternoon turning into Sunday night, the only sound along Ocean Bend Road was the roar of waves crashing onto the beach below the dramatic cliff edge. Fern drove her blue VW from Matt's house inland to her home, about one mile east of Highway 101, the U.S. highway that went directly through the heart of Port Stirling, as it did in almost every coastal town in Oregon.

Although the days were finally starting to grow longer, Fern's house was in darkness. The sky had turned overcast, blocking out any moon or stars. She pulled into her small garage, and quickly used her remote to safely close the garage door behind her.

Surviving the Bushnell case had toughened her up. Fern had been nervous when Emily's killer was on the loose – who wouldn't be? But that case had taught Fern a lot about herself. She didn't back down, and she didn't lose her cool, even in the alarming face of unmasking the killer. Although the crime was horrific, deep down Fern had found her work invigorating and meaningful.

She had time to take stock of the experience, and had grown in the three months since their team, led by Matt, had solved the crime. Fern didn't relish another killer on the loose, especially with this level of violence, but she knew she could handle herself now to do her part. It was a good feeling.

Logging on to her laptop, she checked flights to San Diego, and left a voicemail on Sylvia's office phone telling her that she would book the travel herself because she wanted to get an early start tomorrow. She also left a message on Arlette Sherwin's phone explaining that she was coming, and would like to talk to her at her home tomorrow afternoon, and would confirm with her once she'd landed in San Diego.

She quickly packed her roller bag, and grabbed her travel cosmetic bag filled with small-sized liquids and creams. Even though Fern hadn't left Port Stirling since last fall – a week-long art-focused tour to Spain – she always kept her travel toiletries bag filled and ready to go. She saw that it still held a small plastic bottle of a delicately orange-scented body lotion that she picked up in Madrid. It was lovely, and she'd have to figure out where and how to buy more.

Ready for Monday, she moved into her kitchen to get some dinner going, starting with a small glass of Beefeater gin with two jalapeno-stuffed olives. Fern's kitchen, which faced her private backyard with its small patio, needed some updating, and she had pledged to get it done this summer when she could more easily use her outdoor grill. She peered out the French door and saw that it was dry – for the moment – but she wasn't tempted to cook her pork chop on the BBQ tonight – too dark and chilly out there.

She turned on some music on her favorite cable station, whipped up a good-sized mixed green salad, and futzed around the kitchen while her pork chop cooked. She'd thrown in some cauliflower with sea salt and olive oil to roast with the chop in the oven.

Taking her dinner into the adjacent dining room, which looked out on the street in front of her house, she noticed lights from a car parked across the street come on as she sat down to eat. She watched a Jeep pull away from the curb and head toward the main road.

Hmm. Amy and Scott must have had company tonight.

♦♦♦

Monday, April 8
"Did you authorize travel to San Diego for Fern?" asked Sylvia Hofstetter as she breezed into Matt's office on Monday morning, trailing a vaguely familiar scent. It was pleasant to Matt.

"Yes, ma'am. Did she give you a copy of her itinerary?"

"Uh-huh. She's leaving about now," she said looking at her watch and seeing 10:30 a.m. "She going to interrogate the widow?"

"Good. Yep, she's following up on a few details we've learned since Friday. Might be a wild-goose chase, but we need to know for sure," Matt told his assistant.

"Sometimes when you chase a wild goose, you catch one."

Matt laughed. "Yes, Sylvia, sometimes you do. Keep me posted if you hear from Fern, will you?"

"Will do, chief."

"Are we all set for the county team meeting today?"

"Yes. Four o'clock...that still work for you?"

"That's fine. Anything else happening this morning I should know about?"

"No, it's quiet. Eerily quiet, if you ask me," Sylvia replied. "I'm not crazy about the idea of some maniac running around cutting off heads."

"Me neither. I'm going out with Joe and Rod and look around. We're going to attempt to retrace Clay Sherwin's movements in the days before he disappeared."

"He must have been sniffing something, don't you think? Something awfully bad." Sylvia scratched her chin.

"I'm trying to not jump to conclusions, but, yes, that's what my gut and some evidence we found at his rental is telling me happened. Sherwin was in town for a reason, and he was a smart guy. He figured out something, the bad guys somehow knew he knew, and they had to eliminate him."

"He was a threat."

"Yeah, I think so. Now, the hard part – the feds and I have to crack the puzzle, and get these guys."

"You will." Sylvia pointed at him for emphasis, and sauntered out of Matt's office and back to her squad room desk, her navy pleated skirt and red, white, and blue silk scarf moving along with her.

◆◆◆

"Knock knock," said Bill Abbott, entering Matt's office a couple of minutes later. "Do you have a minute?"

"Yeah, but I was just about to leave to meet the feds."

"This won't take a minute."

Now what? I filled him in on the latest yesterday.

"I'm afraid I don't have anything new to offer up on this Monday morning," Matt said. He didn't want to tell him about Arlette's fencing experience just yet, as there was a good chance it would turn out to not be relevant.

"This is not about the case. Well, not directly anyway," Abbott stuttered. The city manager tugged on one earlobe as he plopped down ungracefully in a chair facing his police chief's desk.

"What then?"

"This is a pain in the ass, Matt, but the district attorney – Dalrymple – called me this morning."

Matt sat up straighter and started to talk, but Abbott held up his hand. "Let me just get this on the table. He says someone told him they saw Fern's car parked in front of your house last night."

"That's right. So what?"

"So what is that Dalrymple says there are rumors about you and Fern, and that it doesn't look good for her to be visiting your cottage on a Sunday night. You being her supervisor and all."

Matt stared at his boss across the desk.

"You've got to be kidding me," he finally said, defensively.

"I told Dalrymple there had to be an explanation," Abbott twitched, and his face was flushed. "Is there?"

"The 'explanation' is that Jay was there, too, and we were having a meeting about the case. They both left by 7:00 p.m. Did Dalrymple see Jay's car, too? It's pretty noticeable – has the word 'POLICE' on the side of it."

"No need to get testy with me. I'm just trying to get to the facts, and to protect my chief of police."

"There's nothing to protect, Bill. Fern works for me, Jay works for me, and we sometimes meet at my place because it's convenient and private. This happens to be a highly sensitive case, and the more we can discuss it out of earshot, the better. What do you want me to do?"

"I want you to tell me that you aren't intimately involved with one of your employees."

"I'm not intimately involved with any of my employees," Matt said icily.

Abbott stood up. "Good. I didn't think so. Although, you could do a lot worse than Fern. Kidding, I'm kidding. This is a small town, Matt, in case you hadn't noticed."

"Oh, I noticed all right."

"People will talk whether there's any there there or not. I don't need to tell you that you are the most visible guy in town these days, and you have to conduct yourself knowing that there are almost always eyes on what you do and say."

"I understand that."

"If you and Fern do decide to give it a go, please tell me in advance and we'll move her to another department."

"Bill!" Exasperated. "There's nothing going on. It's just because she's pretty and single and left Dalrymple in the cold. He's jealous she's working here now because she was the best thing going at the county."

"Agreed. And I have your back. But please understand that I don't want to have this conversation again, OK? It's awkward for an old geezer like me."

Matt had to smile at that, even though he was completely pissed off.

"You've got nothing to worry about, Bill. The feds and my department are doing our jobs, and Dalrymple can fuck off."

"If only he would," Bill said shaking his head. "If only he would. Keep me posted."

"You know I will. Hey, one quick question: were you able to watch your end of the beach last night? See anything?"

"I watched. And I watched. Nothing. No lights, no noise, nothing. I was out on my deck several times from sunset until we went to bed, and, if anything, it was quieter than normal. I'll keep watching, count on it. Good luck with Joe and Rod today…we need a lead, son."

"Yeah, a lead would be good," Matt said.

◆◆◆

Sylvia came flying into Matt's office.

"You again?" he smiled.

"There's a call for you on line 1!" she exclaimed. "Transfer from 911. Hurry, pick it up!"

Without hesitation, Matt did as she told him.

"This is Chief of Police Matt Horning," he said into the mouthpiece. "How can I help you?"

On the other end, a strong woman's voice said "Chief, I just had a situation here I need to tell you about."

"Who is this calling, please, and where is 'here'?"

"My name is Maria Ramos, and I work at the Cup O Joe drive-up kiosk south of town on the highway. Do you know it?"

"Yes, ma'am. I live not too far from there. Good coffee. What can I do for you?"

"I just had a vehicle come through. Two guys in the front, and a young girl in the backseat. They ordered, I gave them their coffees, and as they pulled away, the girl looked directly at me and mouthed 'help me'. It scared the daylights out of me."

"OK, this is good you called 911 immediately," Matt said calmly, grabbing a pen off his desk. "First, what kind of vehicle was it? Make? Color? Did you get a license plate number?"

"It was a Jeep. Kinda old and beat up. I would say it was sand-colored. Sort of desert looking. It had Oregon plates, but I didn't get the whole number. I'm sorry, I was so shook up looking at the girl as they drove off, I didn't recover in time."

"That's OK, Maria," Matt soothed. "You did well. Do you remember any numbers or letters at all?"

"I'm guessing, but I think the letters at the end might have been 'CAP' or 'OCP', something like that. I didn't catch any numbers. Maybe a '2'. I'm sorry, I'm just not sure."

"Which direction did they take off in after they drove away?"

"They definitely turned right – south – on the highway. And they took off fast. Hardly even stopped at the stop sign."

"OK, this is good," Matt said and jotted down notes. "Can you tell me anything about the men? Did you recognize them? Have you seen them before?"

"No. I don't know them. I'm sure they don't live in Port Stirling or any of the neighboring towns, or I would know them," Maria answered.

"OK, so they're visitors. How old would you say they were? Defining characteristics? Race?"

"Latino. Latin America. Both of them. English-speaking but with a strong accent. I'm from Mexico originally, and they aren't Mexican. That's why I know they don't live here. We're a small, tight-knit community. The older man was neat appearing, shaved and trim hair. I remember liking his eyeglasses – they had a gold bar across his nose, and fitted his face well. The younger one was grungier, with messy long hair. I didn't get as good a look at him as I did the driver."

Matt jotted down notes as she spoke. "If they aren't Mexican, and you had to guess what country they're from, what would you say?"

"Maybe Guatemala. Maybe Costa Rica. Not Mexico or South America, pretty sure."

"How old were they?"

"The driver was older than the second guy…probably about thirty. The passenger wasn't much more than mid-twenties."

"Hold on a minute, Maria." Matt held up a piece of paper to Sylvia. He had written "Call Ed Sonders and Jay immediately with this: Sand-colored Jeep, older model, headed south on Hwy 101, two men, girl. Men are Latino, late twenties. All hands bulletin! Go!"

Sylvia grabbed the paper, gave Matt a quick little salute and ran out of his office. The paper trembled in her hand.

"I'm back. How old was the girl?" Matt asked carefully.

"She couldn't have been more than fourteen or fifteen. Poor thing." Maria paused to catch her breath. "What do you think is going on, Chief Horning?"

"It's too soon to say, but I don't like it. Clearly the girl is in some sort of danger, and she reached out to you. Can you describe her?"

"Long dark hair, big eyes, olive skin more on the lighter side than dark, skinny little thing," Maria said. "Reminded me of me before I got fat. She could be Mexican, but I suspect she's from the same country as the men. Hard to say because she didn't speak. She was wearing a blue top – couldn't see anything else."

"Did anything else stand out to you during the encounter?"

"They were in a hurry. Didn't want to talk or engage in any way. Not rude, just not interested in lingering to chat with me. I don't know anything else to tell you."

"This is obviously upsetting to you, Maria, but I need to ask you a favor. I need you to stay at work until the end of your shift. Don't tell anyone what you saw. Anyone. Can you please do that for me?"

"I guess I can. What are you going to do?" she asked.

"I've already directed the Oregon State Police, and a detective in my department to start looking for that Jeep. I will join them as soon as we're finished with this call. I will send another one of my guys out to talk to you further. In the meantime, here's my cell phone number if you think of any-thing else about these two men. Anything at all."

"OK. Got it."

"Thank you, Maria. This is more important than you know. Can't thank you enough for your heads up action!"

"Don't thank me. Just please help her."

◆◆◆

Matt hung up, spun his chair, vacantly looking out his big window overlooking the Port Stirling jetty, lighthouse, and the mouth of the Twisty River as it barreled into the Pacific Ocean. He took just a moment to compose his thoughts and steady his breathing before he picked up his phone again to call Joe Phelps. *Could they have been two of the men in Clay's photo? Is there something really big going on in our small village?* It suddenly felt big – hair standing up on the back of his neck big. International drug-smuggling was one thing, but homicide coupled with potential kidnapping, or even human trafficking, was a horse of a different color.

He didn't know that was what was in play here – it could just be a girl mad at her older brothers. Or, it could be another piece of a very nasty puzzle, and Matt did not like puzzles.

"We're on our way now," Joe Phelps said when he answered Matt's call. "Be at your place in about five."

"Step on it. We've got a new development."

"Tell me."

Matt reported Maria Ramos' call to the federal agent.

"What percentage of Port Stirling's population is Hispanic or Latino?" Phelps asked.

"Less than one-half of one percent. Port Stirling is over 94% white. Another 3% or so is Native American, African American almost 2%, and the remainder is split between Hispanic and Asian. That means that out of about 3,000 residents, there might be ten people total," Matt said. "It's my understanding that we experience a slight uptick of Mexican guests in the summer and early fall to help out during harvest season, but I haven't personally observed that yet."

"So, two Latino gentlemen in an old Jeep would stand out, especially to Maria Ramos?"

"Yes, she doesn't know them, and swears they aren't from around here."

"Holy shit. What are we dealing with here?" Phelps asked rhetorically.

"It could be a coincidence, just a young girl mad at her brothers," Matt said. "But when you add this personal sighting to Clay's photo, it gives me the willies. I am well known for my dislike of coincidence when it comes to crime, and this smacks of a tie-in to Sherwin's murder coming right on the heels of it."

"Are you thinking human trafficking?" asked Phelps. "Clay never mentioned anything of this nature to Rod and me, but that doesn't mean he wasn't on to something. He liked to get his ducks all in a row."

"Something got Sherwin killed, and killed with a message for us. 'Don't interfere in what we're doing in Oregon' was the message that came through loud and clear. That means it's very, very lucrative."

"I hear you. And human trafficking can be just as rewarding, if not more so, than the luxury drug trade. Combine the two, make a few deals, and a guy from Central America is set for life. Pulling into your parking lot. Let's hit the highway and hope we can find that Jeep!"

CHAPTER 15

....

home decor

Shaded from the bright sunshine under an expansive portico, Fern rang the Ring video doorbell at Arlette Sherwin's beautiful La Jolla home. She smoothed the front of her ivory tropical wool skirt. The old skirt worked well with the new peony pink twill jacket and matching tank she'd bought recently for a new spring outfit. It was Fern's belief that not looking like a cop gave her a distinct advantage in her new profession. The element of surprise. And besides, she liked fashion. *So sue me.*

The house was spectacularly situated on the ocean bluff, and was surrounded by what could only be called estate gardens. Fern took it all in quickly, and noted the difference between a Port Stirling cliff-top home, like Matt's rented cottage, and the southern California bluff. Here were lush green lawns punctuated by tropical-looking flowers, healthy palm trees, and manicured everything. There was no wind, and not a cloud to be seen. Back home, the wind-blown trees on top of the 300-foot Port Stirling cliffs were bent backwards from the force of the gales and the relentless weather. This time of year the weeds and the gorse starting taking over. Aside from the Port Stirling Links resort crew, the town was home to one landscape gardener who did his best to keep the city-owned properties and those of the town's wealthier citizens looking as good as possible. But it was always an uphill battle, and no landscape in Port Stirling would ever compare to the perfection Fern was now standing in.

Fern loved her home state, but occasionally, usually at times like this in sunnier, warmer climes, she wondered, *why is it, exactly, that I live in Port Stirling?*

She looked wistfully at the beautiful blue agapanthus growing in the adjacent sunny border while she waited for someone to answer the door.

A wary woman's voice came through the device. "Who's there, please?"

"It's me, Fern Byrne from the Port Stirling police department. We just spoke on the phone."

"Can't be too careful, can we?" Arlette said, opening the door.

"No we can't," agreed Fern, "especially under the circumstances. May I come in?"

"Of course," said Arlette, waving a bracelet-heavy arm in the direction of her ample foyer. Fern stepped onto the marble floor in the high-ceilinged space, and was grateful for the coolness inside compared to the heat outdoors. It was only in the low 80's, but when you'd come from 50 degrees and raining, the difference was stark. A fan suspended from the ceiling spun lazily, like a worker who did barely enough to get the job done.

Fern extended her hand to Arlette, and with her free hand produced her police identity card. Arlette studied it, handed it back, and said "You don't look like a cop."

Fern smiled. "I think that's a good thing, don't you? I'm more like a consultant who is brought in for special investigations." Fern hoped Arlette couldn't see through her teensy white lie. Normally Fern believed in total honesty, but until she knew for certain who she was dealing with, there was no reason to let on to Arlette just how new to the cop game she was.

"You must be good if they sent you down here to talk to me," Arlette observed. "I would think my husband's death is a big case. Let's go in here." She turned and walked into a large room at the far end of the foyer, her white leather flip-flops making a discreet clatter. Arlette was wearing white cotton shorts that ended a tasteful one inch above her knees, and a cutaway tunic top that looked expensive. Fern noticed a small tattoo of what looked like a wave on her right shoulder, and she suspected the cutaway tunic had been chosen specifically because it exposed the tattoo. Arlette's shoulder-length blond hair was definitely in the 'rich California girl' mode…casual, but perfect in every way.

Beyond Arlette, in what was one of the most beautiful rooms she'd ever been in, Fern could see the vast wall of windows that overlooked the Pacific. She was fairly certain she could see Japan.

"Your husband's death is indeed a big case for our little town. Please accept my condolences, and that of the entire Port Stirling police department.

We're very sorry for your loss." Fern reached out and touched Arlette on her arm.

Arlette teared up, cleared her throat, and said "Thank you, Ms. Byrne. It is a shocking loss. I still can't believe I'm never going to see Clay again." She sank into a dove grey leather chair, and motioned for Fern to sit in the matching chair opposite. A white ottoman separated them. It held a tray with an icy pitcher of water and lemons and two glasses.

"Please know that we are doing everything we can to figure out what happened to your husband, and who did this horrible thing," Fern said. "Mr. Sherwin's employers from the State Department are in town now, and are providing the help and resources we will need for a case of this magnitude."

"Are Joe and Rod overseeing the investigation?"

"You know them?"

"We've never met, but Clay worked with them for years, and we've spoken on the phone a few times. They are competent men, and Clay had a lot of respect for both of them."

"Did your husband keep them in the loop of what he was working on daily?"

"I don't know about daily, but I know he reported in from the field on a regular basis," Arlette said. "I do know that Clay had recently told them he had a lead on a smuggling operation — his first lead since they'd sent him to Oregon."

"Did your husband tell you what that lead was?"

"He never went into much detail with me, just a vague sense of the mission. Said it was for my own protection, but the truth is Clay was a secretive man, and, honestly, I preferred to not know the gory details of his work. That system worked well for us. We've been married for twenty years, almost twenty-one."

"Happily married?"

Arlette smiled. "Look around. Wouldn't you be happy here?"

"It's a gorgeous home," Fern smiled back. "But four walls don't necessarily make a happy marriage."

"That's some wisdom in someone your young age. You're right, of course, it takes a whole lot more than money and things for two people to survive over the decades. Clay and I were very compatible. We made the most of it whenever he was at home. And, he loved to travel, and I'm good with solitude, so his job didn't interfere as much as you might think."

"Plus, you've got two great kids," Fern added.

For the first time, Arlette's face broke into a broad grin. "Yes, I've got the two best kids on the planet. I suppose every mom says that, huh?"

"I've talked to both of yours, and I think you may have the best kids on the planet," Fern smiled. "They are both just terrific."

"This is so hard on them. They both had a wonderful, loving relationship with their dad. Can't imagine how I'm going to help them get through this."

"You will. You have to. In my brief experience with death, staying strong for your children will help your grieving process, too. Right now, it looks like a gigantic mountain in front of you, but it truly is one step at a time. You may never make it to the top, but you will make progress."

"I lost both my parents recently, and this doesn't seem fair," Arlette started to softly cry now.

"Do you have a good support system around you? Friends, other family members? Is there anyone I can call for you?"

"I've notified everyone I could think of. Pretty much been on the phone for two days, except for time with the kids. I have wonderful friends, and two in particular have been a real rock. You just missed Rachel, one of my childhood friends. She lives down the street, and has been with me almost non-stop."

"Other family?"

"Not so much. I have a younger sister, but we had some difficulties when our parents died. I tried to take care of her financial needs, but I'm not her favorite person. Clay was an only child, and his parents are gone, too, so there's really no one on that side except for one uncle, who we didn't see too much. He lives in Tennessee. I talked to him yesterday, and he's quite upset."

"Where does your sister live?"

"L.A."

"How did you and Clay meet?"

"At college. USC. He was so handsome. Strong, silent type. At first, I thought he was more trouble than he was worth, but I couldn't quite ignore him. He was originally from Montana, and not the usual SoCal guy. I liked that he was different from the boys I went to high school with."

"Did you meet in class, football game, what?"

"I'd seen him around at a campus coffee shop, and one day I just introduced myself. It took off from there."

Fern frowned, but moved on. "I know this is in his file, but how long had he worked for the State Department?"

"I don't remember exactly, but I would guess it's been about eleven years now. He worked for a time in D.C. after we graduated, but not at the State Department – that came later, after the kids were born and we'd moved back to California."

"What was his previous work? I'm sorry to trouble you with all these questions, but it's part of our investigation."

"It's no problem. I want to help you. Before State, he worked mostly for the GAO, the accountability office that works for Congress."

"What did he do for them? What was his job?"

"You know, I can't tell you for sure," Arlette said thoughtfully. "I think he investigated things and did audits – that kind of thing. Even then, he didn't really talk much about the minutia of his daily work."

"So, he's been a government employee for all of your married life? Is that correct?"

"Yes. He made a good salary, but all of this" – she waved her arm around the room – "came from my parents. We would have had a comfortable living with Clay's job, but my parents were very wealthy when they died."

"Was Clay good with their money? I'm sorry if that sounds personal."

"He was a little intimidated by it at first, but we both got used to it real fast," she smiled. "All money does is make life easier, and we came to realize that there's nothing wrong with that, especially where the kids are concerned."

"Did you have any hobbies together?" *Like fencing?* Fern wanted to ask.

"We play golf and tennis – we're both athletic. We bought a boat about five years ago, and enjoyed that a lot. Not so much recently now that the kids are getting older. We're big college sports fans, and like to watch sports on TV when he's home. It helps him relax. When the PGA is in California, we'll make it to some tournaments. We're both big readers, too. Clay always had a book or two going."

"I'm sorry," Fern said, "but would you mind if I used your restroom?"

"It's down the hall on your right. First door. I'll pour us some water while you're gone," Arlette said, reaching for the pitcher in front of her.

Fern stood up, turned around toward the door, and nearly lost her balance. Behind her was a huge, almost walk-in fireplace, and hanging over it was a very dangerous-looking, shiny sword. She recovered, walked over to it, and said "My, that's a beauty," pointing at the sword. "Scary looking but dramatic."

"That belongs to Clay. He likes fencing, and has several different pieces around the house. That one's his favorite, so I humor him by displaying it in this room."

"You're a good wife," Fern smiled. "Not sure I'd want a weapon like that in my living room."

"Oh, it's not really a weapon…more like a souvenir," Arlette said matter-of-factly. "I don't even notice it anymore."

"Where did he get it? Do you remember?"

"You know, I really don't. It's always been there." Arlette turned away and walked over to the window, her back to Fern.

"I'll be right back," Fern said quickly, and sped down the hall.

Matt and the feds had no luck spotting the suspect Jeep, and after separate calls with Ed Sonders and Jay, they learned that they struck out, too.

"Vehicles can't just disappear," said Joe Phelps, "especially in such a small town."

"Small, yes, but lots and lots of places to hide," said Matt. "We've been looking for Clay's 4Runner for two days now with no luck. Even with a helicopter. What we need to do is to conduct a ground search, and start going house to house and farm to farm."

"I agree with you, chief," said Rod. "But that means all of Chinook and Bell counties will know by tonight that a federal agent got his head chopped off. I don't think we want that news out there yet, do you?"

"We can be discreet, guys," said Matt. "We don't have to shout out the specifics. We can tell folks that we're looking for two suspicious vehicles – an older model sand-colored Jeep and a new black Toyota 4Runner. We don't have to say 'why'. Joe, what do you think?"

"That Jeep and the tire tracks on your cove are the only leads we've got," said Joe. "If the APB on it doesn't turn up that Jeep, the chief is right, Rod – we've got to turn over every rock and every grain of sand in this county until we find it. We've been here 36 hours now, and we've got nothing but one young girl in a Jeep with some potentially bad dudes who needs our help and some tire tracks disappearing into the Pacific."

"And what if that girl isn't the only girl in my town who's in trouble?"

"You think we're dealing with human trafficking here?" asked Rod.

"I believe it's possible, if not probable," Matt answered. "I'm going to the middle school next with this girl's description, and see if anyone knows her. And I would bet the farm that no one will. As I told Joe on the phone, Port Stirling is a very white bread community, and if this child is enrolled in our school, teachers will know who she is. If she's not, as my gut is telling me based on the fact that Maria didn't recognize any of them, then we'll have to figure out how she got here and where she's living."

"And my gut is telling me we'd better do it fast," added Joe. "If we are dealing with trafficking of girls for sex or porn purposes, it will be a fast-moving operation. It could also be forced labor. The stats on that are just as alarming. Modern-day slavery."

"Yeah, it's prevalent in Texas and California. No reason to think it wouldn't have made its way to Oregon." Matt slapped his open hand on his desk so hard his lamp shook. "Dammit! I dealt with it in Texas, where the numbers are unbelievable, and I won't put up with this here."

"The State Department puts it at over 24 million victims world-wide, and it's not just in developing countries. It's a huge crime industry, both international and domestic. Doesn't Oregon have a big agriculture industry?" Joe asked.

"Yeah," Matt said. "It's worth billions to the state's economy. They tell me Oregon is the number one producer of lots of different crops, like blackberries, Christmas trees, and here in Port Stirling, cranberries. Have you seen all those red bogs?"

"Is that what those are?" Rod asked. "We were wondering. Wouldn't surprise me if there is forced labor trafficking around here then – Ag is big. The perpetrators coerce poor people and exploit them in the hard labor industries. That part is most often men, though, whereas the females are forced into domestic work or sexual exploitation. They could be brought in from almost anywhere to here, especially Central or South America where economic conditions and corruption are ripe."

"I've only been here a little over three months," Matt said, "but I haven't seen any evidence of trafficking at all. I like to think I'm pretty observant."

"It can be a silent, hidden crime," Joe said. "Especially if it's forced labor for agriculture because it's easy to hide victims in fields, or in your case, cranberry bogs. It's also extremely lucrative, and if that's what is going on in your town, Matt, they won't let us crash their party easily. Do we have any leads other than the Jeep to follow?"

"No one has come forward with anything else, and we haven't learned enough about the gun yet." Matt said. "Also, my guys can't find Clay's car, and the descriptions of the two men in the Jeep didn't ring any bells with anyone." He paused. "But we may have one other lead."

Joe's head turned sharply towards Matt. "What haven't you told me?" he demanded.

"One of my officers learned something interesting when she was talking to Clay's daughter, Lily. I didn't mention it yesterday because it could be a coincidence. Arlette and Clay Sherwin met while students at USC when they were in the same fencing class. You know – fencing, like with swords," Matt explained.

"I know what fencing is," Joe said. "And a heads up on this nugget of info might have been nice." He looked cranky.

"Sorry, we were so focused on the smuggling angle, and didn't really talk to the family until yesterday. Fern – my colleague – is great at getting people to talk. Warm and trustworthy. Lily Sherwin shared the story about how her parents met with Fern."

"Don't apologize. We dropped the ball not talking to the family first, and that's on me. Same as you, it seems so obvious why Clay was killed – there is something major-league illegal going on here, and he was on to it. But we have to explore all angles. Thanks for being smarter than me, hot shot," Joe said.

"It's easy to have a single-minded focus, especially in a case like Clay's, where we know he was operating in a dangerous arena. The thing with Arlette will likely turn out to be nothing, but I sent Fern down to La Jolla today to talk to Arlette and snoop around a little. Gonna go to USC, too, and confirm Lily's story if she can. I expect to hear from her later this afternoon. I still think it's likely not relevant to Clay's murder, but it is a quirky twist."

"I know Arlette," said Rod, shaking his head. "She's strong and fit, an athletic type, but she's not big enough or smart enough to surprise her husband and kill him."

"My medical examiner said that he died of a gunshot through the heart," said Matt, "then he was decapitated. I haven't met Arlette yet, but couldn't a fit woman who knows how to use a sword do so on an already dead man?"

"Damn straight," said Joe. "I want to know what your officer finds. When is she due back here?"

"Open-ended ticket, but if she gets what she needs this afternoon, she'll be back tonight. Tomorrow at the latest. She'll call me as soon as she has the opportunity."

"And you'll call me, right?" said Joe with a drip of sarcasm. "No more holding back."

CHAPTER 16

....

farms and barns

The wind had picked up, and the sky had turned leaden as Matt headed home following the county crime team meeting. It had lasted over three hours, and everyone had a theory.

In his view, Patty Perkins, as usual, made the most sense. The investigator from the Twisty River PD had made the point that their main priority now had to be to protect any victims, if that's what the Cup O Joe girl and the girls in Clay's photo were. It might be too late to prevent trafficking in their jurisdiction – and this turn of events came as a surprise to every single member of the team – but it wasn't too late to help that girl, and discover if there were others like her, and what they were really dealing with.

Patty had argued that they couldn't do anything for Clay Sherwin now, but they could surely uncover this operation, and prosecute the criminals. Everyone agreed that a massive ground search with all their resources was priority number one, but there was general discomfort around the table of this news going wide. They discussed how to keep the more unsavory details under wraps as much as possible. Cops as a rule liked to keep crime details away from the public whenever they could, primarily because they didn't want to alarm the citizens they worked for. Or – all too frequently – risking them getting in their way. A head cut off from its body and deposited on public lands would be about the most disturbing news possible. Especially when an arrest had not yet been made. Everyone around the table in the conference room had a vested interest in keeping their public from learning how Clay Sherwin had died.

As Matt pulled into his driveway on this Monday night, the moon was flitting in and out of the clouds overhead as it rose in the southeast to begin its trek to the southwest, over the ocean. A steady rain was beading up on the hood of his car, and water was beginning to race down the sides of his driveway. He parked close to his front door, and turned off the key, sitting still in the silence, watching the rain dribble down his windshield.

This is more than I bargained for. Do I want to fight a potential international crime ring? Do I want to deal with officials from the U.S. State Department? What if this is just the beginning? Is my life at risk, and the lives of my colleagues? Will we have to start checking for bombs under our cars? Is this how I want to live? Is it?

Quit whining, and get on with it.

Matt barely made it the few steps into his cottage before tossing his briefcase on the hall table, and collapsing onto his sofa.

After a 20-minute rest, Matt drug himself up, got a fire going in his fireplace, slipped into some grey sweatpants and a Texas 'Horns sweatshirt, and set about getting some dinner going. He grilled a trout that Bill Abbott's admin assistant, Mary Lou, had brought in to City Hall today. Her husband had a good outing on the river yesterday, and she came to work with a cooler loaded with the beautiful fish. Ever efficient, Mary Lou had packed individual bags with ice for them to take their fish home, with the admonition that they should cook it tonight or tomorrow.

As his trout was grilling, Matt made a salad. He was looking forward to planting some lettuce seeds in the raised beds that came with the property, some radish and spinach, too. In this moderate climate, he knew he could have fresh greens and some simple veggies year-round without much effort. It would never be the huge Texas ranch he was raised on and missed, but he didn't have the time or the inclination for that now.

He drank a beer at his kitchen table and finished his dinner, eating an orange for dessert, just as his phone rang. Fern, finally.

"Where are you?" he said as a greeting.

"LAX," she answered. "My flight leaves in about 35 minutes, and since I won't get home until late, I thought I'd try to reach you now. I'm in a cubicle at the United Club. Can you talk?"

"You fly enough to make that membership pay off?"

"I get around," Fern answered. "There is such a thing as vacation, you know."

"Wouldn't know about that. Never take them."

"That explains a lot," she said. "Where are you? Is it private?"

"Yeah, I'm home. Just finished eating some trout that Mary Lou brought in to the office today."

"Damn. I love it when Howard goes fishing. That man can catch fish. Sorry I missed out."

"Was it worth it?"

"Not sure. We know more than we did last night at this time, but I don't know if it's useful or not. I have mixed feelings."

"How so?"

"Well, I confirmed that Lily's story about how her parents met is accurate. I was able to corroborate with USC that Clay Sherwin and Arlette Green both belonged to the Trojan Fencing Club when they were students. Arlette even competed for a while in regional and national competitions."

"So there's some skill there," Matt observed.

"Yes. Earlier in my day, Arlette told me that Clay was the fencer in the family, but there's evidence they were both competent in the sport."

"Did you meet with Arlette at their house?"

"Yep. I went there first, and then drove up to L.A. Have you ever done that drive on I-5? Lots of traffic, but portions of it are really beautiful."

"Haven't spent much time in California. Tell me about Arlette." Matt didn't mean to sound harsh, but they did have a murdered agent and possibly some kidnapped girls on their hands.

"Right, sorry, not the time to talk about scenery," Fern said, realizing how she must have sounded to her stressed-out boss. "Arlette is grieving, and worried about her kids. It sounds like they were a close-knit family, even with Clay's work and travel, and all three of them are very upset. But this is the part where I have mixed feelings."

"How so?"

"There are a bunch of swords and blades in that house, many of them on display in different rooms. When I inquired about them, Arlette didn't want to talk about them, and changed the subject."

"Deliberately, you mean?"

"Yeah, and it felt obvious to me that she didn't want to go there. Maybe it was only because of how her husband died, and she found it too upsetting.

But maybe it was because she wanted to deflect attention away from her fencing experience…just in case."

"So, you didn't hit it head on with her?"

"I tried. I said something like 'Don't you think it's a bit of a coincidence that you and Clay have fencing experience and he was decapitated with some sort of blade?' And she replied that in his line of work, nothing ever surprised her."

"She dodged the question?"

"Yes. At the time I felt she was taking herself as a possible suspect out of the equation. But as I was driving north, I changed my mind and think the subject was too awful for her to think or talk about. I mean, think how you'd feel if someone you loved was decapitated. For self-preservation, you'd want that image to go away and to not dwell on it, wouldn't you? I surely would."

"I suppose," Matt concurred. "But depending on what happens with finding the Jeep, I'll want to bring her in for official questioning. Joe and Rod agree with me, and they're anxious to hear how your day went."

"What Jeep?"

Matt filled her in on the Cup O Joe incident, and detailed what their plans were for a ground search starting tomorrow as soon as it was daylight.

"Well, this makes Arlette look even less guilty, don't you think? We must be dealing with some hardcore criminals."

"Likely. But there's still some doubt. Both in your mind and in mine, and until the facts and evidence completely erase that doubt, we leave no stone unturned. I want you to start checking Arlette's alibi for last week, and see if you can get hold of her phone and credit card records. You'll need warrants, and you'll have to subpoena her credit card issuer."

"Got it, and I'll handle this. Will I see you in the morning?"

"Probably not until about noon after the first wave of the search is over. Also, after you've had some sleep, I'd like you to go to the middle school and talk to teachers and administrators about the girl. There's a police report with the description of the girl on your desk. Talk to Maria Ramos at Cup O Joe if you need to clarify any details – she's our informer, and she's very eager to help us further if she can."

"You want to know if anyone matching the description of this girl is known to them and enrolled in school, right?"

"That's it. I tried to reach the school principal tonight, but she hasn't returned my call. If I hear back from her tonight, I'll leave you a text.

Otherwise, please go there first in the morning, and have Sylvia help you with warrants for Arlette's info. I'll see you at some point tomorrow. Safe travels."

"Your door is locked, right?" Fern said.

Matt laughed. "I've trained you well. Wish I could get everyone else in this village to start locking their doors. Yeah, my door is locked. You keep your eyes and ears open when you get home tonight, OK?"

"Will do, boss. I like my head."

"I like it, too."

◆◆◆

Tuesday, April 9

Last night's rain was the start of a nice little springtime Oregon coast storm. The wind rattled Matt's oceanfront windows and woke him early, just before dawn. He laid there until it started to get light, enjoying Mother Nature's squall. The dribble rain of last night had turned into a deluge, and threw itself hard against his windows and pounded on the roof. A black and heavy sky hung low over the sea, and the grey waves were rambunctious.

He grabbed his royal blue terry robe from its bathroom hook, and slipped into fleece slippers that he placed upside down on a heating vent so they were toasty warm in the morning, and went to the kitchen to make coffee. Often, Roger the seal appeared during stormy weather, as if he enjoyed frolicking in the turbulent surf. Sure enough, there he was, just a few yards out from the beach, bobbing along. Matt waved, and Roger ducked under a breaker and then popped right back up, as if to acknowledge Matt's greeting. He discussed the day's activity with the seal – a one-sided conversation – but Roger appeared to follow along, nodding in agreement. Matt was clear on what he needed to do today. Cheaper than a therapist.

◆◆◆

"Chief, it's Ed Sonders here," the OSP lieutenant said into Matt's ear. "We just got a tip on the state police hotline, and it could be a real break in this sucker."

"I'm listening."

115

"A guy named Marvin Moretti said his son told him last night that he and his girlfriend had found a black Toyota 4Runner under a tarp in an isolated barn just south of Port Stirling."

"No shit!"

"Yeah. It dawned on him this morning that we were looking for that vehicle."

"What was his son doing in an isolated barn last night?" Matt asked.

"What do you think? Teenage boy, teenage girl."

"Oh, yeah. I get it. Duh," Matt laughed. "Do you have the location?"

"Mr. Moretti was very specific on the location. He hesitated before calling the hotline because he didn't want to get his son involved, and the barn is on private property, but then he realized it could be important and did his duty. I'm on my way to your office now, be there in about ten minutes. You there?"

"No, but I will be as quick as I can get dressed. Wait in my office, OK?"

"Roger that," Ed said.

◆◆◆

Two patrol cars from the Port Stirling PD, one Oregon State Police car, a police van carrying Dr. Bernice Ryder and her forensics team, and Joe Phelps and Rod McClellan simultaneously descended on what they had learned was the Rowell Farm in southern Chinook County, about eight miles south of Port Stirling.

They had arranged a search warrant from Circuit Court Judge Hedges, and Matt gripped it tightly in his hand as he approached the farmhouse's front door.

An elderly man dressed in coveralls and a baseball cap answered the door, a couple days of stubble on his face.

"Mr. Rowell, I'm Matt Horning, Chief of the Port Stirling Police Department, and I have a warrant to search your property."

To Matt's surprise, the elderly man laughed. "Whatever for?"

"We have reason to believe that a vehicle we've been searching for is hidden on your farm…in the barn." Matt pointed at a structure several hundred yards beyond the farmhouse. "We believe it's in that building, and this allows us to enter it and search. Do you have any questions for us, or want to make a statement before we begin?"

"I don't know what the hell you're talking about. There's nothing in that barn 'cept hay."

"You're not hiding a black Toyota under a tarp in your barn?" Matt persisted.

"Nope. I have a white Toyota parked in my garage. Just drove it to the store."

"When was the last time you were in your barn, Mr. Rowell?"

"Well, last week sometime. Don't remember the exact day. Do you want to tell me what's going on?"

Matt ignored the question and instead asked, "Do you live here alone, sir? Other family members?"

"My wife died two years ago, and my daughter and her husband live with me now. My son-in-law travels for his job, and they're away this week. My daughter goes with him when he goes to a place she likes. Seattle this week, so she decided to go along."

"Do you have any farmhands or any other people who help you run this place?" Phelps asked, stepping up behind Matt's shoulder.

"I have a crew during hay season, and another one to harvest the Christmas trees, but no one around right now. Who are you?" the old man inquired. It was a logical question, as Joe Phelps somewhat resembled Ichabod Crane…a long-necked, big-eared, lanky, and unattractive man.

Producing his I.D, Phelps said, "I'm Joseph Phelps, United States Department of State. We're here to help Chief Horning and the Oregon State Police."

"State Department? What the hell is this? I'm thinking I should call my lawyer," Mr. Rowell said.

"That's up to you, sir," said Phelps. He cleared his throat. "But for now, we just want to look in your barn." He turned and walked off the front porch.

Matt turned to Jay and said, "Detective Finley, please stay here with Mr. Rowell while we search the barn. Let's go, everyone."

"After you, Chief," Phelps said to Matt, who was already halfway to the barn.

Ed Sonders, donning gloves, opened the small black door immediately to the right of the large, rusted red sliding doors. Bernice rushed to pull even with Ed.

"No one go near these big barn doors," she said, indicating the red metal sliders. "If the victim's vehicle is in here, it likely came in through those doors, and we might pick up some evidence off them. Let's use this entrance door until we see what we've got."

The hulking tarp was just inside the barn to their left, in front of the sliding doors. For a country barn, this one was remarkably clean and tidy. A few hay bales were stacked neatly along part of one wall, and there was a new-ish woodstove with a not-to-code-looking stovepipe angled up and out along the facing wall. One room on the far side of the tarp held gardening tools and two wheelbarrows. Covered outdoor furniture was the only other thing in the recently-swept space.

The forensics crew approached the tarp, which clearly contained a large vehicle under it.

"It could be a tractor," Ed said, while forensics did their thing.

"Could be," agreed Matt, "but why did the kids say it was a black 4Runner?"

"To get attention?"

"Possible. We'll know in a minute," Matt said. He, like the others, stood quietly by and watched forensics, clenching and unclenching his fists during the wait. He looked over at Joe and Rod, and the narcs were staring at the ground, Rod's eyes closed as if he was afraid to see what they were about to see.

"OK," said Bernice, "tarp coming off." She began to tug at one corner of the cover where it snagged, and Matt rushed in to help her.

Black Toyota 4Runner.
Shattered driver's side window.
Front seat covered in blood.

"What a great place to hide Clay's car," said Joe Phelps, shaking his head. "One crusty old man who might not come in his barn until July."

Matt raised his arms and placed his hands, fingers splayed, on the back of his head, rubbing it. "If it hadn't been for those two neighbor kids looking for a place to make out, we would never have discovered it," he said. "Perfect. Obviously, Sherwin was killed in his car. It didn't happen here, however, or there would be shattered glass on the floor. Somebody drove the car here to hide it, and then took his body to the marsh."

"They wanted us to find Clay, but not to find all the blood and other possible evidence," added Phelps.

"How did the killers find this barn?" said Ed to no one in particular. "How did they know about it?"

"It could be someone who knows Rowell or the area well," said Matt. "Or, if it truly is a crime ring, they could have been here longer than Clay even knew, and have spent serious time scoping out the region for their specific needs. Or, Mr. Rowell or someone in his family is our killer."

"Couldn't Arlette Sherwin have been here as well?" asked Phelps. "Does she have an alibi for last week?"

Matt stared at him, and thought about it. "We're working on that as we speak. It's a valid question, for sure, but this is more than a lover's spat, Joe. It's too elaborate."

"But Ms. Byrne said that Arlette lied to her about how she met Clay. I find that suspicious."

"So do I," agreed Matt, "but it might be explainable by something as simple as Arlette not wanting us to know about her fencing experience. Just because we might jump to the conclusion we're jumping to."

"Matt's right," said Rod, "plus, we know for a fact that Clay was on to something. He told me so four days before he went missing. Unless Arlette is somehow involved in an international crime ring, she's not our perp, Joe."

The cops went silent, and all eyes turned to Rod.

"What?!?" Rod said, looking around. "Wait. You don't really think my agent's wife is tangled up with a bunch of Spanish-speaking crime lords. Ridiculous."

CHAPTER 17

∙∙

even bad guys have to eat

They took Mr. Rowell into City Hall for questioning, where he was joined by his lawyer. He denied knowing anything about the 4Runner in his barn. He didn't hear or see anything suspicious last week. Or ever, he said. He lives a quiet life, and has never been in trouble with the law. If there are international smugglers operating near his farm, he knows nothing about them. He would be very surprised to learn that his farm was known to anyone but friends and neighbors. He doesn't take drugs or know anyone who does. His daughter and son-in-law are, in his words, 'health nuts', and don't even drink alcohol. They are steady, hard-working, church-going people who help out their old man. They aren't rich, but they're not poor either, and are comfortably off financially. He'd never heard of Clay Sherwin and didn't recognize him. He'd never met anyone in Port Stirling who spoke Spanish.

In short, Mr. Rowell could not help them in any way. And, Matt believed him.

"He's telling the truth, guys," he said to the assembled cops.

"Do you folks have lie detecting machinery?" asked Joe Phelps. "I agree with you, Matt, but let's be sure."

"Yeah, we have one for the county and it's in Twisty River. The D.A.'s office runs it. I'm OK with sending Rowell over there. Can't hurt. Even if his results turn out to not be admissible in court, I'd like to see how he performs under stress."

◆◆◆

Mr. Rowell was unflinching with the lie detector machine hooked up to his elderly body. "I've never told a lie in my life," he said to Joe Phelps as the test begun. "No point in it."

The machine confirmed it.

"I'm taking my client home now," said Mr. Rowell's annoyed lawyer.

"We'd like to ask him just a few more questions," said Matt. "Please sit. I promise this won't take long."

"Fine with me, chief," said Mr. Rowell, after a quick glance at his lawyer. "I want to cooperate. But make it snappy."

"Your barn was hiding a vehicle used in the commission of a homicide," said Matt. "I know you said you had no idea how it got there, and the machine says you're telling the truth. But it was on your property, and we are having a hard time understanding how it got there without your knowledge. What do you think the answer is?"

"Like my client said," answered the lawyer for his client, "he never locks his barn door. Anyone in town could have gone in there."

"But how could you not have noticed that kind of activity?" Matt persisted.

"Mr. Rowell lives…" his lawyer began, but Joe interrupted him and said, "Let your client answer, please."

Mr. Rowell squirmed in his chair and said, "Everyone knows I live alone most of the time when the kids are away or working. My house is big, and it doesn't face the barn. Plus, I go to bed early. Most folks know that, too. I read a lot, and could have been engrossed in a book. I had no reason to keep an eye on my barn, and anyone could have slipped in there. Especially at night. I don't know what else to tell you, chief." He looked pale, and his eyelids were getting a bit droopy.

"You know you don't have enough evidence to arrest my client," huffed the lawyer. "We're leaving now."

"You are correct," Matt told the lawyer, and then turned to the elderly man, gently putting his hand on Mr. Rowell's shoulder. "Plus, I believe you, Mr. Rowell. We're just doing our job, and we need to be as thorough as possible. Thank you for your cooperation."

Mr. Rowell, in the company of his lawyer, was allowed to return home.

"Now what?" Matt said to Phelps after Mr. Rowell had left the building.

"He's clueless, isn't he?" said Joe.

"That's what my gut instinct, plus the evidence, is telling me, Joe."

"Agree with your gut in this instance," Joe said and paused. "These guys have a hideout somewhere around here. We need to find it."

"We're starting by learning what properties changed hands in Chinook and Bell counties in the past year or so," Matt said. "They could be renting something or even squatting, but that feels risky if it's the kind of operation we suspect. We are working the real estate angle starting with Clay's list, but we have to consider a house-to-house search soon, at least on beachfront or beach-access properties, especially near where we found the tire tracks."

"Agreed," said Phelps. "Let's run the real estate gig, and wait for your medical examiner to give us the forensics report on Clay's car."

"We'll keep going on the search for the Jeep in the meantime, but it looks like they're back in hiding," said Matt. "Who the heck are these guys?"

"And where are they?" asked Phelps, locking eyes with Matt.

Jay reported on Sandy's real estate information to the group gathered in the War Room. Tuesday had been a long day, and everyone was tired and hungry, so Matt asked for some dinner to be sent in for them.

"Where's Fern?" Matt asked.

"Don't know, haven't seen her all day," replied Jay.

"Have you, Ed?" Matt asked looking up at the big guy who was taking a stretch break.

"No, but I haven't been around here much today."

Matt punched a button on the phone in the middle of the table. When Sylvia answered, he said, "Is Fern here?"

"Not right now. She was earlier. After she got back from the school. Do you want me to call her?"

"Yes, please. Let me know."

Turning back to Jay, Matt asked him to elaborate on the three real estate deals that Sandy had brought to his attention.

"The rock band and the Silicon Valley entrepreneur are curious, for sure, but the one that stands out to me is the Seattle couple with the Costa Rica connection."

"Ditto," said Joe Phelps. "Although a possible Chinese link could be intriguing as well. And, not to be obvious, but do you suppose the rock band likes their drugs? Jay, please thank your realtor buddy – this is cracker-jack information, and it's precisely why the State Department needs your help."

"Couldn't agree more. Sandy's the bomb." said Matt. "All three might turn out to be nothing, but it feels like we're zeroing in on the hideout."

A knock on the War Room door was followed quickly by Sylvia's entrance into the room. A powder-blue and ivory scarf flew out behind her as she moved swiftly to Matt's side.

Matt felt a sudden knot in his stomach. "What's the matter, Sylvia? Is it Fern?"

"No, haven't tried her yet because a call for you just came in. Line 1. Says her name is 'Vicki'.

"Vicki the waitress?"

"Yeah, that's the one. Says it's urgent."

Matt lunged for the phone and hit the Line 1 button. "Vicki, it's Matt. What's up?"

"You need to come to the restaurant right now," she said hurriedly. "There's two guys here I want you to see. They're like you said the other night: speaking some language, Spanish I guess, and I've never seen them around here before. And one of them looks like he could be one of the men in the photo you showed me yesterday. They look mean."

"How so?" Matt asked.

"When I took their water to the table, one of them was sorta snarling at the other one, having a heated conversation. Under his breath, but I heard him. And one of them has a tattoo of a snake on his neck – gave me the willies."

"I'll be right there. Act normal until we get there."

"We? Who is 'we'? I just want you to come." She sounded scared.

"I've got a couple of guys with me. Don't worry, we'll be cool." Matt nodded to his colleagues around the table.

"You have to. Don't make a big scene, there's a bunch of customers and I don't want anyone bothered. It might be nothing."

"It might be nothing – eating while speaking Spanish is not a crime, but you did the right thing, Vicki. Stay calm, and we'll be right there. Only a few minutes away from you."

She hung up.

"OK, men, let's go," Matt said to his four colleagues, who were already on their feet grabbing their coats off the rack. "It looks like even bad guys have to eat."

MIDNIGHT BEACH

CHAPTER 18

....

probable cause

"You know we can't just barge in there and detain two guys because the waitress doesn't know them, and they're speaking Spanish?" Phelps said.

"Because this is America, and we have laws?" Matt said. "Yeah, I knew that Joe."

"We can talk to them, though," Ed deadpanned, "because we're friendly guys. And besides," he added in a more serious tone, "if the waitress said they were arguing, that gives us just cause to chat."

Phelps had to smile in spite of himself. Big Ed Sonders looked anything but friendly with his gun slung around his middle. And how the heck did his state police uniform still look crisp after this long day from hell? Phelps' suit hung on him, and he looked and felt like he'd been put through a wringer.

"It would be nicer to meet the potential crooks when we were more refreshed, but it is what it is," Phelps said to the group. "I suggest we split into two groups when we go in – uniforms, and Rod and me. You approach them, Matt, and make them uncomfortable. Antsy people make mistakes. Ed and Jay, just loom over them, and let Matt do the talking. Rod and I will cover."

Vicki was waiting just inside the door by the steps that led down into the glass-walled dining room. Wide-eyed, she jerked her head to her right to indicate her suspicious guests were in the booth in the corner at the end of the room. Matt saw them immediately, and noted they were both facing the entrance in the time-honored crooks' habit of not sitting with your back to the door. He recognized one of the men from Clay's photo.

127

There was only one other table of customers on the right side of the long narrow dining room, and they were in the opposite corner, near the window. The cops nodded a friendly greeting to the senior couple as they passed by their table. The grey-haired rotund man gave them a friendly smile and a quick thumbs up that said to the cops, "I've got everything handled."

The targets shifted in their booth almost simultaneously upon spotting the armed police. There were two men, and in addition to possibly being the men in the photo, they matched the description given by Maria Ramos of the men in the Jeep with the girl: one in his late 20's, the other a few years older, probably about 33 or 34, both Latino.

Matt would have added to her description that the older of the two was nicely groomed – fresh shave, his hair cut and styled simply, pressed red sweater over a clean collared shirt. He wore wire-rimmed eyeglasses with a thin, subtle gold bar over the bridge of his nose. Nice looking and clean cut. Just right for dinner out on the town.

The second, younger, of the two men hadn't fared as well. His black hair was long and unkempt, and his face was stubbly with odd hairs where you didn't want them. He needed an eyebrow trim and some acne medication. He'd made an attempt with a white dress shirt, but a glob of what appeared to be a guacamole spill right in the middle spoiled whatever look he'd been going for.

"Hi, guys," Matt said as they approached the table. "I see you're drinking my favorite brew, and I just wanted to say hello." He pointed at the two cans of Pelican Brewery Pelicano Extra in front of them. It wasn't exactly a lie – he did love Pelican Brewery, but generally preferred their India Pale Ale. He stuck his hand out toward the older of the two, saying "I'm Matt Horning, Port Stirling Chief of Police. Nice to make your acquaintance."

Without budging, the man shook hands and said, "Hello", while the younger man stared, his hands under the table. Nothing more offered from the duo.

"Looks like you've also got a shot of some nice whiskey," Matt said, indicating the tumbler with an amber liquid and no ice sitting in front of the older guy. "A man after my own heart…a shot of whiskey with a beer chaser." He smiled broadly, but got nothing in return.

"Is there something we can do for you, sir?" asked the well-dressed one. Good English with a moderate accent.

"Nope. Just wanted to introduce ourselves. This is Detective Jay Finley, also with the Port Stirling Police Department, and this big guy is Lt. Ed Sonders with the Oregon State Police. We've had a hard day's work and, like you, came to get some grub. What's your name?" Friendly look plastered on Matt's face.

"I'm Octavio and this is Juan."

"Got last names?"

"Not tonight." Octavio stared hard at Matt.

"So this is how it's going to be?" Matt asked coolly.

"Just want to enjoy our 'grub', as you say, sir. Don't want to be hassled."

"No hassle. I just like to know who's in my town. Port Stirling welcomes all guests. Never know when you might need help from the police. Am I right?"

"S'pose so. We won't be here long."

"Exactly how long will you be in town?" Matt followed up. He shifted his feet, widening his stance.

"We'll let you know," said Octavio, taking a small sip of his whiskey.

Matt tried another tact. "No dates tonight? Pretty young women for handsome guys like yourselves?"

"Juan's all the company I need," he smiled. "Now, con permiso, por favor."

"Sorry? I didn't catch that."

"I said 'Excuse me'. Please," Octavio added, looking in turn to all three of the cops standing before his table.

"Sure thing. We'll get out of your way and let you enjoy your dinner. It's nice to meet you fellas, and I hope you have a nice stay in my town." Matt turned to Ed and Jay and said "Let's go get us some food, what do you say?"

"Sounds good, boss," said Jay, his voice only noticeably unsteady to Matt, who knew his young detective well.

"Oh, wait," said Matt, spinning back around to face Octavio. "Is that your Jeep in the parking lot out front? That sandy-colored one?"

"Maybe," answered Octavio. "Why do you ask?"

"I couldn't help noticing that your license plates expire at the end of this month. You'll want to be sure to get that renewed, especially if you stick around here. My department can get picky about things like that. Buenas noches, gentlemen."

Vicki showed the three cops to a large table on the left side of the restaurant where Joe Phelps and Rod McClellan were sipping glasses of water and pretending to look at menus. While they walked, Matt discreetly asked Vicki to save the drinking glasses of Octavio and Juan. "You did good, kid. Don't touch the rims, and place them in a plastic zip bag, OK? Hide them somewhere safe, and I'll come back at the end of your shift for them."

"Yes, Tex. I've got it covered," Vicki replied. The menus she held in her hand were shaking. Matt gently took them from her and said loudly enough for the nearby customers to hear "We'll seat ourselves with our friends, ma'am. Thank you."

The five ordered beers and some food, even though they had no intention – except for Jay – of drinking or eating since they'd already had dinner at City Hall. Only Jay could and would eat two dinners.

"Wimps," he grinned at them, digging into his burger and fries while his colleagues pushed their ordered food around on their plates.

◆◆◆

They settled their bill just after 10:00 p.m., and the restaurant was clearing out. Someone had turned down the classic jazz music coming through the sound system.

At Matt's direction, Ed called one of his state police colleagues, and told him to hot foot it in his unmarked car to the Inn at Whale Rock parking lot, or, better yet, across Ocean Bend Road in the parking lot for the motel directly across from the restaurant. He and his partner were to sit with their lights off facing the restaurant's front door, and watch for two guys getting into the Jeep. They were to follow them as best they could.

Matt knew Octavio and Juan would be looking for a tail, and would somehow find a way to lose the state cops, but he wanted to try anyway and see what happened.

Sure enough. They lost the Jeep.

"How far south did you get?" Matt asked.

"Didn't go south, went north," Officer Terry Parshall said. "Up Ocean Bend Road, through town, and north on Hwy 101."

"North, huh? Where did you lose them?"

"If I knew that, I'd know where they are, wouldn't I?"

Matt frowned. "Let me rephrase the question, Officer. Where were you when you realized they were gone?"

130

"We still had them in our sights when we went past the turnoff to Port Stirling Links, but there were a couple of cars in between us. They must have taken either the road that goes over the hill to Twisty River, or they turned left on a smaller side road that goes off into the dunes. We bet on the Twisty River road, but once we turned on that, they had disappeared."

"Shit," said Matt.

"I know. Sorry, chief. We're usually pretty good at this. Not sure what happened."

"What happened is we're up against pros, I'm afraid. Go home, it's late."

"We'll come back early tomorrow morning, and cover the area like a blanket and see if we can turn up that Jeep."

"If by chance you do find them, call for backup, Terry. These guys should be considered armed and dangerous until we know if they are suspects or not."

"Copy that, chief."

◆◆◆

Matt decided to take his own advice and go home – it was indeed late. He said good night to Jay, Ed, and the two feds at the restaurant, reminding them that the bad guys now knew what they looked like, and they should mind their P's and Q's. Then he went looking for Vicki and their promised rendezvous.

He found her in a dark corner of the Whale Rock's bar, nursing a yellowish drink in an icy martini glass. She had pulled on a bulky black cardigan over the white blouse and short red skirt she'd been wearing earlier.

"What the hell is that?" Matt asked, pointing to it. "I figured you for a bourbon on the rocks kind of gal."

Vicki laughed. "God, do I have to teach you everything? This here is an Alaska cocktail. Tanqueray gin, yellow Chartreuse, a dash of orange bitters so it's not too sweet, and a lemon twist. Want a sip?" She held the glass out to him, and the yellow liquid against her dark red nails was arresting.

"I can do better than that," he said, turning to the bartender. "I'll have what the best waitress on the planet is having."

"Oh? Who would that be?" the bartender grinned.

"You OK?" he said to her.

"I'm all right. I let it get to me tonight, which is why I'm drinking – don't usually do this on work nights. Those slimeballs gave me the heebie jeebies."

"We don't know yet for sure they're slimeballs," Matt cautioned.

"Oh, they're slimeballs all right. I have slimeball radar, and guys who pretend to be all soft-spoken and respectable are slimeballs 99.9% of the time. Like I'm too stupid to know. Take it to the bank."

"Did you wait on them?"

"Yep. The good-looking one was all nicey-nice to me, butter wouldn't melt in his mouth, but it was condescending, and his eyes were cold as a fish. Guys like that don't really like women, don't think we're as good as they are. I can spot it a mile away, and it burns my butt." She was getting riled up.

"What did they eat?" Matt asked, trying to keep the conversation focused.

"Chips and guac to start. The young one had BBQ chicken, slaw, and fries. The smooth one had the fresh halibut, salad, and French green beans. Both had ice cream for dessert."

"Did they drink a lot?"

"You would think so, wouldn't you? But they didn't. One beer each, and Mr. Smooth had one shot of whiskey."

"Just two guys out for a nice dinner."

"So it would appear. Except for the snarling at each other, which was my tipoff – most of my customers are happy…happy to be on vacation, happy to not be cooking, etc." She looked down at her drink. "You wanna tell me what's going on?", she asked and waited.

"I can't. Not yet. But you did the right thing tonight, and we're all grateful. Mad at me?"

"Of course not, hon. It's in my best interests to support you in any way I can. Just do your job."

"If you give me those glasses they drank out of, I will. I promise." He patted her hand. "Thanks, Vicki. I owe you one."

Rising up out of her chair she said "Oh, Lordy, you owe me a lot more than one, Tex, but who's counting?"

◆◆◆

"I didn't expect you to answer your phone – it's so late," Fern said.

"Well, I hope this won't piss you off, but I was worried about you," Matt said. "Why haven't you called me before now?"

"I know. I know. I just saw that you've called twice. I got busy this afternoon, caught up in what I was doing, and missed the team meeting. I should have called earlier. Sorry. I'm home now and so tired I can hardly wash my face. Guess yesterday's down-and-back and late night is getting to me."

"What was so compelling this afternoon? Did you make it to the middle school?"

"That's where it started," Fern said. "I was there for almost three hours, and really made the rounds to teachers, administrators, and some students. No surprise, but no one has seen this girl. She's definitely not enrolled in school."

"Figures. I hate this," Matt said, and Fern heard a tick in his throat.

"There's more. One 8th grade boy told me that he thought he might have seen this girl in the public library last Saturday. He wasn't sure, but says he did see a girl about his age that he'd never noticed before, and it could be this girl. Says she was 'real pretty but different looking'. So next I went to the library."

"Any luck?"

"Afraid not. I described her to all the staff, and no one had seen her."

"Maybe they have different staff working on Saturday than today?"

"They do, and I talked to them, too. Had to track them down around town. That's why I missed the meeting. Unfortunately, I struck out there, too. Maria Ramos appears to be the only person in this entire town who has seen that girl. If I hadn't talked to Maria myself, I might be inclined to think she made up this whole story," Fern said, dejection in her voice.

"She didn't make it up – I saw the guys and the Jeep tonight. It's a long story and we will fill you in tomorrow morning, but we all need to get some sleep. Just know that the bad guys know who we are, and that we've noticed them. Plus, there's a theory bubbling up that involves your new friend Arlette. They'll probably lie low for a few days, but the truth is I don't really have a clue what they'll do next."

"Yikes."

"Yeah, big-time yikes. Please make sure you're safe. Lock all doors and windows, and I would leave any outdoor lights on tonight. I'm doing the same here. I'm also sleeping with my gun on my nightstand for the first time in ten years. It was Ed's suggestion, and I think it's a good one. You should do the same. And, for cryin' out loud, Fern, please stay in touch from now on."

"Yes, boss, I'm sorry. It won't happen again. Good night, chief."

"See that it doesn't."

CHAPTER 19

....

forensics, forensics, oh my

Wednesday, April 10

Matt's day started with a large Americano and the bakery's version of a Sausage McMuffin – there was no McDonald's in Port Stirling, no fast food restaurants at all, actually – at his desk, along with Bernice's autopsy report on Clay Sherwin. He stared out his window, astounded at the juxtaposition between the violent nature of what he was reading, and the idyllic scene before him. The blue of the Pacific, seagulls racing down the Twisty River to meet the high tide coming, calling excitedly from on high. The sparkling white of the lighthouse perched on its rocky promontory with the pristine sandy beach beyond.

Why can't people respect what we've got here and not spoil it with bloodshed and brutality?

Sherwin was killed by a gunshot wound to his heart, which entered through the left front of his chest and exited through the middle of his back. As Bernice expected, the victim's head was separated from his body at some point after he died – she couldn't say exactly when because of the length of time before the body was found. In her additional forensics report on Sherwin's Toyota 4Runner, she noted that no bullet was found in the vehicle. That told Matt that either he was killed while in his car and the killer was smart enough to find and remove the bullet, or he was killed somewhere else.

But all the shattered glass and blood stains in the Toyota indicated he was killed while sitting in the driver's seat, which meant this murder was not the killer's first rodeo. Without the bullet, it was impossible to tell the make of the gun. Bernice said she found a fragment of the bullet, but it was obliterated and couldn't tell them anything. The size of the entry wound was consistent with a .38 caliber, but Matt knew that a 9mm was almost identical in diameter, so it was merely one hypothesis. Bernice's report said the exit wound indicated a hollow-point bullet, due to the fact that the exit wound was bigger, with more tissue damage.

Matt pondered whether it was even worth running gun registrations through the state's database. He was sure they could all but rule out anyone local…there was no motive for an execution-style killing like this one. And he was also certain that his friends at the restaurant last night didn't waltz into Ernie's Gun Shop in Buck Bay to buy their weapons, although he would check it today because it was the only gun shop in the area. Shortly after his arrival in Port Stirling, Matt had taken time to get to know Ernie, the owner, for just this reason. Ernie was one of the good guys, ethical and with a strong moral compass, important in his line of business. Matt was certain that Ernie would keep him in the loop if he suspected any shady deals.

He heard the sound of a helicopter overhead and looked out his window just as two Sikorsky Jayhawks belonging to the Coast Guard flew over the lighthouse, heading north up the coastline. Joe Phelps had arranged for nightly overhead sweeps of the beaches from Buck Bay in the north to a little south of Crescent City, California by the Coast Guard headquartered in Astoria. The Jayhawks were ending their overnight shift and heading back to base.

Phelps had also requested that Astoria's two newly-delivered Sentinel-class cutters be assigned to the south coast for law-enforcement patrols out to sea. The vessels, armed with a remote-controlled autocannon and crew-operated .50 caliber machine guns, were to run parallel with the beach. Matt understood that as long as the ships weren't required for search and rescue operations, the Port Stirling case would be their number one priority, for which he was grateful. Now, if the damn tourists would quit tempting fate by getting too close to rogue waves and being swept out to sea, he would have the firepower he needed to fight whatever these guys were doing. Phelps guaranteed that the nightly stakeouts would continue until they knew what they were up against.

Not surprisingly, OSP Officer Terry Parshall called to tell him this morning's search for Octavio and Juan and the Jeep had failed to discover anything. He had checked in the vicinity of where he suspected they'd lost them last night, but found no clues or evidence at all. He'd driven up and down the road they'd been on, taking several likely turnoffs, all with no luck. He was so sorry. *Yeah, I'm sorry, too.*

By the time Matt had finished his bakery treat, Phelps had called to update him on the reports from last night: Nothing. Zilch. The helicopters had investigated one fire on a hidden beach cove, but it had turned out to be kids enjoying a few beers away from parental eyes. No suspicious boats, no amphibious vehicles, no odd lights for several miles off the coast...quieter than normal.

Matt would be shocked if Octavio, Juan, and whoever else was working with them didn't lie low now that they knew the police were aware of their presence. Octavio was a smooth operator. Matt wondered at his nationality, it was hard to tell. Maria Ramos had been correct in that Octavio was not Mexican, of that he was sure. But beyond that, he could've been from anywhere from Costa Rica to Chile. Matt's Texas experience gave him some insight into the migrant world, and he could often pin down nationality, but his brief run-in with Octavio and Juan had been confusing. It almost seemed as if Octavio had been effecting a certain accent to throw him off.

As sure as Matt was now that they had gone into hiding, he was equally sure that their suspected business would require they get back to work fairly soon. Depending on where home base was, there could even be a shipment on the way to them now that would demand action when the cargo – whatever it was – arrived on the Oregon coast. If drugs were the contraband, they could conceivably loll about out in the Pacific for an unspecified time, but if the traffic was human, they would eventually have to land and unload their goods.

Matt finished reading both of Bernice's forensic reports – the autopsy on Clay Sherwin, and the examination of his car. She found "at least three different blood samples" in the car, and "blood with a different genetic marker than Sherwin's" was also found on the victim. He needed to talk to her.

"Bernice, quick question for you about your autopsy report," Matt said into the phone.

"Can I say something first?" Bernice said.

"What?"

"I don't often get to work with people who have respect for what I do, so I want to say 'thank you' for several things. First, I really appreciate our communication. It's important for the crime scene investigator to understand how the scientist likes to collect and preserve the evidence, and you make an effort to do that. You also have a grip on my lab's capabilities. I'm sure my preferences are different from your Texas forensics people, but you roll with what I need and how I like to do my job. I appreciate it, Matt, and it leads to better results. There, I'm done now. Feeling maudlin today."

"I got a little self-pity going on myself," Matt admitted. "I don't mind telling you that finding your level of expertise in Chinook County was a surprise, so right back at ya."

"We're not all hayseeds."

He smiled through the wires. "I never thought that, just figured you'd have fewer resources, and the job wouldn't attract the best and brightest. I was dead wrong."

"This is my home, and I don't care about being the best and brightest. I just want to be as effective as I can and help protect the people I love. Kinda like you, I suspect. Now, why did you call me?"

"The way I read your reports, it sounds like you found different blood on *both* Clay's body and in his car, different from Clay's, that is. You called it 'suspect genetic markers'. Someone other than Clay's blood in both locations – is that correct?"

"Yes, that's right. That means that your killer was in close proximity to Sherwin, and there was an exchange of blood between them. Probably during the beheading, but it could also have happened during the shooting. Say, if it was at close range, as we've determined, and a piece of the car's shattered window cut the shooter on his hand or arm."

"So if I can get a DNA sample from a suspect, you can compare it to what you've analyzed from the autopsy and from the vehicle bloodstains, and tell me if I have a match or not." This came out more like a question than a statement. Matt had used DNA in previous cases, but he wanted to make sure that he and Bernice were on the same page here.

"Yes, but the caution here is that I can't absolutely link it to a person. I can only testify that the evidence can link to one specific person with a high degree of probability. It's not like a fingerprint that is totally unique, but I can make a strong statistical case for you."

"How strong?"

"I can tell you that one person in several million or even billion has a particular DNA profile. And, if you get me a sample from your suspect, I can then tell you whether or not he has the same DNA profile."

"In other words, it's not a perfect match, but the odds of the matching DNA are very much in my favor," Matt said.

"Yes, it's compelling evidence. It helps rule out suspects completely, and can add beyond a reasonable doubt to whomever is ruled in. All you have to do now is get me samples from the killer to compare," Bernice said.

"I may have already done that," he said.

"Oh?"

"Yeah, because of a heads up from a waitress friend of mine, we may have encountered our villains last night in a local restaurant. I talked to them, and they are smug, smart, and suspicious. We tried to follow them home afterwards, but lost them."

"That's too bad."

"Yeah, but you're going to love this next part. Vicki, the waitress, nabbed their drink glasses for me, and we've got them tucked safely in a plastic bag. They'll be on their way to you as soon as one of my officers gets here this morning. With any luck at all, they've slobbered all over them."

"One can hope," Bernice said. "That's great news for me, but does it put you at risk? I mean, they must know you're on to them."

"Let's just say I double-locked my doors and windows last night. Jay and Ed Sonders were with me, and they got eye-balled as well. Joe Phelps and Rod McClellan were in the restaurant at the time, but they were a little more undercover, and I'm not sure Octavio and Juan made them."

"We have names?"

"First names only. They weren't inclined to share any further info with me once I made them uncomfortable. It's going to be a cat-and-mouse game from here on out, but I'm smarter than they are. I know that because I know that they think they're smarter than us."

"You lost me, but I think you said you'll get them," Bernice said.

"You can bet the farm on it."

◆◆◆

"You're looking very pretty this morning, Fern," said Sylvia, as Fern entered the squad room.

"It's up to you and me to set the standard in this room full of slobs, don't you think?"

It had taken a while for Fern's colleagues to appreciate her sense of humor, but the room laughed out loud this morning.

"You ladies have more to work with than we do," said Walt. The sergeant could be chivalrous when he wanted to be.

It was an unusual police squad room, probably because they had all come together out of a sense of need during the Bushnell case. The small-town police department had been unused to violent crime; most of them had never experienced one in their years on the force. A new boss, a dead child, and the successful resolution of the case, all occurring in one week, had bonded the group to each other as securely as if they'd been glued to one another.

Fern knew that a couple of the officers were a little jealous of her close relationship with Matt – Jay's too – but she also knew they understood why it had happened. Matt, Jay, and Fern had been thrown together under unusual circumstances, the worst possible circumstances, and they had fought their way through together. It was completely natural, once they were on the other side, that the closeness they'd developed during that horrific week would remain in place, probably forever.

Fern had gone out of her way to take the undesirable assignments, to ask for their advice, and to always be the best possible colleague she could be. It had not gone unnoticed by the other officers, and, deep down, to a man they were happy to have someone with Fern's brains on their team. And, she was funny, which certainly didn't hurt in a police squad room. She could both take it and dish it out.

"What do you call the color of that jacket?" Rudy asked Fern now. He was smirking.

"I call it 'peony pink', and it's in honor of spring, which despite what is currently happening outside your window, is just around the corner." It was pouring down rain, beating on the windows as if to tell the humans that it may say 'spring' on the calendar, but the weather wasn't buying it just yet.

"Sylvia's right, you do look pretty today," Rudy admitted. "Matter of fact, you look pretty good, too, Sylvia, for an old broad."

"And you look like hell, Rudy," Sylvia snapped. "Isn't there anyone who can help you find a sweater that didn't come out of the bottom of the laundry bin? Try harder." She turned back to her computer, flinging her also-spring-like lime green scarf around to the back and out of her way.

Rudy gave Sylvia, who was no longer paying attention to him, a firm salute.

Fern made her way across the room to her desk, leaning down to whisper in Sylvia's ear as she passed her "That green looks ab fab on you. Let's keep it going, girlfriend."

Sylvia turned her head ever so slightly, winked, and whispered "girl power", resuming her work immediately.

Joe Phelps had called Fern after reading Bernice's forensics reports, and told her he was going to bring Arlette Sherwin to Port Stirling. The medical examiner had released Clay's body, and it was time for Arlette to deal with arrangements. He and Rod planned to help her, but Phelps had also told Fern that he wanted to get a blood sample from Arlette that Bernice could analyze. He'd called Fern to get a read on how she thought Arlette would react to that.

"She'll be pissed," Fern had told him bluntly. "She thinks you put her husband in a no-win situation, and it cost him his life."

"Clay always knew the risk he was taking, knew it for all the years he worked for us. We tried to talk him into backup on this one, but he refused. He thought his prey would smell two agents, and he was convinced that on his own he could go unobserved. It was an error in judgment on my part, and I'll have to live with it. I don't blame Arlette for feeling the way she does."

"She knows Clay took chances in his work, she told me that. She just needs to blame this on someone, and she'll get over blaming you...someday. But she'll go nuts if she thinks you believe there is a chance she killed her husband. I subtly suggested to her that it was an odd coincidence considering how Clay died that she has swords and blades on display all throughout her home, and she quickly and efficiently shut me down. She's a clever woman. She saw right through me, and she'll know what you're about, too."

"Well, it can't be helped," Phelps said. "The truth is I do believe there's a chance Arlette did it. I give it a one in 100 chance, but still, there's a chance, and I have to rule her out. Your medical examiner did a great job with the forensics, and we have blood evidence from the suspect or suspects. We'd be derelict in our duty if we didn't match the widow's blood to it, just to be positive. Arlette had the means – she knows how to handle a sword – she had the opportunity because she was one of the few people in the world who knew where Clay was. What we don't know – yet – is if she had a motive to want her husband dead."

"She didn't have a financial motive," Fern told him. "Most of their money came from Arlette's parents directly to her. And, according to her and both of the children, Arlette and Clay were happily married. I didn't sense any undercurrents of discord in the marriage when I visited their home. So, if she's got a motive for wanting him dead, I don't see it."

"Where was she at the end of last week? Do we know if she has an alibi?"

"I don't know yet. I did ask the kids if they'd spent time with their mom last week, and they both said 'yes'. I'm making calls today to two of her friends, and to check up on her usual routine, exercise classes, that sort of thing. Do you want me to still do that?"

"Yes, please proceed," Phelps replied.

"Since I have a relationship with her, do you want me to tell her that we will need a blood sample from her?" Fern asked, hoping like hell the answer from Phelps would be 'no'.

"I was her husband's boss, so it's my responsibility to arrange for her to travel here and for the State Department to help her in any way we can. Once she's here, I will tell her the truth: that we need to rule her out as a suspect. If she's pissed, she's pissed, I can't help it because it has to be done."

"OK," Fern said. "I will help you with whatever you need me to do. But I don't believe that Arlette is involved."

"I understand you have a background in psychology, Ms. Byrne, and you spent some time with Arlette, so I respect your opinions. I happen to agree with you, but I have to do what I have to do."

"Of course, sir. I'll be in touch when I have a report."

CHAPTER 20

....

green green grass

Matt went into the squad room, looking for Rudy.

"Hey, boss, what can I do for you?" Rudy said as Matt approached his desk.

"Need you to take these glasses," he replied, holding up the evidence bag, "over to Dr. Ryder in Buck Bay. We encountered two potential suspects last night – Octavio and Juan – and they drank out of these. Dr. Ryder is expecting you."

"Sure thing, chief. This feels like progress," Rudy said hopefully, looking up at Matt with his broad, innocent face and baby blue eyes that contrasted with his muscular, cut physique. Rudy was the gym rat of the department.

"It might be. Dr. Ryder will tell us. Get a move on, OK?"

As he headed back to his office, Matt noticed Sylvia talking to a teenage boy who was hanging out at her desk in the corner.

"Honey, I can't give you any more right now," Sylvia was saying.

Matt strolled over and said to the boy, "What can we do for you, son?"

"This is my grandson, Joshua," Sylvia said. "Say hello to the chief, honey."

The boy frowned but did as his grandmother told him to.

"It's nice to meet you, Joshua," said Matt, sticking his hand out to shake and stubbornly leaving it there until the boy finally reached out.

"Nice to meet you, too," Joshua sullenly uttered.

"Are you here to take your beautiful grandmother out to lunch today?" Matt said with a smile.

Sylvia snorted. "Only if I pay, huh, Josh?" She playfully slugged her grandson in the arm. "He's come up a little short this month, and needs a loan," she explained to Matt.

"Grandma!" Joshua exclaimed and glared at her.

"Ah, I was always short of cash when I was your age, too," Matt lied. The Hornings were a wealthy family in Texas. "Maybe I can help out your cause. Do you have time after school to do a little work in my yard? It doesn't need much, just a little weeding and mowing the grass, but I don't seem to have time to get to it this week."

"Where do you live?" the boy asked, his curiosity piqued.

"On Ocean Bend Road, about five minutes from here. It's just down the road from your school, and you could easily walk there. If you're interested, I can tell you where to find my mower and tools and you can go today. Call me when you're done, and I'll pay you and give you a ride home. How does that sound?"

"OK, I guess," Joshua said, the beginning of a smile trying to work itself out.

"Matter of fact, why don't I just hire you to come a couple of times a month from now through summer? Could you do it?"

"Don't see why not," he said almost pleasantly.

"Deal, then. Here's where to go and here's my cell – call me when you're done." Matt grabbed a Post-it note off Sylvia's desk and scribbled his info.

"Thanks, chief. I'll do a good job. I like working outside."

"Of course you'll do a good job. You're Sylvia's grandson – it's in your bones."

"See you later, grandma," the boy said, bending down to give Sylvia a kiss on the cheek. Off he went.

"That was a nice thing you just did," Sylvia said. "Thank you."

"I remember how important it is to a teenage boy to have some cash in his pocket," Matt said. "And, my yard really needs the help."

"That's no lie," said Fern, coming up to join the conversation. "His yard is sad."

"Oh? You've been there?" inquired Sylvia, a discreet smile on her face.

"Jay and I had a meeting with the chief there on Sunday when this place was locked up," she explained. But a flush crept up her neck, and turned her cheeks the same color as her jacket. There was a good chance that all three of them were thinking the same thing.

"I need to tell you what Joe Phelps is up to," Fern said quickly, changing the subject.

"Take it in the other room, please," said Sylvia, waving her hand toward Matt's office. "I've got to get on the phone."

"Phelps just called me, and he's decided he wants a blood sample from Arlette Sherwin," Fern said, sliding into the armchair facing Matt's desk.

"That's wise," said Matt. "We haven't ruled out anybody yet, especially Arlette. And Bernice got some good samples, both off Clay's body and his vehicle. We can start comparing and see if we get a match from people of interest. How's Joe going to do it?"

"He's bringing her up here now that Clay's body has been released by Bernice. Planning to spring it on her once she arrives. Said to make sure you knew."

"OK! Let's get investigating."

"She's gonna be pissed."

"Tough."

"You sound just like Phelps," Fern said. "She is the widow, you know."

"And if she didn't chop off hubby's head, my heart goes out to her. But if she's part of this — whatever this is — we'll string her up."

"String her up? Who *are* you??"

"Figure of speech left over from Texas," Matt said sheepishly. "Sorry."

"Don't ever say that again. It will make you popular with the people you don't want to be popular with."

"Am I still popular with you?"

"Not at the moment," she said, but smiled a smile that said the opposite.

"Guess what Jay's doing?"

"No idea. Fill me in."

"He's hiring a drone to fly over three properties south of town that changed hands in the past year or so. These three real estate transactions stood out because they were unusual for this area — out of towners, cash deals. We're taking some aerial photos in the hopes we'll see something the bad guys don't want us to see."

"Does Jay think one of them might belong to our criminals?"

Matt filled in Fern on Jay's theory about the access cutoff to the fishing hole, and patrolling big dogs.

"Well, if I were smuggling drugs in international waters, I would first buy a remote piece of land near the beach, and make it as private as I could. So, maybe Jay's onto something."

"I sure as hell hope so," Matt said. "I'm 99.9% positive Octavio's involved, and I want to find him before any more weird shit happens. He's a smart, slippery man, and he's here for a reason. I don't know if he shot Clay Sherwin in the heart himself, but he's entangled in this somehow."

"You had a real moment with that guy, didn't you?" Fern said, fidgeting in her chair.

"Yeah, I guess you could say that. He looked right through me, and it was not a good feeling. There was also a smugness about him, like he knew that I knew but it didn't worry him. Like whatever I did, he could one-up me. I'm not afraid of much, Fern," Matt said looking directly into her beautiful green eyes, "but this guy scared me. Octavio can manipulate people, he knows it, and he uses it. He is not a man to be trifled with."

"Well, if he is what you think he is, he'll slip up somewhere along the line. My money's on you," she smiled. "Smug bad guys can't beat my guy."

"I guess we'll find out, won't we?"

◆◆◆

Matt Googled 'Zhang Chen', and spent some time searching through articles and reading about him. Chinese descent, but born in San Francisco to immigrants. Scholarship to the University of California at Berkeley. Dropped out his junior year and started a technology company that he sold when he was 24 years old for $28 million. No apparent scrapes with the law. Upstanding citizen named "Technology Entrepreneur of the Year" in San Jose four years ago. Thirty-one years old now with a net worth in nine figures.

Does this guy need to smuggle drugs or traffic young women? It can't be him, thought Matt. *Too much to risk.* Chen had paid $410,000 for the 200 acres that included a small house and several out buildings. The property included the gravel road in from Hwy 101, and beach access.

He pulled up Jay's report on the Wasserman property. Sheila and Kenneth Wasserman. Microsoft millionaires. *I should have gone into technology.*

The Wassermans, in contrast to Chen's multiple properties up and down the west coast, owned only four that Matt could find online. Their primary home on Mercer Island in Washington, an apartment in Paris, a house in

146

Sunriver, Oregon, and a small resort in Costa Rica. The 50 acres on Fauna Lake was their most recent purchase.

They employed a general manager to run the Costa Rican resort, a small property on a gorgeous bay on the Pacific side of the country. It was composed of eight two-story units, all with wrap-around porches, set back from the beach in a jungle-like environment. The Wassermans appeared to be doing life right. The Costa Rica connection bothered Matt because Maria Ramos mentioned that country in her description of the two men's accent. And, in addition to its beautiful beaches and lovely people, the country, sadly, has a growing presence in the drug trade. He decided to start with the couple.

"Hey, Sylvia," Matt said into his intercom, "can you get a phone number or email address for Sheila and Kenneth Wasserman for me? They live in Mercer Island, Washington, and our realtor Sandy Vox might be able to help you. They're in Jay's report."

"Yes, I've got that right here. On it."

The rock band, Deep Love, was next on Matt's research. He knew that over the years there had been many links between Hollywood celebrities and Oregon. Not surprising that they might seek out remote, off-the-grid locations just north to unwind out of the spotlight.

The local Buck Bay realtor who had served as the buyers' agent had provided Jay with a contact phone number, the cell phone of the band's agent in Los Angeles. Matt dialed the number now.

To his great surprise, his call was answered. *Who answers their phone these days?*

"I'm calling for Kip Allred," Matt said.

"Speaking. Who are you?"

"Matt Horning, Port Stirling, Oregon, Chief of Police. Do you have a couple of minutes to talk?"

"Ahh, yes, the band's real estate village," said Mr. Allred. "I saw the area code, and thought you might be someone else. Why are you calling? Has there been a break-in?"

"No. I'm investigating a serious crime in Port Stirling, and I'm looking at recent property sales."

"It's not illegal to buy a house," Allred huffed. "Why are you bothering me? I don't like this conversation." He sounded like a child about to have a tantrum.

"I just have a few questions about the property they bought up here last year. But if you don't want to talk now, I can send my L.A. colleagues to your office in uniform. They're an impressive bunch of cops. And, I will tell the media that we tried to talk to Deep Love's manager, but he was uncooperative."

"That won't be necessary, Matt," Allred said, loosening up. "I'm always happy to help out the police in any way I can."

"Great. Let's start with, why did the band buy 150 acres in the middle of nowhere?"

Allred laughed. "That's a valid question, Matt. Can I call you Matt?" He continued talking as if he hadn't asked a question. "My band can't go anywhere in the world without being hounded by paparazzi and fans. Check that: they can go to the ranch in Oregon." He pronounced it 'Ore-gone'. "The only place they can really chill."

"How many times have they been here since they bought it?"

"A couple of times, I think. Once right after the deal was finalized. Only Artie had seen it before they bought it. They all trust him. But they all went up soon after the buy. Stayed about a week if I recall. Then they were up there in the fall. Can't remember if they all went then, but they had a break in the tour schedule and wanted to sleep and drink. Oh, wait, and they went for a long weekend right before Christmas, too. That's it."

Matt recalled that Artie was the base player. "How did Artie find the property?"

"He's from Oregon. Portland. Good music scene up there. He remembered the south coast from hunting trips with his family when he was young. He contacted a local agent, and drove up I-5 to meet her and check out the place. She found two or three properties that matched the band's needs, and he loved the ranch. Wouldn't be surprised if he doesn't buy out the guys when they're finished with this gig and retire up there. He digs the beach, the rain, the wind, all that stuff."

"So, to your knowledge Mr. Allred, Deep Love is not running a drug smuggling ring from their ranch?"

This got a loud, snorted laugh. "When, for fuck's sake, would they have time to do that? In case you haven't noticed, they're kinda busy."

"Yeah, they do seem to keep busy," Matt allowed. "Do me a favor, Kip. Ask them if they noticed any unusual activity near the beach – lights, boats, and so forth – when they were here, especially in December. Can you do that for me? I may have to talk to them directly, but, for now, that will give us a start."

"Sure thing, Matt. I'll ask them."

"Also, a colleague in the LAPD will need to take an official statement from you and/or Artie about the property purchase at some point soon."

"They can talk to me if you have to, but the band is in Dubai currently. So that's not going to happen," he said firmly.

"I'm the police, Kip, and interrogating witnesses is what we do. It is going to happen. When do they return to the states?"

"Not for two weeks. Listen, Matt, buddy, I'll help you, but you have to leave the band alone for now. This trip is worth $75 million, and I don't want them upset. And, if you link me or them to any drug smuggling deal, you'll be the target of a lawsuit faster than you can say "Deep Love". Just deal with whatever is going on up there. I wouldn't want anything to spoil the boys' peace and quiet."

"I'm not your buddy, and we're not crazy about the idea either," Matt said.

Matt never got tired of looking out of his office's window. He could swear that in the three months he'd been on the job, the view had not been the same twice. They had a saying in Oregon: If you don't like the weather, wait five minutes. Other locales said that, too, but here it was really true…the weather could, and did, change on a dime.

At this moment in time, the sky was a mix of blues with a bunch of clouds thrown in to make it interesting. The clouds out to sea on the horizon were heavy and grey, foreboding. But over the river, the lighthouse, and the jetty, they were a fluffier, whiter version. The river, nearing its mouth at the Pacific, was a blue/green color today, but with a few whitecaps forming that didn't look, yet, like they meant business. Matt hoped any rain would hold off until Joshua got out of school this afternoon and mowed his lawn.

He was curious about Sylvia and his staff's private lives, but found it better to let them share things with him rather than him prying too much. He would already have known everything about everybody in Texas, but Oregonians would tell you only what they thought you needed to know. Today he wondered if Joshua's mother or father was Sylvia's child. It didn't matter in the greater scheme of things, he was curious, that's all. He was already fond of the boy.

Matt knew his parents would love to have some grandchildren. Neither he nor his younger brother or sister were parents yet. Mom and Dad were gracious enough to not point it out, but Matt knew his mother, in particular, was getting antsy. *You'll have to wait, mom, no babies in the picture here yet. But a redheaded baby, boy or girl, would be a joy. Where the hell did that come from?* Matt thought and quickly shook it off.

Sylvia came in, and Matt flushed at his thoughts, the color rising in his cheeks. "Here's a phone number for Kenneth Wasserman," she said, pretending not to notice his face, and pushing her glasses on top of her head. "I'd like to know what they're planning for that Fauna Lake property. We used to take the kids water-skiing there when Richard was alive. Lots of fun, and I hope these Microsoft people don't mess it up. Are you going to ask them why they bought it?"

"Yes, ma'am, I am. They also own a small resort on the beach in Costa Rica which they built, so it's valid to wonder if they have the same plans for here. But the house in Sunriver is small, so it's possible they just like to have getaways from Seattle. Plus, there's a lot of real estate investing going on right now, people buying up properties and holding them as the market goes up. That could be the Wasserman's story. Jay tells me it's a real nice piece of land."

"It is," Sylvia confirmed. "Pretty little lake surrounded mostly by forest, close to the beach but out of the wind. It's special."

"How long were you married?"

"Forty-five long years," she grinned. "I'm kidding, Richard was a wonderful man and husband. He's been dead for six years, but I still miss him."

"What did he do for a living?"

"He was an accountant, and a good one. We started out in New York, the Bronx, and he was a banker. When we moved out to Oregon, he decided accounting was his love, and he opened a small business. He provided for me very well. I don't need to work, I do this because I'm not the sit-on-a-beach-in-my-old-age type. One needs to be engaged with something meaningful and social when you reach a certain age, or you will rot in a chair."

"That will never, ever happen to you, Sylvia," he smiled. The truth, she had more energy than some of his officers who were half her age.

"I could have given Joshua all the money he wanted, but his father – my son – and I agree that it's time he started earning it. We've decided we're not going to hand him everything. He's a bright kid, and he'll do well if he wants it bad enough. That's why what you did this morning means so much. Let him understand what work and responsibility feels like. I really appreciate it, chief." She refused to call him 'Matt', it was disrespectful for his position, no matter how informal Port Stirling was.

"It's me that's getting the favor. It's been pointed out to me that my cottage's yard needs some TLC," he smiled. "I was just about to get to it when this case came along. I don't want my yard to be the worst-looking one on Ocean Bend Road. I think I even signed something when I rented it that said I have to maintain the property, so your grandson will likely keep me out of jail."

"Joshua will make sure you don't go to jail. He likes working outdoors, and I think he has a knack for it. Don't go easy on him, OK? If he gets lazy, yank his chain."

"Consider it yanked."

Fern had gone downtown to grab some oyster stew from the Crab Shack Café in between making phone calls to Arlette Sherwin's friends and colleagues. She decided to stay in the Café to eat instead of bringing lunch back to her desk like she usually did. It was the day the weekly local newspaper came out, and she picked one up from the counter.

"You're looking spring-y today in your pretty pink," greeted Gina, the cashier and daughter of the owner. Fern liked Gina, and always admired her flawless skin and lustrous dark hair. With Fern's red hair and freckles, there was no hope of ever being a sensual brunette.

"Well, it's spring, isn't it?" Fern smiled at the girl. Can I have some oyster stew and a grilled cheese sandwich?"

"Half or whole?"

"Half, please, but a big bowl of the stew."

She took her newspaper and sat at the small table in the corner that overlooked the Port Stirling harbor. Today, it was blue sky and white boats with some sunshine sparkling on the water. Very nice, and it was good to get out of the office for a few minutes.

Fern didn't know it, but she was sitting at the exact same table Clay Sherwin had sat at the afternoon he was killed.

CHAPTER 21

....

tires

After about 35 minutes, Fern paid her check and left the Crab Shack Café. She walked down the boardwalk a block or so to the small florist shop at the waterfront, where she bought a replacement rose for the vase on her VW's dashboard. The red rose currently in the vase was done, so today she bought – what else? – a pale pink rose.

Returning to her baby blue VW bug, she settled the new rose in its home for the week, put the key in the ignition, and started the car. She pulled out into Main Street, and headed up the hill toward City Hall, but after one block, she knew something was wrong.

What the heck? she asked herself, as the VW bumped along wildly, and she seemed to be pitched forward. She pulled over to the side of the street, and got out to look at her car. The front two tires had bitten the dust, completely flat. She peered closely at them, and it was obvious both tires had been slashed. *Great, more blade work.*

Normally, Fern would call AAA, and have the nice young man come and change a flat tire, but this felt different, dangerous. She found herself looking over her shoulder and around the area. She didn't see anyone or anything that looked suspicious, and the street was mostly empty after the lunch rush, which in Port Stirling was about ten people. She dialed Matt's cell phone.

He answered with his usual these days, "Where are you?"

"I'm near the Crab Shack Café, and my VW has two flat front tires. They've been slashed with a knife or something," she explained. "I started to

153

call AAA, but not sure I want to hang around here that long and wait for him."

"Smart. I'm on my way. Go inside the café and wait for me." His voice was tense and hurried.

"I don't see anything odd or anyone I don't recognize," Fern told him, looking up and down the street again. "I think the jerk that did this is long gone."

"Humor me," Matt said firmly. "Go back inside the café and wait for me. Am I clear?"

"Yes. Going in now."

Driving to the waterfront with his siren on, Matt called Bernice.

"What's up, chief?" Bernice said.

"Can you spare a forensic guy for a quick job? Fern's tires have been slashed on Main St. and I want to dust them before we move her car."

"You want a forensics team for a tire slashing?" Bernice asked, just to be clear.

"Not any old tire slashing. A double tire slashing on a very identifiable car belonging to an officer investigating a murder and a possible kidnapping. Maybe it's a coincidence, but..."

"But you don't believe in coincidences, I know," Bernice interupted. "Neither do I. Oh, God, is Fern at risk?"

"Don't know. I'm on my way there now to check it out."

"I'll send DJ, he's hanging around waiting for me to finish up something. But it will him take 20 minutes or so to get there. Can you keep people away from her vehicle until then?"

"I'll do my best. Thanks, Bernice."

"Please tell Fern to hang in there."

◆◆◆

Matt pulled bright yellow plastic "POLICE - DO NOT CROSS" tape out of his back seat kit, and, with Fern's help, wrapped it around the VW. As they worked, he asked her "How are you? OK?"

"Uncomfortable."

"Understandable."

"No one would do this to me," she fumed, her fear turning to anger. "Everyone knows my car."

"It is recognizable," Matt agreed.

"So, why me? And in broad daylight? On Main Street even?!? What the hell is wrong with these people?"

"They're trying to scare us. They're bullies and they want us, particularly me, to back off."

"That's not going to happen!" She smacked the roof of her VW. "They can't come in here and turn my town upside down. Not friggin allowed!"

"I'm wondering how they know about you," Matt said quietly, hoping to quiet Fern an octave or two. Fern had a calm, amiable disposition, but every once in a while the volatile redhead temperament showed itself. "You weren't with Jay, Ed, and me in the restaurant last night. In fact, we've barely been in the same room together since this case started."

"Not really since Sunday night at your cottage," Fern said, thinking.

"They must be staking out City Hall and watching who goes in and out."

"Wouldn't we have noticed them? Don't you think?"

"Boy, I would think so. We're all on high alert. It's odd. Maybe they've been watching my house, and saw you leave Sunday." Saying that gave Matt a chill, and he moved closer to Fern.

She felt it and moved in even tighter to him. "You know, now that I think about it, there might have been someone in my neighborhood Sunday night after I got home." She looked up and locked onto Matt's eyes. "There was a car parked in my street. I assumed it was guests of my neighbors Amy and Scott across the street. But maybe it was there to watch my house."

"It wasn't a Jeep, was it?"

"I'm not great at identifying cars, but, yes, I think it might have been a Jeep."

Reflexively, Matt reached out and took Fern's hands in his.

◆◆◆

Once Matt and Fern took care of her car's business, they returned to City Hall. Fern drank a tall glass of water, calmed down, and resumed checking on Arlette Sherwin's schedule last week. Matt retreated to his office to call Sheila and Kenneth Wasserman.

He hadn't completely ruled out the rock band and their ranch, but he had to admit that their agent had a point: they were a highly successful band with an ongoing international tour. Unless they had a trusted lieutenant, Matt didn't see how they would have time to run a smuggling ring. However, a well-connected businesswoman, say, like Arlette Sherwin, also with California ties, and free to come and go as she pleased, could serve as the band's emissary. It was within the realm of possibility.

Kenneth Wasserman had almost immediately returned Matt's call after the chief left a message on his voicemail, but Matt had not taken the call during the VW drama. Now, he dialed him back.

"Thanks for getting back to me so fast," Matt started.

"Sure thing. I can't imagine why the Chief of Police in Port Stirling would be calling me, so I guess you could say I'm curious." He sounded affable.

"It's my understanding that you and your wife bought 50 acres on Fauna Lake last year, and I want to talk to you about that purchase."

"Is something wrong?"

"No, this is just routine. We're looking at all recent property sales to get background on another matter."

"That's a relief. It's a gorgeous piece of property. We were smitten the minute we saw it for the first time."

"If I may inquire, Mr. Wasserman, what do you plan to do with the property? If anything."

"You probably know that there aren't currently any structures on our acreage. There's the beach frontage on the northwest side, which, of course, is fabulous. Our property curves around the north end of the lake to the east side, and most of that is treed. The only infrastructure is a dirt road that comes in from Highway 101, and electrical from the road. We intend to build two structures – a vacation home for our family, which will go on the northwest corner and will give us both a beach and lake view...if we do it right! That project will begin in June. Once the home is built, we are considering another building on the east side of the lake that would become a small bed & breakfast, with 4-5 rooms. Sheila has always fancied herself as an hotelier of sorts, and this would be her project."

"I understand you own a resort in Costa Rica," Matt inserted.

"Yes, that's Sheila's doing as well. We bought that property pretty rough, and it's now a beautiful, successful operation. She thinks Fauna Lake can be that, too, only on a smaller scale. We like that it's convenient to Port Stirling Links, and that high-end, luxury market of golfers is who we'd target. But first, we want to build a house for us, and get to know the area better. We love what we've seen so far, and we're big fans of Oregon. We also own a home in Sunriver and we spend some time down there every summer. But we're both especially fond of the Oregon coast, so this was a natural for us."

"The beach is special, I agree. Have you been to your property recently?"

"No, but we need to get down there soon. We'll be looking to hire a general contractor, and get the building permit going. Do you happen to know of any I might contact?"

"I've only been here for about three months, so can't really help you there. When you bought the property, did you notice any unusual activity on the beach side? Boats coming and going? Traffic and people? Lights at night? That sort of thing?"

Wasserman laughed. "No, chief, just the opposite. That's why we bought it. Nobody around at all, just the sound of the wind in the trees, and the waves breaking on shore. When you've been in a pressure-cooker corporate world as long as Sheila and I have been, you can't even put a price tag on this kind of peace and quiet. The locals may think we paid a lot for this land, but the reality is we consider it below fair market value – we think we got a steal for this serenity."

"I hear you. I'm already addicted to it."

"Are you going to tell me why the Chief of Police is interested in our purchase? Is there anything we should know?" Direct, to the point.

"We're investigating a crime that may involve smuggling somewhere on the Oregon or northern California coastline," Matt said. "I'm checking out beach property purchases in the last year or so, and yours popped up."

"Should I be worried?" Wasserman asked.

"Not unless you're bringing in contraband from the high seas."

Again, Wasserman laughed. "Nope. Not doing that, chief."

"I would ask that you check in with me when you come down, just to meet you. And that you keep your eyes and ears open when you do. Your section of beach access is fairly out in the open, not hidden, so there's likely no action near you, but you never know in this kind of situation."

"I'll look forward to it, Chief Horning. Thanks for the heads up."

◆◆◆

Matt decided to not contact Zhang Chen just yet. *Unless Kip Allred and Kenneth Wasserman were the two best conmen on the planet, I'm 0-for-2 on suspicious beach properties. Don't think I'll tip my hand to the third candidate yet until I check him out further.*

157

Matt would wait to see what the drone flyovers showed. Jay said they were going out about 3:00 p.m. He also confirmed to Matt that he'd booked them to do daily runs for a while so they could compare any movement of equipment or vehicles that might be happening at night.

His intercom buzzed, and Sylvia said, "Dr. Ryder on line 1 for you."

"Thanks, Sylvia. Bernice, what did you find?"

"Absolutely nothing. Just like in Clay Sherwin's vehicle. Whoever killed him and whoever slashed Fern's tires was wearing gloves…no usable prints."

"Figures, doesn't it? I'm of the mind that if it had just been kids playing around, there would have been prints. And, someone would have seen them. These guys are pros, and know how to get in and get out invisibly. They're trying to get me to panic."

"You don't strike me as the panicking kind of guy," Bernice said.

"They don't know that, do they? So they think they can terrorize me until I back off. Well, that's not going to happen," Matt said. "Repeat after me: They're going down."

"They're going down!" Bernice obeyed. Then she unexpectedly laughed. "I love you, chief. You're a breath of fresh air even in the middle of this horror movie."

"That's exactly what this is – a horror movie, and I've never liked those movies."

"Me neither."

"Let's end this one…what do you say?"

"All for it, chief. Go forth and make arrests soon, please."

Joe Phelps and Rod McClellan strode into Matt's office.

"Hi, guys," Matt greeted them. "What's the latest on your end?"

"Did Fern tell you we're bringing Arlette up here?" Phelps asked. Matt nodded. "It's happening tomorrow. She'll be here sometime tomorrow afternoon. She's arranged to have Clay's body removed to California for burial."

"What can I do to help you?"

"She wants to meet with the medical examiner while she's here. Can you arrange that with Dr. Ryder?" Phelps said.

"Of course. It's natural she'd have some questions about how her husband died, don't you think?"

"Yes, but Arlette was quite specific that she wanted to meet with Dr. Ryder alone, or just with you present. She doesn't want Rod or I in the meeting. Not sure why, and I didn't ask."

"Well, you weren't on the scene at the beginning, so that's probably all she wants to know," said Matt.

"We'll still need to inform her we need a blood sample," piped in Rod. "She might not like that."

"Yeah, but it's a solid idea," said Matt. "I would frame it to her in terms of us needing to rule her out, more than anything else. It's true."

"What if it rules her in?" said Phelps. "I will have a tough time explaining how the wife of my star agent is involved with her husband's murder."

"I don't think it will come to that, Joe," said Matt. "I think Octavio is our man. He's onsite and he's running the operation. The two issues are related. I'm certain. We just have to catch him in the act and prove it."

"Is that all?" Phelps said, straight-faced.

"I'll set up a meet with Bernice, and I'll be there, too. I need to meet Arlette and talk face-to-face. After our phone call, I don't have much of a read on her. Fern is convinced she's a grieving widow, and the fencing/blade stuff is just a coincidence."

"I'm with Fern," Phelps said. "But Rod here isn't so sure." He waggled his thumb toward his partner.

"I know Arlette," Rod said, "and I like her. But I also wouldn't put anything past her. She's astute, and she's worldly. She also really likes being rich. Maybe her parents' dough isn't going as far as she wants. Maybe she knows just enough about international smuggling rings to find her way in. I know I'll sleep better if her DNA rules her out of Clay's murder."

"So, you think money is her motivation?" asked Matt. "Enough of a motivation to cut off the head of her husband?"

"Sounds crazy, I agree," said Rod. "But losing an agent this way is crazy. Someone thought Clay was close to outing their operation, and they had to stop him. I hope like hell it wasn't Arlette, but if it was…" his voice trailed off.

"If it was, those poor kids," was Matt's thought. "Are they coming with her?"

"No," said Phelps. "Her best friend and neighbor is staying with the kids in their home while Arlette is here. The daughter has moved home to help her brother while this is going on. I also agreed to put a security guy on house watch; Arlette was nervous about leaving the kids."

"We need one here at City Hall, too," said Matt. "Someone is tracking me and my people." He explained about Fern's car tires and her possibly being watched at home Sunday night.

"Do you think they know she went to Arlette's on Monday?"

"Possible, but I don't know how they would get that info," said Matt. "I really couldn't say. Fern just told me about a strange vehicle on her dead-end street Sunday night. She hadn't made a connection with the case until the episode with her car this afternoon. She couldn't say if she'd been followed anywhere, like the airport on Monday."

"And if your friends Octavio and Juan are involved, they know you, Jay, and Ed, and that City Hall is the hub of the action," said Phelps. "We'd better get you covered. I don't like the way this is trending."

"Agreed," said Matt. He told them about the drone flyover happening about now, and his work on checking out the coastal properties. "Along with the Coast Guard patrols, and my department plus the county help, we're covering all the bases. Something will give. I just hope it's soon."

"Before anyone else gets hurt," added Phelps.

CHAPTER 22

....

drone

Jay was excited. "We found two cool things!" he exclaimed, bursting into Matt's office.

"Have a seat, detective, and tell me. I'm all ears," Matt said.

"First, it turns out that the Coast Guard has a drone, and that's the one we used. And it's the dope best thing I've ever seen. They can make it go anywhere. I want one."

"Put it on the list. Right in front of your next raise. How does it work, and what did you find that's got you all hot and bothered?"

"The one the Coast Guard uses has an ultra-sophisticated camera, GPS and satellite-equipped. You pilot it above the perimeter of the property, and it makes an aerial videotape. Theirs cost about $10,000 he told me, but you can get them for as little as $1,500 that will do essentially the same thing. Theirs is capable of infrared imaging, so it can track people and things at night. Wouldn't that be cool to have?" Jay said, his eyes wide.

"Yes. Cool. Please tell me you did more than make your Christmas list for Santa."

"Funny. We filmed the Wasserman property at Fauna Lake to start, and it's a complete non-starter. There's nothing but trees, water, and sand at their end of the lake. No buildings or structures of any kind. No animals, no vehicles, no equipment, nothing man-made except a sorry one-lane dirt road."

"I talked to Kenneth Wasserman, and their plans are to build a family retreat on the northwest portion of the acreage, and then maybe a luxury B & B on the east side overlooking the lake for the golf crowd."

"There's a perfect spot to build a house," Jay said. "They can get a view of both the beach and the lake from one area."

"Yeah, I think that's the plan. What's the beach access look like from the air?"

"There's a narrow footpath that goes over some reeds and sand, and it's probably about ¼ mile in length. It's not much and barely visible from the drone's altitude. There's no way in hell any vehicle traffic could get from the beach to the dirt road."

"Did you see any movement at all?"

"One lonely seagull – that's it. This isn't the HQ for an international smuggling ring," Jay said.

"OK, next?"

"Next is BINGO!" Jay exclaimed. "Actually, it's more like 'possibly bingo'. Zhang Chen's property. First, it's huge, about four times the size of the Wasserman property. At least 200 acres. And truly in the middle of nowhere. It's about two miles off the highway, and the gravel road we've seen goes to the house and clearing."

"What else?" Matt prompted. "And am I going to get to see the videos and aerial photos at some point?"

"Yes, the Coast Guard is processing everything as we speak. You're going to be blown away. Zhang Chen may not be in the county currently, but somebody is. His property includes a small-ish house, one level, and a barn that's bigger than the house. There's a couple of other buildings too, smaller, and not sure what they're for. One's probably a garage, and looks like it would hold three or four vehicles."

"How do you know someone is there?"

"For starters, we could see the big dogs my buddy mentioned. And, there were several cars in the clearing by the house and barn."

"A sand-colored Jeep, by any chance?" Matt said hopefully.

"Nope, at least not out in the open. The barn's big enough to house about 20 Jeeps. We got photos, including license plate numbers for all the cars. Two had Oregon plates, and three had California. There was one other car we couldn't see the plate for because it was parked up against a hedge on one end, and had a wheelbarrow parked in front of the other end."

"Is the clearing where the house and out-buildings are private?" asked Matt. "If there wasn't a drone overhead, could anyone see them?"

"No, it's completely private, and practically impenetrable. In fact, I'm surprised the state let that whole property sell – the beach side of it looks like it should be retained as a natural resource to me."

"What do you mean?"

"You have to picture this: You turn off 101 onto the gravel road, and go about two miles toward the beach. The road goes through stands of old-growth, and through big meadows. You come through a dense canopy of trees into this clearing where the house sits, and the road dead-ends there. West of the house the trees get sparse, and there's a reedy area with tall grasses about 200 yards wide. Then, get this, there's a kind of river with a spit of sand and grasses on the other side, and then you're on the beach. It's really beautiful, and should be accessible to the public, in my opinion."

"Is there a bridge of any sort over the 'kind of river'? And what does that mean exactly?" Matt asked.

"It's a river, bigger than a creek and with moving water, but it's likely salt water and both enters and exits into the Pacific. And, no, I didn't notice a bridge over it anywhere. But it looks shallow enough, I could wade across it, I'm pretty sure. But there is a mowed path from the house through the reedy, grassy area to the river."

"How wide is it?"

"Wide. Like ten feet, maybe."

"Big enough to drive on?"

"Don't spoil the best part!" Jay said. "I'm getting to it!"

Matt just looked at him, waiting, his fingers intertwined and resting on his stomach as he leaned back in his chair, rocking gently.

"There are tracks on both the mowed grass path, and on the other side of the river down to the beach. The Coast Guard said the tracks were made by some sort of amphibious vehicle. Hence, bingo. And the tracks looked exactly like the ones you and I saw near Bill Abbott's house on Saturday that went right down to the water."

"Did you see the vehicle at the house?"

"Nope. I'm guessing they keep it in the barn."

"Likely," said Matt, and paused, thinking. "So, there's a ship somewhere offshore at night, probably with no running lights. They unload the cargo into the amphibian and sail it and then drive it right up into the barn. The distributors drive into the barn and pick up the cargo and off they go. All under the cover of darkness in a remote part of the world. Brilliant."

"But, wait, there's more," smiled Jay. "The Coast Guard is convinced that Zhang Chen's place is the operation, but we also saw something that I thought was odd at the Deep Love ranch. It, too, is in the middle of nowhere, surrounded by trees, and with access to the beach, although it's a little rougher than and not as easy to get to as Chen's property. They don't have all the outbuildings either, but the house is much bigger. It's a ranch style and sprawls, probably at least 8,000 square feet with garages on both ends of the house. There's no barn, but there's a big asphalt driveway and parking area adjacent to the house, and smack in the middle of that were two big semi-trucks."

"Hmm. Wonder what's in them?"

"Don't know, but don't you think it's odd?"

"Maybe," said Matt, "although it could be band gear…stuff like that."

"Yeah, but *two* big semis?"

"Were there any people around?"

"None that we saw, and there were no visible cars either. No animals."

"You've done nice work here, Jay," said Matt. "There's enough suspicious stuff on these two properties that we can get the court to approve a search on each of them. I'm suspicious of both, and I'm feeling big-time 'probable cause'. But I'll want to talk to Phelps, and we'll need to think it through. Would it be best to conduct a stakeout, or would we realize enough evidence conducting a search? A search would be extremely dangerous, and we might not get what we need."

"I'd rather watch both places for a while," said Jay. "And not because I'm afraid to go in with guns blazing – although I am. But even if we're able to arrest guys on the shore, we risk not catching the guys at sea."

"And that's who we really want," agreed Matt. "Octavio, as clever as I think he is, and Juan are maybe just the operations people. Who's fronting this operation? Is it Zhang Chen or the Deep Love band, or is it someone other than the property owners? We also need to know where the cargo is coming from."

"Yeah, the property owners could just be the front men," Jay said. "Some sort of partner."

"Or, maybe they don't even know how the property is being used. They are both absentee owners. Maybe the smugglers are simply squatting while the owners aren't paying attention. It's not like there is anyone around to notice. Although, the band was here at the end of last year according to their agent, so if it's the Deep Love ranch, it's recent."

"Do you know if Zhang Chen has been here?" Jay asked.

"I don't know. Haven't talked to him yet. I've been holding on that call until I did a little more research on him."

"I've talked to the Coast Guard, and pinpointed the two locations we're staking out. I asked them to pay particular attention tonight."

"Good," said Matt. "Maybe they'll pick up some signaling by lights between guys on the beach and a ship off shore."

"Wouldn't that be lovely," said Jay.

◆◆◆

The Chinook County crime team, with guest member Bell County Sheriff Les Thompson, called today's meeting to order at 4:10 p.m.

"I've been told that you requested two search warrants, chief," started District Attorney David Dalrymple in his best formal, and highly obnoxious D.A-ish tone. "Can you explain your reasoning?"

"Valid question, David," said Matt. *Valid, yes, but a needle in my eye nevertheless, you jerk.* "Detective Finley will give this report. Jay?"

Jay filled in the committee on the drone report, and produced aerial photos for all to see. The amphibious vehicle tracks drew the most interest, although Sheriff Thompson weighed in on the semi-trucks.

"I saw those trucks around Silver River," Thompson said. "I remember them because they're so big and don't have any noticeable markings."

"When was this?" asked Matt.

"I want to say it was right around New Year's, maybe a week after. They were stopped alongside Highway 101, in front of a popular restaurant."

"Did you happen to see the drivers?"

"Nope. Just remember seeing the trucks," said the sheriff.

"That makes it after the band's visit in December," noted Jay. Matt explained to the team what Deep Love's agent had told him about their visits to the property.

"Maybe the band visited in December to get everything ready for the operation to start in January," mused Patty Perkins. "Have you run background checks on the individual band members, chief?"

"Yes, and they are remarkably clean for an internationally renowned rock band," said Matt. "There are two cousins in the band, both from the L.A. area, and one of them – Kirk Parker – got a DUI while both of them were in the car about five years ago. It was a misdemeanor, as it was his first one. He paid a fine, got a six-month suspension of his driver's license, and a three-year probation. Which he's past now with no further violations. That's it."

"So if they are now running an international crime syndicate, there's nothing in their past that would indicate it," said Patty.

"Correct," said Matt. "On the other hand, they probably run in social circles we can only imagine. Who knows where those connections lead? We need to dig deeper."

"Do we have enough probable cause to bring them in for questioning?" asked Phelps. "What do you think, chief?"

"The semi-trucks are suspicious, for sure, but we've got even more at the Zhang Chen site. That's where the amphibious tracks were spotted. Jay," Matt said and nodded at his detective.

"Yeah, the Coast Guard is convinced there's something going on up the road at Chen's property," Jay said. "Looking at the aerials of this place, you'll see the tracks come up from the ocean, across the spit, across the river, and up the mowed pathway through the grasses. Hard to imagine what he could be doing with a vehicle like this other than something he shouldn't be."

"Couldn't it just be an ATV or some recreational thing?" asked Patty.

"The tracks are too big for that, in my view," said Matt. "Heavy looking."

"What's this Chen guy's story, chief, and have you spoken with him yet?" asked the D.A.

"I asked Matt to not call him yet," said Phelps. "I didn't want to alert him that we're on to something, because we think his property is the closest to what Clay reported to Rod."

"Joe's right," said Rod. "When Matt and Jay first described the three unusual real estate transactions and we looked at the map, Chen's property struck a chord with me, thinking back to what Clay told me. But our problem is that this guy's life history doesn't indicate 'cartel boss' any more than the rock stars. We need more info."

"Which is why Joe and I have decided to sit on the search warrants for a while," Matt explained. "It's nice to have them in our hip pocket, but we think we need more time to stakeout both properties, and that process is underway."

"Do you know you only have 15 days to exercise the warrant?" said Dalrymple.

Matt stared at him across the table. "Yes, David, I am aware of that fact, and have been for, oh, twenty years or so. Joe and I will revisit a possible search a few days from now, but first we want to compare drone photos for a couple of days. And we've got the Coast Guard zeroing in on these two locations on their night runs. So, for now, we're going to watch and wait. We don't just want the guys on land, we want their accomplices out to sea, too."

"What if they're laying low and nothing happens during your stakeout?" asked Dalrymple.

"We won't wait forever," said Phelps. "But Matt and I believe we can outwait them, especially if part of their cargo is human. And, remember that only Octavio and Juan have been made; they could be two of dozens involved, and the rest will carry on while those two stay under wraps. Patience is on our side."

"A serious consideration is what a delay might mean for any hostages they might be holding, especially if they're young girls," Matt said. "It upsets the hell out of me to have to wait. If anyone around this table feels that, too, and doesn't agree with the stakeout approach, this is the time to say so." Matt waited.

"It's the right thing to do, Matt," said Patty. "Exercising the warrants might get us something, but it likely won't get us everything, and this feels like one of those 'you get one shot' deals to me."

"What she said," agreed Ed Sonders, pointing at Patty.

Every head around the tabled nodded. All agreed, but there was a silence in the room as the enormity of the decision sunk in.

"Besides," Jay added, "think how much fun it will be swooping in with the feds' aerial and sea might, while we supply the muscle on the ground once we confirm what we suspect."

"You have a different view of fun than I do, son," said Matt, shaking his head at Jay's sarcasm, as the team laughed. It cut the tension that every single person in the room was feeling.

"I understand your joke, Jay, but your point's well taken," said Phelps. "If our stakeout turns up the goods, we will bring the full force of the federal government down on these scumbags' heads."

"What in Chen's personal history makes you doubt he's our guy, chief?" asked Dalrymple.

"He just doesn't need this gig," Matt answered. "He was a boy genius, made his first million by the time he was 25 years old, is a respected Silicon Valley stalwart – I can't understand why he would risk everything to add to his millions."

"Some people, especially men," said Patty, her eyes twinkling, "can't seem to ever get enough. And, it's not always about the money, sometimes they just want to prove they can do it and no one can stop them. Boils down to ego."

"Could be," allowed Matt. "I also need to examine his family in more detail. His parents were immigrants from China, Beijing, I recall, and there might be a story there. Maybe the U.S. did them wrong decades ago, and this is Chen's way of getting even. Who knows? I'll be doing more research as soon as we're done here."

"What about the Wasserman property?" Ed asked. "Assuming we've ruled it out since there are only two warrants. What's the deal?"

Jay explained that the Wasserman property turned up nothing of interest, and Matt said the same of his phone call with Kenneth Wasserman. Fern, the D.A., Patty, and Bernice loved the idea of a new luxury B&B, while Chinook County Sheriff Earl Johnson, he of the Mike Ditka-like haircut, bulging belly, and disdain for the wealthy golfers who descended on his county exclaimed "Jesus Christ! Isn't Port Stirling Links enough?!? Now we're gonna lose another good fishing hole?"

"But sheriff, they will probably have a spa at the new B&B, think how much you'd love a facial and massage," teased Fern.

Earl harrumphed in the classic, cliché, old fart mode, and the meeting was adjourned.

CHAPTER 23

....

stakeout

Matt quietly asked Joe, Rod, Fern, and Jay to stay behind for a minute.

When the others had filed out, Jay said "What's up?"

"There's one other place I'd like staked out, starting tonight if you can spare the resource, Joe."

"Where?" Phelps asked.

"My house," said Matt, glancing at Fern. "I have reason to believe that the bad guys may know where I live, and that they might have been there on their own stakeout a couple of nights ago. They probably ID'd me on Friday when I went to the scene of the crime, watching from afar because they would want to know who was in charge of their murder."

"Not far-fetched," said Rod. "I would do the same, if I were the crooks."

"My department's resources are stretched pretty thin with their investigating, plus I thought your guys would be more experienced."

"Where and when, Matt?" asked Joe.

"Here's what I want to do. Fern and Jay, you come over tonight for a meeting. Drive separately and park in front of my house. Tell your guy to hang out on Ocean Bend Road – he should drive up and down a couple of times after Jay and Fern get there. Then, be back at my driveway about 8:30 p.m., and hang back to see if anyone follows their cars when they leave. If they get a follow, stay well back, but track him."

"And leave you unprotected?" asked Phelps.

"I'm not worried about me," Matt said looking first at Fern, and then Jay. "I'm worried about them. I've had more familiarity with this kind of vermin

169

than they have. I'll be fine, but I don't want either of them to be surprised just because they hang out with me."

"Your call, chief," said Phelps. "We'll get our guy on it. We should set up a call-in for the three of you, plus Ed Sonders who they also made in the restaurant. Everybody call my cell at 10:00 p.m. so we know all are safe. Let's do that for the next couple of nights."

"OK," said Fern. "Appreciate the thought, gentlemen. We'll be right as rain, though. It's not like we're not all paying attention."

"Works for me," agreed Matt.

"Also, I didn't want to say this in the team meeting," said Phelps, "but Arlette is due in town tomorrow about 2:00 p.m. Fern and I will pick her up at the airport and then escort her to the hospital to meet with the medical examiner as she requested. And take a blood sample from her, which she doesn't know yet. Then we'll bring her to Port Stirling and you can chat with her, Matt. That work for you?"

"Sure. Did someone get her a hotel room?"

"I reserved the best suite at the Inn at Whale Rock for her, since it's your budget, Joe," Fern grinned.

"Thanks a lot," Joe said, and tried a smile. "We're going to need security for her, too, while she's in town. I'll handle that as well."

"Are we done here for now?" asked Matt. Affirmative nods around. "OK, kids, I'll see you at 7:00 at my place. I'll bring the booze," he smiled. "Let's see if we can flush out a rat."

◆◆◆

Matt arrived home just before dark, and was thrilled at the progress Joshua had made on the landscaping around his house. His lawn looked nice, and all the dead foliage and blooms on shrubs around the lawn were pruned away. He was weeding the front bed when Matt drove up, and it looked about finished.

"You did a great job," Matt told the young man, climbing out of his car.

"Told you so," Joshua grinned. "It was fun, but it definitely needed work," he added.

"So, you'll come back next week?"

"If you want. I could use the change."

"I hear you, and here you go," said Matt, handing the kid some cash. "Put the tools away, and I'll give you a lift home. Your grandmother said you live nearby."

"Yeah, just on the other side of the highway. I could probably walk home."

"Nope, a deal's a deal. Let's go."

◆◆◆

Matt set out some salami, cheese, and olives, and thawed a baguette he had in the freezer. He cut up some carrot and celery sticks, and threw in a few red radishes. Then he chilled a wine glass – Fern liked her white wine cool – and brought in some extra beers from his garage to stock the frig.

He built a fire which instantly made his cottage cozier, and went the extra step of lighting a couple of candles on the mantle that put out a soft glow. *Not sure why I did that, but what the hell?* thought Matt. *Maybe they could all use a little extra comfort tonight.*

It was starting to rain outside, but it was a gentle rain tonight, and there was still not much wind. While he waited, he stood in front of his big window and looked out to sea. It was too dark to see much, but he could glimpse the white, foamy waves as they crashed on the beach below him. No sign of the Coast Guard ships, but Matt didn't really expect to see them from his lofty perch on the bluff...they would likely be further out to sea, and wouldn't be in place until the later hours of the night.

He also didn't see any signaling lights, but that, too, was expected. The feds told him that, in their experience, if there was anything going down, it would likely be at a time when the crooks expected everyone in Port Stirling to be tucked in for the night, most likely between 2:00 – 4:00 a.m. Matt hoped that the noise generated by the drone wouldn't be too conspicuous tonight. He was comforted by the fact that federal agents and Coast Guard officials were on the job.

Fern was the first to arrive, knocking gently on Matt's door.

She had changed out of her pink blouse and jacket from the business day, and was now wearing a soft blue cashmere sweater and nice-fitting black jeans. Matt missed her long, wavy hair, but reluctantly had to admit that her new shorter contemporary cut looked good on her. A subtle, barely-there floral fragrance came in with her.

"Jesus, what a day, huh?" she said. "Not sure I thanked you for helping with my car." She tossed her handbag down on his foyer table.

"You did, and it's not necessary anyway. We're friends, and friends help each other."

"I'm not the kind of woman who usually gets all flustered over car trouble, I want you to know that. But this threw me."

"Look, this wasn't the usual car trouble, and we both know it."

She looked up into his face, searching for something. "It wasn't, was it?"

He shook his head. "And the best way to move on from this afternoon is with a nice glass of white wine," he said and shifted away from her into his kitchen.

"I didn't know you could read minds."

"I have many skills you don't know about yet," he answered from his kitchen.

"Oh?" she smiled as he handed her the wine. She greedily gulped it.

"That's right. For instance, do you know I'm a 4-handicap golfer?" He retreated back to the kitchen to get himself a beer. "That's really good for an amateur, in case you didn't know."

"I do know that, I play the game, too."

"What's your handicap?"

"Not telling," she grinned, and caressed the curves of her wine glass.

"That bad, huh?"

"Maybe it's lower than yours and I don't want to make you feel bad."

His eyes widened. "Are you telling me you have a lower handicap than mine?" *She does look athletic*, now that he thought about it.

Fern laughed. "I'm bluffing. I'm a 26-handicap, thrilled when I break 100."

"What's your best score ever?"

"89, but it was an easy course in Central Oregon where the ball flies further. I occasionally win 'closest to the pin' when I play in tournaments, however. I'm very accurate. What's yours?"

"I shot a 73 once, but same as yours, it was an easy course."

"We should put on a charity golf tournament at Port Stirling Links! We could plan an event with the fire department – I know there's a couple of firemen who are good golfers. And the Links would love it because they're trying to have more of an impact in the local community."

"Yeah, I've heard that too. Probably because they want to build a second course just north of the Links, and they know they'll have an uphill battle with the county and the environmentalists."

"Cynical you. Maybe they just want to belong."

"And maybe it's all about the $$," Matt said, rubbing his fingers together.

"You're hopeless," she said, taking a seat on his sofa in front of the food, and helping herself to some cheese and a piece of bread.

Matt sat on the other end of the sofa, and rested his arm on top of it. She leaned back and said, "This is nice. I always like a fireplace, it relaxes me."

"I figured we could all use a little relaxation tonight. It's been a hectic, scary five days."

"Very scary. We've got to make some arrests soon, Matt. I'm terrified at the idea that people will find out how Clay Sherwin died. If we can put them behind bars before word gets out, it would make this story easier to digest."

"I believe they won't lay low for long. And I think the drone's aerial photos will show us the location. Things will change as they move people and equipment in and out of the location at night, and the drone will note the difference, allowing us to pinpoint the property. And, when the ship that we all suspect is offshore, moves closer and sends a signal to the land crew, the Coast Guard will spot them. It's just a matter of time now and waiting them out."

"Land, sea, and air," Fern said. "You're right, we have to turn up something. But I don't mind telling you that I don't relish our town thinking we let criminals run around cutting off people's heads."

"My boss said that very thing this morning. His point was well-made," Matt smiled.

"I know you're the chief," Fern said and placed her hand on his, "but we're all responsible now, not just you, Matt. We all have a job to do."

A knock on the door, followed by Jay bounding in out of the rain. He stopped in his tracks when he saw them on the sofa, and a funny look came over his face.

"Am I interrupting something?" he said, looking from Fern to Matt.

"No," Matt said, jumping up to greet Jay. "Come in out of the rain, young man. I'll grab you a beer."

Jay took off his wet jacket and hung it on the rack near the door. He walked over to the fireplace and stood with his back to it, clasping his hands behind him to warm them up.

"I just drove down 101 a little to see if I could see anything interesting," he said to Fern.

"Did you?"

"'Fraid not. If you had to guess, where do you think these guys are?"

"I think they're in the barn on Zhang Chen's property playing poker and smoking crack," Fern said with a straight face, but her hand shook as she brought her glass to her lips.

"You're probably very close to the truth," Matt said, handing a beer to Jay.

"How do you think they're getting food?" Jay asked. "Should we be staking out Goodie's Market, it's the closest one to the south part of town. And we now have a description of potential suspects."

"They do have to eat," Fern agreed.

"It's likely they have a supply of food onsite, wherever they are," Matt said. "But should we consider taking the store manager into our confidence and giving him a description of Octavio and Juan? What do you think?"

"It's risky," said Fern. "Everybody in town shops there, and it would be hard to keep a lid on it."

"What if we put Walt and Rudy on the market tomorrow while we wait for the drone and the Coast Guard to do their thing? Fern, you have to deal with Arlette, and Jay, you're our point person with the feds, but the rest of our department is running out of leads to follow."

"That works for me," said Jay.

"OK, I guess," said Fern, "but what if shoppers start asking them why they're there? I'd like it better if they were in plain clothes rather than their uniforms. Hanging out in the produce aisle, not looking silly."

"I hired a smart woman," Matt said to Jay, as if Fern weren't sitting next to him.

Jay grinned.

The three snacked and drank and talked over every possible angle for the 'case from hell' as Fern called it. A sudden gust of wind sharply rattled Matt's window, and all three of them jumped. Matt got up and checked that his door was securely locked.

And then it was 8:30 p.m. and time for part two of Matt's plan.

"Before we put this operation in gear tonight," Matt started, and then paused, looking down at the floor.

"What is it?" Fern asked.

"I need to know if we're OK," Matt said. "The three of us, I mean."

"Do we trust you, you mean?" Jay said. The gangly detective looked squarely at his boss, with no intention of making this easy for him.

Matt returned Jay's stare. "Yeah, that's what I mean. Do you trust me?"

"Because you lied to us," Jay said. He mopped up some beer that had spilled on his leg when he jerked at the unexpected gale.

"For which I will always be sorry."

Jay looked at Fern and said, "I dunno…do we trust him?"

She shrugged.

Jay looked back at Matt. "Guess we have to. You're the only chief we've got," Jay said seriously, and then, "Maybe if you buy me a drone…"

Jay paused, and all three burst into laughter.

"But don't ever lie to us again," Fern admonished. "No matter how good you think your reason is. It's demeaning to us, and we deserve better."

"I know that now. I may not have known it in January," Matt said quietly, his leg twitching nervously.

"We thought you were Superman," Jay said. "And Superman doesn't lie."

"I am fucking Superman," Matt grinned. "But I still need my two Batmans, so here's what we're going to do. Just act natural," Matt said to Fern, as he placed her coat around her shoulders. "Drive straight home, and go in your house like you always do. You, too, Jay. Straight home, no stopping at your girlfriend's house," he smiled.

"You have a girlfriend?" Fern said, turning to look at Jay. "You? Have. A. Girlfriend?"

"I might," Jay said defensively. "Stranger things have happened."

"Not many," Fern said.

"You're a real comedian," Jay said. "A jealous comedian."

"And on that note, off you both go," said Matt, opening his door. "I don't have to tell you to be careful, but please be careful. No heroics, and don't forget to call Phelps at 10:00 p.m. I'll be close to my phone at all times, so don't hesitate."

"Watch your own back, Matt," said Fern. "Romeo and I will be fine."

Peeking out of a corner window in his kitchen, Matt watched first Jay and then Fern pull out onto Ocean Bend Road and head toward the village. No other car fell in behind them. Finally, he saw the federal agent pull in several hundred yards behind Fern. Matt watched for about ten minutes, not moving a muscle. There didn't appear to be any other action on the road this foggy, damp Wednesday night. *Kidding yourself if you think you're not afraid*, Matt told himself.

CHAPTER 24

....

widow

Thursday, April 11

Fern had been right: she and Jay were both fine this morning. In fact, both reported their best night's sleep since this horrific crime happened, likely due to the presence of federal agents watching their homes.

Matt's night was quiet, too. He arose at dawn and checked in with Roger the seal – frolicking with that smile on his face as always. While shaving, he noticed that he badly needed a haircut, but no time for that right now. He didn't always wear his chief of police uniform to work, but with the Arlette Sherwin meeting in mind, today he donned a crisp, clean one from his closet. Perhaps his official uniform would offset his non-regulation, curly hair.

Fern was wearing a black fit and flare dress and black low heels this morning out of respect for Arlette's widowhood. She added a simple gold hoop earring that hung just below her new blunt-cut hairdo.

Jay was Jay, and managed to look rumpled even in his freshly dry-cleaned uniform. It was obvious that the three of them had dressed for their day ahead. Since his promotion to detective, Jay didn't always wear his police uniform either, but it made him feel more like one of them when he was dealing with the Coast Guard. Those guys, in keeping with tradition, always looked smart and professional, and, to Jay, very clean in their white shirts and navy blue pants. He aspired to that.

Matt's first task this morning was to try to reach Zhang Chen. Google told him that Chen was currently CEO and Chairman of the Board of a company named Redfire, which appeared to be a computer security service business headquartered in San Jose, California. Chen had announced the company's first quarter earnings just yesterday, results which had exceeded Wall Street's expectations. After the bell, Redfire's stock had risen 1.8% on the news.

Again, Matt thought to himself: *Why does this guy need to run a smuggling ring?* He'd heard Patty loud and clear on men's egos and need for more, more, more, but in Chen's case it just didn't ring true to him. He dialed the phone number in the 'Contact Us' section of Redfire's website. A pleasant woman answered "Redfire, how may I direct your call?"

"I'd like to speak to Mr. Zhang Chen, please. This is Chief of Police Matt Horning of Port Stirling, Oregon."

"What is the nature of your business?" the woman asked.

"It's police business, and therefore confidential." He waited.

"I'm not sure Mr. Chen is in yet this morning, I'll have to check with his assistant. Can I take a number and get back to you?"

"No, I'll wait while you check," Matt said.

"Please hold," she said crisply, and he heard a click.

A short while later, another voice, a woman, said "Hello, this is Lan, I'm Mr. Chen's assistant. Can I help you?"

"Thank you for taking my call, but I need to speak directly to Mr. Chen," Matt said patiently.

"Can I tell him what this matter is concerning?"

"All I can say is that Mr. Chen owns property in my town, and it's in connection with that. Is he at work this morning?"

"Yes, but he's in a meeting at this time. I will take your number and let him know you phoned." Curt, but efficient.

"OK, but please tell him that it's most urgent that I speak with him this morning. Will you do that? He needs to return my call at his first opportunity."

"Of course, sir. Mr. Chen is a very busy man, however."

"So am I," Matt said and hung up.

◆◆◆

"Do you want to see the drone aerial photos from this morning?" Jay asked coming in to Matt's office with Fern.

"Sure. What have you got?"

Jay spread the photos out on the small conference table next to Matt's desk, and the three of them leaned in closely. There were the two locations: Deep Love ranch, and Zhang Chen's property. Matt reached over to a file on his desk, and pulled out the drone photos from yesterday morning.

They compared the aerial photos from the Deep Love ranch first, and there didn't appear to be any changes.

"The semi-trucks are in the exact same positions as yesterday," Jay lamented. "No movement there."

Matt placed the photos on top of each other and held them up to his big window. "Identical," he said. "No movement, no tracks, no footprints. Nothing. We need to keep watching those trucks, though. They seem out of place to me, and if Sheriff Thompson really saw them pass through Silver River in January, why are they still just sitting there? It doesn't make sense, does it?"

"Not to me," Jay agreed. "It's like the semis are poised and waiting for something."

"I'm not so sure, guys," said Fern. "Why wouldn't a Los Angeles band store trucks here filled with gear or to use for touring? If you own a huge property in a sparsely-populated part of Oregon, it makes more sense than L.A."

"You could both be right," Matt said. "On the surface it looks odd, but there could be an easy, rational answer. It's a puzzle, and we need more info. I'd like to call Kip Allred, the band's agent, back and ask him why there are two large semi-trucks parked at the ranch, but I can't. If they're up to no good, that would blow our stakeout."

"Yeah, this waiting game sucks," Jay said. "But we all agree it's the smart strategy. It's just hard."

"And it's only been 24 hours," Matt observed. "You and I are so patient."

"Never been a strength of mine."

Matt clipped the two Deep Love ranch photos together and placed them in his file, carefully writing the date of each on the back first.

"Did the Coast Guard send you digital files of these photos as well as the prints?"

"Yeah. On my computer."

"Good. You might forward them to me, too, for extra safe keeping. Next?" Matt said.

"I don't think the Chen property is any different either," Jay said, pointing to the several images left on the table. Matt got out a magnifying glass from his desk drawer, and moved in closer to the photos.

"Not so sure. Take a look at this photo from today compared to yesterday. Look closely at the white Chevy parked close to the barn door. I think it's a little further from the barn than it was yesterday. What do you think?"

Jay held the magnifying glass up to his eye and bent over very close to the table, looking first at today's photo and then at yesterday's. "Man, I don't know, Matt, they look the same to me."

"Look at the front driver's side bumper," Matt persisted. Doesn't it look closer to the barn door in yesterday's photo? I'm only talking a foot or so."

Jay looked again. "Maybe," he said unconvincingly. "I think you're reaching."

Matt continued to run the magnifying glass over the other photos. Suddenly he let out a whoop. "Ahh!" he grunted, and shook his fist in the air.

"What?!?" said Jay.

"Look at this! The mowed path from the river up to the house and barn clearing. Tell me what you see compared to yesterday."

"Wow!" said Fern. "It's been mowed. The amphibious vehicle tracks aren't as noticeable today. I didn't notice that without the magnifying glass."

"I didn't either at first glance, but it's obvious, don't you think? Jay?"

"Yeah," agreed Jay. "Someone mowed the grass. Maybe Chen has a landscape service to keep everything mowed and pruned, so his property doesn't get overgrown. Maybe it's harmless and just a coincidence."

"Maybe," said Matt. "But maybe whoever all those cars belong to is trying to make the tracks in the grass disappear. At the very least, we know someone has been to the Chen property. You're right, Jay, in that we don't know who or why, but this is indisputable evidence that there is some people movement at this site. Mr. Chen has some 'splaining to do."

"Have you talked to him yet?"

"I put in a call to his office just before you came in here, but he's got a wall of two very efficient women guarding his door. I made it clear to his brusque assistant that it was important he call me back. So we'll see if he gets the message."

"I don't want to sound like a radical, but I can't stand these corporate types who hide in their towers," Jay said fiddling with his tie knot.

"It's not as bad on the west coast as it was in Texas," Matt said. "The oilmen, in particular, felt it was their duty to stall the law as long as possible. The law doesn't really apply to them, you know…that's their thinking. Business people out here seem more responsive."

"We'll see if Mr. Chen does his citizen duty, or if we have to go down there and drag him out of his office. If so" – Jay raised his arm in the air – "I volunteer for that duty."

"Tough guy," Fern smiled.

◆◆◆

Joe Phelps and Rod McClellan walked in through Matt's open office door.

"Just the gentlemen I was going to call," said Matt. "Jay, show them the discrepancies on the Zhang Chen photos."

The two men took turns looking through the magnifying glass at the two sets of photos.

"God, I love this drone technology," said Rod. "It's helped us over and over again. These are minute discrepancies, but this thing showcases them brilliantly. Have you talked to this Chen guy yet?"

"I wish people would quit asking me that. I'm trying to reach him this morning."

"If you do, please record your call," said Phelps. "We now have evidence that someone has been on his property yesterday afternoon or last night, and I want to hear his explanation. Do you record official police calls?"

"Line 1 on my phone is automatic record, and that's the number I gave his assistant. We'll get it."

"OK, good. What about the rock band ranch, anything there?"

Jay filled them in.

Joe Phelps twitched in his chair. "So to summarize our stakeout's first 24 hours, what we've got is either the crooks lying low at the Deep Love ranch, with the action being on Zhang Chen's property. Or, they're lying low at the ranch, and there's a simple explanation for the grass getting mowed at Chen's. In other words, maybe we've got nothing so far."

"Or," said Matt, drawing out the word, "the bad guys are lying low at the ranch, and Chen's property is being readied for the next delivery, and both locations are somehow involved. Meaning we've got something even bigger than we first thought."

All four men gazed at each other thoughtfully.

Phelps broke the silence first. "Do we know if there is any connection between Deep Love and Chen?"

"We're working on it," replied Matt. "Patty Perkins, with an assist from Sylvia, is looking into the backgrounds of all the members of the Deep Love band and their agent, Kip Allred, and then comparing it to Zhang Chen to see if there are any obvious connections. They're looking at schools, clubs, business deals and organizations, family connections, any way they might know each other. The band should be easy to track, at least since they came to fame about ten years ago."

"Joe, we need to start thinking about leaving to pick up Arlette," Fern said. "Are you about ready?"

"I'm ready as I'm ever going to be," Joe frowned, standing and straightening his black suit. "Can't say I'm looking forward to this."

"Me neither," said Fern. "But it's got to be done. Let's go. Dr. Ryder is prepared, and I'm to send her a text when we're leaving the airport."

"Ask Arlette if she knows the band and/or Chen, will you?" suggested Matt. "It's a longshot, of course, but it might be interesting."

Fern looked quizzically at Matt. "And what will I say if she asks why, or says 'yes'?"

"Tell her they are all native Californians with an Oregon connection, and you just wondered. It's the truth, right?"

"Right. I guess," said Fern.

Phelps turned to Matt and Jay and said "You know that the Coast Guard struck out last night, don't you? No suspicious activity at all anywhere between Buck Bay and Crescent City."

"Yes, they filled in Jay first thing. The only shred of new info we have is the mowed grass photos."

Phelps wagged his finger at Jay. "Make sure that drone gets in the air again this evening."

"Yes, sir, I'm personally seeing to it. I love that thing."

"I'll marry it, if it gives us evidence to solve this bugger," Phelps said.

◆◆◆

Arlette Sherwin was in a somber mood, as could be expected. As if on cue, the weather had turned nasty – driving, slanting rainstorm, gusty wind, and colder than it should be in April. She huddled in the passenger seat of Phelps' car, pulling her white raincoat closer around her, while the rain battered her window. Fern and Rod sat in the back seat.

The plan was to take Arlette straight to Dr. Ryder's office, where she and Fern would meet with Bernice, and give Arlette a chance to ask her questions regarding her husband's death without the State Department officials present. Once she was satisfied, they would all, including Phelps and McClellan, discuss the logistics of the body's transportation to San Diego, and the specifics of his military burial.

After they were all clear on what would happen next, Bernice would tell Arlette that she wanted to take a blood sample from her 'as a routine matter in a homicide case'. If she balked, Phelps would take over and attempt to explain that they needed to 'rule out' the victim's widow.

As it turns out, Arlette did balk.

"Why on earth would you need a blood sample from me?" she exclaimed, her eyes wide.

"Well, like I said, Mrs. Sherwin," said Bernice, "it's standard operating procedure when we have a homicide. In a case like your husband's where there was quite a lot of blood at the scene of the crime, it's incumbent on me, the medical examiner, to rule out immediate family. It's our practice, especially in violent crimes."

"No, I'm not going to leave some of my blood in this godforsaken place," Arlette said loudly, shaking her head. She stared down Bernice. "I was 1,000 miles away when my husband was murdered, and there's absolutely no reason why I should give you a blood sample. Is this your crazy idea, Joe?" she said turning to Phelps.

Phelps ignored her question, and said "Dr. Ryder is correct, Arlette. It's required in a homicide case, and we are demanding that you cooperate, or we have the legal authority to incarcerate you. It's for your own good."

"Throw me in jail? Are you out of your fucking mind?"

"I'm afraid I'm not, Arlette. This is just a simple step in our investigative process, and you must cooperate."

"The man I loved was brutally murdered, you've made no arrests, and you're wasting time taking blood from me," Arlette said, quiet now. "I can't believe this is happening." She started to cry, and Fern moved to comfort her.

Fern had completed her investigation of Arlette's whereabouts for most of last week, and was confident she hadn't left California during the timeframe in question. She felt sorry for her now.

Arlette looked at Fern and said "Please tell Dr. Ryder to proceed with whatever she needs to do, and then get me the hell out of here." She ignored Joe Phelps, and, in fact, never spoke another word to him the rest of her life.

"If you gentlemen will leave the room now, I'll get this done quickly," Bernice said curtly, donning a clean white lab coat. "Fern, please stay, and help Mrs. Sherwin while I prepare things."

CHAPTER 25

....

kongzi

Matt took himself out to lunch while he waited for Arlette's visit to his office. No one had called him to say how it was going with the widow, and he had a bad feeling. *Maybe a big bowl of clam chowder will help.* It was hot and delicious, but it didn't lift his bad vibes.

He'd brought a piece of apple pie from the restaurant back to his office. He loved the little harborside café's slogan 'Pie fixes everything', and hoped that it would be true on this nasty Thursday afternoon. The rain was now bleating against his window, and the howling wind was becoming more frequent and fiercer. The sky had darkened, and out to sea, the churning waves were beginning to deposit foam high up on the beach.

"Oh, good, you're back," said Sylvia breathlessly as she stood in his office doorway. "Zhang Chen is on line 1 for you. I'll put him on."

"Mr. Chen, this is Chief of Police Matt Horning. Thank you for returning my call," Matt started.

"Of course," Chen's unruffled, clipped voice came on the other end of the line. "Why is it you want to speak with me?"

Matt's first reaction was that Chen sounded older than he knew him to be. He also did not sound worried or upset in the least.

"You own property in Port Stirling, Oregon…is that correct?"

"Technically, it's south of Port Stirling, but, yes, I do. I own about 200 acres, west of Highway 101. Why? What's this about?"

Matt decided to tread lightly and give away as little as possible. "We've had a citizen complaint about some vicious dogs on your property, and I wanted to ask you about that. What can you tell me?"

"That is untrue," said Chen. "I don't own any dogs. In fact, I'm allergic to most breeds, and don't like being around dogs. Are you sure you have the correct property in mind?"

"Yes, we know your property. The local real estate agent who closed your transaction identified it for us. You own a small house, and several out-buildings, including a good-sized barn. Your property also includes a pretty little river, and a good amount of Pacific Ocean beach access."

"Yes, that sounds like my place," Chen said. "But I don't keep dogs there. I can't understand why someone would say that."

"It's also been noted that you closed off a dirt road that lead to a favorite fishing hole."

"I know the place you mean," said Chen, sounding puzzled, "but I didn't do anything to interrupt the locals' access to it. I understood it was a popular spot to fish, and I wouldn't ruin that for the townspeople. What's going on, Mr. Horning?"

"That's Chief Horning."

"Sorry, chief, no offense. I'm not used to dealing with the police."

"I was hoping you could tell me what's going on at your property, Mr. Chen. Do you have a caretaker watching it for you?"

"No, not yet. I was planning to hire a team before summer to do some remodeling on the house, and to take care of the property. I've been told that things really start growing and take over once spring hits. Everyone says it's OK to let it go during the winter, but that it will get out of control once the weather warms up a bit. Is that your experience, chief?"

Matt laughed, in spite of himself. Something about Chen's naivety about Oregon's nature forces reminded him of himself when he first moved here. "The grass in my yard has grown almost a foot in the past two weeks," he said as a way to explain his laughter.

"Oh, my," Chen said. "No way. Is that true?"

"Let me just say that if you don't get a landscape crew in there soon, it will turn into the Zhang Chen Jungle," Matt said. "So, you don't have any-one currently on the property, is that correct?"

"Correct."

"Are you storing any vehicles onsite?"

"I keep an old Jeep in my barn so I'll have something to drive if I ever get up there," Chen said.

Matt swallowed hard. "No other cars or trucks?"

"No, just the Jeep."

"And when was the last time you were here, Mr. Chen?"

"Oh, I've never been there personally. The real estate deal was all done online, and one of my representatives eyeballed the place on my behalf, and judged it suitable for my purposes. I do look forward to seeing it soon."

"It's my understanding you own several properties up and down the west coast. Are they all for investment purposes, or do you hang out at any of them?"

"Mostly investments. I do spend some time in my condo in Vancouver, B.C. when I can get away. One gets tired of the incessant sunshine in California, and I find Vancouver to be a delightful city."

"I've heard it has a vibrant Chinese community; is that part of the draw for you?" Matt asked.

"Only from the food perspective," Chen laughed. "It's very authentic. I don't know many people there, just a few in my building, and I'm not much of a joiner. I mainly eat and walk in Stanley Park when I visit. It's one of the reasons I bought in Oregon. I suspect I may quite enjoy walking on my beach when I do manage to get there."

"Well, I hope you realize that it's not exactly 'your beach', Mr. Chen. The people of Oregon own the Oregon beaches. They passed legislation in the 60's that gave them unfettered access to the state's entire coastline. The beaches are like a public highway."

"But the public can't come on my property to get to the beach – isn't that right?" Chen asked. "I didn't mean that I own the beach itself."

"Yes, that's correct. I think the law starts at the vegetation line on your property. So, that grassy area between the river and the beach is probably your property line. What you can't do is put up barriers on the sandy beach that block people from walking there."

"I would never do that. All citizens should be able to enjoy freely – Kongzi would have it no other way."

"Kongzi?"

"Who you call Confucius, chief. Humanity toward others is a moral philosophy."

"We could certainly use more humanity toward others," Matt said. "Would you mind if I go onto your property and make sure there aren't any wild dogs? You would be held accountable if they injured anyone."

"It's my responsibility as a homeowner," Chen replied quickly. "Let's do this: I will hire a private security firm to patrol the perimeter of my property, and I will personally ask them to make sure there aren't any dogs, and that the access to the fishing hole is not restricted in any way. Would that be sufficient for your needs, chief?"

"I hate to see you go to all that expense when I could just run down there and check."

"I assure you it's not a problem, and I should have done this initially. I just didn't anticipate there would be any interaction with the public and, therefore, no problems. My property is so isolated, but I suppose the locals know of it. I assure you I will take care of the matter, and I appreciate you calling it to my attention. You will have no further issues."

"Thank you for your cooperation, Mr. Chen. I look forward to meeting you if you ever find your way to our little town."

"It would be my pleasure."

"Oh, one other thing," said Matt. "I've also been told your barn will need a new roof soon. You might want to have your representatives look into that. I'd hate for it to be all flooded when you see it for the first time. Thanks again."

◆◆◆

What a load of bullshit, Matt thought. It never failed to amaze him how many people he came into contact with who thought the police were stupid. *Did Zhang Chen really believe I couldn't tell how strongly he didn't want me on his property? And he's sure concerned about people on his beach no matter how much he pretends the public should have access.*

Matt didn't know how much Chen knew, or how much he was personally involved, but he was now 99% sure that this was the location Clay Sherwin was focused on.

Shortly after he hung up with Chen, Matt's phone rang again – Bernice.

"Hi, Bernice. What've you got for me?"

"One big thing. One little thing. What do you want first?"

"The big thing. Lay it on me."

"I just got the results from the Portland lab on the DNA samples from the two drinking glasses your waitress friend got for us."

"And?"

"And, one of them is a perfect match with the blood I took off the window and the front seat of Clay Sherwin's car. It's statistically highly probable that either Octavio or Juan is your killer."

"No shit?"

"No shit," confirmed Bernice.

"You could testify to that in court?"

"I not only could, it would make me very happy to do so. These guys may turn out to be smugglers and traffickers or not, but one of them is most definitely a killer."

"I knew it when I looked into his cold dead eyes at the restaurant," Matt said. "Now all I have to do is find him."

"How hard can that be? There are only ten million rocks and trees in Chinook County – he has to be under one of them," she said wryly.

"Yeah, piece of cake. What was the little thing?"

"Your little party with the victim's widow is on their way to your office – they just left here."

"How did it go with Arlette?"

"Let's just say that no one was smiling when they left. Phelps is tough," she said, and there was admiration in her voice.

"He is, and he's one of the good guys. I'm so glad he's here to help us."

"I should have Arlette's blood sample results in 24-48 hours, and I'll let you know."

"Great. Thanks so much, Bernice. Keep track of Octavio and Juan's results."

"Will do. Hopefully, you'll need them soon."

◆◆◆

Phelps and McClellan dropped off a silent Arlette Sherwin and Fern at Port Stirling City Hall. Fern had agreed to make sure Arlette and Matt talked, and then to ensure she safely got to her accommodations for the night. The State Department had arranged for a security detail to guard the hotel.

Arlette had hired a private plane to ferry Clay's body home to California, and she would travel on the same plane one last time with her husband.

They were scheduled to depart at 9:00 a.m. tomorrow, and Fern would drive her to the airport, and stay with her until the plane was ready to take off. No one had to ask her to do that; Fern's heart went out to Arlette, and she believed the men were way off base with their suspicions about her involvement in Clay's murder. She was certain Arlette's blood sample would show she hadn't been anywhere near the body. Fern, for one, looked forward to Arlette's exoneration so that the police could properly show the widow the compassion and empathy she deserved.

Matt and Arlette had a cordial conversation. He was candid about the investigation, and shared their process with her. She seemed relieved that everything possible was being done to find her husband's killer, and thanked Matt for his efforts. She was particularly intrigued by the drone, and indicated that Clay would have enjoyed that – he liked technology, and she shared that he had been a 'gadget nerd'.

He quizzed her some on her movements the week her husband was murdered, and her answers were in sync with what Fern had told him last night. There didn't appear to be any inconsistencies. Matt was also blunt about the irony of her fencing experience and the blade used on Clay.

"I knew that was going to mean trouble for me, chief," Arlette told Matt. "But I'm telling you it's nothing but a weird coincidence."

"Why didn't you tell me about it the first time we talked?"

"Would you have mentioned it if you were me? Be honest." She ran a hand through her long blonde hair, moving it off her face and placing it behind her shoulder.

"I get your point," Matt said, "but you had to know we would discover the connection, and you would look bad for not telling us upfront."

"Maybe you would and maybe you wouldn't. I figured a small-town police department dealing with what has to be an unusual event around these parts might not be up-to-speed on investigating murders. I took my chances that my fencing background would not come out. I didn't count on a cop as thorough as you," she smiled.

"Thanks for the compliment, but you should have told us. That omission is a big reason why Phelps is suspicious about you."

"Joe doesn't really believe I had anything to do with this," she said softly. "You need to understand the pressure he's under until an arrest is made. He's just grasping at every straw. Deep down, he knows I would never hurt Clay. Joe knows I loved him, and what a team we were. What a team we always would have been if he'd had a different employer, or certainly a different partner than Rod McClellan, who let this horrible thing happen."

Fern surreptitiously wiped away a stray tear.

Although Arlette Sherwin was a beautiful woman, the dark shadows under her eyes and the lines around her mouth told Matt how exhausted she was. *Time to wrap this up,* and he nodded at Fern, who understood and walked to the coat rack to retrieve Arlette's coat and her own.

"Please don't blame Rod," Matt said. "He feels awful, but he was only following your husband's wishes. Rod wanted to send in back-up, but Clay felt it would tip off the bad guys too soon. It wasn't his fault."

"He should have known better," Arlette spit out. "That was his job. His fucking job."

CHAPTER 26

....

a walk on the beach

After walking Fern and Arlette to their car, Matt sat quietly making notes on his phone call with Zhang Chen. *This guy was a cool cucumber*, Matt thought. *Wonder if he's always been that way? I need to talk with some of his co-workers, and maybe I should try to reach his parents tomorrow.* Matt knew he could Google Zhang Chen for all the information about him online, and talk to him directly again until he was blue in the face, and still, Matt understood, he would never get the full picture on this guy. But he could get further insight into what drives Chen by talking to his colleagues and to his mom and dad, he bet.

Matt's own mother once told him that no one understands a person, fully understands them, better than their mother or father. He'd called her on that remark, saying that parents only saw the good in their child. But his mother had argued back, and said "You don't think I knew every time you lied to us? Thankfully, you weren't a child who lied often, but when you did, your father and I didn't buy it for a minute – we could tell because we understood who you are as a person, not just as our baby. We knew when you were being mean, when you were being lazy, when you were being not as good as we knew you could be."

Matt had never forgotten that lesson, and he often talked to parents when he needed more information on what formed a suspect's character. This felt like one of those times. He spent some time online researching Chen's parents, and confirmed that they still lived in San Francisco. They once owned a very successful restaurant in Chinatown, but had sold it several years ago, about the same time that their son had sold his first company. It appeared that today the couple ran an import/export business, focused on Chinese food products and healthy herbal remedies. Matt found a phone number for the company headquarters, also in Chinatown. He started to dial the number when Jay came in.

"Just the man I want to see," Matt said. "Take a chair."

Jay eased his tall, lanky frame into the seat Arlette had recently vacated. "How's your day, boss?"

"Hell if I know," Matt replied. "But I do have some info for you to pass along to the Coast Guard for tonight's run. My call with Zhang Chen was both illuminating and completely puzzling."

"How so?"

"Well, according to him, there is no one on his property, no dogs, no vehicles except, get this, 'an old Jeep' he keeps in his barn for if he ever gets to his property. Says he bought it sight unseen, has never been here, and has no caretaker."

"Are you telling me that his property is being used by squatters and he knows nothing about it?"

"That's what he would like me to believe."

"But you don't believe him?"

"I do not."

"Why not?"

"When I offered to go down there and make sure there weren't any wild dogs on his property, he instantaneously came up with a solution that would keep me from inspecting…he's gonna hire a private security firm to make sure there aren't any dogs, and to make sure the public access to the fishing hole is restored. That was my pretext to call him."

"He was anxious to keep you away from his property?"

"That's what it felt like to me. But my problem is I can't figure out why in hell this guy needs this gig. He's putting a valuable life and career at great risk, and I don't see how the possible reward balances that out."

"Smuggling is very lucrative, and maybe Patty's right – with some guys enough is never enough."

"I guess that's possible. I was just about to phone his parents in San Francisco and see if I could get a better read on their son."

"I wish we could just barge in to the property in broad daylight and see what the heck is going on!" said Jay.

"Yeah. That. But we both know we're handling this stakeout the right way — it's the answer. We need our ducks in a row. I want you to communicate to the Coast Guard that Chen's property needs to be the focus tonight. Whether Chen is involved or whether he's telling me the truth, I believe there is a Jeep in that barn that would match the description of the one carrying Octavio and Juan and that girl through the drive-up, and the one I saw with my own eyes at the restaurant. And somebody mowed that path through the grasses yesterday. I believe Clay Sherwin knew what we know now, and that this is the place he died."

"We just need more evidence from the feds," Jay said.

"Yes. The more I think about it, the more I think the key is going to be spotting a ship offshore on a night when there is some sort of signaling between land and sea. We've seen the tracks made by an amphibious vehicle, so we know it's hidden somewhere on the property. We know for a fact there are cars and, therefore, people at the locale. We know for a fact that there is a young girl that no one in town knows, and who wants help. We simply need a little more evidence about what is being hauled in and out of the property at night, and some hints that a deal is going down soon and how it's likely to unfold."

"I'm still bothered by the semi-trucks sitting on the band's property," Jay said. "Why are they there? What's in them, or are they empty?"

"You don't suppose there's any chance that these guys are using both properties? That maybe the semis are connected with what's going on at Chen's property?"

Jay rubbed his chin. "Even though there's hundreds of acres of land involved, the two places do neighbor each other. So, you think that maybe the bad guys know that the band's property is also absentee-owned with no one paying attention? That they've parked the semis there until they need them for transport?"

"I think that's entirely possible," Matt said. "According to the band's agent, there is nothing going on at their ranch currently. He indicated that no one would be back up here until summer because of their tour commitments."

"Boy, it's risky, though."

"Their whole operation is risky, are you kidding me? Parking a couple of semi-trucks next door requires far less courage than somehow bringing an amphibious vehicle – or maybe there's even more than one of them – into Port Stirling and hoping like hell no one notices you."

"True. Are you worried that Zhang Chen will tip off the bad guys and they'll go completely underground on us?"

"For sure that's a possibility," Matt admitted. "But I keep going back to 'what's their cargo?'. If it's human, they can't lay low indefinitely. People, especially if it's young, vulnerable girls we're talking about, have a much shorter shelf life than drugs. I think time is on our side."

"Here's hoping we get something tonight. This waiting is agonizing."

"Everyone is on standby and ready to hit the minute we get the word from the Coast Guard," said Matt.

◆◆◆

Fern got Arlette settled into her room at the Inn at Whale Rock, and checked to make sure her security detail was in place. They were unobtrusive, and if Fern hadn't known they were to be there, she would have missed the two non-descript, casually dressed men. She said her goodbyes to Arlette, and confirmed her 8:00 a.m. pickup tomorrow morning.

Fern was on her way back to the office when the blustery rain and wind suddenly died down, and brilliant sunshine broke through the clouds. And, just like that, a beautiful spring afternoon jumped up and said 'hi'.

◆◆◆

Napping in his makeshift office in the barn, Octavio was woken by his cell phone's jingle.

The voice on the other end said "You need to do something to get Matt Horning to back off, or you risk our deal blowing up."

"What happened?" asked Octavio.

"Nothing you need to concern yourself with. But if he's not stopped, he will cause an adverse effect on our beautiful planning."

"The feds are snooping around, too. I've heard what sounds like one of those damn Coast Guard drones overhead. They're taking photos, I'm sure."

"Time is of the essence, Octavio. The Anselmo can't sit offshore forever, not with these girls on board. We've come too far to let one cowboy cop stop us now."

"I understand."

"And kill those damn dogs."

◆◆◆

Fern was eager to stretch her legs. She hadn't had any exercise since this ordeal began six days ago, and she was starting to feel the lethargy that comes with no movement. She could go back to the office for an hour or so, considering it was 4:30 p.m., but having discharged her responsibility for Arlette, Fern decided her time would be better spent doing something to replenish her energy. She turned off Ocean Bend Road on to 24th Avenue which would take her across the highway and home for a quick change of clothes.

Slipping into grey Nike sweats over a pink long-sleeved running top, and her waterproof shoes, Fern took a quick minute to slather on sunscreen, and then headed back to her VW.

Although Fern's house was inland from the beach, and therefore, affordable on her single salary, it was only about five minutes from the sea. She liked to drive to a popular wayside on the southern end of Ocean Bend Road with parking, a porta potty, and a well-maintained path and stairs down to the beach.

She was not the only Port Stirling resident who lived by the slogan 'When the sun comes out, go out', as there were several other cars parked in the wayside lot. She locked the VW and zipped the keys into the pocket of her jacket. Her ever-present cell phone went into the other pocket.

As she dodged puddles left over from the earlier showers, and headed for the narrow path down to the open beach, it occurred to her that she should inform the office that she wouldn't be back in this afternoon. She dialed Matt's cell, but her call went straight to voicemail. She left a message saying "I'm going to work out and then home to chill. Call me if you need anything. See you early tomorrow morning if nothing happens tonight."

She met two friends coming up the path as she headed down.

"You beat me!" she greeted them.

"Hey, girl, you gotta get here early or it might start raining again," said her childhood friend Bo. She'd known him and his buddy Rick since the fourth grade.

"Some of us have to work," she grinned. "As it is, I'm skipping out a little early because I need to clear my head."

"I'm sure Port Stirling will be safe long enough for you to take a jog."

If you only knew, Fern thought. Instead, she said, "I'm sure."

"Some of us should have gone into teaching so we'd get off work at a decent hour instead of being a copper," Rick said.

"Touché," Fern said. "See you later." Waving over her head, she took off jogging down the beach steps.

What a glorious day it turned out to be. The ocean's waves had turned from angry, foamy monsters back into blue arching forms breaking gently into ripples on the shore. The air was fresh and clean with just a slight breeze, and she ran for a while on the firm, packed sand close to the water, and then slowed her pace.

Fern was a runner, but now found that she enjoyed a brisk walk almost more. Walking seemed to engage all the senses more than a run did, and she noticed more around her than when she ran for exercise. She moved right along, however, to keep her heart rate up, and made it a point to take long, natural strides, and deep breaths. Her arms pumped in opposition to her legs.

This beach was popular with the locals, and she could see two or three people up ahead of her. She liked the wide open space, but considering the circumstances this week, she was happy there were other people around her.

She looked out to sea and had a moment where this whole scenario seemed impossible. There was nothing except sky, sea, sand, and huge offshore rocks for as far as the eye could see. Pure nature practically untouched by human hands. Fern wondered how people that weren't born around here could even find this place – it was such a remote location, with only one highway to bring them here. *I guess that's part of the draw for the crooks,* she speculated to herself. *No one to snoop on what they're up to.*

Fern had every faith in Matt leading their team, and certainly the combined resources of the United States government would eventually catch up with the killer, or, more likely, killers. But on this gorgeous afternoon, it seemed impossible that there could be such violence in her perfect world, and she picked up her pace down the untrammeled beach.

After about ten minutes, Fern saw two men coming from the opposite direction toward her. Instinctively, she reached for her phone and pretended to have an animated conversation with a non-existent male friend. That was always her trick to give any possibly frisky men the notion that she could easily get help if they made any funny moves. It had worked for her since her college days. Her self-defense training made her confident she could also kick the shit out of anybody if she needed to; it was just easier to avoid it.

She didn't recognize the two men, and they appeared to be tourists, holding their shoes in their hands as they walked barefoot. Nobody around here did that because they knew the packed sand was cold. The closer to them, the faster Fern walked. She stared them down as she passed them, and gave them a brief 'hello' wave, still talking into her phone to dead air. The men smiled and walked on. After a few yards, she glanced back over her shoulder, and, to her relief, saw the men continuing to walk leisurely up the beach, engrossed in their own conversation.

This is what it's come to? she muttered to herself. Fern wasn't foolhardy, but she refused to be scared the rest of her life on her beach. She took off at a brisk run down the sand, and did another mile or so before turning around and heading back.

The hard part of every beach workout was always the stairs back up to the parking lot. Fern had never counted the steps, but she was sure there were at least 200 to the top. By the time she reached her car, she was huffing and puffing, and couldn't wait to get a drink of water from the water bottle in her console. She bent over, hands on her knees to catch her breath, and took a last look out to sea, watching the sun beginning its drop toward the horizon, about 45 minutes from what promised to be a glorious sunset.

A darkly handsome man about her age unlocked the car parked next to hers, and he smiled when he saw her approaching the VW. Nicely dressed and wearing wire-rimmed glasses with a thin gold bar across the bridge of his nose, he casually leaned against the roof of his car.

"This is a cute car, lady, is it yours?" he greeted her. "Love the flower vase!"

Wary, Fern slowed her approach and said "Yes, it's mine, and it is cute, isn't it?" A brief smile to show she was friendly, and a quick glance around to see if they were alone in the parking lot. She saw no one else.

"Had it long?" he asked, as he continued to rest his arms on the roof of his car. Coming a little closer now, Fern could see the unfamiliar man had pronounced cheekbones, deep brown eyes, and close-cropped black hair.

"A couple of years," she answered, making a show of pressing the 'unlock' button on her key, and trying to sound normal while her gut screamed 'Run'! She turned to do just that, when a second man she hadn't noticed jumped out of the passenger side, and quickly placed a cloth over her nose and mouth as he held her tightly to him.

The sweet-smelling, ether odor was the last thing Fern remembered.

CHAPTER 27

....

demands

"Sorry to bother you again, chief," said Joe Phelps into Matt's ear.

"Didn't I talk to you ten minutes ago?" asked Matt. "What's up?"

"Fern didn't phone in."

Matt stopped breathing. "What do you mean, she didn't phone in?"

"She didn't call in at 10:00 p.m. like she's supposed to. I waited about ten minutes to see if she was just late, but I haven't heard from her. I called her cell and there's no answer. Everyone else called on time. Have you heard from her?"

"She left me a voicemail about 4:30 p.m. Said she was going to work out instead of coming back to the office. Then she was going home."

"And you haven't talked to her since then? Tell me the truth, Matt. If she's with you, I need to know that."

"Jesus, Joe, she's not here!" Matt said, grabbing his jacket and car keys off his hall stand. "I'm on my way over to her house. I'll call you back."

"I'll meet you there. What's her address?"

Matt gave Phelps Fern's address, hung up, and immediately dialed Jay. "Don't ask me any questions, just go to Fern's house right now. Even if you're in your PJ's. You live the closest to her. Go!"

Matt screeched to a halt in Fern's driveway and saw Jay on the front porch, knocking loudly on her door. He was wearing a Columbia fleece jacket over what, indeed, looked like pajamas. There were two men Matt didn't know with Jay. Must be the federal agents assigned to watch his and Fern's homes at night.

"She's not answering, boss," Jay said, eyes wide open. "What's going on? Tell me."

"Fern didn't call in to Phelps tonight like the rest of us," Matt choked out. "Something's wrong." He clasped Jay's arm, as if he would fall without it, and appeared unsteady.

But then Matt shook himself free, and started pounding on the door, yelling "Fern! Fern! Wake up! Open the door!" Jay joined in, also pounding and yelling "Fern! Let us in!"

No answer. Lights were coming on across the street.

"Fern! Please! Wake up!" Matt continued hammering with his fists, until Jay finally grabbed his arm and said, "She's not here, Matt. Unless she's unable to come to the door."

Matt glared at Jay. "Do NOT say that, Jay. Do not say that." He was shaking and seemed paralyzed on the spot, but croaked to one of the agents, "Go around the back. See if you can get in the kitchen door."

The other strange man, the agent guarding Fern's house, Jimmy, said "She's not home, guys. I've been here since sunset, and she hasn't come home. Nobody's been here until Jay showed up."

"But she told me she was coming home after she worked out," Matt said, somewhat detached.

"Well, she didn't," Jimmy reiterated.

"Why the hell didn't you call us?" Matt demanded of the agent.

"I figured she'd gone out to eat. Thought she'd be along shortly," he said, morose.

"Looks like you thought wrong, asshole!" Matt screamed and lunged at Jimmy.

"Hey, hey, Matt," Jay said, putting his boss in a bear hold. "It's not Jimmy's fault. He wasn't supposed to follow Fern, just make sure her house was safe at night. It's not his fault and you need to stand down."

Matt sagged into Jay's shoulder for a split second, and then appeared to regain his composure. "How could I let this happen? I'm a fool. I've killed her. Killed her, Jay."

"We don't know that, Matt. She could call us any minute. You need to get a grip. Please, sir. There's probably a real simple answer."

Matt stood up straight, took a step backward to free himself from Jay's hold, took a big gulp of fresh night air, and looked Jay in the eye. "Yes, there is a simple answer, Detective Finley. They've got her. If Fern was able to call in to Phelps at the appointed hour, she would have. She didn't. They've got her. Now, the simple question is what are we going to do to get her back? If they haven't already killed her."

"Stop saying that! You're freaking me out."

"I'm facing facts, and I suggest you do the same," Matt said forcefully. "First, we need to make sure she isn't here. Know for certain. We're going to break in. What's your preference, Detective, break a window or kick the door in?"

"I'm more of a break-the-window kind of cop," Jay said, relieved his chief was back in action.

"Me too," Matt said, reaching for one of the bigger rocks that lined Fern's front sidewalk. In one smooth move, he picked up the rock and threw it as hard as he could, shattering the window to the left of her front door. Jay turned sideways and slid his skinny body through it. He unlocked the front door, and Matt and Jimmy came in.

It was dark inside, and Matt knew instantly that the house was empty. "She's not here, fellas. Turn on all the lights and search every room to confirm, but she's not home, and she hasn't been for a while. Jay, check the garage, and see if her car is there."

Matt went first to the kitchen, and let the other agent in the back door. That door, too, was locked. "See anything odd in the back yard?" Matt asked him.

"No, sir, everything looks normal to me," he replied.

"Help Jay and Jimmy search the house, please. We're looking for a tall, slender woman, about 33 years old, real pretty red hair, chin-length. Her name is Fern."

"Yes, sir."

Matt walked into the bedroom on the east side of the house, and knew it was her bedroom. She had commented once to him how much she loved lying in bed in the morning and watching the sun come up over the Twisty River Valley hills. He'd shared with her how much he was enjoying living on the ocean, and what a treat it was every morning to take in his view. She had laughed and said, "But along with that spectacular view, you have to take the wind, too." He'd acknowledged that was true.

On the bed were the clothes Fern had been wearing, and for the second time that day Matt thought, *a redhead in a black dress has an unfair advantage.* She had obviously come home, changed into workout clothes, and gone out again. Somewhere. Matt touched the sleeve of her black dress, and paused for a moment, lost in thought. Then he joined the others who were gathered in the living room.

"Anything?" he asked.

"No," answered Jay. "Her car is not in the garage, and there's no sign of her. The house is tidy, and there's no sign of a break in, except ours. One water glass on the kitchen counter next to the sink. That's it." The federal agents nodded in agreement.

"OK, put out an APB for her VW," Matt instructed Jay. "We need to find her car. And we need to find it yesterday. Got it?"

"Got it, chief."

"While you do that, I'll call Fern's cell phone. Likely, it will go straight to voicemail," Matt said, his eyes dropping down and looking at his phone screen. He kept staring at it.

Jay placed his hand on Matt's shoulder and said, "Do you want me to dial her number, sir? We need to find out where she is. You'll see. Fern is fine."

Matt pressed the familiar number on his speed dial, and looked at Jay while the phone rang. Suddenly, he looked startled, and moved his phone closer to his ear. Someone had answered the ringing phone.

"Fern!" Matt shouted into his phone. "Are you there? Fern! It's me."

A man answered.

"That was fast. Ms. Byrne has only been our guest for a few short hours."

"You son-of-a-bitch! If you hurt her, Octavio, I'll kill you with my bare hands."

"Ah, you remember me. I thought you might."

"Is she alive?"

"For the moment, yes. She's fine and we are enjoying her company."

"Leave her alone, asshole."

"It's really not necessary for you to keep calling me names, chief. I understand you are unhappy with this turn of events. We planned on that. But it doesn't mean we can't be civil."

Matt took a deep breath. "What do you want, Octavio?"

"I guess this is the part where I give you our list of demands."

"What is it that you want?" Matt said, more calmly now, getting his emotions under control. "Enlighten me."

"We have a ship offshore, the Anselmo, and it's very important that ship be allowed to approach the coastline and discharge its cargo. You need to call off the Coast Guard and allow us to do our job."

"I can't do that, Octavio. I'm not in charge, the feds are."

"Then you will find Ms. Byrne's head as you found Clay Sherwin's. I need to make one thing clear to you. I don't intend to negotiate. There will be no further communication until our work is finished."

"I need to talk to Fern. Put her on the phone."

"You can't make demands, chief, that's my job," said Octavio.

"Put her on the damn phone now or we're done!"

A pause. "Matt?" Fern whispered, but her voice was strong and clear.

"Are you OK, sweetie?"

"I'm OK. They.."

"There," said Octavio, pulling the phone away from Fern. "You can see your employee is fine…for now. Let our ship in, and we'll go quietly on our way, leaving Ms. Byrne in one piece. Make my life difficult, chief, and your life will be forever ruined. Your choice."

But Matt understood that he really didn't have a choice. They would kill her. He took a deep breath and said "You win. Leave her alone and keep her safe, and I'll make sure you can do your job."

"That's the spirit. Let's all get some sleep now, and we'll connect on this phone once we've completed our business. Ms. Byrne will be well-treated in our custody. We're feeding her, and she's free to move about – we are making her as comfortable as possible under the circumstances. Don't worry, chief, you'll survive this and life will go on."

"Oh, I know I'll survive," Matt said angrily. "I'm less confident about your chances."

"We don't negotiate with terrorists," Joe Phelps said flatly.

"They will kill Fern," Matt said. "You know it and I know it. Our hands are tied. We have to let that ship approach and unload their cargo."

"I'm a director with the United States Department of State," Phelps said, becoming a bit more animated and leaning in toward Matt. "Do you actually believe I will tell the United States Coast Guard to cease and desist? 'Just kidding, CG. Go about your business, but leave that ship offshore alone.

The criminals have a job to do. We'll get back to you soon'. Get real, Matt. I would be fired before the phone call ended."

"So you're just going to let them kill Fern?" Matt said desperately. "I can't believe you would do that."

"Fern is a fine officer and a wonderful human being, and I would hate to see a hair on her head harmed. And I didn't say we were just going to let them kill her. I said we don't negotiate with terrorists. That doesn't mean we won't come up with a plan that accomplishes both of our goals: We bust up what's looking more and more like a major international crime ring, and you rescue your employee. We can do both, Matt, we just have to stay calm and cool, and get the right plan in place."

Matt shook his head violently. "No! If we try to get funny, they will kill her, Joe. I know it!" He slammed his fist on his desk. "I will tell the Coast Guard to back off. I don't care if I get fired, I'm going to do the right thing. The only thing we can do. Once we rescue Fern, then we can track these guys down. I'm sorry if you disagree with me, Joe, but that's the way this is going to go." He glared at Joe, his fist balled up.

Jay had called Lt. Ed Sonders of the Oregon State Police, briefly explained what had happened, and asked him if he could come to Matt's office right away. Despite the late hour, Sonders had immediately driven to Port Stirling. The two cops now exchanged looks over the head of Matt, who remained motionless, holding his defiant pose, and Ed subtly nodded.

Jay said, "I know you're upset, Matt. We all are. We all love Fern, and this is our worst nightmare. But, forgive me, you're a little overwrought. We need you to take it easy and listen to Mr. Phelps."

Matt looked over at Jay as if he was seeing him for the first time. His eyes were moist, and his face had turned red and splotchy.

"I'm trying," he said quietly, looking at his fingers now splayed out on his desk as if he was trying to push down the big piece of furniture. "I need to pull it together. This isn't helping her. I know."

Ed got up from his chair and put his big, beefy arm around Matt's shoulders. "We're all in this together, chief, and we're going to find a way. Joe here will help us, and we need his experience in this situation."

Matt visibly pulled back from Ed. "It's not a *situation*. It's Fern! Can't you all understand that?" he pleaded, slumping in his chair.

"We know, we know," Ed said soothingly. "And we'll take care of her. I promise. You and Joe need to come up with a plan. How about we let Joe and Rod talk to the Coast Guard and their office, while Jay and I take you home and you can get a couple of hours' sleep?"

Matt stared at Ed. "You want me to go home? While she's in the grasp of these evil men? You want me to sleep? Are you nuts? That's not going to happen, Ed."

"I'll go with you and stay in your cottage. Just for an hour or two. Don't sleep, then, we'll just catch our breath. What do you say?"

"I'll go, too," said Jay, also purposefully calm. "We'll rest a little and brainstorm next steps."

Matt pushed his chair back and stood up. He scanned his office, stopping to look at each man in turn. "I'm fine, gentlemen," he eventually said, a coldness in his voice. "Yes, I'm upset because a person I care about is in mortal danger. But I'm not nuts, and I'm not falling apart. There's a maniac out there, and we're sitting here doing nothing. I believe that my plan is the only way this can work. We rescue Fern, and then we go after them. You didn't talk to Octavio – I did. You didn't hear the vileness of the man. You don't understand him like I do. He will kill Fern."

He stopped talking and looked around the room again, stopping at Ed. "But we do need a plan – I agree with you on that, Ed. So, we three can go to my house and *rest*, if that's what you think is best." He looked at his watch. "Joe, make the calls you need to make, you can stay here and use my office. We'll go and think this through, then we meet back here at 7:30 a.m."

Resolutely, he strode out of his office, leaving Ed and Jay to catch up with him.

"Talk soon," Ed said, pointing purposefully at Phelps on his way out.

"Yes, lieutenant, talk soon," Phelps said back, locking eyes with the state cop.

♦♦♦

All Fern remembered of her abduction was waking up in a chilly, dark place with a bag over her head. She had no idea how she got here, or where she was. She remembered leaving Arlette's room at the Inn at Whale Rock, but nothing after that. She had no memory of why she was wearing sweats.

Once she began to stir, a man removed the bag. She blinked rapidly, and he said "welcome to paradise" and laughed. She did not recognize her captor.

Fern was surprised at how calm she was. *I've obviously been kidnapped by the bad guys. I don't know exactly where I am, but I might be able to figure that out. Be friendly.*

"Hello," Fern said to the man. "Where am I? Can you tell me that?"

"Hello yourself, Ms. Byrne," he said. "I'm afraid it would serve no purpose of mine to tell you where we are. Would you like a drink of water?"

"Yes, please. If you can't tell me where we are, can you at least tell me why I'm here?"

He handed her a bottle of water. Fern held it in her hand for a moment so as not to appear desperate for a drink, and waited for his response.

"We need the cooperation of your police chief, and it was my thought that he might be more willing to assist us if he thought your life might be at risk," the man said.

Fern nodded. "An honest answer. Is my life at risk?" Gratefully, she drank some water.

"It is not," the man replied. "As long as your friends do what we asked them to do."

"And what is that?"

"It's simple, really. We need them to let us do our job without interference. Then we'll be gone, and you'll be safe."

Fern's heart sank. Matt and the feds would never agree to that. She was screwed.

"Aren't you afraid I'll be able to identify you once this ends?" she asked, cool-headed and unperturbed.

"You and your friends will never find us or see us again," he answered, also coolly.

"You mean you'll just leave Port Stirling and leave us alone?"

"Yes. That is our plan. It has always been our plan."

"What's your freight?" she asked, switching gears. Keeping him talking seemed like the right move. "I assume it's coming here by ship?"

"Again, Ms. Byrne, it's not in my best interests to divulge that information," he smiled at her.

Fern thought there was a certain tranquility about the man.

"I suppose that means you also aren't interested in telling me who you're working for?" she smiled back.

"We're working for the oppressed people of the world."

"Like your banker?"

He tossed his head back and laughed loudly. "You are a worthy opponent, Ms. Byrne."

"Thank you, I guess. But this will go better if you don't patronize me," she glowered at him.

The man considered this. "I do expect to be generously compensated for my work here."

"How much does a teenage girl fetch on the open market these days?" Fern said boldly, looking directly at the man.

His face clouded. "This delightful conversation is over. I'll be back soon with some food for you. Please make yourself comfortable in the meantime."

He walked behind her, and she turned to follow his movements. She didn't appear to be tied up or constrained in any way. *Thank the Lord for small favors.* He exited the large, high-ceilinged room they were in through a small white door about 50 feet away from her chair. He pulled the door tightly shut behind him, and she heard a dead bolt lock swing into place.

She took another swig from the water bottle, and stood up to survey her surroundings. She swayed, feeling a little dizzy, but steadied herself. *I'm OK, and I'm in a barn. Of course.* The barn was huge, and the height of a two-story house. She walked slowly around the dark open space - it appeared to be nighttime – until her balance returned, going into three enclosed rooms, and turning on lights as she found switches. Two of the rooms had multiple cots with blankets and pillows, and several chairs. The third room looked like a make-shift kitchen, with rough, plywood countertops holding a small refrigerator, large microwave, and a stack of dishes. There was also a sink with running water (she checked), and two card tables with seating for eight.

So this is where they've been laying low. She wondered which barn she was in. Wracking her brain to remember the suspected properties, she thought only the Zhang Chen site had outbuildings this big. And it was good-sized; large enough to accommodate two substantial amphibious vehicles in the far end of the barn away from the enclosed rooms.

'Substantial' was maybe not the right word for the vehicles Fern stood looking at. *Terrifying, perhaps?* They were military in appearance, very big with room to carry lots of people, she thought, and each featured a machine gun mounted at the commander's station in the turret. Green in overall color, with some camouflage detail on the sides. She approached one and cautiously touched its side. Dry. So was the second vehicle. The six wheels on the side she was standing had sand and dirt on them.

She could see a small door about two feet above the wheels which was clearly how one entered the beast, and she clambered up to explore. *Locked.* *Natch.* Besides, if it had keys to operate it, the man would surely have removed them. If he didn't feel it necessary to tie her to the chair, he was obviously confident she couldn't escape out of the barn.

There was no way in hell they could have transported these things through Port Stirling with no one noticing, so she figured they must have been brought here on the ship. That meant it had to be a fairly large ship. *Surely the Coast Guard will find that ship soon, but if they do, what happens to me? Will it mean I'm dead?*

CHAPTER 28

....

woodstove

Fern continued her exploration of the barn, getting more and more depressed as she did.

There wasn't a single window in the structure, and the massive barn doors on either end were tightly locked. The small white door the man had gone out of was the only other door in the building. What looked like some sort of translucent panels were high up on one wall, but she couldn't tell what they were made of or if they opened to the outside. Besides, she hadn't spotted a ladder, and had no way to climb up that high.

The only other item of interest in the barn was a woodstove in a corner closest to the enclosed rooms that had a stovepipe extending to the roof. *Could I shimmy up it somehow?* It looked old and fragile, and Fern didn't believe it would support her body. But it was a way out, as it had a cap on the roof that could easily be pushed through. She stared at it for the longest time; there had to be a way.

Climbing up on the stove, which was solid and held her weight easily, she wrapped her arms around the pipe to test it. She gave it a squeeze, and it creaked like an old man getting up out of a chair. Even if she could shimmy up it, it wouldn't hold. And if by some miracle it worked, then what? How would she get off the roof of the barn, especially without being seen? She didn't relish a fall off a two-story roof. Plus, she wouldn't know where to go even if she did make it off the barn roof. *Damn, I wish I'd paid more attention to those aerial photos of the Chen property.*

If she could get out of the barn, she would run west toward the beach if she could get her bearings. She would be a sitting duck on the dirt road in from the highway. But it didn't matter because she couldn't get out of the barn. *Face it, it's hopeless. No, it's not – nothing is ever hopeless. Have to stay focused. That's all. Stay focused.*

She sat back down in 'her' chair to think. *What was that buzzing noise? The drone is overhead!* She frantically waved her arms in the air, a despairing signal from deep inside the barn.

A signal – that's what she needed. She knew Matt and the guys would be looking for her. They would be worried sick. If she could somehow change the scene before the drone flew back over, they might pick up on it and realize it was her telling them where she was.

Could she build a fire in the woodstove? A thorough search of the barn turned up no wood, no paper, and certainly no matches. But she did find a metal pole in a dark, recessed corner on the other side of the amphibians. Was it long enough to reach the ceiling through the stovepipe and knock off the stove's cap? *One way to find out.*

Fern was wrestling with the pole when she heard the dead bolt slide back from the white door. She immediately dropped the pole and moved quickly back toward her chair.

The man came in with a tray of food, and walked toward the 'kitchen' room. "You'll be comfortable eating in here," he said.

"Thank you."

He set the tray down on one of the card tables and found plastic – harmless – utensils for her in a drawer by the microwave. He pulled out a big pot from under the sink and said "use this when you need to."

Fern gave the man a dirty look and didn't respond. She would rather chew off her own arm before giving him the satisfaction of using that pot. He left without saying another word.

It was very quiet now, and the drone had obviously moved on to its next target. Fern laid down on the floor and shut her suddenly heavy eyes.

◆◆◆

The next thing she knew, the man thrust his phone up against her ear, and she heard Matt's voice. She whispered his name and heard him say "Are you OK, sweetie?"

212

Fern told him she was OK. And then added quickly before the man could snatch the phone away, "I'll be better when you get this asshole!"

The man yanked the phone away and kept talking to Matt. Fully awake now, Fern listened carefully to what the man was saying, and tried to decipher what Matt might be saying on the other end. *How in the hell did I get myself in this stupid position?* Upset at the reality of her circumstances, and even more upset that she had put her friends and colleagues in danger, too, Fern started to cry.

The man hit 'end call' and said "Stop your bawling. Your boss is a smart man and he will do the proper thing. You will be free in less than 24 hours. If it's any consolation, Ms. Byrne, he seems quite upset about your absence."

"It's not," she snarled at the man, tears running down her face. She watched him go out through the white door and heard the lock slide into place.

Fern let herself cry for a while because it felt like it needed to come out. *And if I can't cry when I'm about to get my head cut off, when can I?* But amongst the tears, there was also anger and resolve growing inside her. She needed to pull herself together and do something, because now she knew for sure that Matt would be looking for her. She dried her eyes and face with her pink tee shirt, and went back to the far corner and the metal pole.

It was unwieldy, but not particularly heavy, and she maneuvered it close to the woodstove. Looking down to watch her step, the pink of her tee caught her eye, and the idea suddenly came to her: her pink tee shirt. Her flag! All she had to do was tie it by its long sleeves around the end of the pole, and somehow force the pole up the stovepipe and through the roof. Every cop in the Port Stirling PD would recognize the signal and know it was Fern.

She slipped off her grey zipped sweatshirt, took off the pink tee, and put the grey sweatshirt back on, this time zipped all the way up to her neck. Now the hard part.

First, she had to twist and pull off the section of the stovepipe where the curve was – her pole was rigid and couldn't make a corner. Fern struggled to get the corner section off, but finally it came free. The rest of the pipe hung from the roof, and stayed in place. She worried about the noise as she twisted the section loose, but it wasn't as bad as she thought it might be when she began – someone would have to be listening closely outside the barn to hear her work.

She tied her tee shirt to the top of the pole, and gently began to jam it up the stovepipe. About halfway up, after bumping the sides several times, the tee shirt fell off and tumbled down. *Damn.* She lowered the pole and re-tied it.

Her second try went better at first, and then…disaster. The pole wasn't long enough; Fern guessed it was about four feet from the ceiling. *Now what? I have to make this work. If Matt and the guys know where I am, they will stop at nothing to get me out of here. But if I can't send a signal, my odds go way down. This is my only hope at staying alive.*

She looked around the barn again, and her eyes settled on the amphibious vehicles. Behind the commander's station on each vehicle were two very long whip antennas. Could she use them? Unscrew them somehow? Would they be long enough? Again, only one way to find out.

She scrambled up on one of the vehicles and made it to the top. Much to her joy, the antennas appeared to be made of a series of interlocking telescoping tubes that were now retracted. *They're even longer than they look! Yee-haw!*

After a couple of false starts, Fern was able to unscrew one of the antennas from its base. She jumped down off the vehicle, carefully holding the antenna in a death grip. Even more to her joy, she noted that the top of the whip had an expanded section that would be ideal to attach her tee shirt to.

Her nice pink tee was starting to look a little tattered with smudge marks on it from being inside the stovepipe, and as she tied it to the top of the antenna, she promised herself she'd not only buy five more of these tees if this worked, she would also buy stock in Nike.

The antenna was flexible and much easier to maneuver up the stovepipe than the pole had been. Her arms and shoulders were getting tired, but too bad – she kept pushing and shoving it up to the ceiling. She felt it hit the stove's cap, and she forced it higher with all of her might. It sounded and felt like the cap was on a hinge of some sort, and she heard it fall open. The antenna continued to press upward, now with ease.

She had done it! She couldn't see it, but she could hear the gentle flap of her tee flag flying in the breeze. The best sound she'd ever heard in her life.

◆◆◆

Fern sat down at her elegant kitchen card table and wolfed down the by now cold food. She drank some water, and rested her tired body, eyelids drooping. Having done everything she could to help her situation, Fern decided to get some sleep so she would be ready for whatever tomorrow would bring. She laid down on the cleanest cot she could find, and closed her eyes. She was sure it was still the dead of night.

A while later, she heard a noise. She wasn't sure if she was awake or dreaming, but it sounded like the buzz of a drone.

◆◆◆

Matt hauled his house key out of his pocket as Ed pulled the squad car into Matt's driveway. The three cops exited the car, and Jay and Ed moved toward the front door.

"Just a minute, guys, let's go out in the yard and check the night sky," said Matt quietly. He had calmed down from his angry outburst at Joe Phelps, and was once again laser-focused, but there remained a sadness deep within him. It was an unfamiliar, worrisome feeling for Matt, and Jay and Ed, two good friends, recognized it, too, because they had never seen him like this: subdued, withdrawn.

They humored his request, and the three walked past Matt's door and into the front garden on the bluff. It was the dead of night, going on 3:00 a.m., and cold but clear. A nearly-full moon lit up both sky and sea out to the southwest. The only sound was the thunderous crashing of the waves on the beach 300 feet below Matt's cottage.

"Looks like high tide," Matt said.

"Yep," agreed Ed. "You've got quite a view here, chief. Just spectacular. You're going to need more than the one chair, though," Ed continued, "because there's no place for me to sit when I come to have a beer every night for the rest of your life."

Matt looked up at Ed and smiled. "I know what you're doing, Ed, and I appreciate it. You're welcome anytime, and I will get some more chairs. Promise." He paused and looked back out to sea, scanning the horizon. "She's out there. We have to find her. We have to figure out where they've taken her. Ed, remember when you told me we're smarter than they are?"

"We are," Ed said.

"Agreed. So, let's figure out how we're going to get our girl back, and put these bastards behind bars."

Jay put his hand on Matt's shoulder and said, "Can we go inside now? It's colder than a witch's tit out here. I can think better when I'm not freezing my ass off."

"Nah," Matt smiled. "Cold air unleashes your brain neurons. It also builds character."

"Whatever," replied Jay. "I'm going in."

"Wuss," Matt said, as he moved to unlock his front door.

Matt switched on lights, and Jay moved to the fireplace, eager to start a fire. He nimbly stacked up newspaper and kindling from the copper pot Matt kept next to the giant fireplace, and lit it with matches from the box on the mantle. It took off in a blaze, and Jay tended it, adding a couple of chunks of firewood.

Ed had gone into the kitchen and filled the teapot with water. He was dying for a beer, but it wasn't the right time. Ed's English grandmother had convinced him that a strong cup of tea could solve most of the world's woes. If it could work on this mess, God bless her.

The cops settled in, warming to the fire, and sipping their tea. Both Ed and Jay noticed that it seemed to revitalize Matt – he was perking up somewhat.

"We need a plan, guys," Matt affirmed.

Ed said, "We can get her, Matt, we have the full resources of the biggest, baddest, meanest country on earth. We just need the 'how'."

Matt looked at Ed, and there was another silence.

And then, Matt said, "Well, it's obvious, guys – first we need to know FOR SURE where they're holding her. Do we have any drone reports yet from tonight's missions?"

"I haven't checked yet," Jay said.

"What are you waiting for, son? Get to it! Ed, you call the Lieutenant Commander and find out if the Coast Guard cutters sniffed anything out to sea yet tonight. Jay, call your drone guy and see if he's done for the night and has anything for us."

Both cops pulled out their phones, and Jay jumped up and paced the big room. Matt went into the kitchen and poured more tea for all of them. Only a few hours left until daybreak, but it was going to be a long night.

CHAPTER 29

....

roger's advice

Friday, April 12

Dawn rising in the east, and it was a beauty. Matt had stepped outside for some fresh air, and rested his hand on the fence on top of the bluff. He looked back over his shoulder to the eastern hills that separated Port Stirling from the Twisty River valley, and watched the sky turn the wispy cirrus clouds all shades of red, pink, and orange. If Fern were in her own home right now, she would be looking at the same sky from her bedroom window. He hoped wherever she was that she could see this dazzling sunrise.

He could tell by the sound of the waves that it was approaching low tide now. Still noisy down below, but a less violent crashing than hours before. He scanned the surf for Roger. *I need you today, buddy.*

Sure enough, there he was. Same place as always, about twenty yards out, bobbing along. *What's the latest, chief?*

They grabbed Fern. I don't know what to do.

Pull your head out, dude. Forget it's a woman you care about. Do what you would normally do in a hostage crisis situation.

I'm trying.

Try harder. If you wimp out, they will kill her for sure. Come up with a plan, man.

I know you're right.

Then get to work, you bum. Roger disappeared under the surf, and Matt returned to his colleagues inside, squaring his shoulders before he opened the door.

Jay spoke first. "Drone guy is e-mailing the aerial photos to me now. I gave him your email – hope that's OK."

"Sure," Matt said.

"He told me to look hard at the Zhang Chen property, especially the big barn."

"OK, we'll start with that lot."

"I have news, too," said Ed. "The CG commander just now called me."

"Did the cutters spot anything during the night?"

"Maybe," Ed said. "He told me that the captain of one of the ships reported a Panamanian-registered ship anchored several miles off the coast near Port Stirling. About five miles out. They didn't want to get too close to scare them off in case they're our perps, but they took some long-range photos and are running the ship's name through their data base. He thinks the name is 'Anselmo', but they weren't running many lights, and the photos are on the dark side. Said it looks like a mid-sized cargo ship. He waited until now to call me because they wanted to get some photos as the sky started to lighten."

"OK, can we get those photos, too?" Matt asked.

"I gave him your email, as well."

"So now we just wait."

Jay said, "Got any food?"

'Got any food?' being one of Jay's favorite phrases, Matt and Ed laughed. Matt stood up and said "I'm sure I can rustle up something."

Jay motioned with his hands for Matt to sit. "No, no, I'll do it. You rest. I didn't want to go in your kitchen and start banging around without permission."

"There's some bacon in the frig, and I think there are enough eggs for us. Apples in the bowl on the counter. Might or might not be some bread in the drawer under the toaster."

"I could use some coffee if we're going to work," Ed said. "Grandma was apparently right about tea solving all issues, but I prefer the hard stuff. Got any?"

"I'm with you," Matt said. "Jay, make some coffee first, OK?"

"On it."

◆◆◆

While they ate, the three cops discussed who they needed to bring into the loop this morning, and the logistics of a well-planned potential raid.

"The land-based portion will be the most critical," Matt said firmly, "because we have to extract Fern first. That segment will be handled by us, Chinook County sheriff's department with Earl's leadership, all of our crime team member PD's, and whatever help the Oregon State Police can provide. We'll especially need the Buck Bay force because Port Stirling and Twisty River don't have enough boots on the ground for this kind of operation. This land-based attack will be under the direction of me. No compromises on this. Are you with me?"

Jay and Ed nodded, and Matt kept talking. "We need clear evidence of the location first. I think Octavio wants to move tonight or tomorrow night at the latest. That means there has to be some activity on his end. We'll look at the latest aerial photos, and see if we can narrow our focus to one location. If we can, then I want to send the drone back out this morning. Oh, shit!..."

"What?" said Jay.

"Arlette is expecting Fern to pick her up this morning..." Matt checked his watch, "in about an hour from now. To take her to the airport."

"Maybe the widow should stick around for another day or two," Ed suggested.

"I don't think she will," Matt said. "Fern said she was adamant about getting out of here this morning. Anyway, she's Phelps' problem, not ours. I'll call him now."

"Let me call Joe," Jay said. "You keep going on the plan. You were on a roll." He grinned at his boss, and then walked outside to make the call to Phelps.

"The OSP will do whatever we need, and we're skilled at drug busts," Ed said. "Speeding tickets and drug busts – that's mostly what we do these days. The occasional domestic violence case thrown in," shaking his head.

"How many cars can we expect from your outfit?" Matt asked.

"As many as you need. The bigger problem is going to be access. Whether it's the Deep Love ranch or the Zhang Chen property, there's really only one road in to each from Highway 101."

"There must be some dirt roads, paths, or open meadows we could utilize to come in from different directions, don't you think? How well do you know these areas?"

"Better than you, I guess," said Ed, "but that's not saying much. I know that both of these properties are remote and isolated, and the Chen place has a fairly substantial stand of trees around the house and outbuildings. I think we'd also have to go through a bunch of trees between the highway and the Deep Love ranch, too. There might be clearings to the north or south of each property where we could mount an all-out assault, but I couldn't say for sure."

"We'll have to rely on the aerial photos, then," said Matt. "Jay may have more familiarity than we do. Let me ask you this, Ed – does the OSP have any sharpshooters?" Grim set to his jaw, but his eyes flashed.

Ed nodded. "Two guys come to mind, one is up the coast near the Newport area, and the other one is in Portland. They're on our primary tactical squad, and have experience in heavy weapons and close quarters combat. Both young guys and exceptionally well-trained. I've seen the Portland guy take a label off a beer can at 600 yards. "

"Would you categorize either or both of them as true snipers?"

"I would. Both. They stay in tip-top physical condition, but their real strength is mental. They are smart and have ice water in their veins. Do you want to get them?"

"Without talking to Phelps – which I'll do after we look at the aerial photos – I would say 'yes'. We're going to need one or two snipers, and I don't think we have that talent around here. Certainly I don't have it in my department. I can shoot, but not at the level we'll need for this operation." Matt paused and lowered his eyes. "Ironically, I was planning to train Fern in this specialized area. She's one of the better shots in my group. Steady and sure."

"We'll get her out of there, Matt. We will." Ed reached out his mammoth arm and clapped Matt on the shoulder.

Jay came back in and his face was white as a sheet.

"What?" said Matt, looking closely at Jay.

"You're not going to believe this one. Phelps told me that Bernice called him early this morning and said that she can't rule out Arlette. That he should keep her here while she runs more tests on her blood sample."

"What do you mean?" asked Matt.

"All I know is that Bernice said that Arlette is statistically within the realm of possibility of her blood being at the scene of Sherwin's murder."

"But we already know it's Octavio or Juan, and the odds are like three million to one," Matt, exasperated. "It's just not possible."

"That's what Phelps said, too. Bernice says it is statistically impossible that two known suspects would both fall within the DNA profile. But they both do."

"So they both could have been present at the murder?" Matt asked, trying to grasp what he was hearing.

"According to Bernice…yes," said Jay. "Phelps is blown away."

"Ditto. What's he going to do?" asked Matt.

"That's probable cause," Ed chimed in. "He can keep her in jail for 48 hours without an arrest warrant."

"That's how he's leaning, I think," said Jay.

"I don't see Arlette's motive," Matt said. "Octavio's is clear-cut; Clay Sherwin was on to them, and he had to get rid of him before he talked and blew up their deal. And Fern all but confirmed Arlette's alibi – her kids and friends seemed sure she was in California all of last week."

"But the science doesn't lie, boss," said Jay.

"Now you sound like Bernice. It doesn't make any sense. That's all I'm saying. And it doesn't matter to me anyway, not right now. Octavio's got Fern, and he's our target."

"But what if Arlette is the big boss?" Ed asked. "What if she's driving it, and Octavio is simply carrying out orders? Don't you want to know?"

"Yes, I want to know," Matt glared at Ed. "But I'm also going with what I know to be fact: Arlette's in a hotel room alone, and Octavio's holding Fern against her will somewhere. That's a fact, and that's our focus. It has to be. Phelps can do what he wants with Arlette, and sticking her in jail for 48 hours is a good idea. We need Joe's help with the Coast Guard, and I don't want him being distracted."

"Good point," said Jay.

"To be blunt," Matt continued, "if we save Fern, and arrest everyone on the land operation, I'll be happy. And, if Phelps and the Coast Guard get the vessel at sea, and we can safely deliver the cargo, whether it's human or drugs, do we really care who's in charge? At least, right now? Shouldn't it be our intention to bust up this ring in our town first, take care of the victims, get the carriers and distributors off the street, and then go after the brains once we've secured our area?"

"With you, boss," said Jay. "Odds are it's Zhang Chen, someone in the Deep Love band, or Arlette."

"Exactly," said Matt. "Once we take care of business, it shouldn't be that hard to pinpoint the front man…or front woman. But first things first. Tell me if I'm wrong on this." He raised his hands, palms up towards Ed.

"I don't like not making an arrest of the head honcho," Ed said, "but I agree with you on our immediate priorities."

Jay nodded.

Matt's email pinged and he opened the attached file from the Coast Guard. He had a printer in the second bedroom which he used for a home office, and he sent the photos there now. His parents had come to visit after the Bushnell case had ended, and he had a bed for them in that room, but they preferred to stay in one of the ocean-front hotels. So, now it was outfitted with a desk and the accoutrements of a home office.

He ran around the corner of the big stone fireplace to the hallway behind it. The second bedroom was at the end of the hall, on the opposite end of his ocean-view main bedroom. Aerial color photos of the coastline and the target properties were pouring out of his printer.

◆◆◆

Matt spread the photos out on his kitchen table, and found his magnifying glass in his briefcase.

On the advice of drone guy, they started with the Zhang Chen property. Matt divided the photos into three piles, and placed one each in front of Ed and Jay, keeping one pile for himself.

"Holler if you need the magnifying glass," Matt said, as he carefully looked at the top photo in his pile.

"Don't need a magnifying glass to see two big semi-trucks!" whooped Jay, practically jumping up and down. "Look at this! It's like you said earlier, Matt, they're squatting on both properties. These trucks have been at the Deep Love ranch since drone day one, and now here they are smack dab in the middle of Chen's driveway! Look at this!"

"Holy moly!" exclaimed Matt. "Would you look at that? Our boy's getting anxious to move. Ed, you have the photos from Deep Love. Can you find one of their parking lot today so we can make sure it's the same trucks?"

Ed dug through his stack, tossing aside photos of the ranch house and beach access. Finally, he raised his arm in the air gripping a photo tightly in his beefy hand. "This photo is sold to the man with the too-long curly black hair for one million dollars! Raise your paddle, chief!"

The three cops laughed together for the first time in what felt like weeks. The photo showed an empty parking lot in front of the Deep Love ranch house where the semi-trucks had been parked yesterday.

"They're at the Zhang Chen property, hiding in the small house and probably in all the outbuildings too," Matt said with confidence. "And they're ready to roll. They drove the semis over, probably last night right after they grabbed Fern."

"They've been using the Deep Love ranch as a cover for the semis," Jay said. "Doubt if the band knows a thing."

"Agreed," Matt said. "Octavio figured any kind of overhead search would show the trucks and we would get suspicious. Just like you did, Jay. Better to throw us off the track of the real operation property, and get us to focus on the band. The question is does Zhang Chen know his place is being used or not?"

"We need to know more about him," Ed said.

"Patty is looking into any connections between Chen and the band," Matt said. "She'll turn up more info on both. It's too early to call her yet, but I'll do it about 7:30 a.m. Remind me."

The three went back to the photo stacks in front of them, and for a while there was silence in the room, except for the swallowing of coffee around the table.

"Look at this," Matt said eventually, grabbing his magnifying glass from the center of the table. "There's a guy coming out of the house, there by the front door. See him?" he asked excitedly.

"Yeah," said Ed. "Let me use the glass for a minute. It's that weasely little guy that didn't say shit at the restaurant. Jose or Juan or whatever his name is."

"It's Juan," said Matt quietly. "They've got her here, at Chen's house. The bastards."

"You know," started Ed, "I don't think they have any intention whatsoever of killing Fern. These asswipes believe they've got you right where they want you, and that you will call off the Coast Guard tonight and let them be on their merry way. They don't care if she identifies them later on because they'll be long gone by then, back to whatever rock they live under."

"They're underestimating Joe Phelps, then," said Jay.

"I don't think they know they're here," Ed said. "Octavio hasn't mentioned the State Department, only the Coast Guard."

"You think they might be thinking they're mainly dealing with us local cops?" Matt asked.

"I think it's possible," suggested Jay. "I know I was surprised to learn there were federal narcotics agents in our little burg. Maybe they will be, too."

"So if they grab one of our own, it would neutralize us and we'd cave," said Ed.

"And it almost worked," said Matt vigorously. "Almost."

He jumped up and made a second pot of coffee, and they kept studying the photos while the sun climbed a little higher in the sky.

"Can drones take photos through windows?" asked Matt. "It would be great if we could get some visual confirmation that Fern is in that house. What do you think?" He turned to look at Jay.

"No idea. But looking at the house," he held up a photo of it, "the shrubs are kinda overgrown up around the windows, and it looks like there's a bunch of trees in the back yard area. I think it would be tough to get a definitive photo."

"Tough never stopped you before," Matt challenged.

"OK, I'll call drone guy as soon as we've gone through all these and see what he says. And I am fucking tough." He stuck out his chin.

Back to the photos.

"Wait a minute," said Matt and paused. "What the hell is that?" He pulled a photo out of his stack and placed it in the middle of the table. It was a picture of the big barn on the Chen property.

CHAPTER 30

....

old glory

"It looks like a flag of some sort," Ed said. "That wasn't there yesterday, I'd swear."

"Is it some kind of signal for the ship out to sea?" Jay asked. "Could the top of the barn be seen from the water?"

"I believe so," said Matt. "It looks like there aren't any big trees between the barn and the ocean. There's just that grassy meadow with the mown pathway to the little river, and then stubby sand dunes between the river and the ocean. Nothing to really impede the view of the barn. At least, not to the roof of it."

"So, the land crew is telling the ship's crew that it's going down tonight," Ed surmised. "The flag is the signal."

"We need to tell Phelps," Jay said. "Like right now."

"First, let's send the drone out for one other pass over the Chen property now that's it daylight," Matt said. "I want them to try to get photos of the windows in the house, and I want a better photo of the barn and the flag. I'll pay for it if budget's an issue. Call drone guy, Jay."

"Calling," Jay obeyed, and hit his speed dial.

"They might see the drone in daylight," Ed whispered to Matt while Jay talked on his phone.

"I don't care," Matt whispered back. "They'll think we're just watching things more closely."

"OK, drone guy is heading out now," Jay reported. "I told him to only do the Chen property, and to make it snappy. Still think we need to tell Phelps."

"I will," Matt said. "Let's head down to City Hall." He checked his watch. "It's almost 7:30 a.m., and that's when we told Joe we'd be back. Employees will be arriving, too, so if anyone is watching, it will look normal."

"I could use a shower," Ed lamented.

"Yes, you could," agreed Matt, "but there's no time. Fern won't care if we stink when we get her out."

Matt called Joe Phelps on the way in to the office. Phelps was in Twisty River at the county courthouse, where he had booked Arlette Sherwin in on suspicion of murder. He could only hold her for 48 hours on probable cause, and she had already called her lawyer. But she would at least be out of the way for the next two days, and her cell phone was now locked away in the jail storeroom.

David Dalrymple, the district attorney, was working with Phelps to make sure Arlette's arrest was kept quiet. Arlette didn't want her kids to know about this development, and Phelps didn't want *anyone* to know.

Joe Phelps' method of making difficult decisions was to imagine both outcomes, which he'd done here. And if the follow-up lab tests confirmed Bernice's original test, and he'd let Arlette go and she disappeared, that outcome would be worse, in his view, than sustaining her wrath for 48 hours.

Matt filled in Phelps on the latest drone photos, and shared his thinking on a plan.

"Shit," said Phelps. "Tonight? Tonight? I was hoping for one more day."

"We'll be ready," Matt told him. "And we need to get Fern and any other hostages out of there as soon as we can. The Coast Guard is more than ready. They're checking out the ship now in a flyover, and told Jay they would have a full read on it in their data base by noon. There's one other piece of this that I'll share when you get to my office."

Matt didn't want to mention the snipers on the phone. That needed to be an in-person conversation with the State Department director.

Phelps told Matt he and Rod would only be in Twisty River for a few more minutes, and then they'd head to Port Stirling.

At least it's a magnificent day on the Oregon coast, thought Matt. Only a few stray frothy white clouds dotted the bluer than blue sky, and any wind was benign. He hoped like hell this weather would hold until tonight. The success rate for their operation would be much higher if conditions were friendly.

Looking out to the southwest now, Matt saw that it was perfectly clear in that direction. His brief experience with living in Port Stirling had so far been that most of the nasty weather seemed to blow in from the southwest. He was relieved to see now that the only clouds were to the east, toward Twisty River and inland, and even those clouds were few and far between. *Maybe we can finally catch a break in this nightmare.*

While he drove, Matt rehearsed how he would tell his department about Fern. Everyone would be so upset, and he needed to show strength that he wasn't − at the moment − sure he possessed. The first time he said the words aloud to practice, he teared up and choked. *Great.* The second time was a little better, but still his voice quivered. *I've got to get through this; I'm their damn leader.*

He pulled into the City Hall parking lot, and went through his speech one more time before going in.

Sylvia was at her desk, looked up, smiled, and said good morning to her boss. Matt felt his cheeks getting red and his eyes turning misty. He mumbled "good morning" in her direction, and stepped into his office, quickly closing the door behind him. He took a couple of big breaths, and tried to compose himself.

"Knock knock," he heard Sylvia say on the other side of his door. "Let me in. What's wrong?"

"I need a minute, Sylvia," he replied through the closed door.

"Nope," she said bursting in, and nearly knocking him down. "What's the matter with you? Tell me," she demanded.

"They've got Fern," he choked out.

"Who's got Fern?"

"The bad guys."

"This cannot be happening." Sylvia placed her hands on her cheeks, her eyes wide with fear.

"They grabbed her last night. Kidnapped."

"No!"

"I'm so, so sorry."

"Oh, honey, it's not your fault," she said, surrounding him in a cloud of two bright blue long sweaters. She hugged him for a while, and the two just stood there.

In due course, Matt pulled out of her tight grasp and said, "I've talked to her and she's OK. It was only for a split second, but she said my name and told me she's doing all right."

"What do they want you to do? Wait, let me guess," she said snidely while she wiped at her cheeks. "They want to do their damn drug deal and you let them go. Right?"

"That about sums it up," he said glumly.

"Then let them do it. Who gives a poop? Get Fern back."

Matt was pretty sure that Sylvia had actually stamped her foot.

"I'm going to get Fern back, don't you worry," he assured her. "But the feds are determined that we're going to make some arrests. We're developing a plan."

"Is it foolproof?"

"Of course not," he said honestly. "But it will be as close as we can get. We have new evidence this morning that helps a lot. Aerial photos, and we are now sure about the location."

"Well, that's something, I guess," she allowed. "But do you know precisely where Fern is? How will you find that out? What if they kill her anyway?"

"Ed Sonders thinks they have no interest in doing that. He thinks they believe we won't stop their deal tonight and..."

"Tonight?" Sylvia interrupted and exclaimed.

Composed now, Matt said, "We have reason to believe they're ready to move, and that it might be tonight. Tomorrow night at the latest. Ed thinks, and I tend to agree with him, that the bad guys think we're running this operation. That they think they can outsmart us local yokels. And that we'll be so afraid of losing Fern that we'll be paralyzed, and will let them complete their enterprise and leave town."

"They are right about one thing," she said.

"What's that?"

"That we're afraid of losing Fern." Sylvia looked weepy, and now it was Matt's turn to hug her.

Over her head and gazing out his window to the sea, Matt said, "We won't lose her. I won't let that happen. We'll have a good plan, and we'll go in with all the resources of the United States Department of State, the Coast Guard, and the entire county behind us. And, Fern was feisty on the phone – you know she will do whatever she can to help herself. She'll be back with us and safe soon."

"You need to tell the department," she said, wiping her face, straightening up, and smoothing her skirt.

"Let's do this," he agreed.

♦♦♦

As Matt expected, his police department was very upset at this development, but he was ready for that. Jay and Ed had arrived, and their support helped, too.

"The best thing we can do to help Fern is to keep doing our jobs," he told the group now. "I'll be meeting with the federal agents soon, along with Jay and Ed. We're working on a plan with the Coast Guard. Walt," Matt said, addressing his sergeant, "I want you to call the sheriff. Tell Earl to mobilize all his guys, and have them standing by for further orders later this afternoon. And then call the Buck Bay chief and tell him the same thing. Got it?"

"Yes, sir," Walt said, happy to have something to do.

Matt gave them all a brief pep talk, and was relieved to be done with this part of his job. Phelps and McClellan walked into the squad room just as they were wrapping up.

The feds were followed at City Hall by Patty Perkins, who Matt had called earlier to fill her in on last night's kidnapping. After a string of colorful expletives, Patty had said, "Well, now these jackasses have gone too far. I'll be right over."

♦♦♦

Matt herded the feds, Jay, Ed, and Patty into the War Room at the end of the hallway, and they all took seats around the conference table. Patty gave Matt a quick hug on the way in. All the cops were wearing their uniforms this morning, and looked official. Matt had never seen Patty in hers previously, and he could tell she meant business today, all buttoned up and crisp. Matt closed and locked the door behind them. He didn't want any other ears hearing a single word of this conversation.

"Patty, we'd like to hear what you found out about any connection between the Deep Love band and Zhang Chen," Matt said. "Can you go first and share anything with us?"

"This will be a short conversation," Patty said. "I went all the way back to elementary school, and there is no connection between Zhang Chen and any member of the Deep Love band, including their agent, and their wives or girlfriends. I did a full search on each principal, and at no time in their respective lives have they connected on any level."

"None of the same schools?" asked Phelps. "Didn't most of them grow up in California?"

"They all went to school in California, except for the one band member who grew up in northeast Portland, Grant High School. Chen mostly in private schools, and the band guys in public. Two of the band guys went to college, both at Pasadena City College, the agent and the bass player. They had also gone to the same high school, and were friends from a young age. The rest of the band members went to various public high schools, all in the southern California area.

Chen went to an independent Chinese American international school in San Francisco until the ninth grade, then he went to a very exclusive private high school, where he earned a top scholarship to Berkeley. Not to put too fine of a point on it, but the band guys couldn't touch Chen in either privilege or smarts," Patty said. "I'm sure the rock stars have millions now, too, but Chen is loaded. The latest estimate pegs his net worth at around $910 million."

"No clubs, like a fancy golf club, or a country club? Or employers in common either?" Phelps again.

"No, sir."

"Have the band members ever been to China?" Matt asked.

"They played one tour date in Beijing two years ago, and they were only in the country for three days," Patty replied. "And, before you ask me, Sylvia found a notice about Zhang Chen giving a speech at John Hopkins University — that's in Baltimore — at the same time the band was in China. They don't know each other," she said emphatically, leaning forward, "and I will eat this table if it turns out they do. They both ended up buying property here for entirely different reasons — Chen is an investor, and the band wanted a private getaway. The only thing they have in common is that they all live in California. And I might point out that California is a rather large state."

"Does Zhang Chen spend much time in China?" Phelps asked.

"Yes, I would say a fair amount," Patty answered. "There's quite a lot on the internet about him visiting various business groups and manufacturing facilities, factories, etc. throughout China. He seems to have a broad Chinese network, as do his parents who run an import business in San Francisco. They are all three fairly prominent in China, despite their U.S. immigrant status." She paused. "I feel like I know him," Patty mused, "and it's hard for me to understand why he would be involved in anything like this."

"Are there any women in his life?" asked Rod McClellan, speaking for the first time.

"That's a good question, Mr. McClellan," Patty said. "Other than his mother, and I would say his assistant at his current business, Chen appears to not be close to any other women. I don't know about his high school life, but there is no evidence that he had a girlfriend at Berkeley – all he did was study, from what I could tell. No sports, no girls…you get the picture. He's never married, and there isn't a single photo of him anywhere with a woman."

"How does an almost billionaire escape the clutches of a woman at some point along the way?" asked Phelps.

"Maybe he's just too weird," Patty said stiffly. "Lots of us don't really care about the money. It's who the man is as a person."

"I didn't mean to cause offense," Phelps said hurriedly.

"None taken." Patty said, but she stared him down.

"Is he gay?" asked McClellan.

"Well," said Patty, "there's no evidence of that either. He's busy socially with groups he supports and business outings, but he's always alone, at least in the photos. Couldn't tell you."

"Was there any indication he and Arlette Sherwin might have encountered one another?" asked Phelps. "I realize she's southern California and he's northern, but did you see any link at all?"

"No links that I came across so far," said Patty, "but we haven't gone as far on this topic as we can. They do seem to each have interests in the real estate world, however, and Sylvia is investigating this further as we speak. Is that OK with you, boss?" She looked at Matt.

"Couldn't hurt. Arlette's are all commercial properties. If you find that Chen has commercial real estate, too, it's worth a deeper dig. My understanding, though, is that his real estate is either personal use or investment property, but he could have been holding back on me."

"Thank you so much, Patty," Phelps said. "This is all very helpful info. I didn't really think there would be a connection between Chen and the band, but it's useful to be able to rule out the band and concentrate on Chen. Our bigger question now is does he or does he not know how his property in Port Stirling is being used?"

After Patty gave her report, the cops analyzed the drone photos from last night. Phelps and McClellan agreed with Matt that it looked like Octavio and company were getting antsy. They all wanted to see the daylight drone photos first before making a call on a raid for tonight, but they planned for it now, discussing various strategies and possible scenarios.

The feds knew what they were doing, and although Matt would be petrified until the moment Fern was safe, he did believe in their plan. Phelps had agreed to have Matt lead the land-based portion of the raid, once Matt had convinced him that he could not only handle it, but would otherwise immediately file a court order to halt the operation unless he was allowed to direct it. Phelps, by now, knew Matt well enough to trust him, and who the hell knew what a local court might do anyway? He couldn't afford to risk finding out.

And, in the light of a new day, Joe could see that Matt's professional instincts had kicked back in after the shock of last night had worn off somewhat. Phelps, more than anyone in the room, knew what it felt like to lose someone you loved, and to feel some personal responsibility and guilt.

Phelps would oversee and coordinate with the Coast Guard, both in the air and at sea. It was not unusual for the DEA, Customs officials, and the Coast Guard to work with locals on the ground, and Phelps felt confident working with Matt, in spite of the chief's personal feelings for the hostage. It was obvious that the entire Chinook County contingent believed in Matt, and that level of trust in leadership counted for a lot in this type of bust.

They all wanted to meet the Oregon State Police snipers, and Ed arranged for them to be brought to Port Stirling – they were in transit now.

Matt stood up to answer a knock on their door. Sylvia.

"The latest drone photos are here," she said. "I'll send them to the big screen now. Be right back." She turned and hustled down the hallway.

Jay dialed drone guy to thank him for the quick turnaround. Phelps also noted what a good relationship Jay appeared to have developed with the local Coast Guard, and he thought that ongoing communication would help them as well.

"Here they are," Sylvia said connecting a laptop to the large screen in the conference room. Matt pulled up the email, and forwarded it to all of his colleagues, who opened it on their laptops. As she left the room, Sylvia waggled her finger in the direction of Matt's face and said forcefully, "Find her."

For the second time today, Matt asked for all eyes on the photos.

"OK, gentlemen, what I'm mainly interested in is if we can see anything through the windows in the house. I realize it's a long shot, but maybe we'll get lucky and be able to determine what room they're keeping Fern in. That's priority number one.

Priority number two is to get a closer, cleaner look at the flag on top of the barn. Joe, this is the one that wasn't there yesterday, and we think it's their signal to the ship that they're ready to move."

"Understood," said Phelps, and stared at the photos. The rest did the same.

The daylight photos of the house proved to be somewhat of a disappointment. As Jay pointed out, there was simply too much shrubbery around the windows blocking the interior views. The drone was able to capture one decent window photo around the back of the house through the trees, and they could even see the silhouette of a person. But it was clearly a short, fat man, and definitely not Fern. The man was alone in the room, and appeared to be drinking a beer.

The house was small, however, one level only, and the group decided it would be a fairly straightforward task to locate Fern once they were inside.

Suddenly, Jay slapped his hand hard on the table. "We're so stupid!" he yelled.

"What is it, Jay?" asked Matt.

"Look at this photo of the barn's flag," he said animatedly. "It's not Old Glory after all. It's a woman's tee shirt, and it's fucking pink."

Matt zoomed in and leaned over his screen. The image was crystal clear. It was not Old Glory in tatters, but a tattered, soot-covered pink tee shirt.

"That's my girl," smiled Matt, placing his hands on either side of his laptop, and leaning back in his chair. "That's my girl."

CHAPTER 31

••

the anselmo

"What is it about that tee shirt that makes you think it belongs to Fern?" said the ever-cautious Phelps.

Matt, Jay, and Ed looked at each other and laughed.

"She was having a pink week," grinned Matt. "She'd worn a bright pink blouse and jacket to work earlier this week – everyone commented on it. She looked the very essence of spring."

"Is this the blouse?" asked Phelps, pointing to the tee shirt flag.

"No, this top is more casual and a lighter pink. But, it's obvious to me that she went home and changed out of today's black dress for her workout, and she was still in a pink mood," said Matt, and Jay and Ed nodded vigorously in agreement. "Plus, it's a color she wears frequently, and she would know that we would recognize it as a sign from her."

"Got it," grinned McClellan, "we're convinced. She's one smart cookie. Wonder how she did it?"

"Who knows?" said Matt. "But I suspect it's going to make a great story when we get her the hell out of there."

"So," said Phelps. "The barn. Probably easier to extract her from there than the house. More wide open."

"Hope so," said Matt, ignoring a nervous twinge. "The advantage we have is that Fern is very aware of the drone photos, and she will know that we now know precisely where she is. And, she also knows that we" – and he swung his arm out to include Ed and Jay – "will come and get her. So, she'll be ready."

"You seem awfully sure of her reaction," said Phelps. "What if she's terrified or tied up? We don't know."

"I don't think she is tied up. Octavio said he's keeping her comfortable. And, she figured out a way to get her shirt up through what looks like a smokestack to the roof of the barn, didn't she?" Matt said. His eyes narrowed. "Give Fern credit. She'll be ready."

"The bad guys must not have seen it," observed McClellan. "That's another advantage for us."

"We know where she is, and Fern knows that we know, and they don't know that we know," summed up Ed. "That's three against one in my book."

"But they chop off people's heads," Phelps said brusquely.

"They're not going to chop off Fern's beautiful head," declared Matt. "I will personally see to that." He loosened his tie just a little.

"It may be over your dead body, Matt," cautioned Phelps.

"Then so be it."

◆◆◆

To a man, they were all impressed with the two OSP snipers. Brad and Harry − last names not provided − were imposing figures. Brad was 30, Harry 31, and Matt wondered to himself if there was a "sell by" date for snipers.

They explained the operation to them, and their role in it. Matt asked if they had experience in hostage extraction, and they both replied in the positive. Phelps wanted an example, and they gave him one in such graphic detail, Jay had to leave the room for a moment.

"Have you ever missed and killed the hostage by mistake?" Matt had to ask.

"No, sir," replied Brad.

"No, sir," replied Harry.

"Good to know," said Matt. "What's your range? Your comfort level? Brad?"

"I'm good from 1,000 yards, although, obviously, the closer the better," Brad said matter-of-factly. *Like we're talking about killing chickens*, thought Matt, but he only said, "Harry?"

"The same." No change of expression. *Impressive*, thought Matt.

"Have you ever had to shoot perched in a tree?" Matt asked.

Brad and Harry looked at each other and smiled. "It's Oregon, chief," said Brad. "So, um, yeah."

"OK, here's how it's going to work," said Matt.

◆◆◆

Fern woke up and could tell it was daylight. The translucent panels on the high up side of the barn let the light in. Her neck was a little stiff, but otherwise everything seemed to be in working order.

Someone had left her a pot of coffee, which was now stone cold. She must have slept for several hours. There was also a tray with one plate of food – it looked like rice and beans. Also cold.

She poured some coffee in a cup she found in the sink, and nuked it in the microwave. While it wasn't really cold in the barn, it was cool this morning, and it felt nice to wrap her hands around the hot liquid.

She drank one cup of the decent coffee, and then, feeling somewhat revived, she decided to wash her face in the sink. Doing more than that was out of the question since she had no towel, and would only have her same sweats to put back on anyway. Her lips were chapped, and she would kill for a toothbrush, but, oh well. At least she still had her head.

Waiting for the rice and beans to reheat in the microwave, she started thinking about Matt and her team. Would they spot her tee shirt flag in new drone photos? She felt confident they would, and that they would realize it was a signal from her.

But then, what would they do? Would they rush the property? Would Joe Phelps take charge? Fern didn't know what the federal government's response would be in a situation like the one she found herself in, but she had a sinking feeling that her safety would not be Phelps' primary concern. He would want arrests, or, worse, to kill as many members of the crime ring he could.

And, while she'd only personally seen the two men involved in her capture, she could hear more voices outside the barn's walls. Upon waking this morning, she'd also heard more than one car moving in or out, she couldn't tell which. She was getting the distinct feeling that there were many people here, and it also felt as if things were moving.

She stared at the microwave, and contemplated whether she could somehow wire it to create an explosion. Some kind of diversion that would allow her to escape and make a run for it. *Who am I kidding? I know absolutely nothing about microwaves, and would probably blow myself up. Think! Is there anything else I can do to get out of here?*

Walking over to the amphibians, she climbed up and tried the small door. Locked. She also tried to lift up the bubble hatch where the gunner would sit, and it wouldn't budge either.

Next, she moved to the big sliding barn doors on both ends, hoping against hope that maybe someone forgot to lock up last night. Both doors were tightly locked and wouldn't give an inch. Then she methodically moved around the barn, pushing on each wall in a slow and deliberate fashion. *Let there be a hole, gap, or something I can exploit.* Just…nothing.

Fern stood in the middle of the barn, out of ideas. *I am a prisoner.*

She would drink more coffee, eat her plate of food, wash up as best she could, and get herself ready mentally for whatever the day would bring her way.

Thank God she had on her running shoes.

◆◆◆

Sylvia knocked on the War Room door again, and Matt let her in.

"Rudy found Fern's car," she said, "and Bernice is on the way to it with her kit. She also said to tell you that she wants 'Ol George back. She was kidding. I think."

Jay and Ed laughed. Phelps and McClellan didn't get the joke.

"'Ol George was Matt's predecessor as Chief of Police," explained Jay, "and virtually nothing ever happened in his 22 years on the job in Port Stirling. It was only since Matt showed up three months ago that people started getting murdered."

Matt ignored Jay. "Good work," he said to Sylvia, his eyes widening. "Where's the car?"

"It was parked in the wayside at the southern end of Ocean Bend Road. She must have gone there to walk on the beach for her exercise," Sylvia said. She blinked rapidly, and Matt really hoped she wasn't going to cry. But she sucked it up and said, "Let me know if you want any further details, or if I should just handle it."

"You handle it," Matt said thankfully. "Tell Bernice to do her thing, and to call me as soon as she can. Then tell Rudy to leave the car where it is for now. I want to inspect it before it gets moved. And please thank Rudy for me."

Matt patted Sylvia on the back as he walked her to the door, and whispered in her ear, "It's going to be all right, we're going to get her back. You'll see."

She looked up into his eyes and gave him a shaky smile.

Once Matt had closed and locked the door again, Phelps said, "This is going to be a mostly uncomplicated operation on our part. That doesn't mean it will be easy, it won't, but I've had to plan for worse."

He picked up two of the drone photos. "There is only the one road in from the highway, from the east, but look at the north and south end photos. First, on the north of the house and barn in the clearing there is what looks to me like a dirt pathway that extends quite a ways north of the barn. There's a tree canopy obscuring part of it, and I can't tell for sure if the path continues under the trees or not. Worst case scenario we'll have to clear through some brush, but my guess is it's a path."

Jay said, "It's a path the whole way, I know it. It's long, too, and it's how the local fishermen used to access the good fishing hole before Zhang Chen put up a chain gate with a 'No Trespassing' sign."

"Do you know where it starts?" Phelps asked.

"Not exactly, but there's another access road in from the highway about a mile north of the one that leads to the house, and I would guess that this path takes off from that. Chen would own the other access road, too. The new gate and the sign are on that other road. There isn't a street sign or any indication from the highway, you just have to know it's there."

"And you know where it is, right?" asked Phelps. "Could you find it after dark?"

"Sure," Jay said. "Think so."

"Are you thinking we'll send men down that path?" asked Matt.

"Yeah," said Phelps. "There's good cover on the north end with the trees, plus if you look at this photo" – he tapped on his laptop – "it comes out right behind the barn. I'd want 20-30 of your guys, plus the snipers to come in this way." He pointed at the clearly visible dirt path in one of the photos. "We can get some guys in trees to stake it out, and then swoop in if the deal goes down tonight. They would be able to watch the beach from these trees, right?"

"Yes," Matt said. "They would be looking over a grassy area, a small river, and low dunes straight out to the beach. That can work. If we're going to hit, the snipers will be close to the barn to take out anyone guarding Fern, with plenty of backup. What about the south flank?"

Phelps rummaged through the photo stacks for pictures of the other side of the house. "This end is trickier," he said. "It looks like there's a substantial layer of shrubs and small trees with no real access points."

"We call that 'understory'," Jay interrupted, "and it's difficult to penetrate. You almost need a scythe to mow it down."

"I hear you," Phelps said. "But this end is critical, too, because it's where the house is, and there's likely to be men in the house. We'll have to identify some local cops who would be comfortable slogging through this area."

"I'll lead this south flank in," said Ed. "I'm used to struggling through this kind of undergrowth when I'm deer hunting. Give me 10-12 men and we'll make it through."

Matt looked at Ed with such gratitude on his face, the big guy was embarrassed. Ed shrugged his shoulders and said, "It's my job, ain't it? Let's tap some of Earl's men at the sheriff's department for this south approach – they're hunters, too."

"Obviously, there's no place to hide on the west side," Phelps continued. "The best we can do is stake out the off-loading on the beach from the trees. Unless you have any better ideas?" He looked around the table.

Matt pointed to a photo that showed the river bordering the Chen property. "If you look just north of Chen's cove, you can see a small inlet where part of the river branches off into the ocean. See it here? Why couldn't we float a raft from further north down to this inlet and have some spies here? It looks to me like there's a small dune with some vegetation on it that could provide cover."

"So our guys would hide behind the dune with binocs watching Chen's cove?" asked Phelps. "Is that what you mean?"

"Yeah, why not? The men in the trees will be able to see action on the beach, but this would be a closer look. Plus, they would be able to see further out in the water, and might see the amphibious craft approaching sooner. What do you think?"

"I like it," said Phelps, nodding. "We're going to need some walkie-talkies on our own frequencies. These men seem pretty sophisticated, and may have radio equipment that can monitor police and military communications."

"You think so?" asked Matt incredulously. "That never occurred to me."

"They seem to know more about your department than they should," Phelps said. "I'm guessing," he shrugged.

A knock on the door, and Sylvia said, "Matt, ask Mr. Phelps to pick up line one – it's the Coast Guard."

"Phelps here." Pause and dead silence around the table. "I'm here with the Port Stirling Chief of Police, and the Oregon State Police, sir. I'm going to put you on the speaker phone. We're in a secure environment. Go ahead, Captain."

"Hi to all. This is Captain Bob Adams. We've got a report from two of our helicopters from the Buck Bay Flight Station. As you know, gentlemen, we've been tracking a vessel about five miles out to sea called The Anselmo. It's a Panamanian-registered ship, and it's been anchored out there for 24-48 hours. It's been quiet, hardly even a crew sighting. But that changed about thirty minutes ago."

"How so, Captain?" Phelps asked.

"We think they're preparing to pull up anchor. There's been more crew sightings on the main and lower decks, and for the first time since we've been spying on them, there is some activity on the bridge deck. It looks like two men on the bridge, one wearing a captain's hat. We think it's tonight."

"So do we," said Matt. "This is Port Stirling police chief Matt Horning, sir. We're seeing some movement on land, too. They've positioned two large semi-trucks on the property we're watching. Your drone caught them there last night and this morning, and they were in another location yesterday. In my world, semi-trucks are used to move tons of product. We think this is a big deal going down."

"Agreed," said Captain Adams. "The ship's location is due west from your suspect's property. Any ideas on how they're going to get the – as you say – product from the ship ashore?"

"We think they have amphibious craft, sir," answered Matt. "We have photos of tracks on the beach and up a mown path to their house and barn area."

"Ahh," said the captain. "Ducks. Makes sense because this ship is too big to get very close to shore. So, they load the product from the ship to the ducks, swim it and then drive it up to where their trucks are waiting on land. All under the cover of darkness."

"Yep. Right here in my town."

"Let's get these bastards, what do you say?" said Captain Adams.

"With you all the way, sir," said Phelps. "We'll be ready on our end, and we'll talk soon. I'm assuming you are point on your end?"

"Yes, I'm your guy."

"One more thing, sir," Matt interrupted. "You are aware that this is also a hostage situation, correct?" His eyes darted around the room.

"I know they grabbed one of your officers, chief, and we're very sorry about that. Director Phelps has assured me that her safety will be paramount on the land portion of this bust."

Matt looked over at Phelps, who gave Matt a little salute, and an attempt at a smile.

"Thank you, sir," said Matt. "It was your drone that gave us hope. We're sure we know precisely where our hostage is being kept. She was able to give us a signal, and the drone caught it. I can't ever thank you enough, Captain."

"Hold your applause, chief. It's not over until it's over. It's also my understanding that we may be dealing with some human cargo."

"We think there's a strong possibility," Matt said. "We will be prepared on our end to ensure their freedom if it comes to that. And we will stay vigilant."

"You'd better," warned the captain. "Your officer's not out of that snake pit yet."

CHAPTER 32

....

a dark, stormy night

The three cops and two federal agents spent the afternoon at City Hall, hanging out mostly in the War Room. Tension grew as the day wore on, and final plans were put in place.

Under the direction of Port Stirling Chief of Police Matt Horning, the muscle for the land raid was assembled. Over in Twisty River, the county seat, Chinook County Sheriff Earl Johnson gathered every deputy in his department except one – his wife was in labor in the hospital, and Earl allowed that was a good excuse. The sheriff would supply nine men and two women. Earl had worked closely with Fern when she was the county's victims' advocate, and tough cop that he was, he was devastated at the news of her kidnapping.

In Buck Bay, Chinook County's biggest town, Matt's counterpart was able to pull in about twenty of his officers and detectives. Bell County Sheriff Les Thompson down in Silver River wanted to help, too, and he rounded up 13 more deputies. Thompson was sick to death about what illegal drugs were doing to the youth in his county, and making a dent in their distribution had been the platform he'd run on for county sheriff. Nothing would make him happier than stopping these guys from bringing in a new shipload of their shit.

Matt explained the plan to Sheriff Thompson, and had thanked him profusely for going out of his county to help them. The sheriff had replied, "We're locked and loaded. Bring 'em on."

Ed Sonders had marshalled about fifteen of his colleagues who were within driving range of Port Stirling. Oregon is a big state – about nine hours to drive across it – and some of the Oregon State Police couldn't make it on time.

Counting his officers, Matt figured he had about 67 police assembled for the land portion, plus the two snipers.

He and Ed, with Sheriff Earl conferenced in on the phone, divvied up the men into teams based on the skill sets they knew about. Along with the Buck Bay chief, these four would serve as team leaders of the operation. The teams were divided by their locations and approaches to the property. Each of the four team leaders would have walkie-talkies to communicate with each other, and all would serve under Matt's overall direction.

Matt's team, including Jay, would approach on the dirt path that came in from the north and ended at the barn.

Brad and Harry, the two snipers, would be positioned in two Douglas fir trees. Brad would be about 60 yards east of the barn, with an expected clear shot of the white door on the side of it. He would also be positioned to take a shot at the front door of the house to the south, about 300 yards across the parking lot, if that scenario became necessary.

Harry would cover the back sliding door of the barn, also on the east side in a separate tree, but with a different view both north and west. If Fern left the barn, Matt expected them to bring her out the white door rather than struggle with the more cumbersome sliding door. But in the event that they did attempt to sneak out the back through the heavier door, it would be Harry's responsibility.

Ed's team included some of his local hunting buddies from the sheriff's department, and several of his Oregon State Police colleagues. They would be positioned on the south side of the property, and would close in on the house, especially the back and side doors.

Sheriff Earl Johnson would bring his team in from Highway 101 on the property's main access road. They would come in with a bunch of squad cars with lights blazing, and would serve as a distraction for Matt's team and Brad and Harry to extract Fern from the barn. On the off-chance Fern had been moved to the house, it would be up to Ed to manage Plan B, and make sure his team was out of the way for Brad to take a shot, if it came to that.

The Buck Bay police department would send some cars and officers with Earl's team to make as big a splash as possible. The chief and five of his best detectives, two of whom regularly went duck hunting near the inlet, would float the river from the north to the inlet, shown clearly on the drone photos. Once on the beach, they would lay low and await the ship's arrival and the deployment of the amphibious craft. They would alert the other teams to any beach action.

Everyone was standing by, including the Coast Guard who would patrol with the two Sentinel-class cutters – with their autocannon and machine guns – and with two helicopters overhead. The teams would assemble shortly after dark, and begin taking up their positions.

Air, land, and sea, thought Matt, and he felt confident in the plan. *They're not going to get away, and we will save Fern.* Still, he felt some trepidation, only natural, and would be very happy once their operation was successfully concluded with arrests made, and Fern safe. He would be happy to have Jay at his side watching the barn, but he worried about Ed. Matt knew Ed could take care of himself better than almost anyone he knew, but the house part of this raid was highly dangerous because it was mostly an unknown. The drone photos told them there were people in the house, and he suspected that one or more of them would try to escape out the back door once Earl and his team came roaring in.

Having participated in a couple of high-level drug busts in Texas, Matt knew it was normal to worry about his colleagues' safety. But there was something different about this one. The Dallas and Plano police departments were huge with immense resources, and confident in their ability to thwart crime at any level. It was no surprise to anyone when they successfully pulled off a big operation.

But his team here were small-town policemen and women, good cops in it for the right reasons, but they were unaccustomed to this degree of sophisticated international crime. They had skills and many were talented, but this was a whole new ballgame for the majority of them. And there was also the undeniable fact that Matt, in a short three months, had become very close to Jay and Ed. He had relied on both of them so much to show him the local ropes in terms of history, geography, and culture. Both men, along with Fern, of course, had been completely unselfish in trying to ensure that Matt succeeded in his new job. He would always be grateful to – and love – the three of them. Putting them in harm's way was the last thing in the world he wanted to do. *But here we are.*

◆◆◆

They all kept a close eye on the weather, making periodic trips from the War Room outside to check. So far, the mild early spring day was holding, much to everyone's relief. The Coast Guard worried that a blustery, nasty night, especially at sea, might put off the bad guys' plan. Matt worried that the same would make things more difficult for Brad and Harry, and, above all else, he wanted them to be comfortable and at their best.

Sunset was nearing. Jay fidgeted and spooked at the slightest sound. Matt, while appearing calm and composed on the outside, was agitated and skittery on the inside. Ed and Rod McClellan, who had hit it off, kept making corny jokes, but even Ed was starting to look a little queasy. Nothing appeared to faze McClellan and Phelps. Guess it was a case of been there, done that with them.

Sunset tonight was just before 8:00 p.m., with civil twilight lasting about another thirty minutes. Each team would depart from a different location in case the bad guys were watching City Hall. They would not rendezvous, but make their separate approaches from their directions. Dressed in all black with dark face paint, they would disappear into the night.

At the appointed hour, Matt gave the other three team leaders the "Go" word on the walkie-talkies, and got back three "Roger that". Each team took off, and drove to their prearranged positions. Phelps and McClellan stayed behind to coordinate with the Coast Guard. A special circuit had been set up for Phelps and Matt to communicate.

Now the wait began.

◆◆◆

Fern had passed the day alternately napping on the cot and pacing around the barn. She threw in some pushups, sit-ups, squats, and lunges, and a few yoga poses to keep her body and mind sharp. There was a great deal of activity around the property, people coming and going. At some point, and it felt like early afternoon, four men came into the barn.

She moved forcefully out of the cot room, ready for anything, but expecting the worst, and…they ignored her. One man stood guard, facing Fern with an AK-47 assault rifle. One man casually waved at her as they walked past the room, but nobody said a word to her. *Fine with me.*

But then, *oh, no!..they're going to the amphibians.* Fern had replaced the elbow of the stovepipe back as good as she could, and it wasn't obvious it had been tampered with. At least, she didn't think it was obvious.

Two of the men climbed up and used the door to enter each vehicle. The other two men went to the back of the barn and unlocked the big sliding door. It took both of them pushing hard to get it to slide open. The big door looked rusty to Fern.

The two drivers started up the vehicles and, awkwardly to Fern's eyes, the ducks lumbered out of the barn. The door guys slid the barn door back into place and locked it, going out the white side door like they came in. She heard the lock on it snapping into place.

She wondered how long it would take them to realize that one of their whip antennas was missing.

◆◆◆

At 10:34 p.m. Phelps' phone rang. Captain Bob Adams of the United States Coast Guard.

"The Anselmo is on the move," Captain Adams said. "It's headed your way, due east of its current location."

"Thank you, Captain," said Phelps. "Land is in position."

"Moving air and sea into position now," the captain responded.

◆◆◆

Phelps dialed Matt. "The Anselmo is moving. Here they come." He sounded almost animated.

"Roger that," said Matt, and quickly passed it on to his three leaders, and to Brad and Harry. Silently and swiftly, he shifted from his location near the dirt path to a higher knoll where he could track his team more easily, and they would be able to see him when he signaled with his flashlight. He knew Jay was right behind him, even though he couldn't see him in the darkness or hear his stealthy movements. He had asked Jay to make sure Fern got out alive if anything happened to him, and his job was to stay glued to Matt's rear.

The silence and darkness enveloped Matt. It was pitch-black, and all he could hear was the sound of water crashing against the steep rocks that protected each side of the Chen cove. It was more muted here than at his house because he was further away from the ocean's power, but he thought the

Buck Bay team down on the beach would have to raise their voices to talk to each other over the unbounded sea.

He hoped it was his imagination, but he could have sworn he just felt a raindrop on his hand. *Oh, crap, it's starting to rain.* And, now the wind was picking up as well. He turned around to Jay, saw the whites of his eyes, and saw him shrug his shoulders, the movement saying 'What are you going to do – it's raining'.

Nothing to do but to wait for the Anselmo. And wait they did.

And then they waited some more. And while they waited, the rain intensified. Every once in a while it would rain sideways in gusts so hard that Matt was afraid it might wash off his black face paint. The now-howling wind was in symphony with the pounding surf.

About 3:00 a.m., Matt's walkie-talkie vibrated and Buck Bay's chief, Dan McCoy, whispered, "I see it. It's about ½ mile out."

"What's the ocean look like?" Matt asked.

"It's getting rough. Rougher by the minute, and the wind is fierce. Really picked up in the last hour."

"Yeah, the wind is bad here now, too. I'm sure it's worse down on the beach. Can they get the ship in close enough?"

"Don't know yet. We'll watch."

And so they waited some more.

3:30 a.m., McCoy called back. "The Anselmo is signaling by lights to the shore, and there's four guys down here. We think they just launched two ducks from the ship, and they're sailing to the beach now."

"Two, huh? Will they make it in?" Matt asked, apprehensive now.

"I wouldn't want to be in those vehicles," McCoy responded. "The seas are heavy and I think it's too rough to unload. And the tide is coming in, so it's only going to get worse in the next hour or so."

"Shit."

"Ah, no! Shit is right – they're turning around, chief. It's just too rough. The ducks are headed back to the ship."

"Unbelievable," Matt said bitterly. "You'd think Mother Nature could give us one stinkin' break. We'll wait for now to make sure they don't change their mind. Hold your post."

"Roger that."

At 4:20 a.m., McCoy called Matt. "They're leaving. Anselmo is turning and heading back out to sea. Fuck."

"Looks like we'll be back out here tomorrow night," Matt said. Despondent didn't begin to cover his black mood. *I'm so sorry, Fern, we tried. We're ready to come and get you, just hang on one more day. Can you do that for me?*

After what felt like several hours of silence, Fern retreated to her cot of the previous night. She had heard voices and vehicles long after dark, and remained poised and ready for anything. But now, the only sounds she could hear were the rain beating relentlessly on the roof of the barn, and the wind groaning through the trees.

Nothing to see here, she said to the cot. *Looks like it's just you and me again tonight.*

CHAPTER 33

....

what could possibly go wrong?

Saturday, April 13

"If they only have two amphibious craft, it will take them at least two trips from the ship to shore to off-load the contraband," said Matt to Phelps. "And that's if they're just moving drugs. If they've got a bunch of girls on board, it will take them several round trips."

"Well, we don't really know how many ducks they have," said Phelps. "The two your men on the beach saw could have just been testing the seas. It's a fairly large ship out there."

"True. My point is that it will take them at least two trips. So, if we let the first off-load go smoothly, they will get overconfident and think they've scared me off. Let them unload and go back out for a second run. Then, we catch them in the act, and have a surprise advantage for freeing Fern. Having part of the contraband unloaded gives us the hard evidence we need for arrests and trial, with the added plus that their guard is down when they don't get nabbed on their first run."

"Strongly agree, Matt," said Phelps. "Be quiet as mice while they do their test run, and nail them to the wall on their second."

Matt looked out his office window and saw the sun blazing high overhead. Last night's storm had blown over, and today was clear and bright. *It figures.* He'd told everyone to go home and get some sleep when they retreated from the Chen property. He assumed he was too wound up and pissed off to sleep, but the weight of the past 48 hours caught up with him, and he was out by the time his head hit his pillow, sleeping the dreamless sleep of the completely exhausted. Hopefully, the rest of the team did the same.

The idea of Fern having to spend a second night and day in captivity was excruciating to him. But he couldn't control the weather; he could only control that he and the team remained motivated and committed to the plan. He awoke feeling stronger than ever and focused. A hot shower, clean clothes, and a hot breakfast invigorated him, and somehow Matt knew tonight was the night. He would get Fern back, and end this horror movie. His optimistic personality was a real asset today; it didn't allow him to consider that it could all go horribly wrong.

Now the team leaders had reassembled to refine their plan based on what last night taught them. The only element Matt changed was to move three of Dan McCoy's officers from the beach to Sheriff Earl's group. It was decided that Dan and two of his guys were enough to report on the approaching ship and the ducks from the beach, now that they knew exactly where they were planning to land. They would let the amphibious vehicles sail in, drive up to the house and barn clearing, and unload their cargo there, while Earl's group stormed in.

Rod McClellan had been put in charge of how they would handle any human cargo. He'd tapped Patty Perkins from Twisty River to help him marshall the local resources they would need if, indeed, they were trafficking people on the Anselmo, instead of, or in addition to, drugs.

"I wish we knew for sure what we're dealing with here," Patty lamented. "Not only do we not know if there are any prisoners being held on that ship or on the property, we don't know if it could be anywhere between one person and 500."

"The facts we do know are fairly conclusive that there is at least one girl being held against her will, and she is likely on the property still," said Matt. "My gut is telling me that we have to prepare for more, and the odds are that it will be girls, maybe young women."

"Patty checked, and there's nothing going on at Port Stirling High School tonight or tomorrow," Rod said. "So we thought in the worst case scenario, we could use the gym there as a staging area. Bernice and a couple of her guys will be there with an ambulance in case we need to take anyone to the Buck Bay Hospital. This is a night I wish Port Stirling had its own hospital."

"That works," said Matt.

"Once we know what we're dealing with," Patty said, "Sylvia is prepared to help me call around to all the local hardware stores and pharmacies for cots, blankets, bottled water, toiletries, stuff like that. We can't arouse suspicion in the community before tonight, so we'll just have to wait and see how it goes down, and then get busy in a hurry if we have to. If there are people being trafficked, we'll take care of them properly."

"We know you will, Patty, and thanks for your help," Matt said. Patty was a rock. She'd proved her mettle during the Emily Bushnell case, and here she was again, doing what needed to be done. "Did you get any sleep this morning?"

"Of course I slept," she smiled. "No men running around chopping people's heads off is going to interrupt my sleep. But I did need both my husband and my electric blanket to warm up after being outside in the brush for six hours. I'm getting too old for this shit," she said, shaking her head. "Did you sleep, chief?"

"Yeah, I surprised myself."

"Good," Patty said. "We need you in tip-top condition tonight."

"I'll be ready," he said tightly.

◆◆◆

They massed at the rendezvous points at the same time as last night, and took up their positions. Mother Nature was cooperating; it was, so far, anyway, a clear, windless night.

Jay had remarked to Matt earlier in the day that April was usually one of the better months for weather. In fact, golfers in the know often chose April to play Port Stirling Links because they were less likely to get rained on and windblown than in the more traditional golfing months.

"That's a nice story," Matt told Jay, "but what the hell happened last night?"

"Well, it's not a perfect science," Jay smiled. "But my point is the odds are with us tonight."

"Good to know."

◆◆◆

It was a little warmer than last night, too, thought Matt, as he gazed up at the starlit sky. And, unlike last night, the moon was visible. He'd warned the

253

troops that they would have to be extra vigilant tonight to stay hidden, because, while the moon wasn't full it was putting out a lot more light than last night when it was hidden entirely behind the clouds.

Matt was edgy and uneasy, just like last night, but he was more comfortable tonight. The sleep had helped, and he was dry. He hadn't gotten used to the rain in Port Stirling yet, and most of the time it still annoyed the hell out of him. The locals kept telling him that a little rain was nothing, and their mild weather would make up for the searing Texas heat this summer. Everyone in Oregon loved summer, and he was anxious to experience his first one soon. *If only I can get Fern back, I'll never complain about the rain again*, he promised the universe.

2:00 a.m. and nothing yet. *What the hell are they waiting for – Christmas?!?*

2:45 a.m. and nothing. It occurred to Matt that he would have to give every one of his officers a raise if they pulled this off tonight.

Finally, after five hours and ten minutes of waiting, Dan McCoy whispered into Matt's walkie-talkie, "Anselmo in sight, four guys on the beach, and two ducks rolling down from your end toward the water."

As he said that, Matt could hear the vehicles moving. It sounded like they were west of the barn and headed west, away from him.

"Roger that," he said to McCoy. "Tell me when you see ducks on your end – either direction."

"Roger that," and the walkie-talkie went silent.

Matt waited for what felt like an eternity, but was really only six minutes before McCoy came back.

"Two ducks launched from Anselmo, headed to beach. Weather is perfect, surf is calm. They're coming at you, chief."

"Roger that," Matt whispered.

"Holy moly," said McCoy. "I see the two vehicles on land, and they're huge. Looks like they're going to run these four ducks back and forth."

"That ship must be full of something," Matt said.

He immediately conveyed McCoy's intel to the team leaders and Phelps. "OK, everyone sit tight, and let's watch the bad guys be bad. No movement, no noise please, ladies and gentlemen."

Dan McCoy and his two Buck Bay detectives watched, as they laid flat on the beach, the ship signaling to their compatriots on shore. It was a go.

The two amphibians from the ship sailed into the tranquil cove, and drove up onto the beach, the vehicle's wheels now visible. The two drivers waved at the ducks on the beach and kept moving toward the low dunes and the river beyond. The vehicles on the beach, whose drivers both returned the wave, went the other way, into the Pacific Ocean, and out toward the Anselmo.

Ed's team, perched both in the trees and on the ground around the house, had the best view of the courtyard. It was Ed's responsibility to report on the next segment...what, precisely, was being off-loaded from the ducks?

The two vehicles crossed the shallow river, came up the mown path through the grasses, and entered the clearing, coming to a stop next to the semi-trucks. Each driver opened the hatch door and jumped down. Soon after, out came another man from the bowels of the vehicle, pulling on a rope which was tied around the waist of a young girl, and another girl, and another girl. In all, six girls came out of the amphibious vehicle, and were marched up a ramp leading to the inside of one of the semi-trucks.

Ed, hidden in undergrowth beneath a large Douglas fir tree next to the front of the house, watched in horror as the barely-clad teenage girls disappeared from his view into the truck. In all, twelve girls from the two ducks were placed in the truck. Following them came several big metal containers wrapped in cardboard. Ed figured they weighed about 35 pounds each, and he guessed that when they opened them, they would find many, many plastic bags full of drugs.

So, girls and drugs. Nice guys.

Ed raged internally, but quietly and professionally told Matt what he was seeing.

"I lost sight of the ducks when they pulled up on your side of the semis," Matt whispered back to Ed. "But I can clearly see the truck ramp. Our worst fears."

"The girls must be cold," Ed said flatly.

"I know you want to go in, but we have to wait for the other vehicles to get to the Anselmo and then come back here. They won't take off until their truck is filled. Sit tight, buddy. I'm going to talk to Earl now."

Another thirty minutes or so went by, and it was obvious the bad guys thought they had aced their test run. No cops! All night to empty the Anselmo's cargo into the semi-trucks and roll out of here!

Only one man, Octavio, hadn't completely bought it yet, and he stayed safely out of sight in the barn, listening.

"Here comes run #2," said Dan McCoy from the beach into Matt's ear. "They should be up to the clearing in about ten minutes."

"Roger that," snarled Matt. "We're good to go in ten."

♦♦♦

Sheriff Earl's team hadn't had experience with kidnapping or hostage-taking, but they sure as hell knew how to conduct a drug bust. Eleven squad cars with lights and sirens blazing, filled with cops with their weapons at the ready, squealed into the courtyard. Sheriff Earl, looking like a geriatric jogger, jumped out of the lead car before it came to a complete stop. Bullhorn in one hand, shotgun in the other, he screeched into the bullhorn, "This is the police! Stop what you're doing and everybody down on the ground! Now!"

The cops surrounded the semi-truck and the amphibious vehicles, pointing their guns as the bad guys, eight in all, one-by-one dropped to the ground, yelling "Don't shoot! Don't shoot!" Two of Earl's deputies clambered up the truck's ramp, and amid the screaming girls, forced two more men down to the ground, one of whom got off a shot that ricocheted off the wall and landed harmlessly.

Sheriff Earl and ten of his best friends now moved closer to the house, where he shouted into the bullhorn, "Come out of the house! Now! Hands in the air! Now!" The front door slowly opened, and six more bad guys came out with their hands held high. They, too, shouted, "Don't shoot!"

"Ed!" screamed Sheriff Earl, "coming out the back at you!"

Ed was already on it, and he and his troopers were scrambling through the bushes, tracking down a few guys dumb enough to flee. They rounded up four more, and brought them to the courtyard to join their friends on the ground. Ed and three of his team completed a sweep of the house.

"All clear in here!" Ed shouted into the walkie-talkie.

"Roger that!" roared Matt.

That left only the barn.

♦♦♦

Matt and his team approached the barn, coming in from two sides.

"Going in now," Matt said into his walkie-talkie. "Let me hear a Roger from each of you."

"Roger that," said Sheriff Earl.

"Roger that," said Brad, the sniper.

"Roger that," said Lt. Ed Sonders.

256

"Roger that," said Chief Dan McCoy.

Silence.

"Harry, do you read me?" said Matt.

Silence.

"Harry, come in please!" said an increasingly panicked Matt.

Silence.

"Harry, this is Chief Horning. Do you read me?"

Silence.

"Ed! Go check on Harry."

"Roger that, chief."

Matt gave the stop signal to his team, and everyone froze in place. They could hear Sheriff Earl continuing to round up and handcuff the men gathered in the courtyard.

Finally, Ed, speaking into the walkie-talkie.

"Harry is dead, chief," Ed sobbed. "His throat is slit. He's on the ground under his tree."

Matt felt a jolt of terror.

"Brad, do you read me?" he whispered.

"Yes, chief."

Thank God!

"I'm approaching the barn now. Please focus on the white door as planned. Be ready, dude!"

"Roger that."

Matt crept around the side of the barn, his team providing cover, and he was now facing the white door. Raising his bullhorn in his free hand – his other held his gun steady – he coolly, but loudly, said, "Fern, it's Matt. Are you in the barn?"

"Yes!" she screamed at the top of her lungs. "But he's got a knife!"

CHAPTER 34

....

blood-splattered

The white door slowly opened.

"Earl, give me a spotlight!" Matt yelled.

The floodlights immediately lit up the courtyard, the barn, and the open white door. In it stood Octavio, holding Fern in front of him. There was a rather large knife at her throat.

"Hold still, Fern," Matt said as smoothly as he could manage. "Octavio, we can talk this out. I can let you go. No problem."

"Octavio underestimated you, chief. But not totally."

"Oh, right, you're doing the third person thing," Matt said sarcastically.

"I'm going to walk out of here with Ms. Byrne, and get in my Jeep," Octavio said. "Do you understand me so far?" Cool as ice.

"Yes, I understand you. Then what happens?"

"Then I drive out of here, and at some point, I let her out of the Jeep. She will walk back here, and you are all to wait here until she arrives. If any of your men follow me in the Jeep, I will cut her very beautiful neck."

"Like you did to Clay Sherwin?"

"Like I did to Mr. Sherwin."

"How do I know you won't just keep going and take her with you?"

"Because if Ms. Byrne's not back here within one hour, you have my permission to call out all your troopers and stop me. I have nothing against her. In fact, I admire her, and taking her life would be painful to me. My freedom is my concern, however. I will be free."

All Matt could think of is *keep him talking*. "How long have you been operating here?"

"That's not important."

"Why did you hide Clay's car in the Rowell barn?"

Octavio smirked. "Because it was easy, and I didn't want any evidence here. Your citizens should be told to lock up their property. No one does."

"Yeah, I've noticed that, too. We'll work on it. Brad!" Matt suddenly howled.

A shot rang out, and Matt heard a scream. But Octavio did not fall.

Matt knew in an instant that his second sniper had been stopped. *Of course they would know that I'd bring snipers to a hostage situation.* Juan was out there somewhere. In the darkness. Behind him.

Since Matt realized he was probably already a dead man, and trembling with rage, he raised his gun and fired quickly, instinctively. Fern let out a piercing, frenzied cry.

Octavio slumped, and collapsed on the ground, the knife in his hand finding the pavement before his body did.

Matt ran toward Fern, lunging at her and forcefully grabbing her blood-spattered hand. He yanked her through the white door and pulled it shut just as he heard gunfire. It seemed to zing off the barn siding.

He held her tightly to him, enclosing her completely in his long arms and big shoulders, and they both whimpered softly while they listened to the shooting happening outside.

Eventually, after what seemed like a very long time, the gunfire stopped, and Matt and Fern looked at one another.

"Are you OK?" she asked him.

"I'm supposed to ask you that."

"I'm OK."

"So am I. This nightmare is over, Fern, and I'm taking you home as soon as we wrap up here."

One minute later Ed rapped lightly on the white door and said, his voice hoarse, "Can I come in?"

"You may," said Fern, recovering first. Matt was still shaking.

◆◆◆

They walked slowly out of the white door, and Ed yelled, "Oh, no!" when he saw them. He was reacting to all the blood on Fern, and now all over Matt as well.

Matt, looking down at his chest, and sensing Ed's fear, said "It's OK, it's Octavio's blood, not ours. We're both fine."

Ed didn't speak, but wrapped them both up simultaneously in a big bear hug. They stood motionless like that, and then Jay was upon them, trying to get in on the cuddle.

"Let's try to not do this again," said Ed.

"Fine with me," answered Fern. She was grinning broadly.

Breaking free from their cop scrum, Matt leaned down to feel Octavio's pulse.

"He's dead," Ed said seriously. "I checked to make sure before I opened the barn door."

"He sold his soul to the devil," Matt said.

"With some guys, there aren't any other buyers," said Ed.

Matt took off his black jacket and placed it over Octavio, closing his eyes as he did so. The bullet from Matt's gun had entered in the middle of Octavio's forehead, a fact which would scare off Port Stirling's criminals for the decade to come.

"What about his colleague, Juan?" Matt asked Ed. "Did he get both of your snipers?" He knew the answer, but had to be sure.

Ed looked down at the ground before speaking. "Yes, Brad and Harry were both killed by Juan. Harry's throat was slit, and Brad took a bullet in the back of the head."

"Who got Juan?"

"I did," said Ed.

"I don't know what to say," Matt said.

"That's a first," said Ed.

"Thank you," said Matt, his face filled with gratitude. "You saved Fern and me."

"No," said Ed, "you did. You got her safely in the barn before I was even able to take my shot at Juan. That was some quick thinking on your part."

"Where was Juan?" asked Jay.

"In a tree next to Brad's," Ed answered. "When Matt yelled and the shot rang out, I could see Brad with Juan right there. He was able to get off another shot before I got him, but, luckily, his second shot missed you two." He smiled at Fern and Matt.

Fern shuddered. "I felt the bullet whizz by me as we were running. That's likely to be something I'll never forget, right?"

"Unfortunately," said Matt, squeezing her hand, which he was still holding.

She smiled up at him, but then turned serious. "I heard girls earlier, and then some screaming. Are there many, and are they all right now?"

For the first time since coming out of the barn, Matt noticed all the commotion around the semi-trucks. Sheriff Earl and Patty Perkins, along with about 20 deputies and state troopers were gently walking the young girls down the truck ramp, covering each one with a blanket. Soothing sounds were coming from Patty and the men as each girl emerged from the truck.

"How many are there?" asked Matt as he approached Patty.

"Too damn many!" she growled. "What the hell is wrong with people?"

Matt understood that Patty's question was hypothetical, and didn't require an answer. Instead, he asked, "What's your plan for them?"

"We are taking them several at a time in Earl's squad cars back to town. Sylvia and Rudy are arranging for the necessary supplies to be immediately delivered to the high school gym, and that's where we're taking them. So far, there are two girls who need medical attention, and we'll have them taken to the Buck Bay Hospital. The rest are mostly OK, at least physically. Tired, hungry, and in need of cleaning up, but probably in better shape than they should be." Unexpectedly, she snorted a laugh.

"What?" quizzed Matt.

"You need to know that Sylvia called the hardware store owner at home, and woke him up."

"Of course she did," Matt smiled looking at his watch. "It's 4:45 a.m."

"He's on his way to his store, and is lining up what we need to take care of these girls. Rudy is getting Summer's Pharmacy to open up now, too, and he and Sylvia will pick up what we need from there. We'll make them as comfortable as we can tonight, and then start dealing with their harsh realities tomorrow once everyone, including yours truly, has had some sleep."

"In a way, these girls are lucky they ended up in Port Stirling," Matt said, putting his arm around Patty's shoulders.

"They are," she agreed. "We take care of our own, and they are now our own."

"I'll see you later," Matt said. "I need to talk with Phelps."

"See you later, chief." She turned back to the truck, but then immediately spun back to face Matt.

"One more thing, chief," said Patty.

"What's that?"

"I'm so relieved you and Fern are OK."

Matt hugged Patty, and they both held on fiercely.

"Talk to me," said Phelps into his phone.

"It's over on our end," said Matt. "We got everyone. Some of the bad guys fled to the bushes out behind the back of the house, but Ed's team tracked them down. They were sure that all are accounted for."

"What about our friend Octavio?"

"He is deceased," said Matt. "I'm sorry to say that he got shot in the forehead." In a way, Matt was deeply sorry; he didn't get into this profession to kill people. "He confessed to cutting off Clay Sherwin's head."

"Did he confess to shooting him first?"

Momentarily taken aback, Matt said, "No, I forgot to ask that. The other part came up because he was holding a knife to Fern's throat at the time."

"Understandable. Did we lose anybody?"

"'Fraid so. Both of the Oregon State Police snipers are dead. Octavio's backup, Juan, got both of them before we could get a shot off on him. One of the sheriff's deputies got grazed in the shoulder by a wayward shot, but he's fine. Patched up here and on his way to the hospital in Buck Bay. The state troopers who tracked down the runners have a few scrapes and bruises, but nothing serious. Those are tough guys," admired Matt.

"Well, I'm very sorry about the OSP men," said Phelps in a low voice. "I guess they understand the risk every time they're in the field, but still…" his voice trailed off.

"Yeah, they were so young. I don't even know if they have families."

"Please find out," Phelps said. "We need to make it right. This is really the federal government's case, and we must make sure Port Stirling and Oregon are made whole once this is over."

"Thank you for that, Joe. Appreciate the sentiment. Speaking of 'over', has the Coast Guard been advised that they can now move on the Anselmo?"

"I will call the captain next. What's the status of the amphibious vehicles? Four of them that we know of, correct?"

"Yeah. The two that were parked in the barn on land are now back at the ship. And we have two sitting in the courtyard here. Their drivers have been arrested, and are currently being interrogated about what else is on that damn ship. Those two ducks brought in twelve girls, and we're looking after them now."

"Shit. I was hopeful the drive-through coffee girl was just an aberration. Did we find her?"

"Yes," confirmed Matt. "She was in the house. Ed says she smiled at him, and she's doing fine now."

"Any drugs?"

"Oh, yeah." said Matt. "They brought six big aluminum containers in their first run in from the ship, and the state police are opening them now. Looks like they're holding lots and lots and lots of plastic bags filled with the pharmaceutical of your choice. I suspect there are more girls and more drugs on the Anselmo. It looked to us that they planned to run the four ducks back and forth for a while yet. You need to stop that ship, Joe."

◆◆◆

Matt next found some coffee on the kitchen counter in the house, and poured a cup for Fern. She stuck close to him as he checked in with Sheriff Earl and had the call with Phelps.

"You have some, too," she urged. "You're cold." She rubbed her hands on his arms to warm him up. "You still have that Texas blood in you," she smiled.

"I'm fine," Matt said, "but spending an April night outside in Oregon is not my idea of a good time. Come with me while I go talk to some of the bad guys."

"Like I'm going to leave your side," she said seriously.

He took her hand, and they went to the center of the courtyard where Sheriff Earl and the state police had everyone rounded up. As they approached, Fern pulled on Matt's hand, and uncharacteristically backed away, reluctant to get too close to her former captors.

"It's OK, Fern," he said gently, "they're all handcuffed and chained. They can't hurt you now."

"I'm not afraid," Fern said, but she held on securely to Matt's hand. He didn't let go.

He advanced toward one of the prisoners, a pasty white guy with dead-looking eyes and limp blond hair, plastered down, about 25 years old, and engaged him in conversation.

"What's your name and where are you from?" the chief asked.

"Who are you?" the young man replied nervously, looking over Matt's blood-stained apparel.

"I'm Matt Horning, the Chief of Police of Port Stirling, and the man that's going to testify against you in a court of law. What I say in court about you depends on what you do or do not tell me in the next few minutes. Got it?"

The man stiffened, and said, "Sure. Kevin Crown, and I'm from Massachusetts. Boston."

"OK, that's a good start, Kevin." Looking around the courtyard, Matt said, "I notice we've got several different nationalities present tonight. Can you tell me where your colleagues are from?"

"Several are from mainland China. Beijing, I think, but don't quote me on that. Somewhere over there."

"Chinese nationals?" asked Matt. "How many?"

Kevin thought for a moment. "Probably eight all together."

"What about the Hispanic guys? Where were Octavio and Juan from? And was Octavio your leader?"

"Yeah, Octavio recruited me and he's the capo. From Costa Rica originally, but lives somewhere around San Francisco now."

"Lived," Matt corrected. "He's dead."

Kevin's eyes widened. "No shit?"

"No shit," Matt confirmed. "What about Juan? Where's he from?"

"The same. Costa Rica, now San Francisco."

"He's dead, too, by the way. You're lucky you're not. But don't worry, if you were going to die, you'd be dead already."

Kevin was feeling luckier by the minute. "Hey, man, I'm just trying to earn a living."

"You ever think of McDonald's? Minimum wage, but guys don't usually get killed there."

"I'm just supplying what people want," Kevin said, but at least he had the decency to look down at his shoes when he said it.

"Do you have a sister, Kevin?" Fern suddenly spoke up by Matt's side. She moved forward, tentatively taking a step or two toward Kevin.

"Look," started Kevin, "we didn't mean you any harm, lady. You were just our ticket out if things went bad."

"Things went bad," Fern said with steel in her voice. "You didn't answer my question."

"I got two sisters."

"How would you feel if they were snatched from your childhood home and brought here to sell to the highest bidder? Likely some perverted old rich guy? Would you like that for your sisters?"

"Didn't have a home. We were in foster care."

Fern stared hard at Kevin before finally saying, "I'm sorry to hear that. But it still doesn't excuse your role in putting these young girls at such risk."

Kevin looked pleadingly at Matt. "I thought it was just drugs. I didn't know about the girls until we got here."

"Where are the girls from? Do you know?"

"China, and some place in Central America. Costa Rica, I think."

"How does a guy like Octavio from Costa Rica and California know how to get girls from China?" Matt asked.

"He's not the frontman," said Kevin flatly.

"Can you guess what my next question is?"

"I don't know who the big boss is for this deal," said Kevin. "I swear I don't. None of us knew anything except Octavio, and he played his cards close to his vest. I would tell you if I knew, man. I would."

CHAPTER 35

··

cheeseburger and fries

Sunday, April 14
Captain Bob Adams of the U.S. Coast Guard took the call from the State Department's Joe Phelps, who informed him that the land operation had been successfully concluded.

"The hostage is safe?"

"Yes, Captain, the hostages are fine. In addition to Ms. Byrne, we rescued several young girls brought in the first wave. We lost two Oregon State Police snipers, and one of the sheriff's deputies got hit in the shoulder, but he and everyone else are good. Two of the smugglers were killed, including the land-based leader, Octavio something – we're checking on his real identity now. All bad guys rounded up, handcuffed, and arrested."

"Roger that. We're going after the vessel. It's about two miles off-shore. Stay tuned."

Two Coast Guard Sentinel cutters, along with one medium-endurance cutter, and three helicopters from the Buck Bay flight station pursued the Anselmo in open waters. After a one-hour chase that was never going to end well for the Anselmo, four of its remaining crew abandoned ship and attempted to escape via life raft. That escape failed after gunfire was exchanged. Two of the crew were killed, and the others surrendered as the Coast Guard boarded the vessel.

The operation ended as daylight broke. In all, 28 men were arrested and four were killed. Eight were Chinese nationals, six were from Costa Rica, nine from California, four from Massachusetts, three from New Jersey, and two from Oregon.

Sensitive electronic equipment was discovered in the attic of the house, and Joe Phelps believed it had been used to monitor police and government communications.

The drug take was unprecedented on the west coast: 700 aluminum containers, each weighing about 40 pounds, and filled to the brim with their cash product. It took the Coast Guard ten hours to unload the ship, and recover about 250 of the containers that were dumped into the ocean by Anselmo's crew as they attempted to sink the ship before their surrender. Due to the Coast Guard's smart thinking and hard work, the Anselmo was saved and towed to the port of Buck Bay. Overall value of the drugs would later be declared at $130 million.

But the primary product – and the real tragedy – was the trafficking of young girls to ready buyers throughout the country. In addition to the 12 girls who first landed on U.S. soil, another 161 girls between the ages of 13-19 were found below decks of the Anselmo.

That's why two semi-trucks were needed: one for the drugs and one for the girls. Patty Perkins would take on a new job for the next two years, reuniting some of the girls with their Chinese and Costa Rican families, and mostly, finding new homes for the girls who had no real family or life in their home countries, and wanted to stay in the U.S.

Kevin had been right about one thing: none of the crew, even under 'difficult' interrogation, knew who put up the money and infrastructure for the operation. All were recruited by Octavio, and it seemed that any knowledge of his boss died with him.

◆◆◆

Once the men were transported to be arraigned in U.S. District Court in Portland, and the girls were all processed through U.S. Customs, cleaned, fed, and put to bed in the Port Stirling High School gymnasium, the cops disbursed.

Ed Sonders had accompanied the bodies of Brad and Harry, the OSP snipers, to the morgue. Sheriff Earl left saying "I'm going to see how my deputy is doing, and then I'm going to bed. Don't nobody bother me for 24 hours."

Buck Bay Chief of Police Dan McCoy went home and tried to get warm, after laying on the wet beach for most of the night.

Matt and Jay took Fern home, stopping on the way to pick up some cheeseburgers, fries, and milkshakes for all. Jay had gone into the restaurant to pick up the takeout; the feeling being that all the blood on Fern and Matt might disturb the other patrons and staff. As it was, the chef seemed surprised at this order at 9:00 a.m.

"Don't ask," Jay told her.

When they arrived at Fern's home, she said, "Not sure if I'm more anxious to eat this, or to get out of these clothes and take a hot shower."

"Why don't you change first," Matt suggested.

"Will you guys stay here while I shower?" she asked, clearly still jittery.

"Of course," they answered in unison. "And we'll heat up the food when you're ready," added Matt.

She disappeared into her bedroom and bathroom, and came out twenty minutes later, blood-free, with wet hair, and wrapped in her favorite robe. She was carrying her gray sweats and Nikes, straight arms holding them out in front of her away from her body.

Handing them to Jay, she said, "You should probably take these to Bernice for evidence. Please tell her I said when she's finished with them, she should burn them. I don't want a receipt, and I don't want them back. Am I clear?"

"Yes, Officer Byrne," said Jay. "Don't blame you." He went into Fern's kitchen and found a plastic bag to deposit them into. "Let's eat!" he said, and loaded the warm food into the microwave until it was hot again.

The three chowed down, and the at-best mediocre cheeseburgers had never tasted better.

"It's funny the things you think about when your life is at risk," Fern said between bites, pulling a wet strand of auburn hair behind her ear, and tightening her pink fluffy robe about her torso. Matt couldn't take his eyes off her. All the passion that was usually focused on his work was now aimed squarely at this woman sitting across from him.

"I kept thinking about how I've taken care of my body all my life – exercised, eaten only healthy food, been careful about getting my sleep. And, now, was it all for naught? Was some stranger going to kill me, and all my careful living wouldn't matter a whit? That was the moment I promised myself if I got out alive, I would start living a bit more recklessly," she grinned. "Look where playing it safe got me."

"Becoming an officer of the law is not exactly playing it safe," Jay disagreed. "But I get your drift. Which is why I don't eat kale. A long life is against the odds of our profession, so we might as well eat fries."

"Let's all shoot for a happy medium," Matt contributed. "Fries and milkshakes once a week, and plenty of fresh seafood and vegetables in between. How's that sound? Oh, and a great deal of alcohol sprinkled in."

Jay laughed, Fern giggled, and all three felt safe and happy, a spirit of euphoric goodwill filling the air.

◆◆◆

"I have to let Arlette out of jail," Phelps told Matt, the sun blazing high in the sky outside Matt's office window. "I don't have enough evidence to arrest her for her husband's murder, or anything to tie her to this international crime ring. And why aren't you home getting some rest?"

"Loose ends. You were up all night, too, why aren't you resting?"

"Yes, that loose ends thing."

"Arlette couldn't be involved, Joe. She's got the money to front the operation, sure, but we can't find a single connection to China, for instance. I will personally follow up with her friends who gave her an alibi, just to be sure, but I'm betting the farm that Arlette is what she seems – a grieving widow."

"Well, you may be betting our jobs, too. But I don't have any choice. Arlette will sue my pants off if I don't let her go now with no new evidence."

"She's innocent, Joe. Let her get on with her life."

"You've completed your part of this operation, Matt, and now it's up to us to track down the kingpin. Someone masterminded this gig, and fronted all the money, and we'll prove it."

"I'm going to do two last things for you," said Matt, "and then we'll call it a wrap on our end. I will triple-check Arlette's alibi, and prove to you that she never left San Diego last week. Then will you let her be?"

"Probably," said Phelps, non-committedly. "What's the other thing you're going to do?"

"I'm going to dive a little further into Zhang Chen's background, maybe even his childhood. Fern said something this morning that resonated with me: she said that whoever the big cheese is, it's someone with a great deal of anger toward women. I will make a couple of phone calls this afternoon, and turn over my findings to you and Rod."

◆◆◆

"Mr. Zhang Chen, please. This is Port Stirling Chief of Police Matt Horning calling."

"I'm sorry, Mr. Horning, but Mr. Chen is on another call at the moment," said his gatekeeper.

"Then get him off, and put him on the line now, please," Matt barked. "It's an emergency."

"One moment."

"Chief Horning," came Chen's voice. "What can I do for you?" His voice was steady and composed, showing no sign of being rattled.

"Thank you for taking my call, Mr. Chen. I'm calling to inform you that a major police operation took place at your property last night," Matt said, and paused, waiting for a reaction.

"Oh? What kind of operation?"

"I think you know, sir."

"I'm afraid I don't." Still calm and cool. "Can you fill me in on the details, please?"

"Agents from the United States federal government, including the Department of State and the Coast Guard, along with a large contingent of local police officers conducted a raid at your property at approximately 4:00 a.m. today. The raid resulted in the arrests of 28 men. Two of our men were killed in an exchange of gunfire, and we're not real happy about that. Oh, and two of your men were also killed. I believe their names to be Octavio and Juan."

"I don't have any 'men'," Chen protested. "And I don't know anyone named Octavio."

"Whatever you say," Matt said derisively. "Don't you want to know why this happened?"

"I assume you will tell me."

"We confiscated lots of illegal drugs that were brought to our shores by an international ship."

"Oh, my."

"Yeah. Tell me, Mr. Chen, do you like women?" Matt said suddenly.

"What?"

"Simple question, really. Do you like women? Or, better, do you hate women?"

"I don't understand why you are asking me this question," Chen said. "I certainly don't hate women. Why are you asking me this?"

"Because in addition to the illegal drugs, we also now have 173 young Chinese and Costa Rican girls as guests of my town. They were found in the bowels of your ship, the Anselmo. I believe that whoever is the head honcho of this operation would have to hate women to do something like this. Since it was your property, and since you have the financial resources to assemble an international crime ring, and since you have strong ties to China, I believe that head honcho is you. The one thing I don't know is if you hate women enough to initiate such an ugly, appalling crime."

"You have insulted me, Chief Horning," Chen said, his voice icy. "Whatever may have happened on my property has nothing to do with me. I don't know what you are talking about, and it is impossible to even consider that I could be involved in anything of this nature. I have led an admirable, honorable life. I regret this has happened, and I will sell my Oregon property as soon as possible."

"If you're done blustering, I need to advise you that federal agents are at your office now, and will want to take a formal statement from you."

"That's outrageous," Chen exclaimed. "This phone call is over."

And, he hung up.

Matt didn't believe one word.

♦♦♦

After checking to make sure his call with Zhang Chen had recorded, he looked up the phone number for Chen's parents' import business in San Francisco, and dialed the number.

A woman answered in Chinese. Matt said, "I'm sorry, but I speak English. Can you help me?"

"Yes, but of course," she replied.

"I am calling for Biyu or Ju, please."

"Yes, Biyu," she said, and then there was quiet on the line. Matt waited.

"Hello. This is Biyu," a pleasant voice said.

"Hello. Are you the mother of Zhang Chen?" he asked.

Silence, and then, "Yes. My son."

Matt introduced himself, and told her that he was calling to learn about her son's childhood.

"Why?" Chen's mother asked.

"It's routine," Matt answered. "We've had an incident on a property he owns in Oregon, and we're looking into backgrounds."

She accepted that explanation for his call, and was quite forthcoming – much more so than he expected, relating many interesting facts about his young genius, his personality, and his immense financial success. Biyu was very proud of her son, and clearly loved to talk about him.

"Thank you," Matt said graciously. "This has been very helpful to me. I wonder if you could tell me if your son has been married?"

"No, he has not. We keep hoping," she said somewhat wistfully.

"Why do you think he hasn't married?" Matt asked carefully.

She laughed. "The girls that he likes never like him, and the ones who do like him, he doesn't like them."

"Can you help me understand that a little better?" Matt said.

"He has always liked Chinese girls, but they want American husbands," she explained.

"But your son is an American."

"Yes, but he looks Chinese. Chinese girls here want blond, blue-eyed husbands, especially the girls he went to school with. Some of them in college were actually very mean to him. One of his classmates told him that if they chose someone like my son, they would be – how do you say? – settling. All the blond, pretty American women like him, but he thinks they really only like his money. So he waits for a proper Chinese girl who will want him. And we wait for grandchildren."

"I am sure he will find the right woman, and you will be a most excellent grandmother," Matt said. "Thank you for talking with me, and sharing your stories about your son. You are proud of him, I can tell."

"Yes. He's a good son."

CHAPTER 36

···

pink

Bernice called Matt and said, "You're gonna kill me."

"No, I'm not. I've done enough killing today. But what's up?"

"The DNA lab in Portland made a mistake analyzing Arlette's sample. Which they discovered when I asked them to do a follow-up test. It couldn't be her blood in Clay Sherwin's vehicle. I'm so, so sorry."

"Oh, boy. This will cause trouble, for sure. I would ask you how it happened, but I wouldn't understand your answer, so there's no point."

"I'm going to resign as medical examiner," she said.

"No, you're not. I have a confession from Clay's killer. We'll apologize to Arlette. Mistakes happen. Thank God we kept her detainment quiet."

"But she might sue us."

"She might," Matt agreed. "But I think she will happily go straight home and start living her life, and the last thing in the world she wants to think about is Port Stirling, Oregon."

"I hope you're right, chief. I've never had this happen before, and I'm devastated."

"Wait a week, and write her an apology note if that will make you feel better. We're moving on, Bernice."

◆◆◆

And moving on was precisely what Matt intended to do. First, Phelps.

"Arlette was in California during the 24-48 hour timeframe of her husband's death," Matt told Phelps on the phone. "I have visual proof. It turns out that her Pilates studio films their classes, and Arlette is clearly visible in the front row during the time period of Clay's murder. And she had dinner at a local restaurant with two friends during the same period. They both told me the same story in separate interviews, and it was what they told Fern, too. The restaurant manager confirmed the three women ate there twice last week – they are regulars. And, there's one more thing."

"What's that?"

"The lab test on Arlette's blood was messed up. Bernice just found out."

"Are you shitting me?" Phelps groaned. Matt couldn't see it through the wires, but Joe had pulled a really ugly face.

"I wish I was. We are very, very sorry, and Bernice offered to resign. Arlette's blood is not in the same DNA pool as found in Clay's car. All I can say is a mistake was made."

"It's a god-dammed big one!"

"It's unfortunate, I agree, Joe, but there's nothing we can do now except apologize to Arlette and turn her loose."

Silence. Joe was beyond pissed.

"I can offer you a crumb of news on another front, however," Matt said.

"What?" he said, disgusted with this conversation.

Matt briefed Phelps on both of his conversations with Zhang Chen and his mother.

"So, he's mad at all Chinese girls, and this is his revenge?" Phelps said.

"I've heard stranger."

"Well, he does have the means – all the dough in the world – the opportunity – he does own the property – and this might be enough of a motive," Phelps allowed. "I assume he denied any knowledge?"

"Emphatically," Matt said. "And he threw in the 'insult' dodge, too. You should move quickly, Joe, he's threatening to sell the place."

"He can't do that until the federal government releases the crime scene."

"And that will be a looong time, right?"

"Weeks. Maybe months," Phelps grinned into the phone.

◆◆◆

Edgar Emerson, a craggy, old, deep sea fisherman out of Silver River, and his wife, Maude, were drinking their morning coffee at their kitchen table while reading the local newspaper.

"They caught a bunch of smugglers bringing in drugs and girls last night. North of here, up close to Port Stirling," Edgar said.

"Was it that ship you saw, the Anselmo?" Maude asked.

"Yep. Says here the Coast Guard got an anonymous tip."

"It was you told 'em, wasn't it?"

"Maybe."

◆◆◆

Matt went shopping. The saleswoman thought he was crazy.

"But these ten tops are all pink," she said.

"I know," he replied.

◆◆◆

"R U awake yet?" he texted.

"Yes," came her reply.

"Can I come over?"

"Yes, please."

◆◆◆

Fern answered her door still wearing her fluffy robe and slippers, but her hair was combed, and she had on some makeup.

"I brought you a gift," Matt said, handing her the shopping bag.

Fern grabbed his arm and pulled him inside, "Come in. It's raining, silly." She took the bag from his hand.

He hadn't noticed that it had begun to rain. Maybe that was a sign he was getting used to it?

She opened the bag and started pulling out pink tops: tees, blouses, and sweaters. She grinned at him, saying "You are the sweetest man I know."

Matt took the bag out of her hand, brushed her hair away from her face, and pulled her to him.

If you enjoyed Midnight Beach, please take a few minutes and write a review at the place you bought it. If you got this book from a library (yay, libraries!), please tell the librarian you loved it, and she should put it on that stand right inside the front door so everyone will see it.

The third installment in the

Port Stirling mystery series

will be published in late 2020.

So you don't miss a single thing, please go to

www.kayjenningsauthor.com

and sign up for my occasional newsletter

Acknowledgements

While this story was inspired by the 1977 Cigale drug bust in Bandon, Oregon, *Midnight Beach* is a fictionalized version of the actual event. I am indebted to old friend Bill Smith of Bandon for first alerting me to this great story in Oregon history, and to a nice BLM employee at the New River Nature Center who expanded on the story, and whose name I unfortunately failed to get.

Special thanks go to current Coos County Sheriff Craig Zanni, who was a participant in the Cigale raid and added some eye-witness details to my story.

I have taken some liberties with the facts in this story. The two new Sentinel-class cutters to be stationed at the Astoria, OR, Coast Guard headquarters have not actually arrived in the state yet. But they sound cool.

This story required information about weapons, about which, admittedly, I know virtually nothing, although I did pass the Oregon Hunter's Safety exam when I was in the 8th grade. I relied on the knowledge of Scott Westerman, and any errors on guns, bullets, blades or other killing machines are solely mine, not Scott's.

The DNA stuff in this story was a struggle for me. If I've understood it incorrectly, or left out something important, I apologize.

The Cigale drug bust did not include any element of human trafficking – that is solely my imagination at play. And it was never known – although there are plenty of rumors – who actually fronted the Cigale operation. I so love the main rumor in the local law enforcement community, but my research says that gentleman died eight years before the bust. So, I've chosen to ignore the rumors about the operation's leadership, and have instead created my own villain.

Special thanks to developmental editor Selina McLemore.

Special thanks to cover designer Claire Brown.

Special thanks to beta readers MaryCay, Peter, and Jeanette, who uncovered issues and typos that I missed, even after 20 readings.

Finally, all my love to Steve. Day in and day out, this guy rocks.

Printed in the USA
CPSIA information can be obtained
at www.ICGtesting.com
LVHW051210300124
770137LV00005B/659/J